D0114853

LADY SUSAN AND OTHER WORKS

LADY SUSAN
AND OTHER WORKS

◆

Jane Austen

with an Introduction and Notes by
NICHOLAS SEAGER
Keele University

WORDSWORTH CLASSICS

For my husband
ANTHONY JOHN RANSON
with love from your wife, the publisher.
Eternally grateful for your unconditional love.

Readers who are interested in other titles from
Wordsworth Editions are invited to visit our website at
www.wordsworth-editions.com

First published in 2013 by Wordsworth Editions Limited
8B East Street, Ware, Hertfordshire SG12 9HJ

ISBN 978 1 84022 696 6

Text © Wordsworth Editions Limited, 2013
Introduction and Notes © Nicholas Seager 2013

Wordsworth® is a registered trademark of
Wordsworth Editions Limited

Wordsworth Editions
is the company founded in 1987 by
MICHAEL TRAYLER

All rights reserved. This publication may not be
reproduced, stored in a retrieval system or
transmitted, in any form or by any means, electronic,
mechanical, photocopying, recording or otherwise,
without the prior permission of the publishers.

Typeset in Great Britain
Printed and bound by Clays Ltd, Elcograf S.p.A

CONTENTS

GENERAL INTRODUCTION

Wordsworth Classics are inexpensive editions designed to appeal to the general reader and students. We commissioned teachers and specialists to write wide ranging, jargon-free Introductions and to provide Notes that would assist the understanding of our readers rather than interpret the stories for them. In the same spirit, because the pleasures of reading are inseparable from the surprises, secrets and revelations that all narratives contain, we strongly advise you to enjoy this book before turning to the Introduction.

KEITH CARABINE
General Adviser
Rutherford College, University of Kent at Canterbury

INTRODUCTION

Jane Austen's literary reputation rests on the enduring popularity of the six major works of fiction published between 1811 and 1818, which place her at a pivotal point in the development of the English novel. Ian Watt made Austen the endpoint of 'the rise of the novel' that started in the previous century with Daniel Defoe, Samuel Richardson and Henry Fielding, while F. R. Leavis calls her 'the inaugurator of the great tradition of the English novel' that subsequently runs through George Eliot, Henry James and Joseph Conrad.[1] Austen, then, is the bridge between the eighteenth-century origins and the nineteenth-century apogee of the English novel. Critical accounts of Austen, however, have

---

1 Ian Watt, *The Rise of the Novel: Studies in Defoe, Richardson and Fielding*, Chatto and Windus, London, 1957, pp. 296–9; F. R. Leavis, *The Great Tradition: George Eliot, Henry James, Joseph Conrad*, Chatto and Windus, London, 1948, p. 16. Whenever possible, surname and page number will follow in parentheses in this Introduction and references will correspond to items in the Annotated Bibliography that follows.

struggled to come to terms with the shorter works that are collected in this volume, fictions that remained unpublished until long after her death. These comprise, first, Austen's juvenilia: short experimental fictions written in her youth that burlesque popular novels of the period. Second, there are three longer works of fiction that mark significant additions to her output as a novelist. *Lady Susan* is the wickedly funny story of a captivating but unscrupulous widow seeking to snare wealthy husbands for her daughter and herself. *The Watsons* through its sympathetic but isolated heroine explores themes of family relationships, the marriage market, and attitudes to rank, which became the hallmark of Austen's major novels. In *Sanditon*, the novel on which she was working when she died in 1817, Austen exercises her acute powers of social observation in the setting of a newly fashionable seaside resort. The juvenilia and other manuscript fictions were published in dribs and drabs between 1871 and 1954, and their reception was for a long time mixed, although recent scholarship has been more sympathetic.

There are three reasons for the long-standing scholarly discomfort with Austen's shorter fictions. The first is simply that none is a full-length novel: the juvenilia are mostly vignettes, *Lady Susan* is a novella and *The Watsons* and *Sanditon* are incomplete. Second, because these works have survived in manuscript, they often expose the tortuous process behind (rather than the finished product of) Austen's brilliance. In the biographical notice attached to the first edition of *Northanger Abbey* and *Persuasion* in 1818, the year after Austen's death, her brother Henry proclaimed: 'Every thing came finished from her pen; for on all subjects she had ideas as clear as her expressions were well chosen. It is not hazarding too much to say that she never dispatched a note or letter unworthy of publication' (cited in Austen-Leigh, p. 141). Her brother's idea of the facility with which Austen crafted her narratives is contradicted by the erasures and additions on working manuscripts such as those of *The Watsons* and *Sanditon*; and his claim that even a mere note by his sister would merit publication belies the fact that a completed novella, *Lady Susan*, was rejected for publication in the posthumous 1818 volume for which Henry Austen was writing this very note. A third cause for the residual critical discomfort with Austen's juvenilia and shorter fictions is part of the reason they remained unpublished for so long. In brief, they delightfully countervail the polished and proper image of Austen that took shape quite quickly after her death, showing a rambunctious, subversive and satirical edge that, while still in evidence in the published novels, is in them considerably more restrained. James Edward Austen-Leigh's *Memoir* of his aunt, published in 1869, was instrumental in establishing a domestic, decorous image of homely, contented, spinsterish 'Aunt Jane', whose sedentary moral judgements, nurtured in a secluded life and articulated in pleasant stories of English village life, ensured that Austen conformed to what a Victorian readership expected of a lady novelist. The manuscript works challenge this view of Austen quite considerably, and the author is enriched for this reason.

The Juvenilia (1787–93)

Austen's juvenilia were composed between 1787 and 1793, and survive in three 'fair copy' manuscript books which were copied up after a 'working' manuscript stage. She titled the books, with mock solemnity, *Volume the First*, *Volume the Second* and *Volume the Third*.[2] Most of the short fictions that comprise the volumes carry witty dedications, again written in jokingly earnest tones, addressed to her family and friends at Steventon, a circle which collectively read and enjoyed, and occasionally contributed to and furnished subjects for, these stories. For example, Austen's sister, Cassandra, completed the illustrations of kings and queens for the spoof 'History of England', and Austen's brother and cousin lent their first names to 'Henry and Eliza'. A pencil note by her father, George, in *Volume the Third* calls its contents 'Effusions of Fancy by a very Young Lady consisting of Tales in a Style entirely new'. This assessment of their originality is more than just fatherly pride; the parodic style of Austen's juvenilia sees her testing ways of writing fiction by way of mocking romantic and sentimental precedents. The point to realise is that these are extremely self-conscious stories, which indicate that Austen was a voracious, if highly critical, reader of the kinds of fiction available to her in the 1780s and 1790s.

One target of Austen's juvenilia was the popular sentimental novel that had attained huge popularity in the late eighteenth century, following on from such works as Henry Mackenzie's *The Man of Feeling* (1771), the protagonist of which, Harley, is debilitated by an excessive fine feeling (or sensibility) that makes him weep uncontrollably whenever he encounters suffering. Austen mercilessly exposed the artificiality and insincerity of this manner of novel, just as she would uncover the clichéd workings of Ann Radcliffe's brand of Gothic romance in *Northanger Abbey*. As one reviewer wrote in 1870, even before the juvenilia were fully available:

2   *Volume the First* is held in the Bodleian Library, Oxford; the other two are in the British Library, London.

Her parodies were designed not so much to flout at the style as at the unnaturalness, unreality, and fictitious morality, of the romances she imitated. She began by being an ironical critic . . . This critical spirit lies at the foundation of her artistic faculty.   [cited in Litz, p. 7]

Austen developed a sense of the kind of novel she wanted to write by establishing what was wrong with the forms and the ethics of novels she did not value, and she did this initially through parody and pastiche. As R. G. Collingwood states: 'Austen's early work consisted largely of parody or burlesque of the popular literary styles. . . . In Jane Austen's early burlesques one sees the premonition of a quite exceptional sense of language and of literary form' (Collingwood, p. 28). As well as linguistic and formal verve, running through Austen's earliest works is the exposure of folly, hypocrisy, false feeling and callousness to the emotions of other people; this is an aspect of the literature she was sending up, but the critique expands out from there to produce a moral commentary that sits independent of fictional sources.

A good example of Austen's pastiche of novelistic conventions is 'Love and Friendship', narrated in the form of a one-way correspondence from Laura to her friend's daughter, Marianne, apparently as a form of moral lesson to the younger woman. Given that the letter-breaks only puncture anticlimactically Laura's otherwise continuous narration of her tribulations, we must ask why Austen uses the epistolary form. The answer is that she is mocking the mode, especially its pretence to intimacy and sincerity, and its claim to capture the momentary fluctuations of feeling of a character. Laura is, by contrast, crass and self-indulgent, and she tells of events that happened years ago, veering from blithe understatement to emotive over-reaction to the wildly improbable events that furnish her story. She claims to be possessed of the fine feelings of sensibility:

A sensibility too tremblingly alive to every affliction of my friends, my acquaintance and particularly to every affliction of my own, was my only fault, if a fault it could be called. Alas! how altered now! Though indeed my own misfortunes do not make less impression on me than they ever did, yet now I never feel for those of another.

[p. 42]

Laura's words wonderfully undercut her own statements. This passage is a brilliant example of Austen's irony, because Laura's story reveals her to be, as she unwittingly acknowledges, particularly alive to her *own* afflictions; her claim to have been numbed to other people's suffering betrays a comic lack of self-knowledge, as she proceeds to unravel a rambling tale of unthinking, self-centred absurdity. This is the exuberance of a child discovering language and observing people.

Joined to a companion called Sophia and in desperate straits after their husbands have been incarcerated, Laura writes:

> You may perhaps have been somewhat surprised, my dearest Marianne, that in the distress I then endured, destitute of any support, and unprovided with any habitation, I should never once have remembered my father and mother or my paternal cottage in the Vale of Uske. To account for the seeming forgetfulness, I must inform you of a trifling circumstance concerning them which I have as yet never mentioned. The death of my parents a few weeks after my departure is the circumstance I allude to. [p. 51]

Laura's equanimity no less than her delay in reporting the 'trifling circumstance' of her beloved parents' deaths indicates her true nature, if such a two-dimensional heroine can be said to have a true nature. She continues:

> By their decease I became the lawful inheritress of their house and fortune. But alas! the house had never been their own and their fortune had only been an annuity on their own lives. Such is the depravity of the world! [p. 51]

Her materialism and stylised response to what should be a distressing circumstance ensures that the joke is on Laura; but to a greater extent the joke is on the course of action the reader might expect from a novel's plot. The prospect of an inheritance is mooted, but quickly snatched away, a move typical of the jerky, anticlimactic action of this story.

Evicted from their lodgings after they have again illustrated their unworldliness by helping their landlady's daughter elope with a fortune hunter, Laura and Sophia wallow in the countryside, before Laura reports 'the lucky overturning of a gentleman's phaeton . . . a most fortunate accident as it diverted the attention of Sophia from the melancholy reflections which she had been before indulging' (p. 58). The irony bites quickly here, as the crash confronts the women with their own husbands, 'weltering in their blood', a coincidence that licenses more over-reaction:

> Sophia shrieked and fainted on the ground – I screamed and instantly ran mad. We remained thus mutually deprived of our senses some minutes, and on regaining them were deprived of them again. For an

hour and a quarter did we continue in this unfortunate situation –
Sophia fainting every moment and I running mad as often.   [p. 58]

The only moral that is offered amidst all this is that repeated swooning
on wet ground may bring on a fatal chill, which is what happens to
Sophia, whereas Laura's having raved for two hours has kept her warm
enough to avoid this fate. The dying Sophia says:

'I die a martyr to my grief for the loss of Augustus . . . One fatal
swoon has cost me my life . . . Beware of swoons, dear Laura . . . A
frenzy fit is not one quarter so pernicious; it is an exercise to the
body, and if not too violent, is, I dare say, conducive to health in its
consequences. Run mad as often as you choose; but do not faint – '
[p. 60]

There is a loony, wild inconsequentiality to such moments, a raucous
gaiety that places Austen (as G. K. Chesterton recognised) among the
greatest comic writers of fiction in English. It staggers belief to think
that the author was not yet fifteen and yet perhaps *only* someone so
young could have written this with such glee. As with many of Austen's
juvenile stories, the satire of 'Love and Friendship' is directed at both
social and literary targets: she lambasts the 'cult of sensibility' that
encouraged people to indulge emotions that were at best insincere and
at worst pernicious, and she derides sentimental, romantic fictional
modes in which characters are shallow and plot is impelled by artificial
coincidences and sudden turns of fortune. The pure parody of sensibility
and the kinds of fiction that fed it is more submerged and more subtle
by the time of *The Watsons* and *Sense and Sensibility* but is nowhere
funnier than in Austen's juvenilia.

Austen's youthful works were for much of the twentieth century
considered in terms of the part they played in the development of the
mature novelist, a critical reception that fails to deal with children's
writing, or indeed parody on its own terms. Virginia Woolf's 1922
review of 'Love and Friendship' was called 'Jane Austen Practising', and
early- to mid-twentieth-century critics sympathetic to the juvenilia (like
R. Brimley Johnson, Marvin Mudrick and A. Walton Litz) extended
this understanding of the juvenilia as a primitive phase in Austen's
development, as try-outs for the real business of taking that place in the
great tradition. More recent critical directions have taken different tacks.
Feminist critics such as Sandra Gilbert and Susan Gubar and Margaret
Anne Doody have assessed ways in which a feminine voice less attuned
to the requirements of patriarchy is discernible in Austen's earliest

writing. 'Catharine, or The Bower' has received considerable attention in light of this critical emphasis. It depicts a sensitive and sensible heroine constrained by the conduct-book morality of an overbearing aunt whose aggressive promotion of narrow feminine 'accomplishments, which were now to be displayed and in a few years entirely neglected' (p. 138), drives Catharine to take solace in a retreat to the personal space of a solitary bower. As well as this gender-focused angle, Juliet McMaster has led the surge of critical interest in Austen's juvenilia as specifically children's writing which has to be taken on its own terms, not on those established by preconceptions derived from readings of the later novels. It certainly seems the case that, for all their precociousness, works like 'Frederic and Elfrida', 'Jack and Alice' and 'Edgar and Emma' mock adult concerns from a specifically juvenile perspective, innocently making light of such subjects as alcoholism and violence, and delighting in verbal playfulness, paradox and wilful behaviour. When Austen's nephew called these stories 'childish effusions' (Austen-Leigh, p. 42), he was being dismissive, but perhaps their 'childish' qualities are recuperable and to be valued. Furthermore, an interest in textual studies in recent work by Kathryn Sutherland and Michelle Levy, which followed the ground-breaking work of Brian Southam, has turned attention to the material and social literary practices that inform Austen's manuscript works, including an attempt to understand the compositional processes of the juvenilia and their part in the Austens' social life at Steventon. These stories we should recall were not written to be published for a reading public: indeed Austen's dedications often mock the idea of their being received with acclaim and going through 'threescore editions' (p. 134). They were written to make those who knew and loved Austen laugh at her knowingness and ingenuity; nowadays when readers separated from Austen by more than two hundred years feel they know and love her as well as possible, the juvenilia can have the same effect.

Lady Susan (1794)

Austen experimented with epistolary form (in ways which indicate her awareness of its limitations) in juvenile works like 'Love and Friendship', 'The Three Sisters' and 'Lesley Castle'. In *Lady Susan* (not Austen's title), composed in 1794, there is still that sense of the genre's limitations, but also of its potential. Shortly after composing *Lady Susan* in 1794, Austen began other novels in letters, 'Elinor and Marianne' and 'First Impressions', which, after conversion to third-person narrative, would become *Sense and Sensibility* and *Pride and*

Prejudice, respectively. Although Austen transcribed a 'fair copy' of *Lady Susan* in 1805, it remained unpublished until 1871, when it was appended to the second edition of Austen-Leigh's *Memoir*.[3] Caroline Austen wrote in a letter to Austen-Leigh: 'I have never felt quite sure how it would be taken by the public . . . I feared it might be thought too much of a monotone . . . but there must certainly be an interest in its complete contrast to those tales by which she became famous' (cited in Austen-Leigh, p. 191). *Lady Susan*'s critical reception was in fact ambivalent and its road to serious critical attention has not been smooth. A review by E. Quincey in 1871 referred to *Lady Susan* as 'entirely unworthy of Miss Austen's hand . . . thoroughly unpleasant in its characters and its details' (cited in Southam [1987], p. 16). G. K. Chesterton later declared: 'I for one would willingly have left *Lady Susan* in the waste-paper basket' (Chesterton, p. x). Richard Holt Hutton's response is more balanced, but he declares *Lady Susan* a 'failure' because it lacks the subtlety of Austen's best novels and it mishandles the epistolary form (cited in Southam [1987], p. 171). More recent critics have reappraised Austen's handling of fictional correspondence, including Julia Epstein and Deborah Kaplan from a feminist angle, and Roger Gard and David Owen from a formalist one: with *Lady Susan*, such critics suggest, Austen both inscribes herself into a feminine fictional tradition and experiments with new means of characterisation and narrative effect.

The letters in *Lady Susan* are well conceived because they confront us with the brazen truths of the scheming widow as well as her compelling social performances, and we get this from different points of view with various extents of knowledge and trustworthiness. In the process, Lady Susan Vernon, who imposes herself on her deceased husband's brother and his wife, Charles and Catherine Vernon, is undercut by a narrative that ostensibly condemns her actions, at the same time that the reader is encouraged to revel in the energy she brings to staid, conventional social life. The De Courcys and Vernons to whom she performs to perfection, and even her own daughter whom she despises, pale into insignificance beside the magnetic heroine. In the first letter we read Susan's entirely plausible desire to get closer to her late husband's family, before this is promptly contradicted by her next letter to Mrs Johnson, her confidante and accomplice, in which we find that Susan has captivated the affections of two suitors despite being only four months a widow, and one of these is a married man:

3 The manuscript is now held in the Pierpont Morgan Library in New York.

I have admitted no one's attentions but Mainwaring's. I have avoided all general flirtation whatever; I have distinguished no creature besides, of all the numbers resorting hither, except Sir James Martin . . . I have been called an unkind mother, but it was the sacred impulse of maternal affection, it was the advantage of my daughter that led me on; and if that daughter were not the greatest simpleton on earth, I might have been rewarded for my exertions as I ought.   [p. 174]

Perhaps Susan is self-deceiving when she excuses herself in these terms, or perhaps such an unconvincing self-exoneration has become automatic to one accustomed to breaching rules. She gives immediate exceptions to absolute statements about her good conduct ('I have admitted no one's attentions but Mainwaring's . . . I have distinguished no creature besides . . . except Sir James Martin'), and undermines her protestations about maternal solicitude by giving a too-frank, but perhaps not entirely unfair, assessment of her daughter, Frederica. Austen uses Catherine Vernon, Susan's sister-in-law and one of the few not taken in by Susan's performances, to anchor the reader's response when her hapless brother, Reginald De Courcy, who scorns Susan's powers from a distance, swims into her waters. The epistolary technique not only controls and complicates the reader's ethical response to all this eccentric action; it also allows Austen to escalate situations at breakneck speed. In letter 7 Susan reports Reginald's arrival to Mrs Johnson; in letter 8 Mrs Vernon writes to her mother that 'Lady Susan has certainly contrived, in the space of a fortnight, to make my brother like her' (p. 181); and in letter 9 Mrs Johnson advises Susan to marry him. The reader struggles not to be amused by this effortless hypocrisy, which sponsors and licenses so much fun. Susan has the vitality and versatility of Thackeray's Becky Sharp, and it is only once her plans are scotched that the narrative is drained of its energy.

Lady Susan has serious points to make despite occasionally veering towards farce. One is about female education, an important subject raised by such figures as Mary Wollstonecraft in the 1790s, who felt that the emphasis placed on trivial female accomplishments designed to secure a husband inhibited women's capacities to be rational wives, mothers and educators. This is precisely the limited education Susan proposes for Frederica, because knowledge of arts and sciences 'will not add one lover to her list': 'I do not mean, therefore, that Frederica's acquirements should be more than superficial, and I flatter myself that she will not remain long enough at school to understand anything thoroughly' (p. 180). To some extent, moreover, Lady Susan's refusal to settle down to the role of widow is a reasonable response to her predicament as an attractive but impoverished woman who has been raised in the art of husband-hunting. The instability of judgement that Austen cultivates through using multiple limited narrators leaves it finally unclear whether we should extend sympathy to Susan, or read this as a warning for young men to avoid the advances of sexually experienced widows, the moral that Reginald finally extracts with more difficulty than it should have taken: 'My understanding is at length restored, and teaches me no less to abhor the artifices which had subdued me than to despise myself for the weakness on which their strength was founded' (p. 336). The problem is that we despise him and other upstanding characters as much as we do Susan's improprieties.

At the end of *Lady Susan*, order of sorts is restored, though the manner of its imposition continues to parody conventional morality. Mrs Johnson, who has been encouraged by her friend to despise her gouty, moralistic husband, breaks from Susan only when Mr Johnson threatens to remove her from town pleasures to countryside boredom. Accepting the necessity of their separation, Susan looks forward to 'happier times, when your situation is as independent as mine' (p. 222): that is, when Mr Johnson is dead! Reginald we have seen finally sees through Susan's artifice, and the third-person narrator that enters in the 'Conclusion' surmises that he can now be 'talked, flattered and finessed into an affection' for Frederica within twelve months, as the girl has been sent to live with the Vernons after Susan marries the lumpish Sir James Martin (p. 227). On Susan's future prospects, the narrator is playfully ambiguous:

> Whether Lady Susan was or was not happy in her second choice, I do not see how it can ever be ascertained; for who would take her assurance of it on either side of the question? The world must judge from probabilities; she had nothing against her but her husband and her conscience.   [pp. 226–7]

The ironic outlook not only remains but intensifies as we move to the third-person voice that should really bring authoritative judgement: for instance, a widow's 'second choice' ostensibly refers to any remarriage, but here the phrase indecorously recalls Susan's attempts to ensnare Reginald. Sir James is mocked, much as Reginald is in the prospect of his being cajoled into an affection for Frederica, and so is Charles Vernon, 'who, as it must already have appeared, lived only to do what-ever he was desired' by his wife, the narrator archly comments. Male authority seems particularly impotent here, and the narrative ends by pointing out its own indeterminacy and the instability of judgement it has purposefully cultivated. Austen's subsequent works, particularly *Pride and Prejudice*, an epistolary version of which was taking shape at this time, are exercises in stabilising judgement; however, the lack of presiding authority in *Lady Susan* is dexterously managed.

The Watsons (1803–4)

Austen's niece, Caroline, referred to *Lady Susan* and the fragment *The Watsons* (most likely composed in 1803–4) as 'betweenities' (Le Faye [2004], pp. 276 –7), suggesting the difficulty of fitting them into either the early stage of Austen's life or the established, published fiction. We know that *The Watsons* follows the original conception and early efforts of composition of the three 'Steventon' novels, *Northanger Abbey*, *Sense and Sensibility* and *Pride and Prejudice*. The former, in the guise of 'Susan', had already been sold to a publisher, though it would remain unpublished until repurchased by the Austens, and indeed until after Jane's death; 'First Impressions' had been offered to a publisher by Austen's father but apparently rejected, and like 'Elinor and Marianne' would be changed from epistolary to third-person fiction. *The Watsons* sees Austen take strides in developing this third-person narrative style, and because it survives in a working manuscript it provides glimpses into precisely *how* Austen did this.[4] In important thematic ways, *The Watsons* also anticipates the 'Chawton' novels – *Mansfield Park*, *Emma*, and *Persuasion* – so named because they were written at the cottage to which Jane and Cassandra moved with their mother after their father's death in 1805. In particular, *The Watsons* depicts a heroine emotionally isolated within an unsympathetic family group and a callous social world, who is made to feel her economic dependence, and must negotiate complex social and emotional challenges to achieve happiness.

The biographical angle on *The Watsons* has tempted numerous critics who have wanted to relate its contents (and the fact of its non-completion) to circumstances in Austen's life. Austen rejected, after initially accepting, an offer of marriage from Harris Bigg-Wither in December 1802 which would have provided financial security for herself and her female relatives. Emma Watson, like Fanny Price adopted by a childless uncle, finds her anticipated financial security whipped away when her uncle dies and her aunt remarries, thrusting her back upon

---

4 The manuscript has suffered physical separation: a fragment of it is held at the Pierpont Morgan Library, New York, and a larger portion is held at the Bodleian Library, Oxford.

her invalid father and her siblings: the spinsterish Elizabeth; the coquettish Margaret; and Robert, who is accompanied by a vulgar wife. Three suitors quickly appear: Lord Osborne, Tom Musgrave and Mr Howard. According to Cassandra, the story beyond the point at which Austen abandoned it was to pan out as follows:

> Mr Watson was soon to die; and Emma to become dependent for a home on her narrow-minded sister-in-law and brother. She was to decline an offer of marriage from Lord Osborne, and much of the interest of the tale was to arise from Lady Osborne's love for Mr Howard, and his counter affection for Emma, whom he was finally to marry. [p. 268]

This narrative direction has resonances for Austen's past and her near future. As well as the rejection of an eligible match for a young woman who decides to hold out for love – a situation familiar from *Pride and Prejudice* and *Mansfield Park* – the first half of which reflected Austen's situation in the early 1800s, this plot arc is proleptic, as it anticipates the death of Austen's father in 1805, an event which might even explain why the novel was not continued past a scene with Emma at her father's bedside.

What does the manuscript of *The Watsons* show us about Austen's process as a writer? Most obviously that she was extremely careful and undertook extensive, carefully calculated revisions.[5] Emma's eldest sister, Elizabeth, recalls the amorous attention she formerly received from the raffish Tom Musgrave: 'Some people say that he has never seemed to like any girl so well since, though he is always ~~philandering with~~ [behaving in a particular way to] one or another' (p. 232). The more delicate, euphemistic substitution could be designed to maintain our sympathy for a woman who has been passed over and remains unmarried – the complex portrayal of Elizabeth rather anticipates an unfortunate spinster like *Emma*'s Miss Bates. When Miss Osborne reneges on her promise to dance first with ten-year-old Charles Blake, preferring instead the allurements of Colonel Beresford, the boy's mother is shown 'stifling her own ~~angry feelings~~ [mortification]' (p. 243). The change is subtle, but it has at least two effects. The first is to give Mrs Blake, a widowed sister of Mr Howard, an even greater sense of her lowly place in relation to the wealthy Osbornes (she can be

---

5   In what follows I present Austen's deletions with strike through text, and her replaced text (that used in the edition) in square brackets.

mortified by Miss Osborne's slight, but *anger* is too much); the second is to create a situation in which the injured party is stunned by this ill-treatment in a way that makes Emma's generosity in offering her hand all the more magnanimous: 'Emma did not think or reflect; she felt and acted. "I shall be very happy to dance with you, sir, if you like it," said she, holding out her hand with the most unaffected good-humour' (p. 243). Austen was learning the art of controlling readers' responses to characters and situations. Consider this manuscript change: when her youthful dance partner goes to sing her praises to his uncle, Emma 'turned away her eyes in time ~~when she heard~~ [to avoid seeming to hear] her young companion delightedly whisper' to Mr Howard about her beauty (p. 274). The revised version suggests Emma's diffidence and modesty, and makes the aversion of her eyes a more conscious decision to avoid *appearing* to overhear this praise. When she finally faces Mr Howard, she observes his 'quietly cheerful, gentlemanlike air' (p. 245), which Austen initially wrote Emma 'liked', before amending this to 'greatly approved', before finally settling on 'which suited her'. Again, the choice seems to be to emphasise the heroine's diffidence (as well as her compatibility with Mr Howard), but only after Austen had been tempted to escalate mere *liking* to *great approval*.

But Emma Watson is also witty and alive to her situation in ways that elevate her above her family and male admirers like Tom Musgrave and Lord Osborne. The latter presumes to tell her that horse riding becomes a woman and pooh-poohs the idea that some women might lack the financial means, to which Emma states:

'Your lordship thinks we always have our own way. *That* is a point on which ladies and gentlemen have long disagreed; but without pretending to decide it, I may say that there are some circumstances which even *women* cannot control. Female economy will do a great deal, my lord: but it cannot turn a small income into a large one.'

[p. 255]

This rejoinder, 'neither sententious nor sarcastic', has the immediate effect of making him *think* and of making him drop his 'half-awkward, half-fearless style' of addressing her. As well as rebuking a young man used to vacuous conversations with young women, this speech announces Austen's concern with her heroine's emotional and economic plight following the death of her uncle and the remarriage of her aunt, which events have cast her back on her biological family:

From being the life and spirit of a house where all had been comfort

and elegance, and the expected heiress of an easy independence, she
was become of importance to no one . . . a burden on those whose
affections she could not expect, an addition in a house already overstocked, surrounded by inferior minds, with little chance of domestic
comfort, and as little hope of future support. It was well for her that
she was naturally cheerful, for the change had been such as might
have plunged weak spirits in despondence.   [p. 268]

This is a remarkably stark assessment of Emma's situation. The voice
is quite instantly recognisable as that which Austen was to develop as
she emerged as a published author after 1811; it is 'focalised' through
the heroine's perspective, yet it remains objective (in a way that
epistolary narrative, for instance, cannot) to a point slightly beyond
Emma's own awareness. She feels the pinch of her situation and we feel
it with her – we empathise with her sense that she is a burden on her
family, even as we feel she is in fact a blessing to them – and we share
her view that her prospects amidst such unsympathetic people are bleak.
The points about her natural cheerfulness and strength of mind are
narrative commentary, with which the reader concurs, rather than
Emma's (conscious) self-assessment. Austen's control of perspective,
intermingling subjective and objective points of view, marks a stride
forward in the capacity of the novel to express human experience. The
situation threatens to be exacerbated by the death of her father, at whose
bedside the family leave her (as they travel to Croydon) and at which
point Austen leaves her, as the manuscript comes to an abrupt end.

Austen's family was, however, not content to leave things there, as
later generations of the family attempted to complete *The Watsons*.
Anna Lefroy and James Edward Austen-Leigh had attempted to
complete the unfinished stories in *Volume the Third* (1792), 'Evelyn'
and 'Catharine' (see Sabor, pp. 363–70), so unpublished family
continuations were not new. But even before *The Watsons* was published
in the second edition of Austen-Leigh's *Memoir* (1871), another Austen
niece, Catherine Hubback, published *The Younger Sister* (1850), a three-
volume novel that begins by closely approximating the original story
and completes it along the lines Austen apparently intended, which
Cassandra communicated to Catherine. Almost eighty years later,
Catherine Hubback's granddaughter, Edith Brown, wrote, with her
husband Francis, another completion of *The Watsons* (1928). Other
completions have been attempted, of which the most notable are those
by L. Oulton (1923), John Coates (1958) and Joan Aiken (1996). Critical
attention to the work focused for a long time on its place in the genesis

of Austen's later works, particularly *Emma*, indicated by shared first names, and *Persuasion*, inspired by the heroine's awkward place in a family set-up. R. Brimley Johnson considered *The Watsons* 'the first version of *Emma*' (Johnson [1930], p. 86) and Q. D. Leavis traces this putative development at great length: she argues that the faultless Emma Watson is reconceived as the spoilt Emma Woodhouse, the invalid Mr Watson becomes the hypochondriac Mr Woodhouse, Musgrave becomes Frank Churchill, and the annoying brother and sister-in-law, Mr and Mrs Frank Watson, become the Eltons. The limitations of this attitude to *The Watsons* – looking for vestigial signs of the later novels – are revealed by the approach of Joseph Wiesenfarth, who assesses it as 'a pre-text . . . a text that comes before other texts', and states: 'Almost everything that we have in *The Watsons* . . . makes its appearance in Jane Austen's canon in some finished fashion' (Wiesenfarth, p. 109). Of course *The Watsons* has its place in Austen's development, but it deserves consideration beyond that appropriate for a dry-run of canonical and complete novels, as recent work by Sutherland, James-Cavan and McMaster demonstrates.

Sanditon (1817)

Austen's last work was the unfinished *Sanditon*, which was composed between January and March 1817, prior to Austen's death in July.[6] Family rumour records that the book was to be titled 'The Brothers' and the first mention of the title by which it is now known is a letter of 1869 from Anna Lefroy to James Edward Austen-Leigh. When extracts of the work were published as part of the second edition of Austen-Leigh's *Memoir* (1871), it was referred to simply as 'The Last Work'; and when a transcription by R. W. Chapman was published in 1925 it was entitled *Fragment of a Novel*. From her letters to James, it is clear that Anna was concerned that the manuscript (which she inherited from Cassandra) had been copied and that Catherine Hubback would follow up on her version of *The Watsons* (*The Younger Sister* [1850]) by publishing *Sanditon*, perhaps with a new completion. Anna therefore started her own completion, but this too remains unfinished; as Le Faye establishes, the direction in which Anna took the story has no relation to anything Austen would have done (Le Faye [1987]). The novel has also proved attractive to later continuers and a host of completions have been published since the 1930s.

Early commentators were fairly underwhelmed by Austen's last work.

6 The manuscript is held at King's College, Cambridge.

In an early review, E. M. Forster said *Sanditon* was 'of small literary merit', regretted that it was a throwback to the juvenilia, and chauvinistically stated that 'we realise with pain that we are listening to a slightly tiresome spinster, who has talked too much in the past to be silent unaided' (cited in Bree and Todd, p. lxxxix). R. Brimley Johnson said very little about *Sanditon* because he thought it was in nothing more than note form and so little of Austen's intentions could be extracted from the manuscript (Johnson [1930], pp. 181–2). There were more positive assessments. Frank Swinnerton discerned 'great and mature excellence' in *Sanditon*, praising 'a delicacy and sureness unsurpassed in any other of her works', while Wilbur Cross remarked: 'Everywhere throughout the fragment there is promise of consummate art' (cited in Southam [1987], p. 103). As Southam notes, however, the negative assessment of *Sanditon* prevailed in the half-century after its publication. This is possibly due to the difficulty of fitting this abortive effort into any story of Austen's artistic growth: however, when attention turned to Austen's social and political concerns in the 1970s, *Sanditon* was finally given some of the critical attention it deserves. Southam's essay, '*Sanditon*: The Seventh Novel' (1975), signals this change in fortune, attending to *Sanditon*'s satire on the fad for improvement at a moment when English society was undergoing modernisation. Since then its critical reputation has continued to grow.

In *Sanditon* we again have a sympathetic and somewhat isolated heroine, Charlotte Heywood, who is swept up and transplanted to Sanditon, which Mr Thomas Parker is aiming to transform into the latest fashionable watering place. Here, Austen's wry social commentary and observations are rather more explicit than is customary for her work, because she was concerned with exposing this fashion for new seaside resorts, the crass commercialism it involved, as well as the betrayal of the traditional moral values of the country estate and the specious medicine by which coastal towns were promoted as sites that could restore health. These criticisms are all local and particular, yet they speak to larger historical transitions as English society, in Austen's eyes, embraced all forms of money-making and moved away from a traditional association of the landed estate with ethical value – the social outlook with which Austen always sympathised, even as she began to critique ineffectual or misguided landowners like Sir Walter Eliot and Sir Thomas Bertram. This baleful development manifests at every turn in the story. When Charlotte arrives in Sanditon, Mr Parker reveals that he has moved out of his 'old house, the house of my forefathers', described as 'a moderate-sized house, well fenced and planted, and rich in the garden, orchard and meadows which are the best embellishments of such a dwelling' (p. 283), and now lets this to the Hilliers. His new, rented, home – situated on higher ground, exposed to the elements, and without enough by way of gardens that they must *buy* their produce – is called Trafalgar House, though he regrets that he has not named it after the more recent Battle of Waterloo ('for Waterloo is more the thing now' [p. 283]). The social milieu of *Sanditon* licenses Austen's pure parody of all that is modern, fashionable and designed for show not use.

But Austen's satirical methods are indirect as well as direct, subtle as well as scathing. The Parkers, man and wife, are not in themselves evil, but have been swept up by a social evil to which they are culpably blind:

> Upon the whole, Mr Parker was evidently an amiable family man, fond of wife, children, brothers and sisters, and generally kind-hearted; liberal, gentlemanlike, easy to please; of a sanguine turn of mind, with more imagination than judgement. And Mrs Parker was as evidently a gentle, amiable, sweet-tempered woman, the properest wife in the world for a man of strong understanding but not of a capacity to supply the cooler reflection which her own husband sometimes needed; and so entirely waiting to be guided on every occasion that whether he was risking his fortune or spraining his ankle she remained equally useless.   [p. 277]

The Parkers are clearly not a bad sort, rather they are silly, susceptible and suggestible, and either have misdirected their energy (him) or have not enough energy to exert (her), as Austen's subtle inversion of their otherwise benevolent characteristics indicates. Great social evil, Austen often makes clear, is more often the product of unchecked folly than real malevolence.

A motley cast of characters is assembled in this novel. It includes the shrewd wealthy widow, Lady Denham, Mr Parker's partner in developing Sanditon as a tourist destination for convalescents. Lady Denham comes with her poor cousin and companion, Miss Clara Brereton, and her niece and nephew, the reserved Miss Esther Denham and the rakish Sir Edward. Then there are Mr Parker's siblings, the witty Sidney, who does not truly emerge in what we have of *Sanditon*, and the three hypochondriacs, Diana, Susan and Arthur, a set that 'must either be very busy for the good of others or else extremely ill themselves' (p. 308). These parts of the narrative allow for some astute jokes at the expense of *faux* medical jargon, just as Charlotte's bemusing encounters with Sir Edward allow for reflections on the function and value of the novel as a genre. Sir Edward is quick to inform Charlotte that: 'I am no indiscriminate novel reader. The mere trash of the common circulating library I hold in the highest contempt' (p. 300). Austen is mocking ill-informed ethical disapproval of fiction (as she does in *Northanger Abbey* too), which was evidently still around when she was writing. This continues when Charlotte invites Sir Edward to expand on the novels he does read and he produces a ridiculous catalogue of fictional traits that deserves to be quoted at length:

> The novels which I approve are such as display human nature with grandeur; such as show her in the sublimities of intense feeling; such as exhibit the progress of strong passion from the first germ of incipient susceptibility to the utmost energies of reason half-dethroned; where we see the strong spark of woman's captivations elicit such fire in the soul of man as leads him – though at the risk of some aberration from the strict line of primitive obligations – to hazard all, dare all, achieve all to obtain her ... And even when the event is mainly anti-prosperous to the high-toned machinations of the prime character – the potent, pervading hero of the story – it leaves us full of generous emotions for him; our hearts are paralysed. It would be pseudo-philosophy to assert that we do not feel more enwrapped by the brilliancy of his career than by the tranquil and morbid virtues of any opposing character. Our approbation of the latter is but eleemosynary. These are the novels which enlarge the primitive capabilities of the heart, and which it cannot impugn the sense or be any dereliction of the character of the most anti-puerile man to be conversant with.   [p. 301]

This hyperbole is met with a laconic dismissal: ' "If I understand you aright," said Charlotte, "our taste in novels is not at all the same." ' The joke is that Sir Edward's idea of the novel is a masculinist fantasy and the kind of fiction he values bears no relation to the real world at a time when realism, largely through Austen's efforts, was entering the ascendancy. Sir Edward is in fact a Quixote – a character following Cervantes's famous prototype in *Don Quixote* (1605–15), who has confused the books he reads with reality: 'Sir Edward's great object in life was to be seductive . . . He felt that he was formed to be a dangerous man, quite in the line of the Lovelaces' (p. 302). He sees Lovelace, the rake and rapist of Samuel Richardson's *Clarissa* (1747–8), as the 'the character he had to play' (p. 302), whereas Charlotte's novel-reading has kept her feet firmly on the ground, indicated by her recollection of the financial distresses experienced by the eponymous heroine of Frances

Burney's *Camilla* (1796), which ensures that Charlotte does not spend beyond her means. The message is simple: novels, contrary to popular prejudice, are good for young people if they have a modicum of sense.

Even in her last novel, then, Austen was both defensive about the novelist's vocation and was eager to set the terms on which the novel might be elevated to prominence as a literary form, a status that Austen's published novels helped it to achieve in the nineteenth century. It is unfortunate, then, that the juvenilia and manuscript fictions, in which Austen's awareness of the fictional landscape in which she implanted herself is most apparent, have not enjoyed nearly as high a status. These stories repay the attention of readers and students for their thematic complexity, their formal significance, and their acute quality of observing people and manners. Above all, though, they are wonderful exercises of the imagination of a comic genius, both when she was growing up and writing to impress her siblings, and when she was suffering with a fatal illness and aiming to set the world to rights.

NICHOLAS SEAGER
Keele University

ANNOTATED BIBLIOGRAPHY

Editions

Jane Austen, *Juvenilia*, edited by Peter Sabor, *The Cambridge Edition of the Works of Jane Austen*, 9 vols, (general editior Janet Todd), Cambridge University Press, Cambridge, 2006

Jane Austen, *Later Manuscripts*, edited by Janet Todd and Linda Bree, *The Cambridge Edition of the Works of Jane Austen*, 9 vols, (general editior Janet Todd), Cambridge University Press, Cambridge, 2008

These editions represent the best available textual work on Austen's juvenilia and her later manuscripts. The editors offer extensive textual and critical histories; *Later Manuscripts* includes transcriptions of the manuscripts of *The Watsons* and *Sanditon*, and *Juvenilia* includes Austen's annotations on Goldsmith's *The History of England*.

Kathryn Sutherland (ed.), *Jane Austen's Fictional Manuscripts*: <http://www.janeausten.ac.uk>

This website contains digitised images of all the manuscripts of the works in the present volume, along with descriptions, transcriptions and accounts of their provenance.

Criticism and Reception

Christine Alexander and Juliet McMaster (eds), *The Child Writer from Austen to Woolf*, Cambridge University Press, Cambridge, 2005

This collection contains chapters on Austen's juvenilia by Margaret Anne Doody ('Jane Austen, that Disconcerting "Child" ', pp. 101–21) and Rachel M. Brownstein ('Endless Imitation: Austen's and Byron's Juvenilia', pp. 122–37).

James Edward Austen-Leigh, *A Memoir of Jane Austen and Other Family Recollections* (1869), edited by Kathryn Sutherland, Oxford World's Classics, Oxford, 2008

Austen's nephew was her first real biographer (this edition also includes the 1818 biographical notice by her brother Henry), and was the first to make public, albeit with major reservations about its worth, and with a great deal of selectivity, the manuscript remains and what he termed the 'childish effusions' (p. 42). Sutherland's edition of the *Memoir* features a judicious introduction and helpful textual notes.

Arthur M. Axelrad, *Jane Austen Caught in the Act of Greatness: A Diplomatic Transcription and Analysis of the Two Manuscript Chapters of 'Persuasion' and the Manuscript of 'Sanditon'*, AuthorHouse, Bloomington, Illinois, 2003

Arthur M. Axelrad, *Jane Austen's 'Sanditon': A Village by the Sea*, AuthorHouse, Bloomington, Illinois, 2010

These books by Axelrad focus on the manuscript practices of Austen in the last years of her life; he provides a transcription of the manuscript and a close critical commentary on *Sanditon*.

Gerard A. Barker, *Grandison's Heirs: The Paragon's Progress in the Late-Eighteenth-Century English Novel*, University of Delaware Press, Newark, Delaware, 1985

Barker studies the literary influence of Samuel Richardson's *Sir Charles Grandison* (1753–4), which Austen called her favourite novel and which she adapted as a play for children. Barker considers the uses of exemplary characters, such as in Austen's 'Jack and Alice' and 'Evelyn'.

Laura Fairchild Brodie, 'Society and the Superfluous Female: Jane
  Austen's Treatment of Widowhood', *Studies in English Literature
  1500–1900*, Vol. 34/4, 1994, pp. 697–718

Brodie argues that Austen moves from a satirical subversion of the
'Merry Widow' stereotype of *Lady Susan* (compare Levine,1961) to the
psychological complexity surrounding love and loss in later works, like
Persuasion. Widow caricatures are employed in order that they are
challenged.

Antoinette Burton, ' "Invention is What Delights Me": Jane Austen's
  Remaking of "English" History', in *Jane Austen and the Discourses of
  Feminism*, edited by Devoney Looser, St Martin's Press, New York,
  1995, pp. 35–50

Burton identifies Austen's *History of England* as a work of 'feminist
historiography' (p. 37), a parodic protest against the neglect and harsh
treatment of women in traditional national histories, most apparently
Oliver Goldsmith's *History of England*.

G. K. Chesterton, Preface to *Love and Freindship and Other Early
  Works*, Chatto and Windus, London, 1922, pp. ix–xv

Chesterton places Austen's juvenilia in a great (and grotesque) comic
tradition in fiction that extends from François Rabelais's *Gargantua and
Pantagruel* (1532–4) to Charles Dickens's *The Pickwick Papers* (1836–7);
like these authors, Chesterton announces, Austen possessed 'the gigantic
inspiration of laughter' (p. xiv).

R. G. Collingwood, 'Jane Austen' (1921) and 'Jane Austen' (*c.*1934), in
  *The Philosophy of Enchantment: Studies in Folktale, Cultural Criticism,
  and Anthropology*, edited by David Boucher, Wendy James and
  Philip Smallwood, Clarendon Press, Oxford, 2005, pp. 21–33, 34–48

The English philosopher and historian R. G. Collingwood (1889–1943)
remarks on Austen's use of parody in her juvenile writings, asserting
that it betokens a prodigious awareness of literary form.

Eric Daffron, 'Child's Play: A Short Publication and Critical History
  of Jane Austen's Juvenilia', in *A Companion to Jane Austen Studies*,
  edited by Laura Cooner Lambdin and Robert Thomas Lambdin,
  Greenwood, Westport, Connecticut, 2000, pp. 191–7

Daffron surveys the textual and reception history of the juvenilia down to 2000, listing editions and surveying critical responses.

Margaret Ann Doody, 'The Short Fiction', in *The Cambridge Companion to Jane Austen*, edited by Edward Copeland and Juliet McMaster, Cambridge University Press, Cambridge, 1997, pp. 58–83

Doody argues that Austen's transition from the manuscript juvenile short fiction to the published longer novels required her conformity to the domestic novel acceptable to a patriarchal society moving towards Victorianism.

Julia Epstein, 'Jane Austen's Juvenilia and the Female Epistolary Tradition', in *Papers on Language and Literature*, Vol. 21, 1985, pp. 399–416

Epstein discusses Austen's use of epistolary technique as a way of developing an ironical voice in her early writings.

Roger Gard, '*Lady Susan* and the Singular Effect', in *Essays on Criticism*, Vol. 39/4, 1989, pp. 305–25

Gard comments that *Lady Susan* is significant as a *nouvelle*, a short, self-contained prose fiction, and as a particularly economic instance of epistolary fiction. The main precursor in the epistolary tradition was Richardson, whose prolixity and moralism Austen here rejects, aiming for a 'singular effect'.

Sandra M. Gilbert and Susan Gubar, *The Madwoman in the Attic: The Woman Writer and the Nineteenth-Century Literary Imagination*, 2nd edition, Yale University Press, New Haven, Connecticut, 2000

This landmark work of feminist literary criticism features a chapter entitled 'Shut Up in Prose: Gender and Genre in Austen's Juvenilia' (pp. 107–45). Gilbert and Gubar contend that Austen parodies established genres because she recognised that their conventions 'contribute to the enfeebling of women' (p. 121).

J. David Grey (ed.), *Jane Austen's Beginnings: The Juvenilia and Lady Susan*, UMI, Ann Arbor, Michigan, 1989

This is a valuable collection of essays on the juvenilia and *Lady Susan* which relates these works to Austen's later writing.

John Halperin, 'Unengaged Laughter: Jane Austen's Juvenilia', *South Atlantic Quarterly*, Vol. 81, 1982, pp. 286–99

John Halperin, 'Jane Austen's Anti-Romantic Fragment: Some Notes on *Sanditon*', *Tulsa Studies in Women's Literature*, Vol. 2/2, 1983, pp. 183–91

Halperin contends that *Sanditon* tackles 'the question of appearance and reality, true and false moral values, true and false ways of *seeing*' (p. 184). He discusses *Sanditon* in light of Austen's antipathy for urban development, her satirisation of hypochondria, her sense of the inadequacy of conventional female education, and her hostility towards *faux* sentimental and romantic attitudes, including in the novel.

Jill Heydt-Stevenson, ' "Pleasure is, and ought to be your business": Stealing Sexuality in Jane Austen's Juvenilia', in *Historicizing Romantic Sexuality*, edited by Richard C. Sha, January 2006, Romantic Circles Praxis. http://www.rc.umd.edu/praxis/sexuality/heydt/heydt.html. Accessed 22 February 2013

Heydt-Stevenson argues that Austen mocks excessive constraints on women in the juvenilia, especially through comedy and depictions of heroines who 'steal' male prerogatives and men who 'steal' female sexuality. Theft is a literal and figurative occurrence in the juvenilia.

Kathleen James-Cavan, 'Closure and Disclosure: The Significance of Conversation in Jane Austen's *The Watsons*', in *Studies in the Novel*, Vol. 29/4, 1997, pp. 437–52

James-Cavan argues that Emma Watson achieves social inclusion through establishing equal terms on which she can converse with others; this movement from exclusion to inclusion ensures that *The Watsons* is a satisfactory novel, not merely a fragment.

R. Brimley Johnson, 'A New Study of Jane Austen (interpreted through *Love and Freindship*)', in Léonie Villard, *Jane Austen: A French Appreciation*, George Routledge, London, 1924, pp. 3–53

Johnson uses *Love and Freindship*, in the wake of its 1922 publication, to reappraise Austen's novelistic career. He argues that this work demonstrates Austen's immersion in fiction and her sense of the need to use realism to correct romance, suggesting ways in which Austen parodies certain romantic and sentimental fictional precedents.

R. Brimley Johnson, *Jane Austen: Her Life, Her Work, Her Family, and Her Critics*, Dent, London, 1930

Chapter 5 (pp. 62–89) of Johnson's study addresses the juvenilia, focusing on *Love and Freindship*, and on the works from what Johnson terms 'the unsettled period of her life' (p. 83): *Lady Susan* and *The Watsons*. He makes connections between these works and the published novels. *The Watsons*, for example, is considered 'the first version of *Emma*' (p. 86). Johnson writes of *Sanditon* as though it were in mere note form and so Austen's intentions remain unclear to us (pp. 181–2).

Deborah Kaplan, 'Female Friendship and Epistolary Form: *Lady Susan* and the Development of Jane Austen's Fiction', in *Criticism*, Vol. 29/2, 1987, pp. 163–78

Kaplan suggests that epistolary form, in providing an unmediated access to the female voice and to communication between women, presented a potential challenge to patriarchy, and that Austen ultimately pulled back from this challenge.

Q. D. Leavis, 'A Critical Theory of Jane Austen's Writings' (1941–4), in *Collected Essays 1: The Englishness of the English Novel*, edited by G. Singh, Cambridge University Press, Cambridge, 1983, pp. 61–146

Leavis advances the theory that Austen's novels are 'geological structures, the earliest layer going back to her earliest writings' (p. 64). She contends that accounting for the way in which situations and characters from the early fictions are reworked in the published novels allows for an insight into Austen's compositional process. Leavis traces at greatest length the development of *The Watsons* into parts of *Emma*, and of *Lady Susan* into *Mansfield Park*.

Deirdre Le Faye, '*Sanditon*: Jane Austen's Manuscript and Her Niece's Continuation', in *Review of English Studies*, Vol. 38, 1987, pp. 56–61

Le Faye describes the circumstances in which JA's niece, Anna Lefroy, came to write an unpublished, uncompleted continuation of *Sanditon*. Le Faye establishes that Lefroy was *not* encouraged to do this by JA before her death, whereas in the case of *The Watsons*, which another Austen niece, Catherine Hubback, attempted to complete, JA did impart the intended direction of the story.

Deirdre Le Faye, *Jane Austen: A Family Record*, 2nd edn., Cambridge University Press, Cambridge, 2004

Le Faye gathers the biographical knowledge we have on Austen, drawing on documentary sources and the biographies of Austen by family members; this biography is positioned as an expansion and rewriting of *Jane Austen: Her Life and Letters. A Family Record* (1913), by Austen's grandson Richard Arthur Austen-Leigh and his uncle William Austen-Leigh.

John C. Leffel, ' "Everything is going to sixes and sevens": Governing the Female Body (Politic) in Jane Austen's *Catharine, or The Bower*', in *Studies in the Novel*, Vol. 43/2, 2011, pp. 131–51

Leffel contends that *Catharine* critiques gendered discourses that focused on female chastity and which equated governance of female sexuality with political order.

Jay Arnold Levine, '*Lady Susan*: Jane Austen's Character of the Merry Widow', in *Studies in English 1500–1900*, Vol. 1/4, 1961, pp. 23–34

Levine outlines the literary heritage of the 'Merry Widow' from *Lady Susan* back to prototypes from eighteenth-century fiction. The stereotype is of a sexually aggressive older woman, with sexual experience and social status, who competes with younger women for male attention. Brodie (1994) offers a different perspective.

Michelle Levy, 'Austen's Manuscripts and the Publicity of Print', in *English Literary History*, Vol. 77:4, 2010, pp. 1015–40

Levy characterises Austen's early manuscript practices as 'confidential': they were written for and circulated amongst a select group, the family circle. Her consideration of the 'later' manuscripts, *The Watsons*, *Lady Susan* and *Sanditon*, which retain a number of 'confidential' features, lead Levy to claim these occupy a place between private and public kinds of writing and suggest the binaries often established between scribal and print cultures, and amateur and professional writing, should be broken down.

A. Walton Litz, *Jane Austen: A Study of Her Artistic Development*,
  Chatto and Windus, London, 1965

In a detailed and substantial chapter, Litz shows that Austen's juvenile
fictions, in their attacks on the conventions of sentimental novels,
develop her critical irony. Litz also discusses the narrative techniques
and social outlooks of *Lady Susan*, *The Watsons* and *Sanditon*, along with
the six published novels.

Juliet McMaster, 'The Juvenilia: Energy Versus Sympathy', in *A
  Companion to Jane Austen Studies*, edited by Laura Cooner Lambdin
  and Robert Thomas Lambdin, Greenwood, Westport, Connecticut,
  2000, pp. 173–90

Juliet McMaster, 'Young Jane Austen: Author', in *A Companion to Jane
  Austen*, edited by Claudia L. Johnson and Clara Tuite, Wiley–
  Blackwell, Oxford, 2009, pp. 81–90

In these essays, McMaster notes the polarisation of Austen's indecorous
and outrageous juvenilia and her disciplined and measured novels, but
argues that the more rambunctious tones of the former creep into the
more polished novels. McMaster also contends that, in *Catharine*,
Austen attains for the first time the 'developed subjectivity' that places
this work 'on the very threshold of becoming a fully-fledged Austen
novel' (2009, p. 87).

Juliet McMaster, *Jane Austen the Novelist: Essays Past and Present*,
  Macmillan, Houndmills, 1996

McMaster's collection of essays includes one on her experience of
teaching *Love and Freindship* (pp. 18–35) and one on family relationships
in *The Watsons* (pp. 59–75).

Marvin Mudrick, *Jane Austen: Irony as Defense and Discovery*, Princeton
  University Press, Princeton, New Jersey, 1952

An important formalist study of Austen's deployment of irony, which
takes stock of the juvenilia.

James Mulvihull, '*Lady Susan*: Jane Austen's Machiavellian Moment',
  in *Studies in Romanticism*, Vol. 50/4, 2011, pp. 619–37

Mulvihull interprets Austen's 'Machiavellian' protagonist through the
lens of competing political understandings of personality in the wake of
the French Revolution (1789).

David Owen, *Rethinking Jane Austen's 'Lady Susan': The Case for her 'Failed' Epistolary Novella*, Edwin Mellen Press, Lampeter, 2010

This is a book-length critical reappraisal of *Lady Susan*, which seeks to overturn negative criticism by attending to Austen's aims in writing a novel in letters.

Paul Pickrel, *'The Watsons* and the Other Jane Austen', in *English Literary History*, Vol. 55/2, 1988, pp. 443–67

Pickrel discusses the exploration of the unvalued, but clear-sighted, young woman's 'exile' from home and psychological isolation, inaugurated in *The Watsons* and extended in Austen's late fiction. This *motif* is explained in biographical terms.

Peter Sabor and Kathleen James-Cavan, 'Anna Lefroy's Continuation of *Sanditon*: Point and Counterpoint', in *Persuasions*, Vol. 19, 1997, pp. 229–43

Sabor and James-Cavan provide a balanced critical assessment of the unfinished completion of *Sanditon* by Anna Lefroy, Austen's niece.

Melissa Sodeman, 'Domestic Mobility in *Persuasion* and *Sanditon*', in *Studies in English Literature 1500–1900*, Vol. 45/4, 2005, pp. 787–812.

Sodeman notes that *Sanditon* displaces the heroine from a domestic setting but is beset by anxieties about 'domestic travel' and relocation, which it presents as largely whimsical, self-serving and pleasure-seeking activities that disrupt established customs and values. Even so, Austen's heroine's mobility is celebrated as a necessary phase of her development, freeing her from 'psychologically damaging confinement' (p. 807).

B. C. Southam, 'Jane Austen's Juvenilia: The Question of Completeness', in *Notes and Queries*, Vol. 209, 1964, pp. 180–1

From allusions in the dedications to Austen's juvenilia, Southam deduces that there may be more of her youthful writing that was not transcribed into the three volumes we have.

Brian Southam, *Jane Austen's Literary Manuscripts: A Study of the Novelist's Development through the Surviving Papers*, Oxford University Press, Oxford, 1964

Southam's study of Austen's manuscripts reversed earlier dismissals of their importance. Because they exposed Austen's compositional processes and failed to exhibit the formal features for which she was celebrated, the manuscripts embarrassed scholars more interested in the published products than the compositional process. Southam reconstructs the familial contexts and the literary backgrounds for the juvenilia (pp. 1–19), and provides a critical study of these works (pp. 21–44). He discusses *Lady Susan* and the lost originals of this novel, and those of some of the published novels (pp. 45–62). Southam also discusses the manuscripts of *The Watsons* (pp. 63–78) and *Sanditon* (pp. 100–35), and evaluates these works.

Brian Southam, '*Sanditon*: The Seventh Novel', in *Jane Austen's Achievement*, edited by Juliet McMaster, Macmillan, London, 1975, pp. 1–26

Southam reappraises *Sanditon* in light of its development of the theme of cultural 'improvement' at a moment when English society was undergoing modernisation.

Brian Southam, *Jane Austen: The Critical Heritage; Volume 2: 1870–1940*, Routledge and Kegan Paul, London, 1987

This volume contains important pronouncements on Austen following the publication of Austen-Leigh's *Memoir* and during the period in which the juvenilia and manuscript fictions first started to be published.

Brian Southam, *Jane Austen: A Students' Guide to the Later Manuscript Works*, Concord Books, London, 2007

Southam was due to edit the *Later Manuscripts* for the Cambridge Edition (see above), but his work for that edition was instead published separately in this student guide. The explanatory notes are extensive and helpful.

Kathryn Sutherland, *Jane Austen's Textual Lives: From Aeschylus to Bollywood*, Oxford University Press, Oxford, 2005

Sutherland attends to the uses to which Austen's texts have been put, and has chapters on the manuscripts and afterlives (such as continuations) of the juvenilia, *The Watsons* and *Sanditon*.

Tony Tanner, *Jane Austen*, Macmillan, Houndmills, 1986

Tanner's critical study of Austen in relation to the social values of her time has a chapter on *Sanditon*. Tanner describes the representation in that work of the social disintegration and disease that accompanied the advent of commerce, modernisation and the neglect of tradition.

Clara Tuite, *Romantic Austen: Sexual Politics and the Literary Canon*, Cambridge University Press, Cambridge, 2002

Tuite discusses early works, including *The History of England* and *Catharine*, suggesting that these works contest the regulatory aims that Austen's mature works are obliged to serve, though Tuite circles back to *Sanditon* as a repudiation of the more conservative bent of the six major novels.

Mary Waldron, *Jane Austen and the Fiction of Her Time*, Cambridge University Press, Cambridge, 1999

Waldron relates Austen's fiction to popular novels of the time. Of the juvenilia Waldron states, 'her first experimental writing was dominated by attempts to refashion fiction as she knew it', particularly by rejecting language typical of conduct literature that prescribed 'proper' female behaviour (p. 16). Waldron praises *Catharine* for its development of free indirect style, critiques the limitations of the epistolary mode in *Lady Susan*, and posits that *The Watsons* informed *Pride and Prejudice*.

Joseph Wiesenfarth, '*The Watsons* as Pre-text', in *Persuasions*, Vol. 8, 1986, pp. 61–109

Wiesenfarth pursues the idea of *The Watsons* as 'a pre-text – a text that comes before other texts' (p. 109). He argues that its contents are recycled in subsequent Austen novels.

Virginia Woolf, 'Jane Austen', 1925, in *The Common Reader* (First Series), Hogarth Press, London, 1962, pp. 168–83

This essay includes material from Woolf's review of *Love and Freindship* when it was published in 1922; in it Woolf gives sustained, appreciative attention to Austen's juvenilia and *The Watsons*.

Frederic and Elfrida

A NOVEL

To Miss Lloyd [1]

My dear Martha

As a small testimony of the gratitude I feel for your late generosity to me in finishing my muslin cloak, I beg leave to offer you this little production of your sincere friend

The Author

The uncle of Elfrida was the father of Frederic; in other words, they were first cousins by the father's side.

Being both born in one day and both brought up at one school, it was not wonderful that they should look on each other with something more than bare politeness. They loved with mutual sincerity but were both determined not to transgress the rules of propriety[2] by owning their attachment, either to the object beloved or to anyone else.

They were exceedingly handsome and so much alike that it was not everyone who knew them apart. Nay, even their most intimate friends had nothing to distinguish them by but the shape of the face, the colour of the eye, the length of the nose and the difference of the complexion.

Elfrida had an intimate friend to whom, being on a visit to an aunt, she wrote the following letter:

To Miss Drummond
DEAR CHARLOTTE – I should be obliged to you if you would buy me, during your stay with Mrs Williamson, a new and fashionable bonnet to suit the complexion of your

E. FALKNOR

Charlotte, whose character was a willingness to oblige everyone, when she returned into the country brought her friend the wished-for bonnet, and so ended this little adventure, much to the satisfaction of all parties.

On her return to Crankhumdunberry (of which sweet village her father was rector), Charlotte was received with the greatest joy by Frederic and Elfrida, who, after pressing her alternately to their bosoms, proposed to her to take a walk in a grove of poplars which led from the parsonage to a verdant lawn enamelled with a variety of variegated flowers and watered by a purling stream, brought from the Valley of Tempe[3] by a passage underground.

In this grove they had scarcely remained above nine hours, when they were suddenly agreeably surprised by hearing a most delightful voice warble the following stanza.

SONG

'That Damon [4] *was in love with me*
I once thought and believ'd,
But now that he is not I see,
I fear I was deceiv'd.'

No sooner were the lines finished than they beheld by a turning in the grove two elegant young women leaning on each other's arms, who, immediately on perceiving them, took a different path and disappeared from their sight.

❧ 2 ❧

As Elfrida and her companions had seen enough of them to know that they were neither the two Miss Greens nor Mrs Jackson and her daughter, they could not help expressing their surprise at their appearance, till at length, recollecting that a new family had lately taken a house not far from the grove, they hastened home, determined to lose no time in forming an acquaintance with two such amiable and worthy girls, of which family they rightly imagined them to be a part.

Agreeable to such a determination, they went that very evening to pay their respects to Mrs Fitzroy and her two daughters. On being shown into an elegant dressing-room, ornamented with festoons of artificial flowers, they were struck with the engaging exterior and beautiful outside of Jezalinda, the elder of the young ladies; but e'er they had been many minutes seated, the wit and charms which shone resplendent in the conversation of the amiable Rebecca enchanted them so much that they all with one accord jumped up and exclaimed: 'Lovely and too charming fair one, notwithstanding your forbidding squint, your greasy tresses and your swelling back, which are more frightful than imagination can paint or pen describe, I cannot refrain from expressing my raptures, at the engaging qualities of your mind, which so amply atone for the horror with which your first appearance must ever inspire the unwary visitor.

'Your sentiments so nobly expressed on the different excellencies of Indian and English muslins,[5] and the judicious preference you give the former, have excited in me an admiration of which I can alone give an adequate idea by assuring you it is nearly equal to what I feel for myself.'

Then making a profound curtsey to the amiable and abashed Rebecca, they left the room and hurried home.

From this period, the intimacy between the families of Fitzroy,

Drummond and Falknor daily increased till at length it grew to such a pitch that they did not scruple to kick one another out of the window on the slightest provocation.

During this happy state of harmony, the elder Miss Fitzroy ran off with the coachman and the amiable Rebecca was asked in marriage by Captain Roger of Buckinghamshire.

Mrs Fitzroy did not approve of the match on account of the tender years of the young couple, Rebecca being but thirty-six and Captain Roger little more than sixty-three. To remedy this objection, it was agreed that they should wait a little while till they were a good deal older.

❧ 3 ❧

In the meantime, the parents of Frederic proposed to those of Elfrida a union between them, which being accepted with pleasure, the wedding clothes were bought and nothing remained to be settled but the naming of the day.

As to the lovely Charlotte, being importuned with eagerness to pay another visit to her aunt, she determined to accept the invitation and in consequence of it walked to Mrs Fitzroy's to take leave of the amiable Rebecca, whom she found surrounded by patches, powder, pomatum and paint[6] with which she was vainly endeavouring to remedy the natural plainness of her face.

'I am come, my amiable Rebecca, to take my leave of you for the fortnight I am destined to spend with my aunt. Believe me, this separation is painful to me, but it is as necessary as the labour which now engages you.'

'Why, to tell you the truth, my love,' replied Rebecca, 'I have lately taken it into my head to think (perhaps with little reason) that my complexion is by no means equal to the rest of my face and have therefore taken, as you see, to white and red paint, which I would scorn to use on any other occasion as I hate art.'

Charlotte, who perfectly understood the meaning of her friend's speech, was too good-tempered and obliging to refuse her what she knew she wished – a compliment; and they parted the best friends in the world.

With a heavy heart and streaming eyes did she ascend the lovely vehicle – a post-chaise[7] – which bore her from her friends and home; but grieved as she was, she little thought in what a strange and different manner she should return to it.

On her entrance into the city of London, which was the place of Mrs Williamson's abode, the postilion,[8] whose stupidity was amazing, declared – and declared even without the least shame or compunction – that having never been informed, he was totally ignorant of what part of the town he was to drive to.

Charlotte, whose nature we have before intimated was an earnest desire to oblige everyone, with the greatest condescension and good-humour informed him that he was to drive to Portland Place,[9] which he accordingly did, and Charlotte soon found herself in the arms of a fond aunt.

Scarcely were they seated – as usual, in the most affectionate manner in one chair – than the door suddenly opened and an aged gentleman with a sallow face and old pink coat, partly by intention and partly through weakness, was at the feet of the lovely Charlotte, declaring his attachment to her and beseeching her pity in the most moving manner.

Not being able to resolve to make anyone miserable, she consented to become his wife; whereupon the gentleman left the room and all was quiet.

Their quiet, however, continued but a short time, for on a second opening of the door, a young and handsome gentleman with a new blue coat entered and entreated from the lovely Charlotte permission to pay to her his addresses.

There was a something in the appearance of the second stranger that influenced Charlotte in his favour, to the full as much as the appearance of the first: she could not account for it, but so it was.

Having therefore, agreeable to that natural turn of her mind to make everyone happy, promised to become his wife the next morning, he took his leave and the two ladies sat down to supper on a young leveret, a brace of partridges, a leash[10] of pheasants and a dozen of pigeons.

❦ 4 ❦

It was not till the next morning that Charlotte recollected the double engagement she had entered into; but when she did, the reflection of her past folly operated so strongly on her mind that she resolved to be guilty of a greater, and to that end threw herself into a deep stream which ran through her aunt's pleasure grounds[11] in Portland Place.

She floated to Crankhumdunberry where she was picked up and buried; the following epitaph, composed by Frederic, Elfrida and Rebecca, was placed on her tomb:

EPITAPH

Here lies our friend who, having promised
That unto two she would be married,
Threw her sweet body and her lovely face
Into the stream that runs through Portland Place.

These sweet lines, as pathetic as beautiful, were never read by anyone who passed that way without a shower of tears, which if they should fail of exciting in you, reader, your mind must be unworthy to peruse them.

Having performed the last sad office to their departed friend, Frederic and Elfrida, together with Captain Roger and Rebecca, returned to Mrs Fitzroy's, at whose feet they threw themselves with one accord and addressed her in the following manner.

'Madam, when the sweet Captain Roger first addressed the amiable Rebecca, you alone objected to their union on account of the tender years of the parties. That plea can be no more, seven days being now expired, together with the lovely Charlotte, since the captain first spoke to you on the subject.

'Consent then, madam, to their union, and as a reward, this smelling bottle[12] which I enclose in my right hand shall be yours and yours for ever; I never will claim it again. But if you refuse to join their hands in three days' time, this dagger which I enclose in my left shall be steeped in your heart's blood.

'Speak then, madam, and decide their fate and yours.'

Such gentle and sweet persuasion could not fail of having the desired effect. The answer they received was this. 'My dear young friends, the arguments you have used are too just and too eloquent to be withstood; Rebecca, in three days' time, you shall be united to the captain.'

This speech, than which nothing could be more satisfactory, was received with joy by all; and peace being once more restored on all sides, Captain Roger entreated Rebecca to favour them with a song, in compliance with which request, having first assured them that she had a terrible cold, she sang as follows:

SONG

'When Corydon[13] went to the fair
He bought a red ribbon for Bess,
With which she encircled her hair
And made herself look very fess.' [14]

❦ 5 ❧

At the end of three days, Captain Roger and Rebecca were united and immediately after the ceremony set off in the stage-waggon[15] for the captain's seat in Buckinghamshire.

The parents of Elfrida, although they earnestly wished to see her married to Frederic before they died, yet, knowing the delicate frame of her mind could ill bear the least exertion and rightly judging that naming her wedding day would be too great a one, forbore to press her on the subject.

Weeks and fortnights flew away without gaining the least ground; the clothes grew out of fashion and at length Captain Roger and his lady arrived to pay a visit to their mother and introduce to her their beautiful daughter of eighteen.

Elfrida, who had found her former acquaintance were growing too old and too ugly to be any longer agreeable, was rejoiced to hear of the arrival of so pretty a girl as Eleanor, with whom she determined to form the strictest friendship.

But the happiness she had expected from an acquaintance with Eleanor she soon found was not to be received, for she had not only the mortification of finding herself treated by her as little less than an old woman, but had actually the horror of perceiving a growing passion in the bosom of Frederic for the daughter of the amiable Rebecca.

The instant she had the first idea of such an attachment, she flew to Frederic and, in a manner truly heroic, spluttered out to him her intention of being married the next day.

To one in his predicament who possessed less personal courage than Frederic was master of, such a speech would have been death; but he, not being the least terrified, boldly replied, 'Damme, Elfrida, *you* may be married tomorrow but *I* won't.'

This answer distressed her too much for her delicate constitution. She accordingly fainted, and was in such a hurry to have a succession of fainting fits that she had scarcely patience enough to recover from one before she fell into another.

Though in any threatening danger to his life or liberty, Frederic was as bold as brass, yet in other respects his heart was as soft as cotton, and immediately on hearing of the dangerous way Elfrida was in, he flew to her, and finding her better than he had been taught to expect, was united to her for ever.

Jack and Alice

A NOVEL

Is respectfully inscribed to
FRANCIS WILLIAM AUSTEN ESQUIRE[16]
Midshipman on board his Majesty's ship the *Perseverance*
by his obedient humble servant
The Author

Mr Johnson was once upon a time about fifty-three; in a twelvemonth afterwards he was fifty-four, which so much delighted him that he was determined to celebrate his next birthday by giving a masquerade[17] to his children and friends. Accordingly, on the day he attained his fifty-fifth year tickets were dispatched to all his neighbours to that purpose. His acquaintance indeed in that part of the world were not very numerous as they consisted only of Lady Williams, Mr and Mrs Jones, Charles Adams and the three Miss Simpsons, who composed the neighbourhood of Pammydiddle[18] and formed the masquerade.

Before I proceed to give an account of the evening, it will be proper to describe to my reader the persons and characters of the party introduced to his acquaintance.

Mr and Mrs Jones were both rather tall and very passionate, but were, in other respects, good-tempered, well-behaved people. Charles Adams was an amiable, accomplished and bewitching young man, of so dazzling a beauty that none but eagles could look him in the face. Miss Simpson was pleasing in her person, in her manners and in her disposition; an unbounded ambition was her only fault. Her second sister, Sukey, was envious, spiteful and malicious. Her person was short, fat and disagreeable. Cecilia (the youngest) was perfectly handsome but too affected to be pleasing. In Lady Williams every virtue met. She was a widow with a handsome jointure[19] and the remains of a very handsome face. Though benevolent and candid, she was generous and sincere; though pious and good, she was religious and amiable; and though elegant and agreeable, she was polished and entertaining. The Johnsons were a family of love, and, though a little addicted to the bottle and the dice, had many good qualities.

Such was the party assembled in the elegant drawing-room of Johnson Court, among which the pleasing figure of a sultana[20] was the most remarkable of the female masks. Of the males, a mask representing the sun, was the most universally admired. The beams that darted from his eyes were like those of that glorious luminary, though infinitely superior. So strong were they that no one dared venture within half a mile of them; he had therefore the best part of the room to himself, its size not amounting to more than three quarters of a mile in length and half a one in breadth. The gentleman at last finding the fierceness of his beams to be very inconvenient to the concourse by obliging them to crowd together in one corner of the room, half shut his eyes, by which means, the company discovered him to be Charles Adams in his plain green coat, without any mask at all.

When their astonishment was a little subsided their attention was attracted by two dominoes[21] who advanced in a horrible passion; they were both very tall, but seemed in other respects to have many good qualities. 'These,' said the witty Charles, 'these are Mr and Mrs Jones,' and so indeed they were.

No one could imagine who was the sultana! Till at length, on her addressing a beautiful Flora,[22] who was reclining in a studied attitude on a couch, with, 'Oh Cecilia, I wish I was really what I pretend to be,' she was discovered by the never failing genius of Charles Adams to be the elegant but ambitious Caroline Simpson, and the person to whom she addressed herself he rightly imagined to be her lovely but affected sister Cecilia.

The company now advanced to a gaming table where sat three dominoes (each with a bottle in their hand), deeply engaged; but a female in the character of Virtue fled with hasty footsteps from the shocking scene, while a little fat woman representing Envy,[23] sat alternately at the elbows of the three gamesters. Charles Adams was still as bright as ever: he soon discovered the party at play to be the three Johnsons, Envy to be Sukey Simpson and Virtue to be Lady Williams.

The masks were then all removed and the company retired to another room to partake of an elegant and well-managed entertainment, after which the bottle being pretty briskly pushed about by the three Johnsons, the whole party not excepting even Virtue were carried home, dead drunk.

◈ 2 ◈

For three months did the masquerade afford ample subject for conversation to the inhabitants of Pammydiddle; but no character at it was so fully expatiated on as Charles Adams. The singularity of his appearance, the beams which darted from his eyes, the brightness of his wit and the whole *tout ensemble*[24] of his person had subdued the hearts of so many of the young ladies that of the six present at the masquerade but five had returned uncaptivated. Alice Johnson was the unhappy sixth, whose heart had not been able to withstand the power of his charms. But as it may appear strange to my readers that so much worth and excellence as he possessed should have conquered only hers, it will be necessary to inform them that the Miss Simpsons were defended from his power by ambition, envy and self-admiration. Every wish of Caroline was centred in a titled husband; while in Sukey such superior excellence could only raise her envy not her love; and Cecilia was too tenderly attached to herself to be pleased with anyone besides. As for Lady Williams and Mrs Jones, the former of them was too sensible to fall in love with one so much her junior and the latter, though very tall and very passionate, was too fond of her husband to think of such a thing.

Yet in spite of every endeavour on the part of Miss Johnson to discover any attachment to her in him, the cold and indifferent heart of Charles Adams still, to all appearance, preserved its native freedom; polite to all but partial to none, he still remained the lovely, the lively, but insensible Charles Adams.

One evening, Alice finding herself somewhat heated by wine (no very uncommon case), determined to seek a relief for her disordered head and love-sick heart in the conversation of the intelligent Lady Williams.

She found her ladyship at home, as was in general the case, for she was not fond of going out, and like the great Sir Charles Grandison, scorned to deny herself when at home, as she looked on that fashionable method of shutting out disagreeable visitors as little less than downright bigamy.[25]

In spite of the wine she had been drinking, poor Alice was uncommonly out of spirits; she could think of nothing but Charles Adams, she could talk of nothing but him, and in short spoke so openly that Lady Williams soon discovered the unreturned affection she bore him, which excited her pity and compassion so strongly that she addressed her in the following manner.

'I perceive but too plainly, my dear Miss Johnson, that your heart has not been able to withstand the fascinating charms of this young man and I pity you sincerely. Is it a first love?'

'It is.'

'I am still more grieved to hear *that*; I am myself a sad example of the miseries in general attendant on a first love and I am determined for the future to avoid the like misfortune. I wish it may not be too late for you to do the same; if it is not, endeavour, my dear girl, to secure yourself from so great a danger. A second attachment is seldom attended with any serious consequences; against *that* therefore I have nothing to say. Preserve yourself from a first love and you need not fear a second.'

'You mentioned, madam, something of your having yourself been a sufferer by the misfortune you are so good as to wish me to avoid. Will you favour me with your life and adventures?'

'Willingly, my love.'

❦ 3 ❧

'My father was a gentleman of considerable fortune in Berkshire; myself and a few more, his only children. I was but six years old when I had the misfortune of losing my mother, and being at that time young and tender, my father, instead of sending me to school, procured an able-handed governess to superintend my education at home. My brothers were placed at schools suitable to their ages and my sisters, being all younger than myself, remained still under the care of their nurse.

'Miss Dickins was an excellent governess. She instructed me in the paths of virtue; under her tuition I daily became more amiable, and might perhaps by this time have nearly attained perfection, had not my worthy preceptoress been torn from my arms, e'er I had attained my seventeenth year. I never shall forget her last words. "My dear Kitty," she said, "good-night t'ye." I never saw her afterwards,' continued Lady Williams, wiping her eyes. 'She eloped with the butler the same night.

'I was invited the following year by a distant relation of my father's to spend the winter with her in town.²⁶ Mrs Watkins was a lady of fashion, family and fortune; she was in general esteemed a pretty woman, but I never thought her very handsome, for my part. She had too high a forehead, her eyes were too small and she had too much colour.'

'How can *that* be?' interrupted Miss Johnson, reddening with anger. 'Do you think that anyone can have too much colour?'

'Indeed I do, and I'll tell you why I do, my dear Alice; when a person has too great a degree of red in their complexion, it gives their face, in my opinion, too red a look.'

'But can a face, my lady, have too red a look?'

'Certainly, my dear Miss Johnson, and I'll tell you why. When a face has too red a look it does not appear to so much advantage as it would were it paler.'

'Pray, ma'am, proceed in your story.'

'Well, as I said before, I was invited by this lady to spend some weeks with her in town. Many gentlemen thought her handsome but, in my opinion, her forehead was too high, her eyes too small and she had too much colour.'

'In that, madam, as I said before, your ladyship must have been mistaken. Mrs Watkins could not have too much colour since no one can have too much.'

'Excuse me, my love, if I do not agree with you in that particular. Let me explain myself clearly; my idea of the case is this. When a woman has too great a proportion of red in her cheeks, she must have too much colour.'

'But, madam, I deny that it is possible for anyone to have too great a proportion of red in their cheeks.'

'What, my love, not if they have too much colour?'

Miss Johnson was now out of all patience, the more so perhaps as Lady Williams still remained so inflexibly cool. It must be remembered, however, that her ladyship had in one respect by far the advantage of Alice; I mean in not being drunk, for heated with wine and raised by passion she could have little command of her temper.

The dispute at length grew so hot on the part of Alice that 'from words she almost came to blows'[27] – when Mr Johnson luckily entered and with some difficulty forced her away from Lady Williams, Mrs Watkins and her red cheeks.

❧ 4 ❧

My readers may perhaps imagine that after such a fracas, no intimacy could longer subsist between the Johnsons and Lady Williams, but in that they are mistaken, for her ladyship was too sensible to be angry at a conduct which she could not help perceiving to be the natural consequence of inebriety, and Alice had too sincere a respect for Lady Williams and too great a relish for her claret not to make every concession in her power.

A few days after their reconciliation, Lady Williams called on Miss Johnson to propose a walk in a citron grove which led from her ladyship's pigsty to Charles Adams's horse pond. Alice was too sensible of Lady Williams's kindness in proposing such a walk and too much pleased with the prospect of seeing, at the end of it, a horse pond of Charles's, not to accept it with visible delight.

They had not proceeded far before she was roused from the reflection of the happiness she was going to enjoy by Lady Williams's thus addressing her: 'I have as yet forborn, my dear Alice, to continue the narrative of my life from an unwillingness of recalling to your memory a scene which (since it reflects on you rather disgrace than credit) had better be forgot than remembered.'

Alice had already begun to colour up and was beginning to speak, when her ladyship, perceiving her displeasure, continued thus: 'I am afraid, my dear girl, that I have offended you by what I have just said; I assure you I do not mean to distress you by a retrospection of what cannot now be helped; considering all things, I do not think you so much to blame as many people do; for when a person is in liquor, there is no answering for what they may do; a woman in such a situation is particularly off her guard because her head is not strong enough to support intoxication.'

'Madam, this is not to be borne; I insist – '

'My dear girl, don't vex yourself about the matter; I assure you I have entirely forgiven everything respecting it; indeed, I was not angry at the time, because, as I saw all along, you were nearly dead drunk. I knew you could not help saying the strange things you did. But I see I distress you; so I will change the subject and desire it may never again be mentioned; remember it is all forgot – I will now pursue my story; but I must insist upon not giving you any description of Mrs Watkins: it would only be reviving old stories, and as you never saw her, it can be nothing to you if her forehead *was* too high, her eyes *were* too small, or if she *had* too much colour.'

'Again! Lady Williams: this is too much – '

So provoked was poor Alice at this renewal of the old story that I know not what might have been the consequence of it had not their attention been engaged by another object. A lovely young woman, lying apparently in great pain beneath a citron tree, was an object too interesting not to attract their notice.

Forgetting their own dispute, they both with sympathising tenderness advanced towards her and accosted her in these terms: 'You seem, fair nymph, to be labouring under some misfortune which we shall be happy to relieve if you will inform us what it is. Will you favour us with your life and adventures?'

'Willingly, ladies, if you will be so kind as to be seated.' They took their places and she thus began.

ᘐ 5 ᘗ

'I am a native of North Wales and my father is one of the most capital tailors in it. Having a numerous family, he was easily prevailed on by a sister of my mother's, who is a widow in good circumstances and keeps an alehouse in the next village to ours, to let her take me and breed me up at her own expense. Accordingly, I have lived with her for the last eight years of my life, during which time she provided me with some of the first-rate masters, who taught me all the accomplishments requisite for one of my sex and rank. Under their instructions I learned dancing, music, drawing and various languages, by which means I became more accomplished than any other taylor's daughter in Wales. Never was there a happier creature than I was, till within the last half-year – but I should have told you before that the principal estate in our neighbourhood belongs to Charles Adams, the owner of the brick house you see yonder.'

'Charles Adams!' exclaimed the astonished Alice; 'are you acquainted with Charles Adams?'

'To my sorrow, madam, I am. He came about half a year ago to receive the rents of the estate[28] I have just mentioned. At that time I first saw him; as you seem, ma'am, acquainted with him, I need not describe to you how charming he is. I could not resist his attractions – '

'Ah! who can,' said Alice with a deep sigh.

'My aunt, being in terms of the greatest intimacy with his cook, determined, at my request, to try whether she could discover, by means of her friend, if there were any chance of his returning my affection. For this purpose she went one evening to drink tea with Mrs Susan, who in the course of conversation mentioned the goodness of her place[29] and the goodness of her master; upon which my aunt began pumping her with so much dexterity that in a short time Susan owned that she did not think her master would ever marry, "for," said she, "he has often and often declared to me that his wife, whoever she might be, must possess, youth, beauty, birth, wit, merit and money. I have many a time," she continued, "endeavoured to reason him out of his resolution and to convince him of the improbability of his ever meeting with such a lady; but my arguments have had no effect and he continues as firm in his determination as ever." You may imagine, ladies, my distress on hearing this; for I was fearful that though possessed of youth, beauty, wit and merit, and though the probable heiress of my aunt's house and business, he might think me deficient in rank, and, in being so, unworthy of his hand.

'However, I was determined to make a bold push and therefore wrote him a very kind letter, offering him with great tenderness my hand and heart.[30] To this I received an angry and peremptory refusal, but thinking it might be rather the effect of his modesty than anything else, I pressed him again on the subject. But he never answered any more of my letters and very soon afterwards left the country. As soon as I heard of his departure I wrote to him here, informing him that I should shortly do myself the honour of waiting on him at Pammydiddle, to which I received no answer; therefore, choosing to take silence for consent, I left Wales, unknown to my aunt, and arrived here after a tedious journey this morning. On enquiring for his house, I was directed through this wood to the one you there see. With a heart elated by the expected happiness of beholding him, I entered the wood and had proceeded thus far in my progress through it, when I found myself suddenly seized by the leg, and on examining the cause of it, found that I was caught in one of the steel traps[31] so common in gentlemen's grounds.'

'Ah!' cried Lady Williams, 'how fortunate we are to meet with you, since we might otherwise perhaps have shared the like misfortune.'

'It is indeed happy for you, ladies, that I should have been a short time before you. I screamed, as you may easily imagine, till the woods resounded again and till one of the inhuman wretch's servants came to my assistance and released me from my dreadful prison, but not before one of my legs was entirely broken.'

❦ 6 ❧

At this melancholy recital the fair eyes of Lady Williams were suffused in tears and Alice could not help exclaiming, 'Oh! cruel Charles, to wound the hearts and legs of all the fair.'

Lady Williams now interposed and observed that the young lady's leg ought to be set without further delay. After examining the fracture, therefore, she immediately began and performed the operation with great skill, which was the more wonderful on account of her having never performed such a one before. Lucy then arose from the ground, and finding that she could walk with the greatest ease, accompanied them to Lady Williams's house at her ladyship's particular request.

The perfect form, the beautiful face and elegant manners of Lucy so won on the affections of Alice that when they parted, which was not till after supper, she assured her that, except her father, brother, uncles, aunts, cousins and other relations, Lady Williams, Charles Adams and a few dozen more of particular friends, she loved her better than almost any other person in the world.

Such a flattering assurance of her regard would justly have given much pleasure to the object of it, had she not plainly perceived that the amiable Alice had partaken too freely of Lady Williams's claret.

Her ladyship (whose discernment was great) read in the intelligent countenance of Lucy her thoughts on the subject, and as soon as Miss Johnson had taken her leave, thus addressed her: 'When you are more intimately acquainted with my Alice you will not be surprised, Lucy, to see the dear creature drink a little too much; for such things happen every day. She has many rare and charming qualities, but sobriety is not one of them. The whole family are indeed a sad drunken set. I am sorry to say too that I never knew three such thorough gamesters as they are, more particularly Alice. But she is a charming girl. I fancy not one of the sweetest tempers in the world – to be sure, I have seen her in such passions! However, she is a sweet young woman. I am sure you'll like her. I scarcely know anyone so amiable. Oh! that you could but have seen her the other evening! How she raved! And on such a trifle too! She is indeed a most pleasing girl! I shall always love her!'

'She appears by your ladyship's account to have many good qualities,' replied Lucy.

'Oh! a thousand,' answered Lady Williams; 'though I am very partial to her, and perhaps am blinded by my affection to her real defects.'

❧ 7 ☙

The next morning brought the three Miss Simpsons to wait on Lady Williams, who received them with the utmost politeness and introduced to their acquaintance Lucy, with whom the eldest was so much pleased that at parting she declared her sole ambition was to have her accompany them the next morning to Bath, whither they were going for some weeks.

'Lucy,' said Lady Williams, 'is quite at her own disposal, and if she chooses to accept so kind an invitation, I hope she will not hesitate from any motives of delicacy on my account. I know not, indeed, how I shall ever be able to part with her. She never was at Bath and I should think that it would be a most agreeable jaunt to her. Speak, my love,' continued she, turning to Lucy, 'what say you to accompanying these ladies? I shall be miserable without you – 'twill be a most pleasant tour to you – I hope you'll go; if you do, I am sure 'twill be the death of me – pray be persuaded.'

Lucy begged leave to decline the honour of accompanying them, with many expressions of gratitude for the extreme politeness of Miss Simpson in inviting her.

Miss Simpson appeared much disappointed by her refusal. Lady Williams insisted on her going – declared that she would never forgive her if she did not, and that she should never survive it if she did, in short used such persuasive arguments that it was at length resolved she was to go. The Miss Simpsons called for her at ten o'clock the next morning and Lady Williams had soon the satisfaction of receiving from her young friend the pleasing intelligence of their safe arrival in Bath.

It may now be proper to return to the hero of this novel, Jack the brother of Alice, of whom I believe I have scarcely ever had occasion to speak; which may perhaps be partly owing to his unfortunate propensity to liquor, which so completely deprived him of the use of those faculties nature had endowed him with that he never did anything worth mentioning. His death happened a short time after Lucy's departure and was the natural consequence of this pernicious practice. By his decease, his sister became the sole inheritress of a very large fortune, which, as it gave her fresh hopes of rendering herself acceptable as a wife to Charles Adams, could not fail of being most pleasing to her – and as the effect was joyful the cause could scarcely be lamented.

Finding the violence of her attachment to him daily augment, she at length disclosed it to her father and desired him to propose a union between them to Charles. Her father consented and set out one morning to open the affair to the young man. Mr Johnson being a man of few words, his part was soon performed and the answer he received was as follows.

'Sir, I may perhaps be expected to appear pleased at and grateful for the offer you have made me: but let me tell you that I consider it as an affront. I look upon myself to be, sir, a perfect beauty – where would you see a finer figure or a more charming face? Then, sir, I imagine my manners and address to be of the most polished kind; there is a certain elegance, a peculiar sweetness in them that I never saw equalled and cannot describe. Partiality aside, I am certainly more accomplished in every language, every science, every art and everything than any other person in Europe. My temper is even, my virtues innumerable, my self unparalleled. Since such, sir, is my character, what do you mean by wishing me to marry your daughter? Let me give you a short sketch of yourself and of her. I look upon you, sir, to be a very good sort of man in the main; a drunken old dog to be sure, but that's nothing to me. Your daughter, sir, is neither sufficiently beautiful, sufficiently amiable, sufficiently witty, nor sufficiently rich for me. I expect nothing more in my wife than my wife will find in me – perfection. These, sir, are my sentiments and I honour myself for having such. One friend I have and glory in having but one. She is at present preparing my dinner, but if you choose to see her, she shall come and she will inform you that these have ever been my sentiments.'

Mr Johnson was satisfied, and, expressing himself to be much obliged to Mr Adams for the characters he had favoured him with of himself and his daughter, took his leave.

The unfortunate Alice, on receiving from her father the sad account of the ill success his visit had been attended with, could scarcely support the disappointment. She flew to her bottle and it was soon forgot.

While these affairs were transacting at Pammydiddle, Lucy was conquering every heart at Bath. A fortnight's residence there had nearly effaced from her remembrance the captivating form of Charles. The recollection of what her heart had formerly suffered by his charms and her leg by his trap enabled her to forget him with tolerable ease, which was what she determined to do; and for that purpose dedicated five minutes in every day to the employment of driving him from her remembrance.

Her second letter to Lady Williams contained the pleasing intelligence of her having accomplished her undertaking to her entire satisfaction; she mentioned in it also an offer of marriage she had received from the Duke of —, an elderly man of noble fortune whose ill health was the chief inducement of his journey to Bath.[32]

> I am distressed [she continued] to know whether I mean to accept him or not. There are a thousand advantages to be derived from a marriage with the duke, for besides those more inferior ones of rank and fortune it will procure me a home, which of all other things is what I most desire. Your ladyship's kind wish of my always remaining with you is noble and generous, but I cannot think of becoming so great a burden on one I so much love and esteem. That one should receive obligations only from those we despise is a sentiment instilled into my mind by my worthy aunt, in my early years, and cannot in my opinion be too strictly adhered to. The excellent woman of whom I now speak is, I hear, too much incensed by my imprudent departure from Wales to receive me again. I most earnestly wish to leave the ladies I am now with. Miss Simpson is indeed (setting aside ambition) very amiable, but her second sister, the envious and malevolent Sukey, is too disagreeable to live with. I have reason to think that the admiration I have met with in the circles of the great at this place has raised her hatred and envy; for often has she threatened and sometimes endeavoured to cut my throat. Your ladyship will therefore allow that I am not wrong in wishing to leave Bath, and in wishing to have a home to receive me, when I do. I shall expect with impatience your advice concerning the duke and am your most obliged
>
> LUCY

Lady Williams sent her her opinion on the subject in the following manner:

Why do you hesitate, my dearest Lucy, a moment with respect to the duke? I have enquired into his character and find him to be an unprincipled, illiterate man. Never shall my Lucy be united to such a one! He has a princely fortune, which is every day increasing. How nobly will you spend it! what credit will you give him in the eyes of all! How much will he be respected on his wife's account! But why, my dearest Lucy, why will you not at once decide this affair by returning to me and never leaving me again? Although I admire your noble sentiments with respect to obligations, yet let me beg that they may not prevent your making me happy. It will, to be sure, be a great expense to me to have you always with me – I shall not be able to support it – but what is that in comparison with the happiness I shall enjoy in your society? 'Twill ruin me, I know – you will not therefore, surely, withstand these arguments, or refuse to return to yours most affectionately,

C. WILLIAMS

9

What might have been the effect of her ladyship's advice had it ever been received by Lucy is uncertain as it reached Bath a few hours after she had breathed her last. She fell a sacrifice to the envy and malice of Sukey, who, jealous of her superior charms, took her by poison from an admiring world at the age of seventeen.

Thus fell the amiable and lovely Lucy, whose life had been marked by no crime and stained by no blemish but her imprudent departure from her aunt's, and whose death was sincerely lamented by everyone who knew her. Among the most afflicted of her friends were Lady Williams, Miss Johnson and the duke, the two first of whom had a most sincere regard for her, more particularly Alice, who had spent a whole evening in her company and had never thought of her since. His grace's affliction may likewise be easily accounted for, since he lost one for whom he had experienced, during the last ten days, a tender affection and sincere regard. He mourned her loss with unshaken constancy for the next fortnight, at the end of which time he gratified the ambition of Caroline Simpson by raising her to the rank of a duchess. Thus was she at length rendered completely happy in the gratification of her favourite passion. Her sister, the perfidious Sukey, was likewise shortly after exalted in a manner she truly deserved, and by her actions appeared to have always desired. Her barbarous murder was discovered and in spite of every interceding friend she was speedily raised to the gallows.[33] The beautiful but affected Cecilia was too sensible of her own superior charms not to imagine that if Caroline could engage a duke she might without censure aspire to the affections of some prince – and knowing that those of her native country were chiefly engaged,[34] she left England, and I have since heard is at present the favourite sultana of the Great Mogul.[35]

In the meantime, the inhabitants of Pammydiddle were in a state of the greatest astonishment and wonder, a report being circulated of the intended marriage of Charles Adams. The lady's name was still a secret. Mr and Mrs Jones imagined it to be Miss Johnson, but *she* knew better; all *her* fears were centred in his cook, when, to the astonishment of everyone, he was publicly united to Lady Williams.

Edgar and Emma

A TALE

'I cannot imagine,' said Sir Godfrey to his lady, 'why we continue in such deplorable lodgings as these, in a paltry market-town, while we have three good houses of our own situated in some of the finest parts of England, and perfectly ready to receive us!'

'I'm sure, Sir Godfrey,' replied Lady Marlow, 'it has been much against my inclination that we have stayed here so long – and why we should ever have come at all, indeed, has been to me a wonder, as none of our houses has been in the least want of repair.'

'Nay, my dear,' answered Sir Godfrey, 'you are the last person who ought to be displeased with what was always meant as a compliment to you; for you cannot but be sensible of the very great inconvenience your daughters and I have been put to, during the two years we have remained crowded in these lodgings, in order to give you pleasure.'

'My dear,' replied Lady Marlow, 'how can you stand and tell such lies, when you very well know that it was merely to oblige the girls and you that I left a most commodious house, situated in a most delightful country and surrounded by a most agreeable neighbourhood, to live two years cramped up in lodgings three pair of stairs high,[36] in a smoky and unwholesome town which has given me a continual fever and almost thrown me into a consumption.'[37]

As, after a few more speeches on both sides, they could not determine which was the most to blame, they prudently laid aside the debate, and having packed up their clothes and paid their rent, they set out the next morning with their two daughters for their seat in Sussex.

Sir Godfrey and Lady Marlow were indeed very sensible people and though (as in this instance), like many other sensible people, they sometimes did a foolish thing, yet in general their actions were guided by prudence and regulated by discretion.

After a journey of two days and a half they arrived at Marlhurst in good health and high spirits; so overjoyed were they all to inhabit again a place they had left with mutual regret for two years that they ordered the bells to be rung and distributed ninepence[38] among the ringers.

❦ 2 ❧

The news of their arrival, being quickly spread throughout the country, brought in a few days visits of congratulation from every family in it.

Among the rest came the inhabitants of Willmot Lodge, a beautiful
villa[39] not far from Marlhurst. Mr Willmot was the representative of a
very ancient family and possessed, besides his paternal estate, a considerable share in a lead mine and a ticket in the lottery.[40] His lady was
an agreeable woman. Their children were too numerous to be particularly described; it is sufficient to say that in general they were
virtuously inclined and not given to any wicked ways. Their family
being too large to accompany them in every visit, they took nine with
them alternately. When their coach stopped at Sir Godfrey's door, the
Miss Marlows' hearts throbbed in the eager expectation of once more
beholding a family so dear to them. Emma, the younger (who was
more particularly interested in their arrival, being attached to their
eldest son), continued at her dressing-room window in anxious hopes
of seeing young Edgar descend from the carriage.

Mr and Mrs Willmot with their three eldest daughters first appeared
– Emma began to tremble. Robert, Richard, Ralph and Rodolphus
followed – Emma turned pale. Their two youngest girls were lifted
from the coach – Emma sank breathless on a sofa. A footman came to
announce to her the arrival of company; her heart was too full to contain
its afflictions.

A confidante[41] was necessary. In Thomas she hoped to experience a
faithful one – for one she must have and Thomas was the only one at
hand. To him she unbosomed herself without restraint, and after
owning her passion for young Willmot, requested his advice in what
manner she should conduct herself in the melancholy disappointment
under which she laboured. Thomas, who would gladly have been
excused from listening to her complaint, begged leave to decline giving
any advice concerning it, which, much against her will, she was obliged
to comply with.

Having dispatched him therefore with many injunctions of secrecy,
she descended with a heavy heart into the parlour, where she found the
good party seated in a social manner round a blazing fire.

❦ 3 ❧

Emma had continued in the parlour some time before she could
summon up sufficient courage to ask Mrs Willmot after the rest of her
family; and when she did, it was in so low, so faltering a voice that no
one knew she spoke. Dejected by the ill success of her first attempt, she
made no other till, on Mrs Willmot's desiring one of the little girls to
ring the bell for their carriage, she stepped across the room and seizing

the string said in a resolute manner, 'Mrs Willmot, you do not stir from this house till you let me know how all the rest of your family do, particularly your eldest son.'

They were all greatly surprised by such an unexpected address, and the more so on account of the manner in which it was spoken; but Emma, who would not be again disappointed, requesting an answer, Mrs Wilmot made the following eloquent oration: 'Our children are all extremely well, but at present most of them are from home. Amy is with my sister Clayton, Sam at Eton, David with his Uncle John, Jem and Will at Winchester,[42] Kitty at Queen's Square,[43] Ned with his grandmother, Hetty and Patty in a convent at Brussels,[44] Edgar at college,[45] Peter at nurse,[46] and all the rest (except the nine here) at home.'

It was with difficulty that Emma could refrain from tears on hearing of the absence of Edgar; she remained, however, tolerably composed till the Willmots were gone, when, having no check to the overflowings of her grief, she gave free vent to them, and retiring to her own room, continued in tears the remainder of her life.

Henry and Eliza

A NOVEL

Is humbly dedicated to
MISS COOPER[47]
by her obedient humble servant
The Author

A S SIR GEORGE AND LADY HARCOURT were super-intending the labours of their haymakers, rewarding the industry of some by smiles of approbation and punishing the idleness of others by a cudgel, they perceived, lying closely concealed beneath the thick foliage of a haycock,[48] a beautiful little girl not more than three months old.

Touched with the enchanting graces of her face and delighted with the infantine though sprightly answers she returned to their many questions, they resolved to take her home and, having no children of their own, to educate her with care and cost.

Being good people themselves, their first and principal care was to incite in her a love of virtue and a hatred of vice, in which they so well succeeded (Eliza having a natural turn that way herself) that when she grew up, she was the delight of all who knew her.

Beloved by Lady Harcourt, adored by Sir George and admired by all the world, she lived in a continued course of uninterrupted happiness till she had attained her eighteenth year, when, happening one day to be detected in stealing a banknote of £50,[49] she was turned out of doors by her inhuman benefactors. Such a transition to one who did not possess so noble and exalted a mind as Eliza would have been death, but she, happy in the conscious knowledge of her own excellence, amused herself, as she sat beneath a tree, with making and singing the following lines:

> 'Though misfortune my footsteps may ever attend,
> I hope I shall never have need of a friend,
> as an innocent heart I will ever preserve
> and will never from virtue's dear boundaries swerve.'

Having amused herself some hours with this song and her own pleasing reflections, she arose and took the road to M—, a small market town of which place her most intimate friend kept the Red Lion.

To this friend she immediately went, and having recounted her late misfortune, she communicated her wish of getting into some family in the capacity of humble companion.[50]

Mrs Wilson, who was the most amiable creature on earth, was no sooner acquainted with her desire than she sat down in the bar and wrote the following letter to the Duchess of F—, the woman whom of all others she most esteemed.

To the Duchess of F—

Receive into your family, at my request, a young woman of un-exceptionable character, who is so good as to choose your society in preference to going to service. Hasten, and take her from the arms of your

SARAH WILSON

The duchess, whose friendship for Mrs Wilson would have carried her any lengths, was overjoyed at such an opportunity of obliging her, and accordingly set out immediately on the receipt of her letter for the Red Lion, which she reached the same evening. The Duchess of F— was about forty-five and a half; her passions were strong, her friendships firm and her enmities unconquerable. She was a widow and had only one daughter, who was on the point of marriage with a young man of considerable fortune.

The duchess no sooner beheld our heroine than, throwing her arms around her neck, she declared herself so much pleased with her that she was resolved they never more should part. Eliza was delighted with such a protestation of friendship, and after taking a most affecting leave of her dear Mrs Wilson, accompanied her grace the next morning to her seat in Surrey.

With every expression of regard did the duchess introduce her to Lady Harriet, who was so much pleased with Eliza's appearance that she besought her to consider her as her sister, which Eliza with the greatest condescension promised to do.

Mr Cecil, the lover of Lady Harriet, being often with the family was often with Eliza. A mutual love took place, and Cecil, having declared his first, prevailed on Eliza to consent to a private union,[51] which was easy to be effected as the duchess's chaplain, being very much in love with Eliza himself, would, they were certain, do anything to oblige her.

The duchess and Lady Harriet being engaged one evening to an assembly, they took the opportunity of their absence and were united by the enamoured chaplain.

When the ladies returned, their amazement was great at finding instead of Eliza the following note:

MADAM – We are married and gone.

HENRY AND ELIZA CECIL

Her grace as soon as she had read the letter, which sufficiently explained the whole affair, flew into the most violent passion, and after having spent an agreeable half-hour in calling them by all the shocking names her rage could suggest to her, sent out after them three hundred armed men, with orders not to return without their bodies, dead or alive; intending if they should be brought to her in the latter condition to have them put to death in some torturelike manner after a few years' confinement.

In the meantime, Cecil and Eliza continued their flight to the continent, which they judged to be more secure than their native land from the dreadful effects of the duchess's vengeance, which they had so much reason to apprehend.

In France they remained three years, during which time they became the parents of two boys, and at the end of it Eliza became a widow without anything to support either her or her children. They had lived since their marriage at the rate of £12,000 a year,[52] of which Mr Cecil's estate being rather less than the twentieth part, they had been able to save but a trifle, having lived to the utmost extent of their income.

Eliza, being perfectly conscious of the derangement[53] in their affairs, immediately on her husband's death set sail for England, in a man-of-war of fifty-five guns, which they had had built in their more prosperous days. But no sooner had she stepped on shore at Dover, with a child in each hand, than she was seized by the officers of the duchess, and conducted by them to a snug little Newgate[54] of their lady's, which she had erected for the reception of her own private prisoners.

No sooner had Eliza entered her dungeon than the first thought which occurred to her was how to get out of it again. She went to the door, but it was locked. She looked at the window, but it was barred with iron. Disappointed in both her expectations, she despaired of effecting her escape, when she fortunately perceived in a corner of her cell a small saw and ladder of ropes. With the saw she instantly went to work and in a few weeks had displaced every bar but one, to which she fastened the ladder.

A difficulty then occurred which for some time she knew not how to obviate. Her children were too small to get down the ladder by themselves, nor would it be possible for her to take them in her arms when *she* made the descent. At last she determined to fling down all her clothes, of which she had a large quantity, and then, having given them strict charge not to hurt themselves, throw her children after them. She herself with ease descended by the ladder, at the bottom of which she had the pleasure of finding her little boys in perfect health and fast asleep.

Her wardrobe she now saw a fatal necessity of selling, both for the preservation of her children and herself. With tears in her eyes, she parted with these last relics of her former glory, and with the money she got for them, bought others more useful, some playthings for her boys and a gold watch for herself.

But scarcely was she provided with the above-mentioned necessaries than she began to find herself rather hungry, and had reason to think, by their biting off two of her fingers, that her children were much in the same situation.

To remedy these unavoidable misfortunes, she determined to return to her old friends, Sir George and Lady Harcourt, whose generosity she had so often experienced and hoped to experience as often again.

She had about forty miles to travel before she could reach their hospitable mansion; having walked thirty without stopping, she found herself at the entrance of a town where often in happier times she had accompanied Sir George and Lady Harcourt to there regale themselves with a cold collation[55] at one of the inns.

The reflections that her adventures since the last time she had partaken of these happy junketings[56] afforded her occupied her mind for some time as she sat on the steps at the door of a gentleman's house. As soon as these reflections were ended, she arose and determined to take her station at the very inn she remembered with so much delight, from the company of which, as they went in and out, she hoped to receive some charitable gratuity.

She had but just taken her post at the inn-yard before a carriage drove out of it, and on turning the corner at which she was stationed, stopped to give the postilion[57] an opportunity of admiring the beauty of the prospect. Eliza then advanced to the carriage, and was going to request their charity, when, on fixing her eyes on the lady within it, she exclaimed, 'Lady Harcourt!'

To which the lady replied, 'Eliza!'

'Yes, madam, it is the wretched Eliza herself.'

Sir George, who was also in the carriage, but too much amazed to speak, was proceeding to demand an explanation from Eliza of the situation she was then in, when Lady Harcourt, in transports of joy, exclaimed, 'Sir George, Sir George, she is not only Eliza our adopted daughter, but our real child.'

'Our real child! What, Lady Harcourt, do you mean? You know you never even were with child. Explain yourself, I beseech you.'

'You must remember, Sir George, that when you sailed for America, you left me breeding.'

'I do, I do. Go on, dear Polly.'

'Four months after you were gone, I was delivered of this girl, but dreading your just resentment at her not proving the boy you wished, I took her to a haycock and laid her down. A few weeks afterwards, you returned, and, fortunately for me, made no enquiries on the subject. Satisfied within myself of the welfare of my child, I soon forgot I had one, insomuch that when we shortly after found her in the very haycock I had placed her, I had no more idea of her being my own than you had, and nothing, I will venture to say, would have recalled the circumstance to my remembrance but my thus accidentally hearing her voice, which now strikes me as being the very counterpart of my own child's.'

'The rational and convincing account you have given of the whole affair,' said Sir George, 'leaves no doubt of her being our daughter and as such I freely forgive the robbery she was guilty of.'

A mutual reconciliation then took place, and Eliza, ascending the carriage with her two children, returned to that home from which she had been absent nearly four years.

No sooner was she reinstated in her accustomed power at Harcourt Hall than she raised an army with which she entirely demolished the duchess's Newgate, snug as it was, and by that act gained the blessings of thousands and the applause of her own heart.

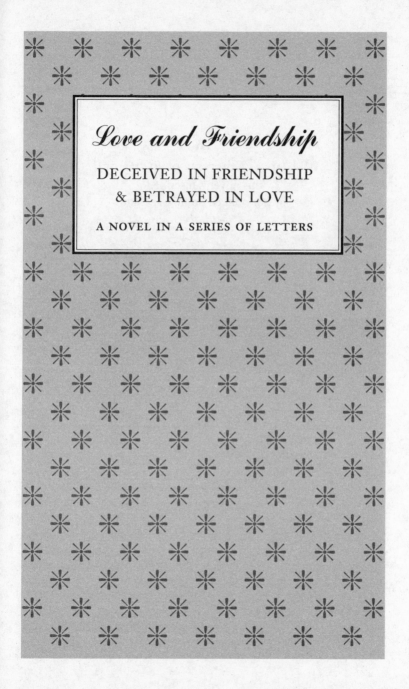

Love and Friendship

DECEIVED IN FRIENDSHIP
& BETRAYED IN LOVE

A NOVEL IN A SERIES OF LETTERS

To

Madame la Comtesse de Feuillide [58]

this novel is inscribed
by her obliged humble servant
the Author

Letter 1

ISABEL TO LAURA

How often, in answer to my repeated entreaties that you would give my daughter a regular detail of the misfortunes and adventures of your life, have you said, 'No, my friend, never will I comply with your request till I may be no longer in danger of again experiencing such dreadful ones.'

Surely that time is now at hand. You are this day fifty-five. If a woman may ever be said to be in safety from the determined perseverance of disagreeable lovers and the cruel persecutions of obstinate fathers, surely it must be at such a time of life.

ISABEL

Letter 2

LAURA TO ISABEL

Although I cannot agree with you in supposing that I shall never again be exposed to misfortunes as unmerited as those I have already experienced, yet to avoid the imputation of obstinacy or ill-nature, I will gratify the curiosity of your daughter; and may the fortitude with which I have suffered the many afflictions of my past life prove to her a useful lesson for the support of those which may befall her in her own.

LAURA

Letter 3

LAURA TO MARIANNE

As the daughter of my most intimate friend I think you entitled to that knowledge of my unhappy story, which your mother has so often solicited me to give you.

My father was a native of Ireland and an inhabitant of Wales; my mother was the natural[59] daughter of a Scotch peer by an Italian opera girl;[60] I was born in Spain and received my education at a convent in France. When I had reached my eighteenth year, I was recalled by my parents to my paternal roof in Wales. Our mansion was situated in one of the most romantic parts of the Vale of Uske.[61] Though my charms are now considerably softened and somewhat impaired by the misfortunes I have undergone, I was once beautiful. But lovely as I was, the graces of my person were the least of my perfections. Of every accomplishment accustomary [62] to my sex, I was mistress. When in the convent, my progress had always exceeded my instructions, my acquirements had been wonderful for my age, and I had shortly surpassed my masters.

In my mind, every virtue that could adorn it was centred; it was the rendezvous [63] of every good quality and of every noble sentiment.

A sensibility [64] too tremblingly alive to every affliction of my friends, my acquaintance and particularly to every affliction of my own, was my only fault, if a fault it could be called. Alas! how altered now! Though indeed my own misfortunes do not make less impression on me than they ever did, yet now I never feel for those of another. My accomplishments, too, begin to fade – I can neither sing so well nor dance so gracefully as I once did – and I have entirely forgot the *Minuet Dela Cour*.[65]

Adieu,

LAURA

Letter 4

LAURA TO MARIANNE

Our neighbourhood was small,[66] for it consisted only of your mother. She may probably have already told you that, being left by her parents in indigent circumstances, she had retired into Wales on economical motives. There it was our friendship first commenced. Isabel was then one-and-twenty. Though pleasing both in her person and manners, between ourselves she never possessed the hundredth part of my beauty or accomplishments. Isabel had seen the world. She had passed two years at one of the first boarding-schools in London; had spent a fortnight in Bath and had supped one night in Southampton.

'Beware, my Laura,' she would often say, 'beware of the insipid vanities and idle dissipations of the Metropolis of England. Beware of the unmeaning luxuries of Bath and of the stinking fish of Southampton.'

'Alas!' exclaimed I, 'how am I to avoid those evils I shall never be exposed to? What probability is there of my ever tasting the dissipations of London, the luxuries of Bath or the stinking fish of Southampton? I who am doomed to waste my days of youth and beauty in a humble cottage in the Vale of Uske.'

Ah! little did I then think I was ordained so soon to quit that humble cottage for the deceitful pleasures of the world.

Adieu,

LAURA

Letter 5

LAURA TO MARIANNE

One evening in December as my father, my mother and myself were arranged in social converse round our fireside, we were on a sudden greatly astonished by hearing a violent knocking on the outward door of our rustic cot.[67]

My father started – 'What noise is that,' said he. 'It sounds like a loud rapping at the door,' replied my mother. 'It does indeed,' cried I. 'I am of your opinion;' said my father, 'it certainly does appear to proceed from some uncommon violence exerted against our unoffending door.' 'Yes,' exclaimed I. 'I cannot help thinking it must be somebody who knocks for admittance.'

'That is another point,' replied he. 'We must not pretend to determine on what motive the person may knock – though that someone *does* rap at the door, I am partly convinced.'

Here, a second tremendous rap interrupted my father in his speech, and somewhat alarmed my mother and me.

'Had we not better go and see who it is?' said she. 'The servants are out.' 'I think we had,' replied I. 'Certainly,' added my father, 'by all means.' 'Shall we go now?' said my mother. 'The sooner the better,' answered he. 'Oh! let no time be lost,' cried I.

A third, more violent rap than ever again assaulted our ears. 'I am certain there is somebody knocking at the door,' said my mother. 'I think there must be,' replied my father. 'I fancy the servants are returned,' said I. 'I think I hear Mary going to the door.' 'I'm glad of it,' cried my father, 'for I long to know who it is.'

I was right in my conjecture; for Mary, instantly entering the room, informed us that a young gentleman and his servant were at the door; they had lost their way, were very cold and begged leave to warm themselves by our fire.

'Won't you admit them?' said I. 'You have no objection, my dear?' said my father. 'None in the world,' replied my mother.

Mary, without waiting for any further commands, immediately left the room and quickly returned, introducing the most beauteous and amiable youth I had ever beheld. The servant, she kept to herself.

My natural sensibility had already been greatly affected by the sufferings of the unfortunate stranger and no sooner did I first behold him than I felt that on him the happiness or misery of my future life must depend.

Adieu,

LAURA

Letter 6

LAURA TO MARIANNE

The noble youth informed us that his name was Lindsay – for particular reasons, however, I shall conceal it under that of Talbot. He told us that he was the son of an English baronet,[68] that his mother had been many years no more and that he had a sister of the middle size. 'My father,' he continued, 'is a mean and mercenary wretch – it is only to such particular friends as this dear party that I would thus betray his failings. Your virtues, my amiable Polydore,' addressing himself to my father, 'yours, dear Claudia,[69] and yours, my charming Laura, call on me to repose in you my confidence.' We bowed. 'My father, seduced by the false glare of fortune and the deluding pomp of title, insisted on my giving my hand to Lady Dorothea. "No never!" exclaimed I. "Lady Dorothea is lovely and engaging; I prefer no woman to her; but know, sir, that I scorn to marry her in compliance with your wishes." No! Never shall it be said that I obliged my father.'

We all admired the noble manliness of his reply.

He continued. 'Sir Edward was surprised; he had perhaps little expected to meet with so spirited an opposition to his will. "Where, Edward, in the name of wonder," said he, "did you pick up this un-meaning gibberish? You have been studying novels,[70] I suspect." I scorned to answer: it would have been beneath my dignity. I mounted my horse and followed by my faithful William set forwards for my aunt's.

'My father's house is situated in Bedfordshire, my aunt's in Middlesex, and though I flatter myself with being a tolerable proficient in geography,[71] I know not how it happened, but I found myself entering this beautiful Vale, which I find is in South Wales, when I had expected to have reached my aunt's.

'After having wandered some time on the banks of the Uske without knowing which way to go, I began to lament my cruel destiny in the bitterest and most pathetic manner. It was now perfectly dark, not a single star was there to direct my steps, and I know not what might have befallen me had I not at length discerned through the solemn gloom that surrounded me a distant light, which, as I approached it, I discovered to be the cheerful blaze of your fire. Impelled by the combination of misfortunes under which I laboured, namely fear, cold and hunger, I hesitated not to ask admittance, which at length I have gained; and now, my adorable Laura,' continued he, taking my hand, 'when may I hope to receive that reward for all the painful sufferings I have undergone during the course of my attachment to you to which I have ever aspired? Oh! when will you reward me with yourself?' 'This instant, dear and amiable Edward,' replied I.

We were immediately united by my father, who though he had never taken orders[72] had been bred to the Church.

Adieu,

LAURA

Letter 7

LAURA TO MARIANNE

We remained but a few days after our marriage in the Vale of Uske. After taking an affecting farewell of my father, my mother and my Isabel, I accompanied Edward to his aunt's in Middlesex. Philippa received us both with every expression of affectionate love. My arrival was indeed a most agreeable surprise to her as she had not only been totally ignorant of my marriage with her nephew, but had never even had the slightest idea of there being such a person in the world.

Augusta, the sister of Edward, was on a visit to her when we arrived. I found her exactly what her brother had described her to be – of the middle size. She received me with equal surprise, though not with equal cordiality, as Philippa. There was a disagreeable coldness and forbidding reserve in her reception of me which was equally distressing and unexpected; none of that interesting sensibility or amiable sympathy in her manners and address to me when we first met which should have distinguished our introduction to each other. Her language was neither warm, nor affectionate, her expressions of regard were neither animated nor cordial; her arms were not opened to receive me to her heart, though my own were extended to press her to mine.

A short conversation between Augusta and her brother, which I accidentally overheard, increased my dislike of her, and convinced me that her heart was no more formed for the soft ties of love than for the endearing intercourse of friendship.

'But do you think that my father will ever be reconciled to this imprudent connection?' said Augusta.

'Augusta,' replied the noble youth, 'I thought you had a better opinion of me than to imagine I would so abjectly degrade myself as to consider my father's concurrence in any of my affairs either of consequence or concern to me. Tell me, Augusta, tell me with sincerity, did you ever know me consult his inclinations or follow his advice in the least trifling particular since the age of fifteen?'

'Edward,' replied she, 'you are surely too diffident in your own praise. Since you were fifteen only! My dear brother, since you were five years old, I entirely acquit you of ever having willingly contributed to the satisfaction of your father. But still I am not without apprehensions of your being shortly obliged to degrade yourself in your own eyes by seeking a support for your wife in the generosity of Sir Edward.'

'Never, never, Augusta, will I so demean myself,' said Edward. 'Support! What support will Laura want which she can receive from him?'

'Only those very insignificant ones of victuals and drink,' answered she.

'Victuals and drink!' replied my husband in a most nobly contemptuous manner; 'and dost thou then imagine that there is no other support for an exalted mind (such as is my Laura's) than the mean and indelicate employment of eating and drinking?'

'None, that I know of, so efficacious,' returned Augusta.

'And did you then never feel the pleasing pangs of love, Augusta?' replied my Edward. 'Does it appear impossible, to your vile and corrupted palate, to exist on love? Can you not conceive the luxury of living in every distress that poverty can inflict with the object of your tenderest affection?'

'You are too ridiculous,' said Augusta, 'to argue with; perhaps, however, you may in time be convinced that . . . '

Here I was prevented from hearing the remainder of her speech by the appearance of a very handsome young woman, who was ushered into the room at the door of which I had been listening. On hearing her announced by the name of 'Lady Dorothea', I instantly quitted my post and followed her into the parlour, for I well remembered that she was the lady proposed as a wife for my Edward by the cruel and unrelenting baronet.

Although Lady Dorothea's visit was nominally to Philippa and Augusta, yet I have some reason to imagine that (acquainted with the marriage and arrival of Edward) to see me was a principal motive to it.

I soon perceived that though lovely and elegant in her person and though easy and polite in her address, she was of that inferior order of beings with regard to delicate feeling, tender sentiments and refined sensibility of which Augusta was one.

She stayed but half an hour and in the course of her visit neither confided to me any of her secret thoughts nor requested me to confide in her any of mine. You will easily imagine therefore, my dear Marianne, that I could not feel any ardent affection or very sincere attachment for Lady Dorothea.

Adieu,

LAURA

Letter 8

LAURA TO MARIANNE, *in continuation*

Lady Dorothea had not left us long before another visitor, as unexpected a one as her ladyship, was announced. It was Sir Edward, who, informed by Augusta of her brother's marriage, came doubtless to reproach him for having dared to unite himself to me without his knowledge. But Edward, foreseeing his design, approached him with heroic fortitude as soon as he entered the room, and addressed him in the following manner.

'Sir Edward, I know the motive of your journey here – you come with the base design of reproaching me for having entered into an indissoluble engagement with my Laura without your consent. But, sir, I glory in the act. It is my greatest boast that I have incurred the displeasure of my father!'

So saying, he took my hand and, while Sir Edward, Philippa and Augusta were doubtless reflecting with admiration on his undaunted bravery, led me from the parlour to his father's carriage which yet remained at the door and in which we were instantly conveyed from the pursuit of Sir Edward.

The postilions[73] had at first received orders only to take the London road; as soon as we had sufficiently reflected, however, we ordered them to drive to M—, the seat of Edward's most particular friend, which was but a few miles distant.

At M— we arrived in a few hours, and on sending in our names were immediately admitted to Sophia, the wife of Edward's friend. After having been deprived during the course of three weeks of a real friend (for such I term your mother), imagine my transports at beholding one most truly worthy of the name. Sophia was rather above the middle size and most elegantly formed. A soft languor spread over her lovely features, but increased their beauty. It was the characteristic of her mind. She was all sensibility and feeling. We flew into each other's arms, and after having exchanged vows of mutual friendship for the rest of our lives, instantly unfolded to each other the most inward secrets of our hearts. We were interrupted in the delightful employment by the entrance of Augustus, (Edward's friend) who was just returned from a solitary ramble.

Never did I see such an affecting scene as was the meeting of Edward and Augustus.

'My life! my soul!' exclaimed the former. 'My adorable angel!' replied the latter, as they flew into each other's arms. It was too pathetic[74] for the feelings of Sophia and myself – we fainted alternately on a sofa.

Adieu,

LAURA

Letter 9

The same to the same

Towards the close of the day we received the following letter from Philippa.

Sir Edward is greatly incensed by your abrupt departure; he has taken back Augusta with him to Bedfordshire. Much as I wish to enjoy again your charming society, I cannot determine to snatch you from that of such dear and deserving friends – When your visit to them is terminated, I trust you will return to the arms of your

PHILIPPA

We returned a suitable answer to this affectionate note and after thanking her for her kind invitation assured her that we would certainly avail ourselves of it whenever we might have no other place to go to. Though certainly nothing could, to any reasonable being, have appeared more satisfactory than so grateful a reply to her invitation, yet I know not how it was, but she was certainly capricious enough to be displeased with our behaviour and in a few weeks after, either to revenge our conduct or relieve her own solitude, married a young and illiterate fortune-hunter. This imprudent step (though we were sensible that it would probably deprive us of that fortune which Philippa had ever taught us to expect) could not on our own accounts excite from our exalted minds a single sigh; yet fearful lest it might prove a source of endless misery to the deluded bride, our trembling sensibility was greatly affected when we were first informed of the event. The affectionate entreaties of Augustus and Sophia, that we would for ever consider their house as our home, easily prevailed on us to determine never more to leave them. In the society of my Edward and this amiable pair, I passed the happiest moments of my life; our time was most delightfully spent in mutual protestations of friendship and in vows of unalterable love, in which we were secure from being interrupted by intruding and disagreeable visitors as Augustus and Sophia had, on their first entrance in the neighbourhood, taken due care to inform the surrounding families that as their happiness centred wholly in themselves they wished for no other society. But alas! my dear Marianne, such happiness as I then enjoyed was too perfect to be lasting. A most severe and unexpected blow at once destroyed every sensation of pleasure. Convinced as you must be from what I have already told you concerning Augustus and Sophia that there never were a happier couple, I need not, I imagine, inform you that their union had been contrary to the inclinations of their cruel and mercenary parents, who had vainly endeavoured with obstinate perseverance to force them into marriages with those whom they had ever abhorred; but, with an heroic fortitude worthy to be related and admired, they had both constantly refused to submit to such despotic power.

After having so nobly disentangled themselves from the shackles of parental authority by a clandestine marriage,[75] they were determined never to forfeit the good opinion they had gained in the world, in so doing, by accepting any proposals of reconciliation that might be offered them by their fathers; to this further trial of their noble independence, however, they never were exposed.

They had been married but a few months when our visit to them commenced, during which time they had been amply supported by a considerable sum of money which Augustus had gracefully purloined from his unworthy father's escritoire,[76] a few days before his union with Sophia.

By our arrival their expenses were considerably increased though their means for supplying them were then nearly exhausted. But they, exalted creatures! scorned to reflect a moment on their pecuniary distresses and would have blushed at the idea of paying their debts. Alas! what was their reward for such disinterested behaviour! The beautiful Augustus was arrested and we were all undone. Such perfidious treachery in the merciless perpetrators of the deed will shock your gentle nature, dearest Marianne, as much as it then affected the delicate sensibility of Edward, Sophia, your Laura and of Augustus himself. To complete such unparalleled barbarity we were informed that an execution in the house[77] would shortly take place. Ah! what could we do but what we did! We sighed and fainted on the sofa.

Adieu,

LAURA

Letter 10

LAURA in continuation

When we were somewhat recovered from the overpowering effusions of our grief, Edward desired that we would consider what was the most prudent step to be taken in our unhappy situation while he repaired to his imprisoned friend to lament over his misfortunes. We promised that we would, and he set forwards on his journey to town. During his absence, we faithfully complied with his desire, and after the most mature deliberation, at length agreed that the best thing we could do was to leave the house – of which we every moment expected the Officers of Justice[78] to take possession. We waited, therefore, with the greatest impatience, for the return of Edward in order to impart to him the result of our deliberations. But no Edward appeared. In vain did we count the tedious moments of his absence – in vain did we weep – in vain even did we sigh – no Edward returned. This was too cruel, too unexpected a blow to our gentle sensibility – we could not support it – we could only faint. At length, collecting all the resolution I was mistress of, I arose, and after packing up some necessary apparel for Sophia and myself, I dragged her to a carriage I had ordered and we instantly set out for London. As the habitation of Augustus was within twelve miles of town, it was not long e'er we arrived there, and no sooner had we entered Holborn than, letting down one of the front glasses, I enquired of every decent-looking person that we passed if they had seen my Edward?

But as we drove too rapidly to allow them to answer my repeated enquiries, I gained little or, indeed, no information concerning him. 'Where am I to drive?' said the postilion. 'To Newgate,[79] gentle youth,' replied I, 'to see Augustus.' 'Oh! no, no,' exclaimed Sophia, 'I cannot go to Newgate; I shall not be able to support the sight of my Augustus in so cruel a confinement – my feelings are sufficiently shocked by the *recital* of his distress, but to behold it will overpower my sensibility.' As I perfectly agreed with her in the justice of her sentiments, the postilion was instantly directed to return into the country. You may perhaps have been somewhat surprised, my dearest Marianne, that in the distress I then endured, destitute of any support, and unprovided with any habitation, I should never once have remembered my father and mother or my paternal cottage in the Vale of Uske. To account for the seeming forgetfulness, I must inform you of a trifling circumstance concerning them which I have as yet never mentioned. The death of my parents a few weeks after my departure is the circumstance I allude to. By their decease I became the lawful inheritress of their house and fortune. But alas! the house had never been their own and their fortune had only been an annuity[80] on their own lives. Such is the depravity of the world! To your mother I should have returned with pleasure, should have been happy to have introduced to her my charming Sophia and should with cheerfulness have passed the remainder of my life in their dear society in the Vale of Uske, had not one obstacle to the execution of so agreeable a scheme intervened, which was the marriage and removal of your mother to a distant part of Ireland.

Adieu,

LAURA

Letter 11

LAURA *in continuation*

'I have a relation in Scotland,' said Sophia to me as we left London, 'who I am certain would not hesitate in receiving me.' 'Shall I order the boy to drive there?' said I, but instantly recollecting myself, exclaimed, 'Alas I fear it will be too long a journey for the horses.' Unwilling, however, to act only from my own inadequate knowledge of the strength and abilities of horses, I consulted the postilion, who was entirely of my opinion concerning the affair. We therefore determined to change horses at the next town and to travel post[81] the remainder of the journey. When we arrived at the last inn we were to stop at, which was but a few miles from the house of Sophia's relation, unwilling to intrude our society on him unexpected and unthought of, we wrote a very elegant and well-penned note to him containing an account of our destitute and melancholy situation, and of our intention to spend some months with him in Scotland. As soon as we had dispatched this letter, we immediately prepared to follow it in person and were stepping into the carriage for that purpose when our attention was attracted by the entrance of a coroneted coach and four [82] into the inn-yard. A gentleman considerably advanced in years descended from it. At his first appearance my sensibility was wonderfully affected, and e'er I had gazed at him a second time, an instinctive sympathy whispered to my heart that he was my grandfather. Convinced that I could not be mistaken in my conjecture, I instantly sprang from the carriage I had just entered, and following the venerable stranger into the room he had been shown to, I threw myself on my knees before him and besought him to acknowledge me as his grandchild. He started, and after having attentively examined my features, raised me from the ground and, throwing his grandfatherly arms around my neck, exclaimed, 'Acknowledge thee! Yes, dear resemblance of my Laurina and Laurina's daughter, sweet image of my Claudia and my Claudia's mother, I do acknowledge thee as the daughter of the one and the granddaughter of the other.' While he was thus tenderly embracing me, Sophia, astonished at my precipitate departure, entered the room in search of me. No sooner had she caught the eye of the venerable peer, than he exclaimed with every mark of astonishment – 'Another granddaughter! Yes, yes, I see you are the daughter of my Laurina's eldest girl; your resemblance to the beauteous Matilda sufficiently proclaims it.' 'Oh!' replied Sophia, 'when I first beheld you the instinct of nature whispered me that we were in some degree related. But whether grandfathers, or grandmothers, I could not pretend to determine.' He folded her in his arms, and while they were tenderly embracing, the door of the apartment opened and a most beautiful young man appeared. On perceiving him, Lord St Clair started and retreating back a few paces, with uplifted hands, said, 'Another grandchild! What an unexpected happiness is this! to discover in the space of three minutes, as many of my descendants! This, I am certain, is Philander, the son of my Laurina's third girl, the amiable Bertha; there wants now but the presence of Gustavus to complete the union of my Laurina's grandchildren.'

'And here he is,' said a graceful youth who that instant entered the room, 'here is the Gustavus you desire to see. I am the son of Agatha, your Laurina's fourth and youngest daughter.' 'I see you are indeed,' replied Lord St Clair. 'But tell me,' continued he, looking fearfully towards the door, 'tell me, have I any other grandchildren in the house?' 'None, my lord.' 'Then I will provide for you all without further delay. Here are four banknotes of £50 each – take them and remember I have done the duty of a grandfather.' He instantly left the room and immediately afterwards the house.

Adieu,

LAURA

Letter 12

LAURA *in continuation*

You may imagine how greatly we were surprised by the sudden departure of Lord St Clair. 'Ignoble grandsire!' exclaimed Sophia. 'Unworthy grandfather!' said I, and instantly we fainted in each other's arms. How long we remained in this situation I know not; but when we recovered we found ourselves alone, without either Gustavus, Philander, or the banknotes. As we were deploring our unhappy fate, the door of the apartment opened and Macdonald was announced. He was Sophia's cousin. The haste with which he came to our relief so soon after the receipt of our note, spoke so greatly in his favour that I hesitated not to pronounce him, at first sight, a tender and sympathetic friend. Alas! he little deserved the name – for though he told us that he was much concerned at our misfortunes, yet by his own account it appeared that the perusal of them had neither drawn from him a single sigh, nor induced him to bestow one curse on our vindictive stars. He told Sophia that his daughter depended on her returning with him to Macdonald Hall, and that as his cousin's friend he should be happy to see me there also. To Macdonald Hall, therefore, we went, and were received with great kindness by Janetta, the daughter of Macdonald and the mistress of the mansion. Janetta was then only fifteen; naturally well disposed, endowed with a susceptible heart and a sympathetic disposition, she might, had these amiable qualities been properly encouraged, have been an ornament to human nature; but unfortunately her father possessed not a soul sufficiently exalted to admire so promising a disposition, and had endeavoured by every means in his power to prevent its increasing with her years. He had actually so far extinguished the natural noble sensibility of her heart as to prevail on her to accept an offer from a young man of his recommendation. They were to be married in a few months, and Graham was in the house when we arrived. *We* soon saw through his character. He was just such a man as one might have expected to be the choice of Macdonald. They said he was sensible, well informed, and agreeable; we did not pretend to judge of such trifles, but as we were convinced he had no soul, that he had never read *The Sorrows of Werther*,[83] and that his hair bore not the least resemblance to auburn, we were certain that Janetta could feel no affection for him, or at least that she ought to feel none. The very circumstance of his being her father's choice, too, was so much in his disfavour, that had he been deserving her in every other respect, yet *that* of itself ought to have been a sufficient reason in the eyes of Janetta for rejecting him. These considerations we were determined to represent to her in their proper light and doubted not of meeting with the desired success from one naturally so well disposed, whose errors in the affair had only arisen from a want of proper confidence in her own opinion and a suitable contempt for her father's. We found her indeed all that our warmest wishes could have hoped for; we had no difficulty to convince her that it was impossible she could love Graham and that it was her duty to disobey her father; the only thing at which she rather seemed to hesitate was our assertion that she must be attached to some other person. For some time, she persevered in declaring that she knew no other young man for whom she had the smallest affection; but upon our explaining the impossibility of such a thing, she said that she believed she *did* like Captain McKenzie better than anyone she knew besides. This confession satisfied us and after having enumerated the good qualities of McKenzie and assured her that she was violently in love with him, we desired to know whether he had ever in any wise declared his affection to her.

'So far from having ever declared it, I have no reason to imagine that he has ever felt any for me,' said Janetta. 'That he certainly adores you,' replied Sophia, 'there can be no doubt. The attachment must be reciprocal. Did he never gaze on you with admiration – tenderly press your hand – drop an involuntary tear – and leave the room abruptly?' 'Never,' replied she, 'that I remember; he has always left the room indeed when his visit has been ended, but has never gone away particularly abruptly or without making a bow.' 'Indeed, my love,' said I, 'you must be mistaken – for it is absolutely impossible that he should ever have left you but with confusion, despair and precipitation. Consider but for a moment, Janetta, and you must be convinced how absurd it is to suppose that he could ever make a bow, or behave like any other person.' Having settled this point to our satisfaction, the next we took into consideration was to determine in what manner we should inform McKenzie of the favourable opinion Janetta entertained of him ... We at length agreed to acquaint him with it by an anonymous letter which Sophia drew up in the following manner.

Oh! happy lover of the beautiful Janetta, oh! enviable possessor of *her* heart whose hand is destined to another, why do you thus delay a confession of your attachment to the amiable object of it? Oh! consider that a few weeks will at once put an end to every flattering hope that you may now entertain by uniting the unfortunate victim of her father's cruelty to the execrable and detested Graham.

Alas! why do you thus so cruelly connive at the projected misery of her and of yourself by delaying to communicate that scheme which has doubtless long possessed your imagination? A secret union will at once secure the felicity of both.

The amiable McKenzie, whose modesty, as he afterwards assured us, had been the only reason of his having so long concealed the violence of his affection for Janetta, on receiving this billet flew on the wings of love to Macdonald Hall, and so powerfully pleaded his attachment to her who inspired it that after a few more private interviews Sophia and I experienced the satisfaction of seeing them depart for Gretna Green,[84] which they chose for the celebration of their nuptials in preference to any other place, although it was at a considerable distance from Macdonald Hall.

Adieu,

LAURA

Letter 13

LAURA *in continuation*

They had been gone nearly a couple of hours, before either Macdonald or Graham had entertained any suspicion of the affair. And they might not even then have suspected it, but for the following little accident. Sophia happening one day to open a private drawer in Macdonald's library with one of her own keys, discovered that it was the place where he kept his papers of consequence and among them some banknotes of considerable amount. This discovery she imparted to me; and having agreed together that it would be a proper treatment of so vile a wretch as Macdonald to deprive him of money perhaps dishonestly gained, it was determined that the next time we should either of us happen to go that way, we would take one or more of the banknotes from the drawer. This well-meant plan we had often successfully put in execution; but alas! on the very day of Janetta's escape, as Sophia was majestically removing the fifth banknote from the drawer to her own purse, she was suddenly most impertinently interrupted in her employment by the entrance of Macdonald himself, in a most abrupt and precipitate manner. Sophia (who, though naturally all winning sweetness, could when occasion demanded it call forth the dignity of her sex) instantly put on a most forbidding look, and darting an angry frown on the undaunted culprit, demanded in a haughty tone of voice, 'Wherefore her retirement was thus insolently broken in on?' The unblushing Macdonald, without even endeavouring to exculpate himself from the crime he was charged with, meanly endeavoured to reproach Sophia with ignobly defrauding him of his money . . . The dignity of Sophia was wounded; 'Wretch,' exclaimed she, hastily replacing the banknote in the drawer, 'how darest thou to accuse me of an act of which the bare idea makes me blush?' The base wretch was still unconvinced and continued to upbraid the justly offended Sophia in such opprobious language that at length he so greatly provoked the gentle sweetness of her nature as to induce her to revenge herself on him by informing him of Janetta's elopement, and of the active part we had both taken in the affair. At this period of their quarrel, I entered the library and was, as you may imagine, equally offended as Sophia at the ill grounded accusations of the malevolent and contemptible Macdonald. 'Base miscreant!' cried I, 'how canst thou thus undauntedly endeavour to sully the spotless reputation of such bright excellence? Why dost thou not suspect *my* innocence as soon?' 'Be satisfied, madam,' replied he, 'I *do* suspect it, and therefore must desire that you will both leave this house in less than half an hour.'

'We shall go willingly,' answered Sophia. 'Our hearts have long detested thee, and nothing but our friendship for thy daughter could have induced us to remain so long beneath thy roof.'

'Your friendship for my daughter has indeed been most powerfully exerted by throwing her into the arms of an unprincipled fortune-hunter,' replied he.

'Yes,' exclaimed I, 'amidst every misfortune, it will afford us some consolation to reflect that by this one act of friendship to Janetta we have amply discharged every obligation that we have received from her father.'

'It must indeed be a most grateful reflection to your exalted minds,' said he.

As soon as we had packed up our wardrobe and valuables, we left Macdonald Hall, and after having walked about a mile and a half, we sat down by the side of a clear limpid stream to refresh our exhausted limbs. The place was suited to meditation. A grove of full-grown elms sheltered us from the east. A bed of full-grown nettles from the west. Before us ran the murmuring brook and behind us ran the turnpike road.[85] We were in a mood for contemplation and in a disposition to enjoy so beautiful a spot. A mutual silence which had for some time reigned between us was at length broken by my exclaiming – 'What a lovely scene! Alas why are not Edward and Augustus here to enjoy its beauties with us?'

'Ah! my beloved Laura,' cried Sophia, 'for pity's sake forbear recalling to my remembrance the unhappy situation of my imprisoned husband. Alas, what would I not give to learn the fate of my Augustus! to know if he is still in Newgate, or if he is yet hung. But never shall I be able so far to conquer my tender sensibility as to enquire after him. Oh! do not, I beseech you, ever let me again hear you repeat his beloved name. It affects me too deeply. I cannot bear to hear him mentioned, it wounds my feelings.'

'Excuse me, my Sophia, for having thus unwillingly offended you,' replied I – and then, changing the conversation, desired her to admire the noble grandeur of the elms which sheltered us from the eastern zephyr.[86]

'Alas! my Laura,' returned she, 'avoid so melancholy a subject, I entreat you. Do not again wound my sensibility by observations on those elms. They remind me of Augustus. He was like them, tall, majestic – he possessed that noble grandeur which you admire in them.'

I was silent, fearful lest I might any more unwillingly distress her by fixing on any other subject of conversation which might again remind her of Augustus.

'Why do you not speak, my Laura?' said she after a short pause. 'I cannot support this silence – you must not leave me to my own reflections; they ever recur to Augustus.'

'What a beautiful sky!' said I. 'How charmingly is the azure varied by those delicate streaks of white!'

'Oh! my Laura,' replied she, hastily withdrawing her eyes from a momentary glance at the sky, 'do not thus distress me by calling my attention to an object which so cruelly reminds me of my Augustus's blue satin waistcoat striped with white! In pity to your unhappy friend, avoid a subject so distressing.' What could I do? The feelings of Sophia were at that time so exquisite, and the tenderness she felt for Augustus so poignant, that I had not power to start any other topic, justly fearing that it might in some unforeseen manner again awaken all her sensibility by directing her thoughts to her husband. Yet to be silent would be cruel; she had entreated me to talk.

From this dilemma I was most fortunately relieved by an accident truly apropos; it was the lucky overturning of a gentleman's phaeton[87] on the road which ran murmuring behind us. It was a most fortunate accident as it diverted the attention of Sophia from the melancholy reflections which she had been before indulging. We instantly quitted our seats and ran to the rescue of those who but a few moments before had been in so elevated a situation as a fashionably high phaeton, but who were now laid low and sprawling in the dust. 'What an ample subject for reflection on the uncertain enjoyments of this world would not that phaeton and the life of Cardinal Wolsey[88] afford a thinking mind!' said I to Sophia as we were hastening to the field of action.

She had not time to answer me, for every thought was now engaged by the horrid spectacle before us. Two gentlemen most elegantly attired but weltering in their blood was what first struck our eyes; we approached – they were Edward and Augustus. Yes, dearest Marianne, they were our husbands! Sophia shrieked and fainted on the ground – I screamed and instantly ran mad. We remained thus mutually deprived of our senses some minutes, and on regaining them were deprived of them again. For an hour and a quarter did we continue in this unfortunate situation – Sophia fainting every moment and I running mad as often. At length, a groan from the hapless Edward (who alone retained any share of life) restored us to ourselves. Had we indeed before imagined that either of them lived, we should have been more sparing of our grief – but as we had supposed when we first beheld them that they were no more, we knew that nothing could remain to be done but what we were about. No sooner, therefore, did we hear my Edward's groan than, postponing our lamentations for the present, we hastily ran to the dear youth and kneeling on each side of him implored him not to die. 'Láura,' said he fixing his now languid eyes on me, 'I fear I have been overturned.'

I was overjoyed to find him yet sensible.

'Oh! tell me, Edward,' said I, 'tell me, I beseech you, before you die, what has befallen you since that unhappy day in which Augustus was arrested and we were separated – '

'I will,' said he, and instantly, fetching a deep sigh, expired. Sophia immediately sank again into a swoon. *My* grief was more audible. My voice faltered, my eyes assumed a vacant stare, my face became as pale as death, and my senses were considerably impaired.

'Talk not to me of phaetons,' said I, raving in a frantic, incoherent manner. 'Give me a violin. I'll play to him and soothe him in his melancholy hours – Beware, ye gentle nymphs, of Cupid's thunderbolts, avoid the piercing shafts of Jupiter [89] – Look at that grove of firs – I see a leg of mutton – They told me Edward was not dead; but they deceived me – they took him for a cucumber.' Thus I continued wildly exclaiming on my Edward's death. For two hours did I rave thus madly and should not then have left off, as I was not in the least fatigued, had not Sophia, who was just recovered from her swoon, entreated me to consider that night was now approaching and that the damps began to fall. 'And whither shall we go,' said I, 'to shelter us from either?' 'To that white cottage,' replied she, pointing to a neat building which rose up amidst the grove of elms and which I had not before observed. I agreed and we instantly walked to it; we knocked at the door and it was opened by an old woman; on being requested to afford us a night's lodging, she informed us that her house was but small, that she had only two bedrooms, but that we should, however, be welcome to one of them. We were satisfied and followed the good woman into the house, where we were greatly cheered by the sight of a comfortable fire. She was a widow and had only one daughter, who was then just seventeen – one of the best of ages; but alas! she was very plain and her name was Bridget . . . Nothing therefore could be expected from her – she could not be supposed to possess either exalted ideas, delicate feelings or refined sensibilities. She was nothing more than a mere good-tempered, civil and obliging young woman; as such we could scarcely dislike her – she was only an object of contempt.

Adieu,

LAURA

Letter 14

LAURA *in continuation*

Arm yourself my amiable young friend with all the philosophy you are mistress of; summon up all the fortitude you possess; for alas! in the perusal of the following pages your sensibility will be most severely tried. Ah! what were the misfortunes I had before experienced, and which I have already related to you, to the one I am now going to inform you of. The deaths of my father, my mother and my husband, though almost more than my gentle nature could support, were trifles in comparison to the misfortune I am now proceeding to relate. The morning after our arrival at the cottage, Sophia complained of a violent pain in her delicate limbs, accompanied by a disagreeable headache. She attributed it to a cold caught by her continued faintings in the open air as the dew was falling the evening before. This I feared was but too probably the case; since how could it be otherwise accounted for that I should have escaped the same indisposition but by supposing that the bodily exertions I had undergone in my repeated fits of frenzy had so effectually circulated and warmed my blood as to make me proof against the chilling damps of night; whereas Sophia, lying totally inactive on the ground, must have been exposed to all their severity. I was most seriously alarmed by her illness, which, trifling as it may appear to you, a certain instinctive sensibility whispered me would in the end be fatal to her.

Alas! my fears were but too fully justified; she grew gradually worse – and I daily became more alarmed for her. At length, she was obliged to confine herself solely to the bed allotted us by our worthy landlady. Her disorder turned to a galloping consumption[90] and in a few days carried her off. Amidst all my lamentations for her (and violent you may suppose they were), I yet received some consolation in the reflection of my having paid every attention to her that could be offered in her illness. I had wept over her every day – had bathed her sweet face with my tears and had pressed her fair hands continually in mine. 'My beloved Laura,' said she to me, a few hours before she died, 'take warning from my unhappy end and avoid the imprudent conduct which occasioned it . . . Beware of fainting-fits . . . Though at the time they may be refreshing and agreeable, yet believe me they will in the end, if too often repeated and at improper seasons, prove destructive to your constitution . . . My fate will teach you this . . . I die a martyr to my grief for the loss of Augustus . . . One fatal swoon has cost me my life . . . Beware of swoons, dear Laura . . . A frenzy fit is not one quarter so pernicious; it is an exercise to the body, and if not too violent, is, I dare say, conducive to health in its consequences. Run mad as often as you choose; but do not faint – '

These were the last words she ever addressed to me. It was her dying advice to her afflicted Laura, who has ever most faithfully adhered to it.

After having attended my lamented friend to her early grave, I immediately (though late at night) left the detested village in which she died, and near which had expired my husband and Augustus. I had not walked many yards from it before I was overtaken by a stagecoach, in which I instantly took a place, determined to proceed in it to Edinburgh, where I hoped to find some kind, some pitying friend who would receive and comfort me in my afflictions.

It was so dark when I entered the coach that I could not distinguish the number of my fellow-travellers; I could only perceive that they were many. Regardless, however, of anything concerning them, I gave myself up to my own sad reflections. A general silence prevailed – a silence, which was by nothing interrupted but by the loud and repeated snores of one of the party.

'What an illiterate villain must that man be!' thought I to myself. 'What a total want of delicate refinement must he have, who can thus shock our senses by such a brutal noise! He must, I am certain, be capable of every bad action! There is no crime too black for such a character!' Thus reasoned I within myself, and doubtless such were the reflections of my fellow travellers.

At length, returning day enabled me to behold the unprincipled scoundrel who had so violently disturbed my feelings. It was Sir Edward, the father of my deceased husband. By his side, sat Augusta, and on the same seat with me were your mother and Lady Dorothea. Imagine my surprise at finding myself thus seated among my old acquaintance. Great as was my astonishment, it was yet increased when, on looking out of the windows, I beheld the husband of Philippa, with Philippa by his side, on the coach box, and when, on looking behind, I beheld Philander and Gustavus in the basket.[91] 'Oh, heavens!' exclaimed I, 'is it possible that I should so unexpectedly be surrounded by my nearest relations and connections?' These words roused the rest of the party, and every eye was directed to the corner in which I sat. 'Oh! my Isabel,' continued I throwing myself across Lady Dorothea into her arms, 'receive once more to your bosom the unfortunate Laura. Alas! when we last parted in the Vale of Usk, I was happy in being united to the best of Edwards; I had then a father and a mother, and had never known misfortunes. But now deprived of every friend but you – '

'What!' interrupted Augusta, 'is my brother dead then? Tell us, I entreat you, what is become of him?'

'Yes, cold and insensible nymph,' replied I, 'that luckless swain your brother is no more, and you may now glory in being the heiress of Sir Edward's fortune.'

Although I had always despised her from the day I had overheard her conversation with my Edward, yet in civility I complied with her and Sir Edward's entreaties that I would inform them of the whole melancholy affair. They were greatly shocked – even the obdurate heart of Sir Edward and the insensible one of Augusta were touched with sorrow by the unhappy tale. At the request of your mother, I related to them every other misfortune which had befallen me since we parted. Of the imprisonment of Augustus and the absence of Edward – of our arrival in Scotland – of our unexpected meeting with our grandfather and our cousins – of our visit to Macdonald Hall – of the singular service we there performed towards Janetta – of her father's ingratitude for it – of his inhuman behaviour, unaccountable suspicions and barbarous treatment of us in obliging us to leave the house – of our lamentations on the loss of Edward and Augustus – and finally of the melancholy death of my beloved companion.

Pity and surprise were strongly depicted in your mother's countenance during the whole of my narration, but I am sorry to say that, to the eternal reproach of her sensibility, the latter infinitely predominated. Nay, faultless as my conduct had certainly been during the whole course of my late misfortunes and adventures, she pretended to find fault with my behaviour in many of the situations in which I had been placed. As I was sensible myself that I had always behaved in a manner which reflected honour on my feelings and refinement, I paid little attention to what she said, and desired her to satisfy my curiosity by informing me how she came there, instead of wounding my spotless reputation with unjustifiable reproaches. As soon as she had complied with my wishes in this particular and had given me an accurate detail of everything that had befallen her since our separation (the particulars of which, if you are not already acquainted with, your mother will give you), I applied to Augusta for the same information respecting herself, Sir Edward and Lady Dorothea.

She told me that having a considerable taste for the beauties of nature, her curiosity to behold the delightful scenes it exhibited in that part of the world had been so much raised by Gilpin's *Tour to the Highlands*[92] that she had prevailed on her father to undertake a tour to Scotland and had persuaded Lady Dorothea to accompany them. That they had arrived at Edinburgh a few days before and from thence had made daily excursions into the country around in the stagecoach[93] they were then in, from one of which excursions they were at that time returning. My next enquiries were concerning Philippa and her husband, the latter of whom had, I learned, having spent all her fortune, had recourse for subsistence to the talent in which he had always most excelled, namely, driving, and that having sold everything which belonged to them except their coach, had converted it into a stage and, in order to be removed from any of his former acquaintance, had driven it to Edinburgh from whence he went to Sterling every other day; that Philippa, still retaining her affection for her ungrateful husband, had followed him to Scotland and generally accompanied him in his little excursions to Sterling. 'It has only been to throw a little money into their pockets,' continued Augusta, 'that my father has always travelled in their coach to view the beauties of the country since our arrival in Scotland – for it would certainly have been much more agreeable to us to visit the Highlands in a post-chaise,[94] than merely to travel from Edinburgh to Sterling and from Sterling to Edinburgh every other day in a crowded and uncomfortable stage.' I perfectly agreed with her in her sentiments on the affair, and secretly blamed Sir Edward for thus sacrificing his daughter's pleasure for the sake of a ridiculous old woman whose folly in marrying so young a man ought to be punished. His behaviour, however, was entirely of a piece with his general character; for what could be expected from a man who possessed not the smallest atom of sensibility, who scarcely knew the meaning of sympathy, and who actually snored.

Adieu,

LAURA

Letter 15

LAURA *in continuation*

When we arrived at the town where we were to breakfast, I was determined to speak with Philander and Gustavus, and to that purpose as soon as I left the carriage, I went to the basket and tenderly enquired after their health, expressing my fears of the uneasiness of their situation. At first, they seemed rather confused at my appearance, dreading no doubt that I might call them to account for the money which our grandfather had left me and which they had unjustly deprived me of, but finding that I mentioned nothing of the matter, they desired me to step into the basket as we might there converse with greater ease. Accordingly, I entered, and while the rest of the party were devouring green tea[95] and buttered toast, we feasted ourselves in a more refined and sentimental manner by a confidential conversation. I informed them of everything which had befallen me during the course of my life, and at my request they related to me every incident of theirs.

'We are the sons, as you already know, of the two youngest daughters which Lord St Clair had by Laurina, an Italian opera girl. Our mothers could neither of them exactly ascertain who were our fathers, though it is generally believed that Philander is the son of one Philip Jones, a bricklayer, and that my father was Gregory Staves, a stay-maker[96] of Edinburgh. This is, however, of little consequence, for as our mothers were certainly never married to either of them it reflects no dishonour on our blood, which is of a most ancient and unpolluted kind. Bertha (the mother of Philander) and Agatha (my own mother) always lived together. They were neither of them very rich; their united fortunes had originally amounted to nine thousand pounds, but as they had always lived upon the principal[97] of it, when we were fifteen it was diminished to nine hundred. This nine hundred, they always kept in a drawer in one of the tables which stood in our common sitting-parlour, for the convenience of having it always at hand. Whether it was from this circumstance, of its being easily taken, or from a wish of being independent, or from an excess of sensibility (for which we were always remarkable), I cannot now determine, but certain it is that when we had reached our fifteenth year, we took the nine hundred pounds and ran away. Having obtained this prize we were determined to manage it with economy and not to spend it either with folly or extravagance. To this purpose we therefore divided it into nine parcels, one of which we devoted to victuals, the second to drink, the third to housekeeping, the fourth to carriages, the fifth to horses, the sixth to servants, the seventh to amusements, the eighth to clothes and the ninth to silver buckles. Having thus arranged our expenses for two months (for we expected to make the nine hundred pounds last as long), we hastened to London and had the good luck to spend it in seven weeks and a day, which was six days sooner than we had intended. As soon as we had thus happily disencumbered ourselves from the weight of so much money, we began to think of returning to our mothers, but accidentally hearing that they were both starved to death, we gave over the design and determined to engage ourselves to some strolling company of players,[98] as we had always a turn for the stage. Accordingly, we offered our services to one and were accepted; our company was indeed rather small, as it consisted only of the manager, his wife and ourselves, but there were fewer to pay and the only inconvenience attending it was the scarcity of plays which, for want of people to fill the characters, we could perform. We did not mind trifles, however. One of our most admired performances was *Macbeth*, in which we were truly great. The manager always played Banquo himself, his wife my Lady Macbeth. I did the Three Witches and Philander acted all the rest. To say the truth, this tragedy was not only the best, but the only play we ever performed; and after having acted it all over England and Wales, we came to Scotland to exhibit it over the remainder of Great Britain. We happened to be quartered in that very town where you came and met your grandfather. We were in the inn-yard when his carriage entered and perceiving by the arms to whom it belonged, and knowing that Lord St Clair was our grandfather, we agreed to endeavour to get something from him by discovering the relationship. You know how well it succeeded. Having obtained the two hundred pounds, we instantly left the town, leaving our manager and his wife to act *Macbeth* by themselves, and took the road to Sterling, where we spent our little fortune with great *éclat*. We are now returning to Edinburgh in order to get some preferment in the acting way; and such, my dear cousin, is our history.'

I thanked the amiable youth for his entertaining narration, and after expressing my wishes for their welfare and happiness, left them in their little habitation and returned to my other friends, who impatiently expected me.

My adventures are now drawing to a close, my dearest Marianne; at least for the present.

When we arrived at Edinburgh, Sir Edward told me that, as the widow of his son, he desired I would accept from his hands the sum of four hundred a year. I graciously promised that I would, but could not help observing that the unsympathetic baronet offered it more on account of my being the widow of Edward than in being the refined and amiable Laura.

I took up my residence in a romantic[99] village in the Highlands of Scotland, where I have ever since continued, and where I can, un-interrupted by unmeaning visits, indulge, in a melancholy solitude, my unceasing lamentations for the death of my father, my mother, my husband and my friend.

Augusta has been for several years united to Graham, the man of all others most suited to her; she became acquainted with him during her stay in Scotland.

Sir Edward, in hopes of gaining an heir to his title and estate, at the same time married Lady Dorothea. His wishes have been answered.

Philander and Gustavus, after having raised their reputation by their performances in the theatrical line at Edinburgh, removed to Covent Garden, where they still exhibit under the assumed names of Lewis and Quick.[100]

Philippa has long paid the debt of nature;[101] her husband, however, still continues to drive the stagecoach from Edinburgh to Sterling.

Adieu, my dearest Marianne.

LAURA

A History of England

FROM THE REIGN OF HENRY THE 4TH
TO THE DEATH OF CHARLES THE 1ST
BY A PARTIAL, PREJUDICED AND
IGNORANT HISTORIAN

With illustrations by her sister Cassandra

N.B. There will be very few dates in this history

To

Miss Austen,
elder daughter of the
Revd George Austen,[102]
this work is inscribed with
all due respect by
The Author

Henry the 4th ascended the throne of England much to his own satisfaction in the year 1399, after having prevailed on his cousin and predecessor, Richard the 2nd, to resign it to him, and to retire for the rest of his life to Pomfret Castle,[104] where he happened to be murdered. It is to be supposed that Henry was married, since he had certainly four sons, but it is not in my power to inform the reader who was his wife.[105] Be this as it may, he did not live for ever, but falling ill, his son the Prince of Wales came and took away the crown; whereupon the king made a long speech, for which I must refer the reader to Shakespeare's plays,[106] and the prince made a still longer. Things being thus settled between them, the king died, and was succeeded by his son Henry who had previously beat Sir William Gascoigne.[107]

HENRY THE 5TH [108]

This prince after he succeeded to the throne grew quite reformed and amiable, forsaking all his dissipated companions, and never thrashing Sir William again. During his reign, Lord Cobham[109] was burnt alive, but I forget what for. His Majesty then turned his thoughts to France, where he went and fought the famous Battle of Agincourt.[110] He afterwards married the king's daughter Catherine, a very agreeable woman by Shakespeare's account.[111] In spite of all this however he died, and was succeeded by his son Henry.

HENRY THE 6TH [112]

I cannot say much for this monarch's sense.[113] Nor would I if I could, for he was a Lancastrian. I suppose you know all about the wars between him and the Duke of York[114] who was of the right side; if you do not, you had better read some other history, for I shall not be very diffuse in this, meaning by it only to vent my spleen[115] *against* and show my hatred *to* all those people whose parties or principles do not suit with mine, and not to give information. This king married Margaret of Anjou,[116] a woman whose distresses and misfortunes were so great as almost to make me, who hate her, pity her. It was in this reign that Joan of Arc[117] lived and made such a *row* among the English. They should not have burnt her – but they did. There were several battles between the Yorkists and Lancastrians, in which the former (as they ought) usually conquered. At length they were entirely overcome; the king was murdered – the queen was sent home – and Edward the 4th ascended the throne.

EDWARD THE 4TH [118]

This monarch was famous only for his beauty and his courage, of which the picture we have here given of him, and his undaunted behaviour in marrying one woman while he was engaged to another, are sufficient proofs. His wife was Elizabeth Woodville,[119] a widow who, poor woman! was afterwards confined in a convent[120] by that monster of iniquity and avarice Henry the 7th. One of Edward's mistresses was Jane Shore,[121] who has had a play written about her, but it is a tragedy and therefore not worth reading. Having performed all these noble actions, his Majesty died, and was succeeded by his son.

EDWARD THE 5TH [122]

This unfortunate prince lived so little a while that nobody had time to draw his picture. He was murdered by his uncle's contrivance, whose name was Richard the 3rd.

RICHARD THE 3RD [123]

The character of this prince has been in general very severely treated by historians, but as he was a *York*, I am rather inclined to suppose him a very respectable man. It has indeed been confidently asserted that he killed his two nephews and his wife,[124] but it has also been declared that he did *not* kill his two nephews, which I am inclined to believe true; and if this is the case, it may also be affirmed that he did not kill his wife, for if Perkin Warbeck[125] was really the Duke of York, why might not Lambert Simnel[126] be the widow of Richard? Whether innocent or guilty, he did not reign long in peace, for Henry Tudor, Earl of Richmond, as great a villain as ever lived, made a great fuss about getting the crown and having killed the king at the Battle of Bosworth,[127] he succeeded to it.

Henry the 7th [128]

This monarch soon after his accession married the Princess Elizabeth of York,[129] by which alliance he plainly proved that he thought his own right inferior to hers, though he pretended to the contrary. By this marriage he had two sons and two daughters, the elder of which daughters was married to the King of Scotland and had the happiness of being grandmother to one of the first characters in the world.[130] But of *her*, I shall have occasion to speak more at large in future. The youngest, Mary, married first the King of France and secondly the Duke of Suffolk,[131] by whom she had one daughter, afterwards the mother of Lady Jane Grey,[132] who though inferior to her lovely cousin the Queen of Scots, was yet an amiable young woman and famous for reading Greek while other people were hunting. It was in the reign of Henry the 7th that Perkin Warbeck and Lambert Simnel before mentioned made their appearance, the former of whom was set in the stocks, took shelter in Beaulieu Abbey,[133] and was beheaded with the Earl of Warwick,[134] and the latter was taken into the king's kitchen. His Majesty died and was succeeded by his son Henry, whose only merit was his not being *quite* so bad as his daughter Elizabeth.

HENRY THE 8TH [135]

It would be an affront to my readers were I to suppose that they were not as well acquainted with the particulars of this king's reign as I am myself. It will therefore be saving *them* the task of reading again what they have read before, and *myself* the trouble of writing what I do not perfectly recollect, by giving only a slight sketch of the principal events which marked his reign. Among these may be ranked Cardinal Wolsey's telling the father abbott of Leicester Abbey that 'he was come to lay his bones among them',[136] the reformation in religion[137] and the king's riding through the streets of London with Anna Bullen.[138] It is however but justice, and my duty, to declare that this amiable woman was entirely innocent of the crimes with which she was accused, and of which her beauty, her elegance, and her sprightliness were sufficient proofs, not to mention her solemn protestations of innocence, the weakness of the charges against her, and the king's character; all of which add some confirmation, though perhaps but slight ones when in comparison with those before alleged in her favour. Though I do not profess giving many dates, yet as I think it proper to give some and shall of course make choice of those which it is most necessary for the reader to know, I think it right to inform him that her letter to the king was dated on the 6th of May. The crimes and cruelties of this prince were too numerous to be mentioned (as this history I trust has fully shown), and nothing can be said in his vindication, but that his abolishing religious houses and leaving them to the ruinous depredations of time has been of infinite use to the landscape of England in general, which probably was a principal motive for his doing it, since otherwise why should a man who was of no religion himself be at so much trouble to abolish one which had for ages been established in the kingdom. His Majesty's fifth wife was the Duke of Norfolk's niece[139] who, though universally acquitted of the crimes for which she was beheaded, has been by many people supposed to have led an abandoned life before her marriage – of this however I have many doubts, since she was a relation of that noble Duke of Norfolk[140] who was so warm in the Queen of Scotland's cause, and who at last fell a victim to it. The king's last wife[141] contrived to survive him, but with difficulty effected it. He was succeeded by his only son Edward.

Edward the 6th [142]

As this prince was only nine years old at the time of his father's death he was considered by many people as too young to govern, and the late king happening to be of the same opinion, his mother's brother the Duke of Somerset[143] was chosen Protector of the realm during his minority. This man was on the whole of a very amiable character, and is somewhat of a favourite with me, though I would by no means pretend to affirm that he was equal to those first of men Robert, Earl of Essex, Delamere, or Gilpin.[144] He was beheaded, of which he might with reason have been proud, had he known that such was the death of Mary Queen of Scotland; but as it was impossible that he should be conscious of what had never happened, it does not appear that he felt particularly delighted with the manner of it. After his decease the Duke of Northumberland[145] had the care of the king and the kingdom, and performed his trust of both so well that the king died and the kingdom was left to his daughter-in-law, the Lady Jane Grey, who has been already mentioned as reading Greek. Whether she really understood that language, or whether such a study proceeded only from an excess of vanity, for which I believe she was always rather remarkable, is uncertain. Whatever might be the cause, she preserved the same appearance of knowledge, and contempt of what was generally esteemed pleasure, during the whole of her life, for she declared herself displeased with being appointed queen, and while conducting to the scaffold, she wrote a sentence in Latin and another in Greek on seeing the dead body of her husband accidentally passing that way.

Mary [146]

This woman had the good luck of being advanced to the throne of England, in spite of the superior pretensions, merit, and beauty of her cousins Mary Queen of Scotland and Jane Grey. Nor can I pity the kingdom for the misfortunes they experienced during her reign, since they fully deserved them for having allowed her to succeed her brother – which was a double piece of folly, since they might have foreseen that if she died without children she would be succeeded by that disgrace to humanity, that pest of society, Elizabeth. Many were the people who fell martyrs to the Protestant religion during her reign; I suppose not fewer than a dozen.[147] She married Philip King of Spain who in her sister's reign was famous for building Armadas.[148] She died without issue, and then the dreadful moment came in which the destroyer of all comfort, the deceitful betrayer of trust reposed in her, and the murderess of her cousin succeeded to the throne.

Elizabeth [149]

It was the peculiar misfortune of this woman to have bad ministers, since, wicked as she herself was, she could not have committed such extensive mischief had not these vile and abandoned men connived at and encouraged her in her crimes. I know that it has by many people been asserted and believed that Lord Burleigh, Sir Francis Walsingham,[150] and the rest of those who filled the chief offices of state, were deserving, experienced and able ministers. But oh! how blinded such writers and such readers must be to true merit, to merit despised, neglected and defamed, if they can persist in such opinions when they reflect that these men, these boasted men, were such scandals to their country and their sex as to allow and assist their queen in confining, for the space of nineteen years, a woman who, if the claims of relationship and merit were of no avail, yet as a queen and as one who condescended to place confidence in her, had every reason to expect assistance and protection; and at length in allowing Elizabeth to bring this amiable woman to an untimely, unmerited and scandalous death.[151] Can anyone if he reflects but for a moment on this blot, this everlasting blot upon their understanding and their character, allow any praise to Lord Burleigh or Sir Francis Walsingham? Oh! what must this bewitching princess, whose only friend was then the Duke of Norfolk,[152] and whose only ones are now Mr Whitaker, Mrs Lefroy, Mrs Knight[153] and myself, who was abandoned by her son, confined by her cousin, abused, reproached and vilified by all, what must not her most noble mind have suffered when informed that Elizabeth had given orders for her death!

Yet she bore it with a most unshaken fortitude, firm in her mind; constant in her religion; and prepared herself to meet the cruel fate to which she was doomed with a magnanimity that would alone proceed from conscious innocence. And yet could you, reader, have believed it possible that some hardened and zealous Protestants have even abused her for that steadfastness in the Catholic religion which reflected on her so much credit? But this is a striking proof of *their* narrow souls and prejudiced judgements who accuse her. She was executed in the Great Hall at Fotheringay Castle (sacred place!) on Wednesday the 8th of February 1586[154] – to the everlasting reproach of Elizabeth, her ministers, and of England in general. It may not be unnecessary, before I entirely conclude my account of this ill-fated queen, to observe that she had been accused of several crimes during the time of her reigning in Scotland, of which I now most seriously do assure my reader that she was entirely innocent; having never been guilty of anything more than imprudencies into which she was betrayed by the openness of her heart, her youth and her education. Having I trust by this assurance entirely done away with every suspicion and every doubt which might have arisen in the reader's mind from what other historians have written of her, I shall proceed to mention the remaining events that marked Elizabeth's reign. It was about this time that Sir Francis Drake,[155] the first English navigator who sailed round the world, lived, to be the ornament of his country and his profession. Yet great as he was, and justly celebrated as a sailor, I cannot help foreseeing that he will be equalled in this or the next century by one who though now but young,[156] already promises to answer all the ardent and sanguine expectations of his relations and friends, among whom I may class the amiable lady to whom this work is dedicated, and my no less amiable self.

Though of a different profession, and shining in a different sphere of life, yet equally conspicuous in the character of an *Earl*, as Drake was in that of a *sailor*, was Robert Devereux, Lord Essex.[157] This unfortunate young man was not unlike in character to that equally unfortunate one Frederic Delamere. The simile may be carried still further, and Elizabeth the torment of Essex may be compared to the Emmeline of Delamere. It would be endless to recount the misfortunes of this noble and gallant Earl. It is sufficient to say that he was beheaded on the 25th of February, after having been Lord Lieutenant of Ireland, after having clapped his hand on his sword, and after performing many other services to his country. Elizabeth did not long survive his loss, and died *so* miserable that, were it not an injury to the memory of Mary, I should pity her.

JAMES THE 1ST [158]

Though this king had some faults, among which and as the most principal was his allowing his mother's death, yet considered on the whole I cannot help liking him. He married Anne of Denmark,[159] and had several children; fortunately for him his eldest son Prince Henry died before his father or he might have experienced the evils which befell his unfortunate brother.[160]

As I am myself partial to the Roman Catholic religion, it is with infinite regret that I am obliged to blame the behaviour of any member of it: yet truth being I think very excusable in an historian, I am necessitated to say that in this reign the Roman Catholics of England did not behave like gentlemen to the Protestants. Their behaviour indeed to the Royal Family and both Houses of Parliament might justly be considered by them as very uncivil, and even Sir Henry Percy, though certainly the best bred man of the party, had none of that general politeness which is so universally pleasing, as his attentions were entirely confined to Lord Mounteagle.[161]

Sir Walter Raleigh[162] flourished in this and the preceding reign, and is by many people held in great veneration and respect – but as he was an enemy of the noble Essex, I have nothing to say in praise of him, and must refer all those who may wish to be acquainted with the particulars of his life, to Mr Sheridan's play of *The Critic*,[163] where they will find many interesting anecdotes as well of him as of his friend Sir Christopher Hatton.[164] His Majesty was of that amiable disposition which inclines to friendship, and in such points was possessed of a keener penetration in discovering merit than many other people. I once heard an excellent charade on a carpet, of which the subject I am now on reminds me, and as I think it may afford my readers some amusement to *find it out*, I shall here take the liberty of presenting it to them.

CHARADE

My first is what my second was to King James the 1st,
and you tread on my whole.

The principal favourites of his Majesty were Car,[165] who was afterwards created Earl of Somerset and whose name perhaps may have some share in the above-mentioned charade, and George Villiers afterwards Duke of Buckingham.[166] On his Majesty's death he was succeeded by his son Charles.

CHARLES THE 1ST [167]

This amiable monarch seems born to have suffered misfortunes equal to those of his lovely grandmother;[168] misfortunes which he could not deserve since he was her descendant. Never certainly were there before so many detestable characters at one time in England as in this period of its history; never were amiable men so scarce. The number of them throughout the whole kingdom amounting only to *five*, besides the inhabitants of Oxford who were always loyal to their king and faithful to his interests. The names of his noble five who never forgot the duty of the subject, or swerved from their attachment to his Majesty, were as follows: the king himself – ever steadfast in his own support – and Archbishop Laud, Earl of Strafford, Viscount Faulkland and Duke of Ormond,[169] who were scarcely less strenuous or zealous in the cause. While the *villains* of the time would make too long a list to be written or read; I shall therefore content myself with mentioning the leaders of the gang. Cromwell, Fairfax, Hampden and Pym[170] may be considered as the original causers of all the disturbances, distresses and civil wars in which England for many years was embroiled. In this reign, as well as in that of Elizabeth, I am obliged, in spite of my attachment to the Scotch, to consider them as equally guilty with the generality of the English, since they dared to think differently from their sovereign, to forget the adoration which as *Stuarts* it was their duty to pay them, to rebel against, dethrone and imprison the unfortunate Mary and to oppose, to deceive, and to sell the no less unfortunate Charles. The events of this monarch's reign are too numerous for my pen, and indeed the recital of any events (except what I make myself) is uninteresting to me; my principal reason for undertaking the *History of England* being to prove the innocence of the Queen of Scotland, which I flatter myself with having effectually done, and to abuse Elizabeth, though I am rather fearful of having fallen short in the latter part of my scheme. As therefore it is not my intention to give any particular account of the distresses into which this king was involved through the misconduct and cruelty of his Parliament, I shall satisfy myself with vindicating him from the reproach of arbitrary and tyrannical government with which he has often been charged. This, I feel, is not difficult to be done, for with one argument I am certain of satisfying every sensible and well-disposed person whose opinions have been properly guided by a good education – and this argument is that he was a STUART.

Saturday, November 26th, 1791

The Three Sisters

A NOVEL

To

EDWARD AUSTEN ESQUIRE [171]

The following unfinished novel is respectfully
inscribed by his obedient humble servant

The Author

My dear Fanny – I am the happiest creature in the world, for I have received an offer of marriage from Mr Watts. It is the first I have ever had and I hardly know how to value it enough. How I will triumph over the Duttons! I do not intend to accept it, at least I believe not, but as I am not quite certain I gave him an equivocal answer and left him. And now, my dear Fanny, I want your advice whether I should accept his offer or not, and that you may be able to judge of his merits and the situation of affairs I will give you an account of them. He is quite an old man, about two-and-thirty, very plain, *so* plain that I cannot bear to look at him. He is extremely disagreeable and I hate him more than anybody else in the world. He has a large fortune and will make great settlements[172] on me; but then he is very healthy. In short, I do not know what to do. If I refuse him he as good as told me that he should offer himself to Sophia and if *she* refused him to Georgiana, and I could not bear to have either of them married before me. If I accept him I know I shall be miserable all the rest of my life, for he is very ill tempered and peevish, extremely jealous, and so stingy that there is no living in the house with him. He told me he should mention the affair to mama, but I insisted upon it that he did not, for very likely she would make me marry him whether I would or no; however, probably he *has* before now, for he never does anything he is desired to do. I believe I shall have him. It will be such a triumph to be married before Sophy, Georgiana and the Duttons. And he promised to have a new carriage on the occasion, but we almost quarrelled about the colour, for I insisted upon its being blue spotted with silver, and he declared it should be a plain chocolate; and to provoke me more, said it should be just as low[173] as his old one. I won't have him, I declare. He said he should come again tomorrow and take my final answer, so I believe I must get him while I can. I know the Duttons will envy me and I shall be able to chaperone[174] Sophy and Georgiana to all the winter balls. But then what will be the use of that when very likely he won't let me go myself, for I know he hates dancing, and what he hates himself he has no idea of any other person's liking; and, besides, he talks a great deal of women always staying at home and such stuff. I believe I shan't have him; I would refuse him at once if I were certain that neither of my sisters would accept him, and that if they did not, he would not offer to the Duttons. I cannot run such a risk, so, if he will promise to have the carriage ordered as I like, I will have him, if not he may ride in it by himself for me. I hope you like my determination; I can think of nothing better.

And am your ever affectionate

MARY STANHOPE

❧ 2 ❧

DEAR FANNY – I had but just sealed my last letter to you when my mother came up and told me she wanted to speak to me on a very particular subject.

'Ah! I know what you mean,' said I; 'that old fool Mr Watts has told you all about it, though I bid him not. However, you shan't force me to have him if I don't like it.'

'I am not going to force you, child, but only want to know what your resolution is with regard to his proposals, and to insist upon your making up your mind one way or t'other so that if *you* don't accept him *Sophy* may.'

'Indeed,' replied I hastily, 'Sophy need not trouble herself for I shall certainly marry him myself.'

'If that is your resolution,' said my mother, 'why should you be afraid of my forcing your inclinations?'

'Why, because I have not settled whether I shall have him or not.'

'You are the strangest girl in the world, Mary. What you say one moment, you unsay the next. Do tell me, once for all, whether you intend to marry Mr Watts or not?'

'Lor,[175] mama, how can I tell you what I don't know myself ?'

'Then I desire you will know, and quickly too, for Mr Watts says he won't be kept in suspense.'

'That depends upon me.'

'No, it does not, for if you do not give him your final answer tomorrow when he drinks tea with us, he intends to pay his addresses to Sophy.'

'Then I shall tell all the world that he behaved very ill to me.'

'What good will that do? Mr Watts has been too long abused by all the world to mind it now.'

'I wish I had a father or a brother because then they should fight him.'

'They would be cunning if they did, for Mr Watts would run away first; and therefore you must and shall resolve either to accept or refuse him before tomorrow evening.'

'But why, if I don't have him, must he offer to my sisters?'

'Why! because he wishes to be allied to the family and because they are as pretty as you are.'

'But will Sophy marry him, mama, if he offers to her?'

'Most likely. Why should not she? If, however, she does not choose it, then Georgiana must, for I am determined not to let such an opportunity escape of settling one of my daughters so advantageously. So, make the most of your time; I leave you to settle the matter with yourself.'

And then she went away. The only thing I can think of, my dear Fanny, is to ask Sophy and Georgiana whether they would have him were he to make proposals to them, and if they say they would not I am resolved to refuse him too, for I hate him more than you can imagine. As for the Duttons, if he marries one of *them* I shall still have the triumph of having refused him first. So, adieu, my dear friend –

Yours ever,   M. S.

❦ 3 ❧

MISS GEORGIANA STANHOPE TO MISS —

Wednesday

MY DEAR ANNE – Sophy and I have just been practising a little deceit on our eldest sister, to which we are not perfectly reconciled, and yet the circumstances were such that if anything will excuse it, they must. Our neighbour Mr Watts has made proposals to Mary: proposals which she knew not how to receive, for though she has a particular dislike to him (in which she is not singular) yet she would willingly marry him sooner than risk his offering to Sophy or me, which, in case of a refusal from herself, he told her he should do, for you must know the poor girl considers our marrying before her as one of the greatest misfortunes that can possibly befall her, and to prevent it would willingly ensure herself everlasting misery by a marriage with Mr Watts. An hour ago she came to us to sound our inclinations respecting the affair, which were to determine hers. A little before she came my mother had given us an account of it, telling us that she certainly would not let him go farther than our own family for a wife. 'And therefore,' said she, 'if Mary won't have him, Sophy must, and if Sophy won't, Georgiana *shall*.' Poor Georgiana! We neither of us attempted to alter my mother's resolution, which I am sorry to say is generally more strictly kept than rationally formed. As soon as she was gone, however, I broke silence to assure Sophy that if Mary should refuse Mr Watts, I should not expect her to sacrifice *her* happiness by becoming his wife from a motive of generosity to me, which I was afraid her good nature and sisterly affection might induce her to do.

'Let us flatter ourselves,' replied she, 'that Mary will not refuse him. Yet how can I hope that my sister may accept a man who cannot make her happy!'

'*He* cannot, it is true, but his fortune, his name, his house, his carriage will, and I have no doubt but that Mary will marry him; indeed, why should she not? He is not more than two-and-thirty, a very proper age for a man to marry at. He is rather plain, to be sure, but then what is beauty in a man? If he has but a genteel figure and a sensible-looking face it is quite sufficient.'

'This is all very true, Georgiana, but Mr Watts's figure is unfortunately extremely vulgar and his countenance is very heavy.'[176]

'And then as to his temper: it has been reckoned bad, but may not the world be deceived in their judgement of it. There is an open frankness in his disposition which becomes a man. They say he is stingy; we'll call that prudence. They say he is suspicious. *That* proceeds from a warmth of heart always excusable in youth, and in short I see no reason why he should not make a very good husband, or why Mary should not be very happy with him.'

Sophy laughed; I continued, 'However, whether Mary accepts him or not I am resolved. My determination is made. I never would marry Mr Watts were beggary the only alternative. So deficient in every respect! Hideous in his person and without one good quality to make amends for it! His fortune to be sure is good. Yet not so very large! Three thousand a year.[177] What is three thousand a year? It is but six times as much as my mother's income. It will not tempt me.'

'Yet it will be a noble fortune for Mary,' said Sophy, laughing again.

'For Mary! Yes indeed it will give me pleasure to see *her* in such affluence.'

Thus I ran on to the great entertainment of my sister till Mary came into the room to appearance in great agitation. She sat down. We made room for her at the fire. She seemed at a loss how to begin and at last said in some confusion. 'Pray, Sophy, have you any mind to be married?'

'To be married! None in the least. But why do you ask me? Are you acquainted with anyone who means to make me proposals?'

'I – no, how should I? But mayn't I ask a common question?'

'Not a very *common* one, Mary, surely,' said I.

She paused and after some moments' silence went on, 'How should you like to marry Mr Watts, Sophy?'

I winked at Sophy and replied for her. 'Who is there but must rejoice to marry a man of three thousand a year who keeps a post-chaise and pair, with silver harness, a boot before and a window to look out at behind?'[178]

'Very true,' she replied, 'that's very true. So you would have him if he would offer, Georgiana? – and would *you*, Sophy?'

Sophy did not like the idea of telling a lie and deceiving her sister; she prevented the first and saved half her conscience by equivocation.

'I should certainly act just as Georgiana would do.'

'Well then,' said Mary, with triumph in her eyes, '*I* have had an offer from Mr Watts.'

We were, of course, very much surprised: 'Oh! do not accept him,' said I, 'and then perhaps he may have me.'

In short, my scheme took and Mary is resolved to do that to prevent our supposed happiness which she would not have done to ensure it in reality. Yet, after all, my heart cannot acquit me and Sophy is even more scrupulous. Quiet our minds, my dear Anne, by writing and telling us you approve our conduct. Consider it well over. Mary will have real pleasure in being a married woman, and able to chaperone us, which she certainly shall do, for I shall think myself bound to contribute as much as possible to her happiness in a state I have made her choose. They will probably have a new carriage, which will be paradise to her, and if we can prevail on Mr W. to set up his phaeton[179] she will be too happy. These things, however, would be no consolation to Sophy or me for domestic misery. Remember all this and do not condemn us.

Friday

Last night, Mr Watts by appointment drank tea with us. As soon as his carriage stopped at the door, Mary went to the window.

'Would you believe it, Sophy,' said she, 'the old fool wants to have his new chaise[180] just the colour of the old one, and hung as low too. But it shan't – I *will* carry my point. And if he won't let it be as high as the Duttons', and blue spotted with silver, I won't have him. Yes, I will too. Here he comes. I know he'll be rude; I know he'll be ill tempered and won't say one civil thing to me! nor behave at all like a lover.' She then sat down and Mr Watts entered.

'Ladies, your most obedient servant.'

We paid our compliments and he seated himself.

'Fine weather, ladies.' Then, turning to Mary, 'Well, Miss Stanhope, I hope you have *at last* settled the matter in your own mind, and will be so good as to let me know whether you will *condescend* to marry me or not.'

'I think, sir,' said Mary, 'you might have asked in a genteeler way than that. I do not know whether I *shall* have you if you behave so odd.'

'Mary!' said my mother.

'Well, mama, if he will be so cross . . . '

'Hush, hush, Mary, you shall not be rude to Mr Watts.'

'Pray, madam, do not lay any restraint on Miss Stanhope by obliging her to be civil. If she does not choose to accept my hand, I can offer it elsewhere, for as I am by no means guided by a particular preference to you above your sisters, it is equally the same to me which I marry of the three.'

Was there ever such a wretch! Sophy reddened with anger and I felt *so* spiteful!

'Well then,' said Mary, in a peevish accent, 'I *will* have you if I *must*.'

'I should have thought, Miss Stanhope, that when such settlements are offered as I have offered to you there can be no great violence done to the inclinations in accepting of them.'

Mary mumbled out something, which I who sat close to her could just distinguish to be, 'What's the use of a great jointure[181] if men live for ever?' And then audibly, 'Remember the pin money;[182] two hundred a year.'[183]

'A hundred and seventy-five, madam.'

'Two hundred indeed, sir,' said my mother.

'And remember I am to have a new carriage hung as high as the Duttons', and blue spotted with silver; and I shall expect a new saddle horse, a suit of fine lace, and an infinite number of the most valuable jewels. Diamonds such as never were seen, pearls as large as those of the Princess Badroulbadour in the fourth volume of *The Arabian Nights*, and rubies, emeralds, topazes, sapphires, amethysts, turkeystones, agate, beads, bugles and garnets, and pearls, rubies, emeralds and beads out of number. You must set up your phaeton, which must be cream-coloured, with a wreath of silver flowers round it, you must buy four of the finest bays in the kingdom and you must drive me in it every day. This is not all; you must entirely new furnish your house after my taste, you must hire two more footmen to attend me, two women to wait on me, must always let me do just as I please and make a very good husband.' Here she stopped, I believe rather out of breath.

'This is all very reasonable, Mr Watts, for my daughter to expect.'

'And it is very reasonable, Mrs Stanhope, that your daughter should be disappointed.' He was going on but Mary interrupted him.

'You must build me an elegant greenhouse and stock it with plants. You must let me spend every winter in Bath, every spring in town,[184] every summer in taking some tour,[185] and every autumn at a watering place,[186] and if we are at home the rest of the year,' Sophy and I laughed, 'you must do nothing but give balls and masquerades.[187] You must build a room on purpose and a theatre[188] to act plays in. The first play we have shall be *Which is the Man*, and I will do Lady Bell Bloomer.'[189]

'And pray, Miss Stanhope,' said Mr Watts, 'what am I to expect from you in return for all this?'

'Expect? why you may expect to have me pleased.'

'It would be odd if I did not. Your expectations, madam, are too high for me, and I must apply to Miss Sophy, who perhaps may not have raised hers so much.'

'You are mistaken, sir, in supposing so,' said Sophy, 'for though they may not be exactly in the same line, yet my expectations are to the full as high as my sister's; for I expect my husband to be good tempered and cheerful; to consult my happiness in all his actions, and to love me with constancy and sincerity.'

Mr Watts stared. 'These are very odd ideas truly, young lady. You had better discard them before you marry, or you will be obliged to do it afterwards.'

My mother in the meantime was lecturing Mary, who was sensible that she had gone too far, and when Mr Watts was just turning towards me in order, I believe, to address me, she spoke to him in a voice half-humble, half-sulky.

'You are mistaken, Mr Watts, if you think I was in earnest when I said I expected so much. However, I must have a new chaise.'

'Yes, sir, you must allow that Mary has a right to expect that.'

'Mrs Stanhope, I *mean* and have always meant to have a new one on my marriage. But it shall be the colour of my present one.'

'I think, Mr Watts, you should pay my girl the compliment of consulting her taste on such matters.'

Mr Watts would not agree to this, and for some time insisted upon its being a chocolate colour, while Mary was as eager for having it blue with silver spots. At length, however, Sophy proposed that to please Mr W. it should be a dark brown and to please Mary it should be hung rather high and have a silver border. This was at length agreed to, though reluctantly on both sides, as each had intended to carry their point entire. We then proceeded to other matters, and it was settled that they should be married as soon as the writings[190] could be completed. Mary was very eager for a special licence and Mr Watts talked of banns. A common licence[191] was at last agreed on. Mary is to have all the family jewels which are very inconsiderable, I believe, and Mr W. promises to buy her a saddle horse;[192] but, in return, she is not to expect to go to town or any other public place for these three years. She is to have neither greenhouse, theatre or phaeton; to be contented with one maid without an additional footman. It engrossed the whole evening to settle these affairs; Mr W. supped with us and did not go till twelve.

As soon as he was gone, Mary exclaimed, 'Thank heaven! he's off at last; how I do hate him!'

It was in vain that mama represented to her the impropriety she was guilty of in disliking him who was to be her husband, for she persisted in declaring her aversion to him and hoping she might never see him again. What a wedding will this be! Adieu, my dear Anne. Your faithfully sincere

GEORGIANA STANHOPE

❦ 4 ❦

The same to the same

Saturday

DEAR ANNE – Mary, eager to have everyone know of her approaching wedding and more particularly desirous of triumphing as she called it over the Duttons, desired us to walk with her this morning to Stoneham.[193] As we had nothing else to do we readily agreed, and had as pleasant a walk as we could have with Mary, whose conversation entirely consisted in abusing the man she is so soon to marry and in longing for a blue chaise spotted with silver. When we reached the Duttons' we found the two girls in the dressing-room with a very handsome young man, who was of course introduced to us. He is the son of Sir Henry Brudenell of Leicestershire. Mr Brudenell is the handsomest man I ever saw in my life; we are all three very much pleased with him. Mary, who from the moment of our reaching the dressing-room had been swelling with the knowledge of her own importance and with the desire of making it known, could not remain long silent on the subject after we were seated, and soon addressing herself to Kitty said, 'Don't you think it will be necessary to have all the jewels new set?'

'Necessary for what?'

'For what! Why, for my appearance.'[194]

'I beg your pardon, but I really do not understand you. What jewels do you speak of, and where is your appearance to be made?'

'At the next ball, to be sure, after I am married.'

You may imagine their surprise. They were at first incredulous, but on our joining in the story they at last believed it. 'And who is it to?' was of course the first question. Mary pretended bashfulness, and answered in confusion, her eyes cast down, 'To Mr Watts.' This also required confirmation from us, for that anyone who had the beauty and fortune (though small, yet a provision[195]) of Mary would willingly marry Mr Watts could by them scarcely be credited. The subject being now fairly introduced and herself the object of everyone's attention in the company, she lost all her confusion and became perfectly unreserved and communicative.

'I wonder you should never have heard of it before, for in general things of this nature are very well known in the neighbourhood.'

'I assure you,' said Jemima, 'I never had the least suspicion of such an affair. Has it been in agitation long?'

'Oh, yes! ever since Wednesday.'

They all smiled, particularly Mr Brudenell.

'You must know Mr Watts is very much in love with me, so that it is quite a match of affection on his side.'

'Not on his only, I suppose,' said Kitty.

'Oh! when there is so much love on one side there is no occasion for it on the other. However, I do not much dislike him, though he is very plain to be sure.'

Mr Brudenell stared, the Miss Duttons laughed and Sophy and I were heartily ashamed of our sister.

She went on. 'We are to have a new post-chaise and very likely may set up our phaeton.'

This we knew to be false, but the poor girl was pleased at the idea of persuading the company that such a thing was to be and I would not deprive her of so harmless an enjoyment.

She continued. 'Mr Watts is to present me with the family jewels, which I fancy are very considerable.'

I could not help whispering to Sophy, 'I fancy not.'

'These jewels are what I suppose must be new set before they can be worn. I shall not wear them till the first ball I go to after my marriage. If Mrs Dutton should not go to it, I hope you will let me chaperone you; I shall certainly take Sophy and Georgiana.'

'You are very good,' said Kitty, 'and since you are inclined to undertake the care of young ladies, I should advise you to prevail on Mrs Edgecumbe to let you chaperone her six daughters, who with your two sisters and ourselves will make your entrée[196] very respectable.'

Kitty made us all smile except Mary, who did not understand her meaning and coolly said that she should not like to chaperone so many. Sophy and I now endeavoured to change the conversation but succeeded only for a few minutes, for Mary took care to bring back their attention to her and her approaching wedding. I was sorry for my sister's sake to see that Mr Brudenell seemed to take pleasure in listening to her account of it and even encouraged her by his questions and remarks, for it was evident that his only aim was to laugh at her. I am afraid he found her very ridiculous. He kept his countenance extremely well, yet it was easy to see that it was with difficulty he kept it. At length, however, he seemed fatigued and disgusted with her ridiculous conversation, as he turned from her to us, and spoke but little to her for about half an hour before we left Stoneham. As soon as we were out of the house we all joined in praising the person and manners of Mr Brudenell.

We found Mr Watts at home.

'So, Miss Stanhope,' said he, 'you see I am come a-courting in a true lover-like manner.'

'Well, you need not have *told* me that. I knew why you came very well.'

Sophy and I then left the room, imagining, of course, that we must be in the way if a scene of courtship were to begin. We were surprised at being followed almost immediately by Mary.

'And is your courting so soon over?' said Sophy.

'Courting!' replied Mary, 'we have been quarrelling. Watts is such a fool! I hope I shall never see him again.'

'I am afraid you will,' said I, 'as he dines here today. But what has been your dispute?'

'Why, only because I told him that I had seen a man much handsomer than he was this morning he flew into a great passion and called me a vixen, so I only stayed to tell him I thought him a blackguard[197] and came away.'

'Short and sweet,' said Sophy; 'but pray, Mary, how will this be made up?'

'He ought to ask my pardon; but if he did, I would not forgive him.'

'His submission then would not be very useful.'

When we were dressed[198] we returned to the parlour where mama and Mr Watts were in close conversation. It seems that he had been complaining to her of her daughter's behaviour, and she had persuaded him to think no more of it. He therefore met Mary with all his accustomed civility, and, except one touch at the phaeton and another at the greenhouse, the evening went off with great harmony and cordiality. Watts is going to town to hasten the preparations for the wedding.

I am your affectionate friend,   G.S.

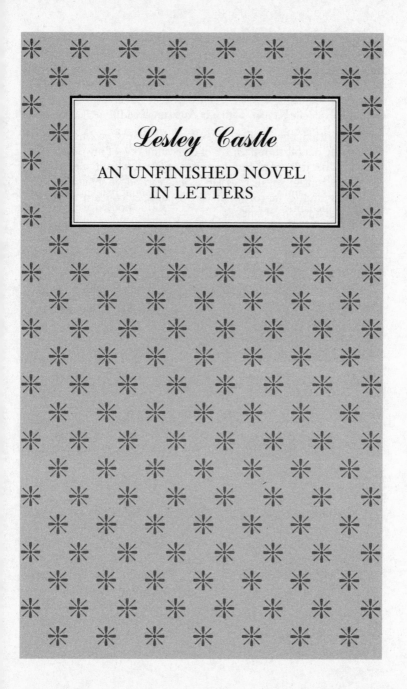

Lesley Castle

AN UNFINISHED NOVEL
IN LETTERS

To

HENRY THOMAS AUSTEN ESQ.[199]

SIR – I am now availing myself of the liberty you have frequently honoured me with[200] of dedicating one of my novels to you. That it is unfinished, I grieve; yet fear that from me, it will always remain so; that, as far as it is carried, it should be so trifling and so unworthy of you, is another concern to your obliged humble servant

The Author

Messrs Demand & Co – Please to pay Jane Austen Spinster the sum of one hundred guineas on account of your humble servant.

H. T. AUSTEN [201]

£105. 0. 0

MISS MARGARET LESLEY TO MISS CHARLOTTE LUTTERELL

Lesley Castle, January 3rd, 1792

My brother has just left us. 'Matilda,' said he at parting, 'you and Margaret will I am certain take all the care of my dear little one that she might have received from an indulgent, and affectionate, and amiable mother.' Tears rolled down his cheeks as he spoke these words – the remembrance of her, who had so wantonly disgraced the maternal character and so openly violated the conjugal duties, prevented his adding anything further; he embraced his sweet child and after saluting[202] Matilda and me hastily broke from us, and seating himself in his chaise,[203] pursued the road to Aberdeen. Never was there a better young man! Ah! how little did he deserve the misfortunes he has experienced in the marriage state. So good a husband to so bad a wife! for you know, my dear Charlotte, that the worthless Louisa left him, her child and reputation a few weeks ago in company with Danvers and dishonour.[204] Never was there a sweeter face, a finer form, or a less amiable heart than Louisa owned! Her child already possesses the personal charms of her unhappy mother! May she inherit from her father his mental ones! Lesley is at present but five-and-twenty, and has already given himself up to melancholy and despair; what a difference between him and his father! Sir George is fifty-seven and still remains the beau, the flighty stripling, the gay lad and sprightly youngster that his son was really about five years back, and that *he* has affected to appear ever since my remembrance. While our father is fluttering about the streets of London, gay, dissipated and thoughtless at the age of fifty-seven, Matilda and I continue secluded from mankind in our old and mouldering castle, which is situated two miles from Perth on a bold projecting rock, and commands an extensive view of the town and its delightful environs. But though retired from almost all the world (for we visit no one but the McLeods, the McKenzies, the McPhersons, the McCartneys, the McDonalds, the McKinnons, the McLellans, the McKays, the Macbeths and the Macduffs), we are neither dull nor unhappy; on the contrary there never were two more lively, more agreeable or more witty girls than we are; not an hour in the day hangs heavy on our hands. We read, we work,[205] we walk, and when fatigued with these employments, relieve our spirits either by a lively song, a graceful dance, or by some smart *bon mot* and witty repartée. We are handsome, my dear Charlotte, very handsome and the greatest of our perfections is that we are entirely insensible of them ourselves. But why do I thus dwell on myself? Let me rather repeat the praise of our dear little niece, the innocent Louisa, who is at present sweetly smiling in a gentle nap, as she reposes on the sofa. The dear creature is just turned of two years old; as handsome as though two-and-twenty, as sensible as though two-and-thirty, and as prudent as though two-and-forty. To convince you of this, I must inform you that she has a very fine complexion and very pretty features, that she already knows the two first letters in the alphabet, and that she never tears her frocks. If I have not now convinced you of her beauty, sense and prudence, I have nothing more to urge in support of my assertion, and you will therefore have no way of deciding the affair but by coming to Lesley Castle, and by a personal acquaintance with Louisa determining for yourself. Ah! my dear friend, how happy should I be to see you within these venerable walls! It is now four years since my removal from school separated me from you; that two such tender hearts, so closely linked together by the ties of sympathy and friendship, should be so widely removed from each other, is vastly moving. I live in Perthshire, you in Sussex. We might meet in London, were my father disposed to carry me there, and were your mother to be there at the same time. We might meet at Bath, at Tunbridge,[206] or anywhere else indeed, could we but be at the same place together. We have only to hope that such a period may arrive. My father does not return to us till autumn; my brother will leave Scotland in a few days; he is impatient to travel. Mistaken youth! He vainly flatters himself that change of air will heal the wounds of a broken heart! You will join with me I am certain, my dear Charlotte, in prayers for the recovery of the unhappy Lesley's peace of mind, which must ever be essential to that of your sincere friend.

M. LESLEY

Letter 2

MISS C. LUTTERELL TO MISS M. LESLEY *in answer*

Glenford, February 12th

I have a thousand excuses to beg for having so long delayed thanking you, my dear Peggy, for your agreeable letter, which believe me I should not have deferred doing had not every moment of my time during the last five weeks been so fully employed in the necessary arrangements for my sister's wedding as to allow me no time to devote either to you or myself. And now what provokes me more than any-thing else is that the match is broke off, and all my labour thrown away. Imagine how great the disappointment must be to me, when you consider that after having laboured both by night and by day in order to get the wedding dinner ready by the time appointed, after having roasted beef, broiled mutton, and stewed soup[207] enough to last the new-married couple through the honeymoon, I had the mortification of finding that I had been roasting, broiling and stewing both the meat and myself to no purpose. Indeed, my dear friend, I never remember suffering any vexation equal to what I experienced on last Monday when my sister came running to me in the storeroom, with her face as white as a whipped syllabub,[208] and told me that Henry had been thrown from his horse, had fractured his skull and was pronounced by his surgeon to be in the most imminent danger. 'Good God!' said I, 'you don't say so? Why! what in the name of heaven will become of all the victuals! We shall never be able to eat them while they are good. However, we'll call in the surgeon to help us. I shall be able to manage the sirloin myself, my mother will eat the soup, and you and the doctor must finish the rest.' Here I was interrupted, by seeing my poor sister fall down to appearance lifeless upon one of the chests, where we keep our table linen. I immediately called my mother and the maids, and at last we brought her to herself again; as soon as ever she was sensible, she expressed a determination of going instantly to Henry, and was so wildly bent on this scheme that we had the greatest difficulty in the world to prevent her putting it in execution; at last, however, more by force than entreaty, we prevailed on her to go into her room; we laid her upon the bed, and she continued for some hours in the most dreadful convulsions. My mother and I continued in the room with her, and when any intervals of tolerable composure in Eloisa[209] would allow us, we joined in heartfelt lamentations on the dreadful waste in our provisions which this event must occasion, and in concerting some plan for getting rid of them. We agreed that the best thing we could do was to begin eating them immediately, and accordingly we ordered up the cold ham and fowls, and instantly began our devouring plan on them with great alacrity. We would have persuaded Eloisa to have taken a wing of a chicken, but she would not be persuaded. She was, however, much quieter than she had been, the convulsions she had before suffered having given way to an almost perfect insensibility. We endeavoured to rouse her by every means in our power, but to no purpose. I talked to her of Henry. 'Dear Eloisa,' said I, 'there's no occasion for your crying so much about such a trifle' (for I was willing to make light of it in order to comfort her). 'I beg you would not mind it. You see it does not vex me in the least; though perhaps *I* may suffer most from it after all; for I shall not only be obliged to eat up all the victuals I have dressed already, but must if Henry should recover (which, however, is not very likely) dress as much for you again; or should he die (as I suppose he will) I shall still have to prepare a dinner for you whenever you marry anyone else. So you see that though perhaps for the present it may afflict you to think of Henry's sufferings, yet I dare say he'll die soon, and then his pain will be over and you will be easy, whereas my trouble will last much longer, for, work as hard as I may, I am certain that the pantry cannot be cleared in less than a fortnight.' Thus I did all in my power to console her, but without any effect, and at last, as I saw that she did not seem to listen to me, I said no more, but leaving her with my mother, I took down the remains of the ham and chicken, and sent William to ask how Henry did. He was not expected to live many hours; he died the same day. We took all possible care to break the melancholy event to Eloisa in the tenderest manner; yet, in spite of every precaution, her sufferings on hearing it were too violent for her reason, and she continued for many hours in a high delirium. She is still extremely ill, and her physicians are greatly afraid of her going into a decline.[210] We are therefore preparing for Bristol,[211] where we mean to be in the course of the next week. And now, my dear Margaret, let me talk a little of your affairs; and in the first place I must inform you that it is confidently reported that your father is going to be married; I am very unwilling to believe so unpleasing a report, and at the same time cannot wholly discredit it. I have written to my friend Susan Fitzgerald for information concerning it, which, as she is at present in town, she will be very able to give me. I know not who is the lady. I think your brother is extremely right in the resolution he has taken of travelling, as it will perhaps contribute to obliterate from his remembrance those disagreeable events which have lately so much afflicted him – I am happy to find that though secluded from all the world, neither you nor Matilda are dull or unhappy – that you may never know what it is to be either is the wish of your sincerely affectionate

C. L.

PS I have this instant received an answer from my friend Susan, which I enclose to you, and on which you will make your own reflections.

The enclosed letter

MY DEAR CHARLOTTE – You could not have applied for information concerning the report of Sir George Lesley's marriage to anyone better able to give it you than I am. Sir George is certainly married; I was myself present at the ceremony, which you will not be surprised at when I subscribe myself your affectionate

SUSAN LESLEY

Letter 3

MISS MARGARET LESLEY TO MISS C. LUTTERELL

Lesley Castle, February 16th

I have made my own reflections on the letter you enclosed to me, my dear Charlotte, and I will now tell you what those reflections were. I reflected that if by this second marriage Sir George should have a second family, our fortunes must be considerably diminished; that if his wife should be of an extravagant turn, she would encourage him to persevere in that gay and dissipated way of life to which little encouragement would be necessary, and which has I fear already proved but too detrimental to his health and fortune; that she would now become mistress of those jewels which once adorned our mother, and which Sir George had always promised us; that if they did not come into Perthshire, I should not be able to gratify my curiosity of beholding my mother-in-law,[212] and that if they did, Matilda would no longer sit at the head of her father's table. These, my dear Charlotte, were the melancholy reflections which crowded into my imagination after perusing Susan's letter to you, and which instantly occurred to Matilda when she had perused it likewise. The same ideas, the same fears, immediately occupied her mind, and I know not which reflection distressed her most, whether the probable diminution of our fortunes or her own consequence. We both wish very much to know whether Lady Lesley is handsome and what is your opinion of her; as you honour her with the appellation of your friend, we flatter ourselves that she must be amiable. My brother is already in Paris. He intends to quit it in a few days, and to begin his route to Italy. He writes in a most cheerful manner, says that the air of France has greatly recovered both his health and spirits; that he has now entirely ceased to think of Louisa with any degree either of pity or affection, that he even feels himself obliged to her for her elopement, as he thinks it very good fun to be single again. By this, you may perceive that he has entirely regained that cheerful gaiety, and sprightly wit, for which he was once so remarkable. When he first became acquainted with Louisa, which was little more than three years ago, he was one of the most lively, the most agreeable young men of the age. I believe you never yet heard the particulars of his first acquaintance with her. It commenced at our cousin Colonel Drummond's, at whose house in Cumberland[213] he spent the Christmas in which he attained the age of two-and-twenty. Louisa Burton was the daughter of a distant relation of Mrs Drummond, who, dying a few months before in extreme poverty, left his only child, then about eighteen, to the protection of any of his relations who would protect her. Mrs Drummond was the only one who found herself so disposed – Louisa was therefore removed from a miserable cottage in Yorkshire to an elegant mansion in Cumberland, and from every pecuniary distress that poverty could inflict, to every elegant enjoyment that money could purchase. Louisa was naturally ill-tempered and cunning; but she had been taught to disguise her real disposition, under the appearance of insinuating sweetness, by a father who but too well knew that to be married would be the only chance she would have of not being starved, and who flattered himself that with such an extraordinary share of personal beauty, joined to a gentle-ness of manners, and an engaging address, she might stand a good chance of pleasing some young man who might afford to marry a girl without a shilling. Louisa perfectly entered into her father's schemes and was determined to forward them with all her care and attention. By dint of perseverance and application, she had at length so thoroughly disguised her natural disposition under the mask of innocence, and softness, as to impose upon everyone who had not by a long and constant intimacy with her discovered her real character. Such was Louisa when the hapless Lesley first beheld her at Drummond House. His heart, which (to use your favourite comparison) was as delicate, as sweet and as tender as a whipped syllabub, could not resist her attractions. In a very few days, he was falling in love; shortly after actually fell; and before he had known her a month, he had married her. My father was at first highly displeased at so hasty and imprudent a connection; but when he found that they did not mind it, he soon became perfectly reconciled to the match. The estate near Aberdeen which my brother possesses by the bounty of his great uncle, independent of Sir George, was entirely sufficient to support him and my sister in elegance and ease. For the first twelvemonth, no one could be happier than Lesley, and no one more amiable to appearance than

Louisa, and so plausibly did she act and so cautiously behave that though Matilda and I often spent several weeks together with them, yet we neither of us had any suspicion of her real disposition. After the birth of Louisa, however, which one would have thought would have strengthened her regard for Lesley, the mask she had so long supported was by degrees thrown aside, and as probably she then thought herself secure in the affection of her husband (which did indeed appear, if possible, augmented by the birth of his child), she seemed to take no pains to prevent that affection from ever diminishing. Our visits therefore to Dunbeath[214] were now less frequent and by far less agreeable than they used to be. Our absence was, however, never either mentioned or lamented by Louisa, who in the society of young Danvers, with whom she became acquainted at Aberdeen (he was at one of the universities[215] there), felt infinitely happier than in that of Matilda and your friend, though there certainly never were pleasanter girls than we are. You know the sad end of all Lesley's connubial happiness; I will not repeat it. Adieu, my dear Charlotte; although I have not yet mentioned anything of the matter, I hope you will do me the justice to believe that I *think* and *feel*, a great deal for your sister's affliction. I do not doubt but that the healthy air of the Bristol downs[216] will entirely remove it by erasing from her mind the remembrance of Henry. I am, my dear Charlotte, yours ever,

M. L.

Letter 4

MISS C. LUTTERELL TO MISS M. LESLEY

Bristol, February 27th

MY DEAR PEGGY – I have but just received your letter, which being directed to Sussex while I was at Bristol was obliged to be forwarded to me here, and from some unaccountable delay has but this instant reached me. I return you many thanks for the account it contains of Lesley's acquaintance, love and marriage with Louisa, which has not the less entertained me for having often been repeated to me before.

I have the satisfaction of informing you that we have every reason to imagine our pantry is by this time nearly cleared, as we left particular orders with the servants to eat as hard as they possibly could, and to call in a couple of charwomen[217] to assist them. We brought a cold pigeon-pie, a cold turkey, a cold tongue and half a dozen jellies[218] with us, which we were lucky enough, with the help of our landlady, her husband

and their three children, to get rid of in less than two days after our arrival. Poor Eloisa is still so very indifferent, both in health and spirits, that I very much fear the air of the Bristol downs, healthy as it is, has not been able to drive poor Henry from her remembrance.

You ask me whether your new mother-in-law is handsome and amiable – I will now give you an exact description of her bodily and mental charms. She is short, and extremely well made; is naturally pale, but rouges a good deal; has fine eyes, and fine teeth, as she will take care to let you know as soon as she sees you, and is altogether very pretty. She is remarkably good-tempered when she has her own way, and very lively when she is not out of humour. She is naturally extravagant and not very affected; she never reads anything but the letters she receives from me, and never writes anything but her answers to them. She plays, sings and dances, but has no taste for either, and excels in none, though she says she is passionately fond of all. Perhaps you may flatter me so far as to be surprised that one of whom I speak with so little affection should be my particular friend; but to tell you the truth, our friendship arose rather from caprice on her side than esteem on mine. We spent two or three days together with a lady in Berkshire with whom we both happened to be connected. During our visit, the weather being remarkably bad, and our party particularly stupid,[219] she was so good as to conceive a violent partiality for me, which very soon settled in a downright friendship and ended in an established correspondence. She is probably by this time as tired of me as I am of her; but as she is too polite and I am too civil to say so, our letters are still as frequent and affectionate as ever, and our attachment as firm and sincere as when it first commenced. As she had a great taste for the pleasures of London, and of Brighthelmstone,[220] she will, I dare say, find some difficulty in prevailing on herself, even to satisfy the curiosity she no doubt feels of beholding you, to go to the expense of quitting those favourite haunts of dissipation for the melancholy though venerable gloom of the castle you inhabit. Perhaps, however, if she finds her health impaired by too much amusement, she may acquire fortitude sufficient to undertake a journey to Scotland in the hope of its proving at least beneficial to her health, if not conducive to her happiness. Your fears, I am sorry to say, concerning your father's extravagance, your own fortunes, your mother's jewels and your sister's consequence, I should suppose are but too well founded. My friend herself has four thousand pounds, and will probably spend nearly as much every year[221] in dress and public places, if she can get it – she will certainly not endeavour to reclaim Sir George from the manner of living to which he has been so long accustomed, and there is therefore some reason to fear that you will be very well off if you get any fortune at all. The jewels, I should imagine, too will undoubtedly be hers, and there is too much reason to think that she will preside at her husband's table in preference to his daughter. But as so melancholy a subject must necessarily extremely distress you, I will no longer dwell on it.

Eloisa's indisposition has brought us to Bristol at so unfashionable a season of the year that we have actually seen but one genteel family since we came. Mr and Mrs Marlowe are very agreeable people; the ill health of their little boy occasioned their arrival here; you may imagine that their being the only family with whom we can converse, we are of course on a footing of intimacy with them; we see them indeed almost every day, and dined with them yesterday. We spent a very pleasant day, and had a very good dinner, though to be sure the veal was terribly underdone, and the curry had no seasoning. I could not help wishing all dinner-time that I had been at the dressing of it. A brother of Mrs Marlowe, Mr Cleveland, is with them at present; he is a good-looking young man, and seems to have a good deal to say for himself. I tell Eloisa that she should set her cap at him,[222] but she does not at all seem to relish the proposal. I should like to see the girl married and Cleveland has a very good estate. Perhaps you may wonder that I do not consider *myself* as well as my sister in my matrimonial projects; but to tell you the truth I never wish to act a more principal part at a wedding than that of superintending and directing the dinner, and therefore while I can get any of my acquaintance to marry for me, I shall never think of doing it myself, as I very much suspect that I should not have so much time for dressing my own wedding-dinner as for dressing that of my friends.

Yours sincerely,

C. L.

Letter 5

MISS MARGARET LESLEY TO MISS CHARLOTTE LUTTERELL

Lesley Castle, March 18th

On the same day that I received your last kind letter, Matilda received one from Sir George, which was dated from Edinburgh, and informed us that he should do himself the pleasure of introducing Lady Lesley to us on the following evening. This, as you may suppose, considerably surprised us, particularly as your account of her ladyship had given us reason to imagine there was little chance of her visiting Scotland at a time that London must be so gay. As it was our business, however, to be delighted at such a mark of condescension as a visit from Sir George and Lady Lesley, we prepared to return them an answer expressive of the happiness we enjoyed in expectation of such a blessing, when luckily, recollecting that as they were to reach the castle the next evening, it would be impossible for my father to receive it before he left Edinburgh, we contented ourselves with leaving them to suppose that we were as happy as we ought to be. At nine in the evening on the following day, they came, accompanied by one of Lady Lesley's brothers. Her ladyship perfectly answers the description you sent me of her, except that I do not think her so pretty as you seem to consider her. She has not a bad face, but there is something so extremely unmajestic in her little diminutive figure as to render her, in comparison with the elegant height of Matilda and myself, an insignificant dwarf. Her curiosity to see us (which must have been great to bring her more than four hundred miles) being now perfectly gratified, she already begins to mention their return to town, and has desired us to accompany her. We cannot refuse her request since it is seconded by the commands of our father, and thirded by the entreaties of Mr Fitzgerald, who is certainly one of the most pleasing young men I ever beheld. It is not yet determined when we are to go, but whenever we do we shall certainly take our little Louisa with us. Adieu, my dear Charlotte; Matilda unites in best wishes to you and Eloisa with yours ever,

M. L.

Letter 6

LADY LESLEY TO MISS CHARLOTTE LUTTERELL

Lesley Castle, March 20th

We arrived here, my sweet friend, about a fortnight ago, and I already heartily repent that I ever left our charming house in Portman Square[223] for such a dismal old weather-beaten castle as this. You can form no idea sufficiently hideous of its dungeon-like form. It is actually perched upon a rock to appearance so totally inaccessible that I expected to have been pulled up by a rope; and sincerely repented having gratified my curiosity to behold my daughters at the expense of being obliged to enter their prison in so dangerous and ridiculous a manner. But as soon as I once found myself safely arrived in the inside of this tremendous building, I comforted myself with the hope of having my spirits revived by the sight of two beautiful girls, such as the Miss Lesleys had been represented to me at Edinburgh. But here again, I met with nothing but disappointment and surprise. Matilda and Margaret Lesley are two great, tall, out of the way, overgrown girls, just of a proper size to inhabit a castle almost as large in comparison as themselves. I wish, my dear Charlotte, that you could but behold these Scotch giants; I am sure they would frighten you out of your wits. They will do very well as foils to myself, so I have invited them to accompany me to London where I hope to be in the course of a fortnight. Besides these two fair damsels, I found a little humoured[224] brat here, who I believe is some relation to them; they told me who she was, and gave me a long rigmarole story of her father and a Miss *Somebody* which I have entirely forgot. I hate scandal and detest children. I have been plagued ever since I came here with tiresome visits from a parcel of Scotch wretches, with terrible hard names; they were so civil, gave me so many invitations, and talked of coming again so soon, that I could not help affronting them. I suppose I shall not see them any more, and yet as a family party we are so stupid that I do not know what to do with myself. These girls have no music but Scotch airs, no drawings but Scotch mountains, and no books but Scotch poems – and I hate everything Scotch. In general I can spend half the day at my toilette[225] with a great deal of pleasure, but why should I dress here, since there is not a creature in the house whom I have any wish to please. I have just had a conversation with my brother in which he has greatly offended me, and which, as I have nothing more entertaining to send you, I will give you the particulars of. You must know that I have for these four or five days past strongly suspected William of entertaining a partiality to my elder daughter. I own indeed that had *I* been inclined to fall in love with any woman, I should not have made choice of Matilda Lesley for the object of my passion, for there is nothing I hate so much as a tall woman; but, however, there is no accounting for some men's taste, and as William is himself nearly six feet high, it is not wonderful that he should be partial to that height. Now, as I have a very great affection for my brother and should be extremely sorry to see him unhappy, which I suppose he means to be if he cannot marry Matilda, and as, moreover, I know that his circumstances will not allow him to marry anyone without a fortune, and that Matilda's is entirely dependent on her father, who will have neither his own inclination nor my permission to give her anything at present, I thought it would be doing a good-natured action by my brother to let him know as much, in order that he might choose for himself whether to conquer his passion or love and despair. Accordingly, finding myself this morning alone with him in one of the horrid old rooms of this castle, I opened the cause to him in the following manner.

'Well, my dear William, what do you think of these girls? For my part, I do not find them so plain as I expected; but perhaps you may think me partial to the daughters of my husband and perhaps you are right. They are indeed so very like Sir George that it is natural to think – '

'My dear Susan!' cried he in a tone of the greatest amazement. 'You do not really think they bear the least resemblance to their father! He is so very plain! But I beg your pardon – I had entirely forgotten to whom I was speaking – '

'Oh! pray don't mind me,' replied I; 'everyone knows Sir George is horribly ugly, and I assure you I always thought him a fright.'

'You surprise me extremely,' answered William, 'by what you say both with respect to Sir George and his daughters. You cannot think your husband so deficient in personal charms as you speak of, nor can you surely see any resemblance between him and the Miss Lesleys who are in my opinion perfectly unlike him and perfectly handsome.'

'If that is your opinion with regard to the girls it certainly is no proof of their father's beauty, for if they are perfectly unlike him and very handsome at the same time, it is natural to suppose that he is very plain.'

'By no means,' said he, 'for what may be pretty in a woman, may be very unpleasing in a man.'

'But you yourself,' replied I, 'but a few minutes ago allowed him to be very plain.'

'Men are no judges of beauty in their own sex,' said he.

'Neither men nor women can think Sir George tolerable.'

'Well, well,' said he, 'we will not dispute about *his* beauty, but your opinion of his *daughters'* is surely very singular, for if I understood you right, you said you did not find them so plain as you expected to do!'

'Why, do *you* find them plainer then?' said I.

'I can scarcely believe you to be serious,' returned he, 'when you speak of their persons in so extraordinary a manner. Do not you think the Miss Lesleys are two very handsome young women?'

'Lord! No!' cried I. 'I think them terribly plain!'

'Plain!' replied he. 'My dear Susan, you cannot really think so! Why, what single feature in the face of either of them can you possibly find fault with?'

'Oh! trust me for that,' replied I. 'Come I will begin with the elder – with Matilda. Shall I, William?' I looked as cunning as I could when I said it, in order to shame him.

'They are so much alike,' said he, 'that I should suppose the faults of one would be the faults of both.'

'Well, then, in the first place; they are both so horribly tall!'

'They are *taller* than you are indeed,' said he with a saucy smile.

'Nay,' said I, 'I know nothing of that.'

'Well, but,' he continued, 'though they may be above the common size, their figures are perfectly elegant; and as to their faces, their eyes are beautiful.'

'I never can think such tremendous, knock-me-down figures in the least degree elegant, and as for their eyes, they are so tall that I never could strain my neck enough to look at them.'

'Nay,' replied he, 'I know not whether you may not be in the right in not attempting it, for perhaps they might dazzle you with their lustre.'

'Oh! Certainly,' said I, with the greatest complacency, for I assure you, my dearest Charlotte, I was not in the least offended – though by what followed, one would suppose that William was conscious of having given me just cause to be so, for coming up to me and taking my hand, he said, 'You must not look so grave, Susan; you will make me fear I have offended you!'

'Offended me! Dear brother, how came such a thought in your head!' returned I. 'No really! I assure you that I am not in the least surprised at your being so warm an advocate for the beauty of these girls' –

'Well, but,' interrupted William, 'remember that we have not yet concluded our dispute concerning them. What fault do you find with their complexion?'

'They are so horridly pale.'

'They have always a little colour, and after any exercise it is considerably heightened.'

'Yes, but if there should ever happen to be any rain in this part of the world, they will never be able to raise more than their common stock – except indeed they amuse themselves with running up and down these horrid old galleries and antechambers.'

'Well,' replied my brother in a tone of vexation, and glancing an impertinent look at me, 'if they *have* but little colour, at least it is all their own.'

This was too much, my dear Charlotte, for I am certain that he had the impudence, by that look, of pretending to suspect the reality of mine. But you, I am sure, will vindicate my character whenever you may hear it so cruelly aspersed, for you can witness how often I have protested against wearing rouge, and how much I always told you I disliked it. And I assure you that my opinions are still the same.

Well, not bearing to be so suspected by my brother, I left the room immediately, and have been ever since in my own dressing-room writing to you. What a long letter have I made of it! But you must not expect to receive such from me when I get to town; for it is only at Lesley Castle that one has time to write even to a Charlotte Lutterell. I was so much vexed by William's glance that I could not summon patience enough to stay and give him that advice respecting his attachment to Matilda which had first induced me from pure love for him to begin the conversation; and I am now so thoroughly convinced by it of his violent passion for her that I am certain he would never hear reason on the subject, and I shall therefore give myself no more trouble either about him or his favourite. Adieu, my dear girl –

Yours affectionately,

SUSAN L.

Letter 7

MISS C. LUTTERELL TO MISS M. LESLEY

Bristol, March 27th

I have received letters from you and your mother-in-law within this week which have greatly entertained me, as I find by them that you are both downright jealous of each other's beauty. It is very odd that two pretty women, though actually mother and daughter, cannot be in the same house without falling out about their faces. Do be convinced that you are both perfectly handsome and say no more of the matter. I suppose this letter must be directed to Portman Square, where probably (great as is your affection for Lesley Castle) you will not be sorry to find yourself. In spite of all that people may say about green fields and the country, I was always of opinion that London and its amusements must be very agreeable for a while, and should be very happy could my mother's income allow her to jockey us into its public places during winter. I always longed particularly to go to Vauxhall, to see whether the cold beef there is cut so thin[226] as it is reported, for I have a sly suspicion that few people understand the art of cutting a slice of cold beef so well as I do: nay it would be hard if I did not know something of the matter, for it was a part of my education that I took by far the most pains with. Mama always found me *her* best scholar, though when papa was alive Eloisa was *his*. Never to be sure were there two more different dispositions in the world. We both loved reading. *She* preferred histories, and *I* receipts.[227] She loved drawing pictures, and I drawing pullets. No one could sing a better song than she, and no one make a better pie than I. And so it has always continued since we have been no longer children. The only difference is that all disputes on the superior excellence of our employments *then* so frequent are now no more. We have for many years entered into an agreement always to admire each other's works: I never fail listening to *her* music, and she is as constant in eating *my* pies. Such at least was the case till Henry Hervey made his appearance in Sussex. Before the arrival of his aunt in our neighbour-hood, where she established herself, you know, about a twelvemonth ago, his visits to her had been at stated times, and of equal and settled duration; but on her removal to the Hall, which is within a walk from our house, they became both more frequent and longer. This, as you may suppose, could not be pleasing to Mrs Diana, who is a professed enemy to everything which is not directed by decorum and formality or which bears the least resemblance to ease and good-breeding. Nay, so great was her aversion to her nephew's behaviour that I have often heard her give such hints of it before his face, that had not Henry at such times been engaged in conversation with Eloisa, they must have caught his attention and have very much distressed him. The alteration in my sister's behaviour, which I have before hinted at, now took place. The agreement we had entered into of admiring each other's pro-ductions she no longer seemed to regard, and though I constantly applauded even every country-dance she played, yet not even a pigeon-pie of my making could obtain from her a single word of approbation. This was certainly enough to put anyone in a passion; however, I was as cool as a cream-cheese, and having formed my plan and concerted a scheme of revenge, I was determined to let her have her own way and not even to make her a single reproach. My scheme was to treat her as she treated me, and, though she might even draw my own picture or play Malbrouck[228] (which is the only tune I ever really liked), not to say so much as, 'Thank you, Eloisa,' when I had for many years constantly hollowed, whenever she played, *Bravo, Bravissimo, Encore, Da capo, Allegretto, Con expressione* and *Poco presto*,[229] with many other such out-landish words, all of them as Eloisa told me expressive of my admiration; and so indeed I suppose they are, as I see some of them in every page of every music book, being the sentiments I imagine of the composer.

I executed my plan with great punctuality. I cannot say success, for alas! my silence while she played seemed not in the least to displease her; on the contrary she actually said to me one day, 'Well, Charlotte, I am very glad to find that you have at last left off that ridiculous custom of applauding my execution on the harpsichord till you made my head ache and yourself hoarse. I feel very much obliged to you for keeping your admiration to yourself.' I never shall forget the very witty answer I made to this speech. 'Eloisa,' said I, 'I beg you would be quite at your ease with respect to all such fears in future, for be assured that I shall always keep my admiration to myself and my own pursuits and never extend it to yours.' This was the only very severe thing I ever said in my life; not but that I have often felt myself extremely satirical, but it was the only time I ever made my feelings public.

I suppose there never were two young people who had a greater affection for each other than Henry and Eloisa; no, the love of your brother for Miss Burton could not be so strong though it might be more violent. You may imagine therefore how provoked my sister must have been to have him play her such a trick. Poor girl! she still laments his death with undiminished constancy, notwithstanding he has been dead more than six weeks; but some people mind such things more than others. The ill state of health into which his loss has thrown her makes her so weak, and so unable to support the least exertion, that she has been in tears all this morning merely from having taken leave of Mrs Marlowe, who with her husband, brother and child is to leave Bristol this morning. I am sorry to have them go because they are the only family with whom we have here any acquaintance, but I never thought of crying; to be sure Eloisa and Mrs Marlowe have always been more together than with me, and have therefore contracted a kind of affection for each other, which does not make tears so inexcusable in them as they would be in me. The Marlowes are going to town; Cleveland accompanies them, as neither Eloisa nor I could catch him; I hope you or Matilda may have better luck. I know not when we shall leave Bristol. Eloisa's spirits are so low that she is very averse to moving, and yet is certainly by no means mended by her residence here. A week or two will I hope determine our measures – in the meantime believe me, &c., &c.,

CHARLOTTE LUTTERELL

Letter 8

MISS LUTTERELL TO MRS MARLOWE

Bristol, April 4th

I feel myself greatly obliged to you, my dear Emma, for such a mark of your affection as I flatter myself was conveyed in the proposal you made me of our corresponding; I assure you that it will be a great relief to me to write to you, and as long as my health and spirits will allow me, you will find me a very constant correspondent; I will not say an entertaining one, for you know my situation sufficiently not to be ignorant that in me mirth would be improper and I know my own heart too well not to be sensible that it would be unnatural. You must not expect news for we see no one with whom we are in the least acquainted, or in whose proceedings we have any interest. You must not expect scandal for by the same rule we are equally debarred either from hearing or inventing it. You must expect from me nothing but the melancholy effusions of a broken heart which is ever reverting to the happiness it once enjoyed and which ill supports its present wretchedness. The possibility of being able to write, to speak, to you of my lost Henry will be a luxury to me, and your goodness will not, I know, refuse to read what it will so much relieve my heart to write. I once thought that to have what is in general called a friend (I mean one of my own sex to whom I might speak with less reserve than to any other person), independent of my sister, would never be an object of my wishes, but how much was I mistaken! Charlotte is too much engrossed by two confidential correspondents of that sort to supply the place of one to me, and I hope you will not think me girlishly romantic when I say that to have some kind and compassionate friend, who might listen to my sorrows without endeavouring to console me, was what I had for some time wished for when our acquaintance with you, the intimacy which followed it and the particular affectionate attention you paid me almost from the first, caused me to entertain the flattering idea of those attentions being improved on a closer acquaintance into a friendship which, if you were what my wishes formed you, would be the greatest happiness I could be capable of enjoying. To find that such hopes are realised is a satisfaction indeed, a satisfaction which is now almost the only one I can ever experience. I feel myself so languid that I am sure were you with me you would oblige me to leave off writing, and I cannot give you a greater proof of my affection for you than by acting as I know you would wish me to do, whether absent or present. I am my dear Emma's sincere friend,

E. L.

Letter 9

MRS MARLOWE TO MISS LUTTERELL

Grosvenor Street,[230] *April 10th*

Need I say, my dear Eloisa, how welcome your letter was to me? I cannot give a greater proof of the pleasure I received from it, or of the desire I feel that our correspondence may be regular and frequent, than by setting you so good an example as I now do in answering it before the end of the week. But do not imagine that I claim any merit in being so punctual; on the contrary, I assure you that it is a far greater gratification to me to write to you than to spend the evening either at a concert or a ball. Mr Marlowe is so desirous of my appearing at some of the public places every evening that I do not like to refuse him, but, at the same time, I so much wish to remain at home that, independent of the pleasure I experience in devoting any portion of my time to my dear Eloisa, the liberty I claim from having a letter to write of spending an evening at home with my little boy, you know me well enough to be sensible, will of itself be a sufficient inducement (if one is necessary) to my maintaining with pleasure a correspondence with you. As to the subject of your letters to me, whether grave or merry, if they concern you they must be equally interesting to me; not but that I think the melancholy indulgence of your own sorrows by repeating them and dwelling on them to me will only encourage and increase them, and that it will be more prudent in you to avoid so sad a subject; but, yet knowing as I do what a soothing and melancholy pleasure it must afford you, I cannot prevail on myself to deny you so great an indulgence, and will only insist on your not expecting me to encourage you in it by my own letters; on the contrary, I intend to fill them with such lively wit and enlivening humour as shall even provoke a smile in the sweet but sorrowful countenance of my Eloisa.

In the first place you are to learn that I have met your sister's three friends, Lady Lesley and her daughters, twice in public since I have been here. I know you will be impatient to hear my opinion of the beauty of three ladies of whom you have heard so much. Now, as you are too ill and too unhappy to be vain, I think I may venture to inform you that I like none of their faces so well as I do your own. Yet they are all handsome – Lady Lesley indeed I have seen before; her daughters, I believe, would in general be said to have a finer face than her ladyship, and yet what with the charms of a blooming complexion, a little affectation and a great deal of smart-talk (in each of which she is superior to the young ladies), she will I dare say gain herself as many admirers as the more regular features of Matilda and Margaret. I am sure you will agree with me in saying that they can none of them be of a proper size for real beauty, when you know that two of them are taller and the other shorter than ourselves. In spite of this defect (or rather by reason of it), there is something very noble and majestic in the figures of the Miss Lesleys, and something agreeably lively in the appearance of their pretty little mother-in-law. But though one may be majestic and the other lively, yet the faces of neither possess that bewitching sweetness of my Eloisa's, which her present languor is so far from diminishing. What would my husband and brother say of us if they knew all the fine things I have been saying to you in this letter. It is very hard that a pretty woman is never to be told she is so by any one of her own sex without that person's being suspected to be either her determined enemy or her professed toad-eater.[231] How much more amiable are women in that particular! One man may say forty civil things to another without our supposing that he is ever paid for it, and provided he does his duty by our sex, we care not how polite he is to his own.

Mrs Lutterell will be so good as to accept my compliments, Charlotte, my love, and Eloisa, the best wishes for the recovery of her health and spirits that can be offered by her affectionate friend

E. MARLOWE

I am afraid this letter will be but a poor specimen of my powers in the witty way; and your opinion of them will not be greatly increased when I assure you that I have been as entertaining as I possibly could.

Letter 10

MISS MARGARET LESLEY TO MISS CHARLOTTE LUTTERELL

Portman Square, April 13th

MY DEAR CHARLOTTE – We left Lesley Castle on the 28th of last month, and arrived safely in London after a journey of seven days; I had the pleasure of finding your letter here waiting my arrival, for which you have my grateful thanks. Ah! my dear friend, I every day more regret the serene and tranquil pleasures of the castle we have left in exchange for the uncertain and unequal amusements of this vaunted city. Not that I will pretend to assert that these uncertain and unequal amusements are in the least degree unpleasing to me; on the contrary, I enjoy them extremely and should enjoy them even more were I not certain that every appearance I make in public but rivets the chains of those unhappy beings whose passion it is impossible not to pity, though it is out of my power to return. In short, my dear Charlotte, it is my sensibility[232] for the sufferings of so many amiable young men, my dislike of the extreme admiration I meet with, and my aversion to being so celebrated both in public, in private, in papers and in print shops,[233] that are the reasons why I cannot more fully enjoy the amusements so various and pleasing of London. How often have I wished that I possessed as little personal beauty as you do: that my figure was as inelegant; my face as unlovely; and my appearance as unpleasing as yours! But ah! what little chance is there of so desirable an event; I have had the smallpox,[234] and must therefore submit to my unhappy fate.

I am now going to entrust you, my dear Charlotte, with a secret which has long disturbed the tranquillity of my days, and which is of a kind to require the most inviolable secrecy from you. Last Monday se'night[235] Matilda and I accompanied Lady Lesley to a rout[236] at the Honourable Mrs Kickabout's; we were escorted by Mr Fitzgerald, who is a very amiable young man in the main, though perhaps a little singular in his taste – he is in love with Matilda. We had scarcely paid our compliments to the lady of the house and curtseyed to half a score different people when my attention was attracted by the appearance of a young man, the most lovely of his sex, who at that moment entered the room with another gentleman and lady. From the first moment I beheld him, I was certain that on him depended the future happiness of my life. Imagine my surprise when he was introduced to me by the name of Cleveland – I instantly recognised him as the brother of Mrs Marlowe, and the acquaintance of my Charlotte at Bristol. Mr and Mrs M. were the gentleman and lady who accompanied him. (You do not think Mrs Marlowe handsome?) The elegant address of Mr Cleveland, his polished manners and delightful bow, at once confirmed my attachment. He did not speak; but I can imagine everything he would have said had he opened his mouth. I can picture to myself the cultivated understanding, the noble sentiments and elegant language which would have shone so conspicuous in the conversation of Mr Cleveland. The approach of Sir James Gower (one of my too numerous admirers) prevented the discovery of any such powers by putting an end to a conversation we had never commenced and by attracting my attention to himself. But oh! How inferior are the accomplishments of Sir James to those of his so greatly envied rival! Sir James is one of the most frequent of our visitors, and is almost always of our parties. We have since often met Mr and Mrs Marlowe but no Cleveland – he is always engaged somewhere else. Mrs Marlowe fatigues me to death every time I see her by her tiresome conversations about you and Eloisa. She is so stupid! I live in the hope of seeing her irresistible brother tonight, as we are going to Lady Flambeau's,[237] who is, I know, intimate with the Marlowes. Our party will be Lady Lesley, Matilda, Fitzgerald, Sir James Gower and myself. We see little of Sir George, who is almost always at the gaming-table. Ah! my poor fortune, where art thou by this time? We see more of Lady L., who always makes her appearance (highly rouged) at dinner-time. Alas! what delightful jewels will she be decked in this evening at Lady Flambeau's! Yet I wonder how she can herself delight in wearing them; surely she must be sensible of the ridiculous impropriety of loading her little diminutive figure with such superfluous ornaments; is it possible that she cannot know how greatly superior an elegant simplicity is to the most studied apparel? Would she but present them to Matilda and me, how greatly should we be obliged to her. How becoming would diamonds be on our fine majestic figures! And how surprising it is that such an idea should never have occurred to *her*. I am sure if I have reflected in this manner once, I have fifty times. Whenever I see Lady Lesley dressed in them, such reflections immediately come across me. My own mother's jewels, too! But I will say no more on so melancholy a subject. Let me entertain you with something more pleasing – Matilda had a letter this morning from Lesley, by which we have the pleasure of finding that he is at Naples, has turned Roman Catholic, obtained one of the Pope's Bulls[238] for annulling his first marriage and has since actually married a Neapolitan lady of great rank and fortune. He tells us, moreover, that much the same sort of affair has befallen his first wife, the worthless Louisa, who is likewise at Naples, has turned Roman-Catholic and is soon to be married to a Neapolitan nobleman of great and distinguished merit. He says that they are at present very good friends, have quite forgiven all past errors and intend in future to be very good neighbours. He invites Matilda and me to pay him a visit to Italy and to bring him his little Louisa, whom both her mother, stepmother and he himself are equally desirous of beholding. As to our accepting his invitation, it is at present very uncertain; Lady Lesley advises us to go without loss of time; Fitzgerald offers to escort us there, but Matilda has some doubts of the propriety of such a scheme – she owns it would be very agreeable. I am certain she likes the fellow. My father desires us not to be in a hurry, as perhaps if we wait a few months both he and Lady Lesley will do themselves the pleasure of attending us. Lady Lesley says no, that nothing will ever tempt her to forgo the amusements of Brighthelmstone for a journey to Italy merely to see our brother. 'No,' says the disagreeable woman; 'I have once in my life been fool enough to travel, I don't know how many hundred miles, to see two of the family, and I found it did not answer; so deuce take me if ever I am so foolish again.' So says her ladyship, but Sir George still perseveres in saying that perhaps in a month or two they may accompany us.

Adieu, my dear Charlotte,
Your faithful

MARGARET LESLEY

Evelyn

To

MISS MARY LLOYD [239]

The following novel is by permission dedicated
by her obedient humble servant

The Author

IN A RETIRED PART OF THE COUNTY OF SUSSEX there is a village (for what I know to the contrary) called Evelyn, perhaps one of the most beautiful spots in the south of England. A gentleman, passing through it on horseback about twenty years ago, was so entirely of my opinion in this respect that he put up at the little alehouse in it and enquired with great earnestness whether there were any house to be let in the parish.

The landlady, who as well as everyone else in Evelyn was remarkably amiable, shook her head at this question, but seemed unwilling to give him any answer. He could not bear this uncertainty – yet knew not how to obtain the information he desired. To repeat a question which had already appeared to make the good woman uneasy was impossible. He turned from her in visible agitation. 'What a situation am I in!' said he to himself as he walked to the window and threw up the sash. He found himself revived by the air, which he felt to a much greater degree when he had opened the window than he had done before. Yet it was but for a moment. The agonising pain of doubt and suspense again weighed down his spirits. The good woman who had watched in eager silence every turn of his countenance with that benevolence which characterises the inhabitants of Evelyn, entreated him to tell her the cause of his uneasiness. 'Is there anything, sir, in my power to do that may relieve your griefs? Tell me in what manner I can soothe them and, believe me, the friendly balm of comfort and assistance shall not be wanting; for indeed, sir, I have a sympathetic soul.'

'Amiable woman,' said Mr Gower, affected almost to tears by this generous offer, 'this greatness of mind, in one to whom I am almost a stranger, serves but to make me the more warmly wish for a house in this sweet village. What would I not give to be your neighbour, to be blessed with your acquaintance and with the further knowledge of your virtues! Oh! with what pleasure would I form myself by such an example! Tell me then, best of women, is there no possibility? I cannot speak – you know my meaning – '

'Alas! sir,' replied Mrs Willis, 'there is *none*. Every house in this village, from the sweetness of the situation and the purity of the air, in which neither misery, ill health or vice are ever wafted, is inhabited. And yet,' after a short pause, 'there is a family, who though warmly attached to the spot, yet from a peculiar generosity of disposition would perhaps be willing to oblige you with their house.'

He eagerly caught at this idea, and having gained a direction to the place, he set off immediately on his walk to it. As he approached the house, he was delighted with its situation. It was in the exact centre of a small circular paddock, which was enclosed by a regular paling[240] and bordered with a plantation of Lombardy poplars and spruce firs alternatively placed in three rows. A gravel walk ran through this beautiful shrubbery, and as the remainder of the paddock was unencumbered with any other timber, the surface of it perfectly even and smooth and grazed by four white cows, which were disposed at equal distances from each other, the whole appearance of the place as Mr Gower entered the paddock was uncommonly striking. A beautifully rounded, gravel road without any turn or interruption led immediately to the house.

Mr Gower rang – the door was soon opened. 'Are Mr and Mrs Webb at home?'

'My good sir, they are,' replied the servant; and leading the way, conducted Mr Gower upstairs into a very elegant dressing-room, where a lady, rising from her seat, welcomed him with all the generosity which Mrs Willis had attributed to the family.

'Welcome, best of men – welcome to this house, and to everything it contains. William, tell your master of the happiness I enjoy – invite him to partake of it. Bring up some chocolate[241] immediately; spread a cloth in the dining-parlour and carry in the venison pasty. In the meantime, let the gentleman have some sandwiches, and bring in a basket of fruit – send up some ices[242] and a basin of soup, and do not forget some jellies and cakes.' Then turning to Mr Gower, and taking out her purse, 'Accept this, my good sir – believe me you are welcome to everything that is in my power to bestow. I wish my purse were weightier, but Mr Webb must make up my deficiencies. I know he has cash in the house to the amount of a hundred pounds,[243] which he shall bring you immediately.'

Mr Gower felt overpowered by her generosity as he put the purse in his pocket, and from the excess of his gratitude, could scarcely express himself intelligibly when he accepted her offer of the hundred pounds. Mr Webb soon entered the room, and repeated every protestation of friendship and cordiality which his lady had already made. The chocolate, the sandwiches, the jellies, the cakes, the ice and the soup soon made their appearance, and Mr Gower having tasted something of all, and pocketed the rest, was conducted into the dining-parlour, where he eat a most excellent dinner and partook of the most exquisite wines, while Mr and Mrs Webb stood by him still pressing him to eat and drink a little more.

'And now, my good sir,' said Mr Webb, when Mr Gower's repast was concluded, 'what else can we do to contribute to your happiness and express the affection we bear you. Tell us what you wish more to receive, and depend upon our gratitude for the communication of your wishes.'

'Give me then your house and grounds; I ask for nothing else.'

'They are yours,' exclaimed both at once; 'from this moment they are yours.' The agreement concluded on and the present accepted by Mr Gower, Mr Webb rang to have the carriage ordered, telling William at the same time to call the young ladies.

'Best of men,' said Mrs Webb, 'we will not long intrude upon your time.'

'Make no apologies, dear madam,' replied Mr Gower. 'You are welcome to stay this half-hour if you like it.'

They both burst forth into raptures of admiration at his politeness, which they agreed served only to make their conduct appear more inexcusable in trespassing on his time.

The young ladies soon entered the room. The elder of them was about seventeen, the other, several years younger. Mr Gower had no sooner fixed his eyes on Miss Webb than he felt that something more was necessary to his happiness than the house he had just received.

Mrs Webb introduced him to her daughter. 'Our dear friend Mr Gower, my love – he has been so good as to accept of this house, small as it is, and to promise to keep it for ever.'

'Give me leave to assure you, sir,' said Miss Webb, 'that I am highly sensible of your kindness in this respect, which from the shortness of my father's and mother's acquaintance with you, is more than usually flattering.'

Mr Gower bowed. 'You are too obliging, ma'am – I assure you that I like the house extremely – and if they would complete their generosity by giving me their elder daughter in marriage, with a handsome portion,[244] I should have nothing more to wish for.'

This compliment brought a blush into the cheeks of the lovely Miss Webb, who seemed, however, to refer herself to her father and mother. *They* looked delighted at each other.

At length Mrs Webb, breaking silence, said, 'We bend under a weight of obligations to you which we can never repay. Take our girl, take our Maria, and on her must the difficult task fall of endeavouring to make some return to so much beneficence.'

Mr Webb added, 'Her fortune is but ten thousand pounds,[245] which is almost too small a sum to be offered.'

This objection, however, being instantly removed by the generosity of Mr Gower, who declared himself satisfied with the sum mentioned, Mr and Mrs Webb, with their younger daughter, took their leave, and on the next day, the nuptials of their elder with Mr Gower were celebrated.

This amiable man now found himself perfectly happy: united to a very lovely and deserving young woman, with a handsome fortune and an elegant house, settled in the village of Evelyn and by that means enabled to cultivate his acquaintance with Mrs Willis. Could he have a wish ungratified? For some months he found that he could *not*, till one day, as he was walking in the shrubbery with Maria leaning on his arm, they observed a rose full-blown lying on the gravel; it had fallen from a rose tree which with three others had been planted by Mr Webb to give a pleasing variety to the walk. These four rose trees served also to mark the quarters of the shrubbery, by which means the traveller might always know how far in his progress round the paddock he was got.

Maria stooped to pick up the beautiful flower, and with all her family generosity presented it to her husband. 'My dear Frederic,' said she, 'pray take this charming rose.'

'Rose!' exclaimed Mr Gower. 'Oh, Maria! of what does not that remind me! Alas, my poor sister, how have I neglected you!'

The truth was that Mr Gower was the only son of a very large family, of which Miss Rose Gower was the thirteenth daughter. This young lady, whose merits deserved a better fate than she met with, was the darling of her relations. From the clearness of her skin and the brilliancy of her eyes, she was fully entitled to all their partial affection. Another circumstance contributed to the general love they bore her, and that was one of the finest heads of hair in the world. A few months before her brother's marriage, her heart had been engaged by the attentions and charms of a young man whose high rank and expectations seemed to foretell objections from his family to a match which would be highly desirable to theirs. Proposals were made on the young man's part, and proper objections on his father's – he was desired to return from Carlisle, where he was with his beloved Rose, to the family seat in Sussex. He was then obliged to comply, and the angry father then finding from his conversation how determined he was to marry no other woman, sent him for a fortnight to the Isle of Wight under the care of the family chaplain, with the hope of overcoming his constancy by time and absence in a foreign country. They accordingly prepared to bid a long adieu to England; the young nobleman was not allowed to see his Rose. They set sail but a storm arose which baffled the arts of the seamen. The vessel was wrecked on the coast of Calshot and every soul on board perished. The sad event soon reached Carlisle, and the beautiful Rose was affected by it beyond the power of expression. It was to soften her affliction by obtaining a picture of her unfortunate lover that her brother undertook a journey into Sussex, where he hoped that his petition would not be rejected by the severe yet afflicted father. When he reached Evelyn he was not many miles from — Castle, but the pleasing events which befell him in that place had for a while made him totally forget the object of his journey and his unhappy sister. The little incident of the rose, however, brought everything concerning her to his recollection again, and he bitterly repented his neglect. He returned to the house immediately, and agitated by grief, apprehension and shame, wrote the following letter to Rose.

July 14th, Evelyn

My dearest sister – As it is now four months since I left Carlisle, during which period I have not once written to you, you will perhaps unjustly accuse me of neglect and forgetfulness. Alas! I blush when I own the truth of your accusation. Yet if you are still alive, do not think too harshly of me, or suppose that I could for a moment forget the situation of my Rose. Believe me, I will forget you no longer, but will hasten as soon as possible to — Castle if I find by your answer that you are still alive. Maria joins me in every dutiful and affectionate wish, and I am yours sincerely

F. Gower

He waited in the most anxious expectation for an answer to his letter, which arrived as soon as the great distance from Carlisle would admit of. But, alas, it came not from Rosa.

Carlisle, July 17th

Dear brother – My mother has taken the liberty of opening your letter to poor Rose, as she has been dead these six weeks. Your long absence and continued silence gave us all great uneasiness and hastened her to the grave. Your journey to — Castle therefore may be spared. You do not tell us where you have been since the time of your quitting Carlisle, nor in any way account for your tedious absence, which gives us some surprise. We all unite in compliments to Maria, and beg to know who she is.

Your affectionate sister,

M. Gower

This letter, by which Mr Gower was obliged to attribute to his own conduct his sister's death, was so violent a shock to his feelings that in spite of his living at Evelyn, where illness was scarcely ever heard of, he was attacked by a fit of the gout,[246] which, confining him to his own room, afforded an opportunity to Maria of shining in that favourite character of Sir Charles Grandison's, a nurse.[247] No woman could ever appear more amiable than Maria did under such circumstances, and at last by her unremitting attentions she had the pleasure of seeing him gradually recover the use of his feet. It was a blessing by no means lost on him, for he was no sooner in a condition to leave the house, than he mounted his horse, and rode to — Castle, wishing to find whether his lordship, softened by his son's death, might have been brought to consent to the match, had both he and Rose been alive. His amiable Maria followed him with her eyes till she could see him no longer, and then sinking into her chair, overwhelmed with grief, found that in his absence she could enjoy no comfort.

Mr Gower arrived late in the evening at the castle, which was situated on a woody eminence commanding a beautiful prospect of the sea. Mr Gower did not dislike the situation, though it was certainly greatly inferior to that of his own house. There was an irregularity in the fall of the ground, and a profusion of old timber which appeared to him ill suited to the style of the castle, for it being a building of a very ancient date, he thought it required the paddock of Evelyn Lodge to form a contrast, and enliven the structure. The gloomy appearance of the old castle, frowning on him as he followed its winding approach, struck him with terror. Nor did he think himself safe till he was introduced into the drawing-room where the family were assembled to tea. Mr Gower was a perfect stranger to everyone in the circle, but though he was always timid in the dark and easily terrified when alone, he did not want that more necessary and more noble courage which enabled him without a blush to enter a large party of superior rank, whom he had never seen before, and to take his seat among them with perfect indifference.

The name of Gower was not unknown to Lord —. He felt distressed and astonished, yet rose and received him with all the politeness of a well-bred man. Lady —, who felt a deeper sorrow at the loss of her son than his lordship's harder heart was capable of, could hardly keep her seat when she found that he was the brother of her lamented Henry's Rose.

'My lord,' said Mr Gower, as soon as he was seated, 'You are perhaps surprised at receiving a visit from a man whom you could not have the least expectation of seeing here. But my sister, my unfortunate sister, is the real cause of my thus troubling you. That luckless girl is now no more – and though *she* can receive no pleasure from the intelligence, yet for the satisfaction of her family I wish to know whether the death of this unhappy pair has made an impression on your heart sufficiently strong to obtain that consent to their marriage – which in happier circumstances you would not be persuaded to give – supposing that they now were both alive.'

His lordship seemed lost in astonishment. Lady — could not support the mention of her son, and left the room in tears; the rest of the family remained attentively listening, almost persuaded that Mr Gower was distracted.[248] 'Mr Gower,' replied his lordship, 'this is a very odd question – it appears to me that you are supposing an impossibility. No one can more sincerely regret the death of my son than I have always done, and it gives me great concern to know that Miss Gower's was hastened by his. Yet to suppose them alive is destroying at once the motive for a change in my sentiments concerning the affair.'

'My lord,' replied Mr Gower in anger, 'I see that you are a most inflexible man, and that not even the death of your son can make you wish his future life happy. I will no longer detain your lordship. I see, I plainly see that you are a very vile man – and now I have the honour of wishing all your lordships and ladyships a good night.'

He immediately left the room, forgetting in the heat of his anger the lateness of the hour, which at any other time would have made him tremble, and leaving the whole company unanimous in their opinion of his being mad. When, however, he had mounted his horse and the great gates of the castle had shut him out, he felt a universal tremor throughout his whole frame. If we consider his situation, indeed – alone, on horseback, as late in the year as August[249] and in the day as nine o'clock, with no light to direct him but that of the moon almost full, and the stars which alarmed him by their twinkling – who can refrain from pitying him? No house within a quarter of a mile, and a gloomy castle, blackened by the deep shade of walnuts and pines, behind him. He felt indeed almost distracted with his fears, and shutting his eyes till he arrived at the village, to prevent his seeing either gypsies or ghosts, he rode on a full gallop all the way.

On his return home, he rang the house-bell, but no one appeared, a second time he rang, but the door was not opened, a third and a fourth with as little success. Observing the dining-parlour window open, he leapt in and pursued his way through the house till he reached Maria's dressing-room, where he found all the servants assembled at tea. Surprised at so very unusual a sight, he fainted; on his recovery he found himself on the sofa, with his wife's maid kneeling by him, chafing his temples with Hungary water.[250] From her he learned that his beloved Maria had been so much grieved at his departure that she had died of a broken heart about three hours after his departure.

He then became sufficiently composed to give the necessary orders for her funeral, which took place the Monday following, this being the Saturday. When Mr Gower had settled the order of the procession, he set out himself to Carlisle to give vent to his sorrow in the bosom of his family. He arrived there in high health and spirits, after a delightful journey of three days and a half. What was his surprise on entering the breakfast parlour to see Rose, his beloved Rose, seated on a sofa; at the sight of him she fainted, and would have fallen had not a gentleman, sitting with his back to the door, started up and saved her from sinking to the ground. She very soon came to herself and then introduced this gentleman to her brother as her husband, a Mr Davenport.

'But, my dearest Rose,' said the astonished Gower, 'I thought you were dead and buried.

'Why, my dear Frederick,' replied Rose, 'I wished you to think so, hoping that you would spread the report about the country and it would thus by some means reach — Castle. By this I hoped somehow or other to touch the hearts of its inhabitants. It was not till the day before yesterday that I heard of the death of my beloved Henry, which I learned from Mr Davenport, who concluded by offering me his hand. I accepted it with transport, and was married yesterday.' .

Mr Gower embraced his sister and shook hands with Mr Davenport; he then took a stroll into the town. As he passed by a public house, he called for a pot of beer, which was brought him immediately by his old friend Mrs Willis.

Great was his astonishment at seeing Mrs Willis in Carlisle. But not forgetful of the respect he owed her, he dropped on one knee, and received the frothy cup from her, more grateful to him than nectar.[251] He instantly made her an offer of his hand and heart, which she graciously condescended to accept, telling him that she was only on a visit to her cousin, who kept the Anchor,[252] and should be ready to return to Evelyn whenever he chose. The next morning they were married and immediately proceeded to Evelyn. When he reached home, he recollected that he had never written to Mr and Mrs Webb to inform them of the death of their daughter, which he rightly supposed they knew nothing of, as they never took in any newspapers. He immediately dispatched the following letter.

Evelyn. August 19th, 1809

DEAREST MADAM – How can words express the poignancy of my feelings! Our Maria, our beloved Maria, is no more; she breathed her last on Saturday the 12th of August. I see you now in an agony of grief, lamenting not your own, but my loss. Rest satisfied, I am happy – possessed of my lovely Sarah, what more can I wish for?

Remain

Respectfully yours,

F. GOWER

Westgate Buildings, August 22nd

GENEROUS, BEST OF MEN – How truly we rejoice to hear of your present welfare and happiness! and how truly grateful are we for your unexampled generosity in writing to condole with us on the late unlucky accident which befell our Maria. I have enclosed a draught on our banker for £30,[253] which Mr Webb joins with me in entreating you and the amiable Sarah to accept.

Your most grateful

ANNE AUGUSTA WEBB

Mr and Mrs Gower resided many years at Evelyn, enjoying perfect happiness, the just reward of their virtues. The only alteration which took place at Evelyn was that Mr and Mrs Davenport settled there in Mrs Willis's former abode and were for many years the proprietors of the White Horse Inn.

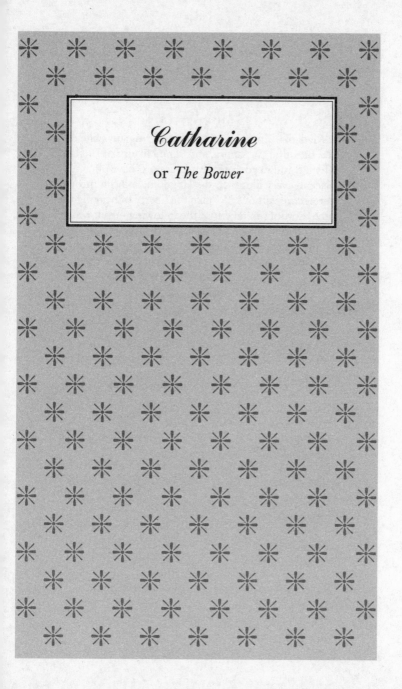

Catharine

or *The Bower*

To

Miss Austen

Madam – Encouraged by your warm patronage of
The Beautiful Cassandra, and 'The History of England',
which through your generous support, have obtained a
place in every library in the kingdom, and run through
threescore editions,[254] I take the liberty of begging the
same exertions in favour of the following novel, which I
humbly flatter myself, possesses merit beyond any already
published, or any that will ever in future appear,
except such as may proceed from the pen of
your most grateful humble servant

The Author

CATHARINE HAD THE MISFORTUNE, as many heroines have had before her, of losing her parents when she was very young, and of being brought up under the care of a maiden aunt, who, while she tenderly loved her, watched over her conduct with so scrutinising a severity as to make it very doubtful to many people, and to Catharine among the rest, whether she loved her or not. She had frequently been deprived of a real pleasure through this jealous caution, had been sometimes obliged to relinquish a ball because an officer was to be there, or to dance with a partner of her aunt's introduction in preference to one of her own choice. But her spirits were naturally good, and not easily depressed, and she possessed such a fund of vivacity and good humour as could only be damped by some serious vexation.

Besides these antidotes against every disappointment, and consolations under them, she had another, which afforded her constant relief in all her misfortunes, and that was a fine shady bower,[255] the work of her own infantine labours, assisted by those of two young companions who had resided in the same village. To this bower, which terminated a very pleasant and retired walk in her aunt's garden, she always wandered whenever anything disturbed her, and it possessed such a charm over her senses as constantly to tranquillise her mind and quiet her spirits. Solitude and reflection might perhaps have had the same effect in her bedchamber, yet habit had so strengthened the idea which fancy had first suggested that such a thought never occurred to Kitty, who was firmly persuaded that her bower alone could restore her to herself.

Her imagination was warm, and in her friendships, as well as in the whole tenure[256] of her mind, she was enthusiastic. This beloved bower had been the united work of herself and two amiable girls, for whom, since her earliest years, she had felt the tenderest regard. They were the daughters of the clergyman of the parish with whose family, while it had continued there, her aunt had been on the most intimate terms, and the three little girls, though separated for the greatest part of the year by the different modes of their education, were constantly together during the holidays of the Miss Wynnes. In those days of happy childhood, now so often regretted by Kitty, this arbour had been formed, and now that she was separated perhaps for ever from these dear friends, it encouraged more than any other place the tender and melancholy recollections of hours rendered pleasant by them, at once so sorrowful, yet so soothing!

It was now two years since the death of Mr Wynne, and the consequent dispersion of his family, who had been left by it in great distress. They had been reduced to a state of absolute dependence on some relations, who, though very opulent and very nearly connected with them, had with difficulty been prevailed on to contribute anything towards their support. Mrs Wynne was fortunately spared the knowledge and participation of their distress by her release from a painful illness a few months before the death of her husband.

The elder daughter had been obliged to accept the offer of one of her cousins to equip her for the East Indies,[257] and though infinitely against her inclinations, had been necessitated to embrace the only possibility that was offered to her of a maintenance; yet it was one so opposite to all her ideas of propriety, so contrary to her wishes, so repugnant to her feelings, that she would almost have preferred servitude to it, had choice been allowed her. Her personal attractions had gained her a husband as soon as she had arrived at Bengal,[258] and she had now been married nearly a twelvemonth. Splendidly, yet unhappily married – united to a man of double her own age, whose disposition was not amiable, and whose manners were unpleasing, though his character was respectable. Kitty had heard twice from her friend since her marriage, but her letters were always unsatisfactory, and though she did not openly avow her feelings, yet every line proved her to be unhappy. She spoke with pleasure of nothing but of those amusements which they had shared together and which could return no more, and seemed to have no happiness in view but that of returning to England again.

Her sister had been taken by another relation, the Dowager[259] Lady Halifax, as a companion[260] to her daughters, and had accompanied the family into Scotland about the same time of Cecilia's leaving England. From Mary, therefore, Kitty had the power of hearing more frequently, but her letters were scarcely more comfortable. There was not indeed that hopelessness of sorrow in her situation as in her sister's; she was not married, and could yet look forward to a change in her circumstances; but situated for the present without any immediate hope of it, in a family where though all were her relations she had no friend, she wrote usually in depressed spirits, which her separation from her sister and her sister's marriage had greatly contributed to make so.

Divided thus from the two she loved best on earth, while Cecilia and Mary were still more endeared to her by their loss, everything that brought a remembrance of them was doubly cherished, and the shrubs they had planted, and the keepsakes they had given, were rendered sacred.

The living of Chetwynde[261] was now in the possession of a Mr

Dudley, whose family, unlike the Wynnes, were productive only of vexation and trouble to Mrs Percival and her niece. Mr Dudley, who was the younger son of a very noble family, of a family more famed for their pride than their opulence, tenacious of his dignity, and jealous of his rights, was forever quarrelling, if not with Mrs Percival herself, with her steward and tenants concerning tithes,[262] and with the principal neighbours themselves concerning the respect and parade he exacted. His wife, an ill-educated, untaught woman of ancient family, was proud of that family almost without knowing why, and like him too was haughty and quarrelsome, without considering for what. Their only daughter, who inherited the ignorance, the insolence and pride of her parents, was, from that beauty of which she was unreasonably vain, considered by them as an irresistible creature, and looked up to as the future restorer, by a splendid marriage, of the dignity which their reduced situation and Mr Dudley's being obliged to take orders[263] for a country living had so much lessened. They at once despised the Percivals as people of mean family, and envied them as people of fortune. They were jealous of their being more respected than themselves, and while they affected to consider them as of no consequence, were continually seeking to lessen them in the opinion of the neighbourhood[264] by scandalous and malicious reports. Such a family as this was ill-calculated to console Kitty for the loss of the Wynnes, or to fill up by their society those occasionally irksome hours which in so retired a situation would sometimes occur for want of a companion.

Her aunt was most excessively fond of her, and miserable if she saw her for a moment out of spirits; yet she lived in such constant apprehension of her marrying imprudently if she were allowed the opportunity of choosing, and was so dissatisfied with her behaviour when she saw her with young men – for it was, from her natural disposition, remarkably open and unreserved – that though she frequently wished for her niece's sake that the neighbourhood were larger, and that she had used herself to mix more with it, yet the recollection of there being young men in almost every family in it always conquered the wish.

The same fears that prevented Mrs Percival's joining much in the society of her neighbours, led her equally to avoid inviting her relations to spend any time in her house. She had therefore constantly regretted the annual attempt of a distant relation to visit her at Chetwynde, as there was a young man in the family of whom she had heard many traits that alarmed her. This son was, however, now on his travels,[265] and the repeated solicitations of Kitty, joined to a consciousness of having declined with too little ceremony the frequent overtures of her friends to be admitted, and a real wish to see them herself, easily prevailed on her to press with great earnestness the pleasure of a visit from them during the summer. Mr and Mrs Stanley were accordingly to come, and Catharine, in having an object to look forward to, a something to expect that must inevitably relieve the dullness of a constant tête-à-tête with her aunt, was so delighted, and her spirits so elevated, that for the three or four days immediately preceding their arrival she could scarcely fix herself to any employment. In this point Mrs Percival always thought her defective, and frequently complained of a want of steadiness and perseverance in her occupations, virtues by no means congenial to the eagerness of Kitty's disposition and perhaps not often met with in any young person. The tediousness too of her aunt's conversation and the want of agreeable companions greatly increased this desire of change in her employments, for Kitty found herself much sooner tired of reading, working[266] or drawing in Mrs Percival's parlour than in her own arbour, where Mrs Percival for fear of its being damp never accompanied her.

As her aunt prided herself on the exact propriety and neatness with which everything in her family was conducted, and had no higher satisfaction than that of knowing her house to be always in complete order, as her fortune was good, and her establishment[267] ample, few were the preparations necessary for the reception of her visitors. The day of their arrival, so long expected, at length came, and the noise of the coach and four as it drove round the sweep[268] was to Catharine a more interesting sound than the music of an Italian opera, which to most heroines is the height of enjoyment. Mr and Mrs Stanley were people of large fortune and high fashion. He was a member of the House of Commons, and they were therefore most agreeably necessitated to reside half the year in town;[269] where Miss Stanley had been attended by the most capital masters from the time of her being six years old to the last spring, which comprehending a period of twelve years had been dedicated to the acquirement of accomplishments which were now to be displayed and in a few years entirely neglected.

She was not inelegant in her appearance, rather handsome, and naturally not deficient in abilities; but those years which ought to have been spent in the attainment of useful knowledge and mental improvement had been all bestowed in learning drawing, Italian and music, more especially the latter, and she now united to these accomplishments an understanding unimproved by reading and a mind totally devoid either of taste or judgement. Her temper was by nature good, but unassisted by reflection, she had neither patience under disappointment, nor could sacrifice her own inclinations to promote the happiness of others. All her ideas were towards the elegance of her appearance, the fashion of her dress, and the admiration she wished them to excite. She professed a love of books without reading, was lively without wit, and generally good humoured without merit.

Such was Camilla Stanley; and Catharine, who was prejudiced by her appearance, and who from her solitary situation was ready to like anyone, though her understanding and judgement would not otherwise have been easily satisfied, felt almost convinced when she saw her that Miss Stanley would be the very companion she wanted and in some degree make amends for the loss of Cecilia and Mary Wynne. She therefore attached herself to Camilla from the first day of her arrival, and from being the only young people in the house, they were by inclination constant companions. Kitty was herself a great reader, though perhaps not a very deep one, and felt therefore highly delighted to find that Miss Stanley was equally fond of it. Eager to know that their sentiments as to books were similar, she very soon began questioning her new acquaintance on the subject; but though she was well read in modern history herself, she chose rather to speak first of books of a lighter kind, of books universally read and admired.

'You have read Mrs Smith's novels,[270] I suppose?' said she to her companion.

'Oh! yes,' replied the other, 'and I am quite delighted with them. They are the sweetest things in the world – '

'And which do you prefer of them?'

'Oh! dear, I think there is no comparison between them – *Emmeline* is *so much* better than any of the others – '

'Many people think so, I know; but there does not appear so great a disproportion in their merits to *me*; do you think it is better written?'

'Oh! I do not know anything about *that* – but it is better in *everything*. Besides, *Ethelinde* is so long – '

'That is a very common objection, I believe,' said Kitty, 'but for my own part, if a book is well written, I always find it too short.'

'So do I, only I get tired of it before it is finished.'

'But did not you find the story of *Ethelinde* very interesting? And the descriptions of Grasmere, are not they beautiful?'

'Oh! I missed them all, because I was in such a hurry to know the end of it – ' Then from an easy transition she added, 'We are going to the Lakes[271] this autumn, and I am quite mad with joy; Sir Henry Devereux has promised to go with us, and that will make it so pleasant, you know – '

'I dare say it will; but I think it is a pity that Sir Henry's powers of pleasing were not reserved for an occasion where they might be more wanted. However, I quite envy you the pleasure of such a scheme.'

'Oh! I am quite delighted with the thoughts of it; I can think of nothing else. I assure you I have done nothing for this last month but plan what clothes I should take with me, and I have at last determined to take very few indeed besides my travelling dress,[272] and so I advise you to do, whenever you go; for I intend, in case we should fall in with any races, or stop at Matlock or Scarborough,[273] to have some things made for the occasion.'

'You intend then to go into Yorkshire?'

'I believe not – indeed I know nothing of the route, for I never trouble myself about such things. I only know that we are to go from Derbyshire to Matlock and Scarborough, but to which of them first, I neither know nor care. I am in hopes of meeting some particular friends of mine at Scarborough. Augusta told me in her last letter that Sir Peter talked of going; but then you know that is so uncertain. I cannot bear Sir Peter, he is such a horrid creature – '

'He *is*, is he?' said Kitty, not knowing what else to say.

'Oh! he is quite shocking.'

Here the conversation was interrupted, and Kitty was left in a painful uncertainty as to the particulars of Sir Peter's character; she knew only that he was horrid and shocking, but why, and in what, yet remained to be discovered. She could scarcely resolve what to think of her new acquaintance; she appeared to be shamefully ignorant as to the geography of England, if she had understood her right, and equally devoid of taste and information. Kitty was, however, unwilling to decide hastily; she was at once desirous of doing Miss Stanley justice, and of having her own wishes in her answered; she determined therefore to suspend all judgement for some time. After supper, the conversation turning on the state of affairs in the political world,[274] Mrs Percival, who was firmly of the opinion that the whole race of mankind was degenerating, said that, for her part, everything she believed was going to rack and ruin, all order was destroyed over the face of the world, the House of Commons she heard did not break up sometimes till five in the morning, and depravity never was so general before, and she concluded with a wish that she might live to see the manners of the people in Queen Elizabeth's[275] reign restored again.

'Well, ma'am,' said her niece, 'I believe you have as good a chance of it as anyone else, but I hope you do not mean with the times to restore Queen Elizabeth herself.'

'Queen Elizabeth,' said Mrs Stanley, who never hazarded a remark on history that was not well founded, 'lived to a good old age, and was a very clever woman.'

'True, ma'am,' said Kitty; 'but I do not consider either of those circumstances as meritorious in herself, and they are very far from making me wish her return, for if she were to come again with the same abilities and the same good constitution she might do as much mischief and last as long as she did before – ' Then, turning to Camilla who had been sitting very silent for some time, she added, 'What do *you* think of Elizabeth, Miss Stanley? I hope you will not defend her.'

'Oh! dear,' said Miss Stanley, 'I know nothing of politics, and cannot bear to hear them mentioned.'

Kitty started at this repulse, but made no answer; that Miss Stanley must be ignorant of what she could not distinguish from politics she felt perfectly convinced. She retired to her own room, perplexed in her opinion about her new acquaintance, and fearful of her being very unlike Cecilia and Mary. She arose the next morning to experience a fuller conviction of this, and every future day increased it. She found no variety in her conversation; she received no information from her but in fashions, and no amusement but in her performance on the harpsichord; and after repeated endeavours to find her what she wished, she was obliged to give up the attempt and to consider it as fruitless. There had occasionally appeared a something like humour in Camilla which had inspired her with hopes that she might at least have a natural genius, though not an improved one, but these sparklings of wit happened so seldom, and were so ill-supported, that she was at last convinced of their being merely accidental. All her stock of knowledge was exhausted in a very few days, and when Kitty had learnt from her how large their house in town was, when the fashionable amusements began, who were the celebrated beauties and who the best milliner, Camilla had nothing further to teach, except the characters of any of her acquaintance as they occurred in conversation, which was done with equal ease and brevity, by saying that the person was either the sweetest creature in the world, and one of whom she was dotingly fond, or horrid, shocking, and not fit to be seen.

As Catharine was very desirous of gaining every possible information as to the characters of the Halifax family, and concluded that Miss Stanley must be acquainted with them, as she seemed to be so with everyone of any consequence, she took an opportunity as Camilla was one day enumerating all the people of rank that her mother visited, of asking her whether Lady Halifax were among the number.

'Oh! Thank you for reminding me of her, she is the sweetest woman in the world, and one of our most intimate acquaintances. I do not suppose there is a day passes, during the six months that we are in town, but what we see each other in the course of it. And I correspond with all the girls.'

'They *are* then a very pleasant family?' said Kitty. 'They ought to be so indeed, to allow of such frequent meetings, or all conversation must be at end.'

'Oh! dear, not at all,' said Miss Stanley, 'for sometimes we do not speak to each other for a month together. We meet perhaps only in public, and then, you know, we are often not able to get near enough; but in that case we always nod and smile.'

'Which does just as well. But I was going to ask you whether you have ever seen a Miss Wynne with them?'

'I know who you mean perfectly – she wears a blue hat. I have frequently seen her in Brook Street,[276] when I have been at Lady Halifax's balls – she gives one every month during the winter. But only think how good it is in her to take care of Miss Wynne, for she is a very distant relation, and so poor that, as Miss Halifax told me, her mother was obliged to find her in clothes.[277] Is not it shameful?'

'That she should be so poor? It is indeed, with such wealthy connections as the family have.'

'Oh! no; I mean, was not it shameful in Mr Wynne to leave his children so distressed, when he had actually the living of Chetwynde and two or three curacies,[278] and only four children to provide for. What would he have done if he had had ten, as many people have?'

'He would have given them all a good education and have left them all equally poor.'

'Well I do think there never was so lucky a family. Sir George Fitzgibbon, you know, sent the elder girl to India entirely at his own expense, where they say she is most nobly married and the happiest creature in the world. Lady Halifax, as you see, has taken care of the younger and treats her as if she were her daughter; she does not go out into public with her, to be sure; but then she is always present when her ladyship gives her balls, and nothing can be kinder to her than Lady Halifax is; she would have taken her to Cheltenham[279] last year, if there had been room enough at the lodgings, and therefore I don't think that *she* can have anything to complain of. Then there are the two sons: one of them the Bishop of M— has got into the army, as a lieutenant, I suppose; and the other is extremely well off, I know, for I have a notion that somebody puts him to school somewhere in Wales. Perhaps you knew them when they lived here?'

'Very well. We met as often as your family and the Halifaxes do in town, but as we seldom had any difficulty in getting near enough to speak, we seldom parted with merely a nod and a smile. They were, indeed, a most charming family, and I believe have scarcely their equals in the world; the neighbours we now have at the parsonage appear to more disadvantage in coming after them.'

'Oh! horrid wretches! I wonder you can endure them.'

'Why, what would you have one do?'

'Oh! Lord, if I were in your place, I should abuse them all day long.'

'So I do, but it does no good.'

'Well, I declare it is quite a pity that they should be suffered to live. I wish my father would propose knocking all their brains out, some day or other when he is in the House. So abominably proud of their family! And I dare say, after all, that there is nothing particular in it.'

'Why yes, I believe they *have* reason to value themselves on it, if anybody has; for you know he is Lord Amyatt's brother.'

'Oh! I know all that very well, but it is no reason for their being so horrid. I remember I met Miss Dudley last spring with Lady Amyatt at Ranelagh,[280] and she had such a frightful cap on that I have never been able to bear any of them since. And so you used to think the Wynnes very pleasant?'

'You speak as if their being so were doubtful! Pleasant! Oh! they were everything that could interest and attach. It is not in my power to do justice to their merits, though not to feel them, I think, must be impossible. They have unfitted me for any society but their own!'

'Well, that is just what I think of the Miss Halifaxes; by the by, I must write to Caroline tomorrow, and I do not know what to say to her. The Barlows, too, are just such other sweet girls; but I wish Augusta's hair was not so dark. I cannot bear Sir Peter – horrid wretch! He is *always* laid up with the gout,[281] which is exceedingly disagreeable to the family.'

'And perhaps not very pleasant to *himself*. But as to the Wynnes; do you really think them very fortunate?'

'Do I? Why, does not everybody? Miss Halifax and Caroline and Maria all say that they are the luckiest creatures in the world. So does Sir George Fitzgibbon and so do everybody.'

'That is, everybody who have themselves conferred an obligation on them. But do you call it lucky for a girl of genius and feeling to be sent in quest of a husband to Bengal, to be married there to a man of whose disposition she has no opportunity of judging till her judgement is of no use to her, who may be a tyrant, or a fool, or both for what she knows to the contrary? Do you call *that* fortunate?'

'I know nothing of all that; I only know that it was extremely good in Sir George to fit her out and pay her passage, and that she would not have found many who would have done the same.'

'I wish she had not found *one*,' said Kitty with great eagerness, 'she might then have remained in England and been happy.'

'Well, I cannot conceive the hardship of going out in a very agreeable manner with two or three sweet girls for companions, having a delightful voyage to Bengal or Barbados[282] or wherever it is, and being married soon after one's arrival to a very charming man immensely rich. I see no hardship in all that.'

'Your representation of the affair,' said Kitty, laughing, 'certainly gives a very different idea of it from mine. But supposing all this to be true, still, as it was by no means certain that she would be so fortunate either in her voyage, her companions, or her husband, in being obliged to run the risk of their proving very different, she undoubtedly experienced a great hardship. Besides, to a girl of any delicacy, the voyage in itself, since the object of it is so universally known, is a punishment that needs no other to make it very severe.'

'I do not see that at all. She is not the first girl who has gone to the East Indies for a husband, and I declare I should think it very good fun if I were as poor.'

'I believe you would think very differently *then*. But at least you will not defend her sister's situation? Dependent even for her clothes on the bounty of others, who of course do not pity her, as, by her own account, they consider her as very fortunate.'

'You are extremely nice[283] upon my word; Lady Halifax is a delightful woman, and one of the sweetest tempered creatures in the world; I am sure I have every reason to speak well of her, for we are under most amazing obligations to her. She has frequently chaperoned[284] me when my mother has been indisposed, and last spring she lent me her own horse three times, which was a prodigious favour, for it is the most beautiful creature that ever was seen, and I am the only person she ever lent it to.

'And then,' continued she, 'the Miss Halifaxes are quite delightful. Maria is one of the cleverest girls that ever were known – draws in oils,[285] and plays anything by sight. She promised me one of her drawings before I left town, but I entirely forgot to ask her for it. I would give anything to have one.'

'But was not it very odd,' said Kitty, 'that the Bishop should send Charles Wynne to sea, when he must have had a much better chance of providing for him in the Church, which was the profession that Charles liked best, and the one for which his father had intended him? The Bishop, I know, had often promised Mr Wynne a living, and as he never gave him one, I think it was incumbent on him to transfer the promise to his son.'

'I believe you think he ought to have resigned his bishopric to him; you seem determined to be dissatisfied with everything that has been done for them.'

'Well,' said Kitty, 'this is a subject on which we shall never agree, and therefore it will be useless to continue it further, or to mention it again – '

She then left the room, and running out of the house was soon in her dear bower where she could indulge in peace all her affectionate anger against the relations of the Wynnes, which was greatly heightened by finding from Camilla that they were in general considered as having acted particularly well by them. She amused herself for some time in abusing and hating them all, with great spirit, and when this tribute to her regard for the Wynnes was paid, and the bower began to have its usual influence over her spirits, she contributed towards settling them by taking out a book, for she had always one about her, and reading.

She had been so employed for nearly an hour, when Camilla came running towards her with great eagerness, and apparently great pleasure. 'Oh! my dear Catharine,' said she, half out of breath, 'I have such delightful news for you – but you shall never guess what it is. We are all the happiest creatures in the world! Would you believe it? The Dudleys have sent us an invitation to a ball at their own house. What charming people they are! I had no idea of there being so much sense in the whole family – I declare I quite dote upon them. And it happens so fortunately too, for I expect a new cap from town tomorrow which will just do for a ball – gold net – it will be a most angelic thing – everybody will be longing for the pattern.'[286]

The expectation of a ball was indeed very agreeable intelligence to Kitty, who, fond of dancing and seldom able to enjoy it, had reason to feel even greater pleasure in it than her friend; for to *her*, it was now no novelty. Camilla's delight, however, was by no means inferior to Kitty's, and she rather expressed the most of the two. The cap came and every other preparation was soon completed; while these were in agitation the days passed gaily away, but when directions were no longer necessary, taste could no longer be displayed, and difficulties no longer overcome, the short period that intervened before the day of the ball hung heavily on their hands, and every hour was too long. The very few times that Kitty had ever enjoyed the amusement of dancing was an excuse for *her* impatience, and an apology for the idleness it occasioned to a mind naturally very active; but her friend without such a plea was infinitely worse than herself. She could do nothing but wander from the house to the garden, and from the garden to the avenue, wondering when Thursday would come, which she might easily have ascertained, and counting the hours as they passed, which served only to lengthen them.

They retired to their rooms in high spirits on Wednesday night, but Kitty awoke the next morning with a violent toothache. It was in vain that she endeavoured at first to deceive herself; her feelings were witnesses too acute of its reality; with as little success did she try to sleep it off, for the pain she suffered prevented her closing her eyes. She then summoned her maid, and with the assistance of the housekeeper, every remedy that the receipt book[287] or the head of the latter contained was tried, but ineffectually; for though for a short time relieved by them, the pain still returned. She was now obliged to give up the endeavour, and to reconcile herself not only to the pain of a toothache, but to the loss of a ball; and though she had with so much eagerness looked forward to the day of its arrival, had received such pleasure in the necessary preparations, and promised herself so much delight in it, yet she was not so totally void of philosophy as many girls of her age might have been in her situation. She considered that there were misfortunes of a much greater magnitude than the loss of a ball experienced every day by some part of mortality, and that the time might come when she would herself look back with wonder and[288] perhaps with envy on her having known no greater vexation.

By such reflections as these, she soon reasoned herself into as much resignation and patience as the pain she suffered would allow of, which after all was the greatest misfortune of the two, and told the sad story when she entered the breakfast room, with tolerable composure. Mrs Percival more grieved for her toothache than her disappointment, having feared that it would not be possible to prevent her dancing with a man if she went, was eager to try everything that had already been applied to alleviate the pain, while at the same time she declared it was impossible for her to leave the house. Miss Stanley, who joined to her concern for her friend a mixture of dread lest her mother's proposal that they should all remain at home might be accepted, was very violent in her sorrow on the occasion, and though her apprehensions on the subject were soon quieted by Kitty's protesting that sooner than allow anyone to stay with her she would herself go, she continued to lament it with such unceasing vehemence as at last drove Kitty to her own room.

Her fears for herself being now entirely dissipated left her more than ever at leisure to pity and persecute her friend, who though safe when in her own room, was frequently removing from it to some other in hopes of being more free from pain, and then had no opportunity of escaping her.

'To be sure, there never was anything so shocking,' said Camilla; 'to come on such a day too! For one would not have minded it, you know, had it been at *any other* time. But it always is so. I never was at a ball in my life but what something happened to prevent somebody from going! I wish there were no such things as teeth in the world; they are nothing but plagues to one, and I dare say that people might easily invent something to eat with instead of them; poor thing! what pain you are in! I declare it is quite shocking to look at you. But you won't have it out, will you? For heaven's sake don't; for there is nothing I dread so much. I declare I had rather undergo the greatest tortures in the world than have a tooth drawn. Well! how patiently you do bear it! how can you be so quiet? Lord, if I were in your place I should make such a fuss there would be no bearing me. I should torment you to death.'

'So you do, as it is,' thought Kitty.

'For my own part, Catharine,' said Mrs Percival, 'I have not a doubt but that you caught this toothache by sitting so much in that arbour, for it is always damp. I know it has ruined your constitution entirely; and indeed I do not believe it has been of much service to mine; I sat down in it last May to rest myself, and I have never been quite well since. I shall order John to pull it all down, I assure you.'

'I know you will not do that, ma'am,' said Kitty, 'as you must be convinced how unhappy it would make me.'

'You talk very ridiculously, child; it is all whim and nonsense. Why cannot you fancy this room an arbour?'

'Had this room been built by Cecilia and Mary, I should have valued it equally, ma'am, for it is not merely the name of an arbour, which charms me.'

'Why indeed, Mrs Percival,' said Mrs Stanley, 'I must think that Catharine's affection for her bower is the effect of a sensibility[289] that does her credit. I love to see a friendship between young persons and always consider it as a sure mark of an amiable affectionate disposition. I have from Camilla's infancy taught her to think the same, and have taken great pains to introduce her to young people of her own age who were likely to be worthy of her regard. There is something mighty pretty, I think, in young ladies corresponding with each other, and nothing forms the taste more than sensible and elegant letters. Lady

Halifax thinks just like me. Camilla corresponds with her daughters, and I believe I may venture to say that they are none of them *the worse* for it.'

These ideas were too modern to suit Mrs Percival, who considered a correspondence between girls as productive of no good and as the frequent origin of imprudence and error, by the effect of pernicious advice and bad example. She could not therefore refrain from saying that for her part, she had lived fifty years in the world without having ever had a correspondent, and did not find herself at all the less respectable for it. Mrs Stanley could say nothing in answer to this, but her daughter, who was less governed by propriety, said in her thoughtless way, 'But who knows what you might have been, ma'am, if you *had* had a correspondent; perhaps it would have made you quite a different creature. I declare I would not be without those I have for all the world. It is the greatest delight of my life, and you cannot think how much their letters have formed my taste, as mama says, for I hear from them generally every week.'

'You received a letter from Augusta Barlow today, did not you, my love?' said her mother. 'She writes remarkably well, I know.'

'Oh! Yes, ma'am, the most delightful letter you ever heard of. She sends me a long account of the new Regency walking dress[290] Lady Susan has given her, and it is so beautiful that I am quite dying with envy for it.'

'Well, I am prodigiously happy to hear such pleasing news of my young friend; I have a high regard for Augusta, and most sincerely partake in the general joy on the occasion. But does she say nothing else? it seemed to be a long letter – Are they to be at Scarborough?'

'Oh! Lord, she never once mentions it, now I recollect it; and I entirely forgot to ask her when I wrote last. She says nothing indeed except about the Regency.'

'She *must* write well,' thought Kitty, 'to make a long letter upon a bonnet and pelisse.'[291]

She then left the room, tired of listening to a conversation which, though it might have diverted her had she been well, served only to fatigue and depress her while in pain. Happy was it for *her*, when the hour of dressing came, for Camilla, satisfied with being surrounded by her mother and half the maids in the house, did not want her assistance, and was too agreeably employed to want her society. She remained therefore alone in the parlour, till joined by Mr Stanley and her aunt, who, however, after a few enquiries, allowed her to continue undisturbed and began their usual conversation on politics. This was a subject on which they could never agree, for Mr Stanley, who considered himself as perfectly qualified by his seat in the House to decide on it without hesitation, resolutely maintained that the kingdom had not for ages been in so flourishing and prosperous a state, and Mrs Percival, with equal warmth, though perhaps less argument, as vehemently asserted that the whole nation would speedily be ruined, and everything, as she expressed herself, be at sixes and sevens. It was not, however, unamusing to Kitty to listen to the dispute, especially as she began then to be more free from pain, and without taking any share in it herself, she found it very entertaining to observe the eagerness with which they both defended their opinions and could not help thinking that Mr Stanley would not feel more disappointed if her aunt's expectations were fulfilled than her aunt would be mortified by their failure. After waiting a considerable time, Mrs Stanley and her daughter appeared, and Camilla, in high spirits and perfect good humour with her own looks, was more violent than ever in her lamentations over her friend as she practised her Scotch steps[292] about the room.

At length they departed, and Kitty, better able to amuse herself than she had been the whole day before, wrote a long account of her misfortunes to Mary Wynne. When her letter was concluded, she had an opportunity of witnessing the truth of that assertion which says that sorrows are lightened by communication, for her toothache was then so much relieved that she began to entertain an idea of following her friends to Mr Dudley's. They had been gone an hour, and as everything relative to her dress was in complete readiness, she considered that in another hour, since there was so little a way to go, she might be there. They were gone in Mr Stanley's carriage and therefore she might follow in her aunt's. As the plan seemed so very easy to be executed, and promised so much pleasure, it was after a few minutes' deliberation finally adopted, and running upstairs, she rang in great haste for her maid. The bustle and hurry which then ensued for nearly an hour was at last happily concluded by her finding herself very well dressed and in high beauty.

Anne was then dispatched in the same haste to order the carriage, while her mistress was putting on her gloves, and arranging the folds of her dress. In a few minutes she heard the carriage drive up to the door, and though at first surprised at the expedition with which it had been got ready, she concluded after a little reflection that the men had received some hint of her intentions beforehand, and was hastening out of the room when Anne came running into it in the greatest hurry and agitation, exclaiming, 'Lord, ma'am! Here's a gentleman in a chaise and four[293] come, and I cannot for my life conceive who it is! I happened to be crossing the hall when the carriage drove up, and I knew nobody would be in the way to let him in but Tom, and he looks so awkward, you know, ma'am, now his hair is just done up,[294] that I was not willing the gentleman should see him, and so I went to the door myself. And he is one of the handsomest young men you would wish to see; I was almost ashamed of being seen in my apron, ma'am, but however he is vastly handsome and did not seem to mind it at all. And he asked me whether the family were at home; and so I said everybody was gone out but you, ma'am, for I would not deny you because I was sure you would like to see him. And then he asked me whether Mr and Mrs Stanley were not here, and so I said yes, and then – '

'Good heavens!' said Kitty, 'what can all this mean! And who can it possibly be! Did you never see him before? And did not he tell you his name?'

'No, ma'am, he never said anything about it. So then I asked him to walk into the parlour, and he was prodigious agreeable, and – '

'Whoever he is,' said her mistress, 'he has made a great impression upon you, Nanny – But where did he come from? and what does he want here?'

'Oh! ma'am, I was going to tell you that I fancy his business is with you; for he asked me whether you were at leisure to see anybody, and desired I would give his compliments to you, and say he should be very happy to wait on you. However, I thought he had better not come up into your dressing-room, especially as everything is in such a litter, so I told him if he would be so obliging as to stay in the parlour, I would run upstairs and tell you he was come, and I dared to say that you would wait upon *him*. Lord, ma'am, I'd lay anything that he is come to ask you to dance with him tonight, and has got his chaise ready to take you to Mr Dudley's.'

Kitty could not help laughing at this idea, and only wished it might be true, as it was very likely that she would be too late for any other partner. 'But what, in the name of wonder, can he have to say to me? Perhaps he is come to rob the house – he comes in style at least; and it will be some consolation for our losses to be robbed by a gentleman in a chaise and four. What livery[295] has his servants?'

'Why that is the most wonderful thing about him, ma'am, for he has not a single servant with him, and came with hack horses;[296] but he is as handsome as a prince for all that, and has quite the look of one. Do, dear ma'am, go down, for I am sure you will be delighted with him – '

'Well, I believe I must go; but it is very odd! What can he have to say to me.' Then giving one look at herself in the glass, she walked with great impatience, though trembling all the while from not knowing what to expect, downstairs, and after pausing a moment at the door to gather courage for opening it, she resolutely entered the room.

The stranger, whose appearance did not disgrace the account she had received of it from her maid, rose up on her entrance, and laying aside the newspaper he had been reading, advanced towards her with an air of the most perfect ease and vivacity, and said to her, 'It is certainly a very awkward circumstance to be thus obliged to introduce myself, but I trust that the necessity of the case will plead my excuse, and prevent your being prejudiced by it against me. *Your* name, I need not ask, ma'am. Miss Percival is too well known to me by description to need any information of that.'

Kitty, who had been expecting him to tell his own name, instead of hers, and who from having been little in company, and never before in such a situation, felt herself unable to ask it, though she had been planning her speech all the way downstairs, was so confused and distressed by this unexpected address that she could only return a slight curtsey to it, and accepted the chair he reached[297] her, without knowing what she did.

The gentleman then continued. 'You are, I dare say, surprised to see me returned from France so soon, and nothing indeed but business could have brought me to England; a very melancholy affair has now occasioned it, and I was unwilling to leave it without paying my respects to the family in Devonshire whom I have so long wished to be acquainted with.'

Kitty, who felt much more surprised at his supposing her to be so than at seeing a person in England whose having ever left it was perfectly unknown[298] to her, still continued silent from wonder and perplexity, and her visitor still continued to talk.

'You will suppose, madam, that I was not the *less* desirous of waiting on you, from your having Mr and Mrs Stanley with you. I hope they are well? And Mrs Percival, how does *she* do?' Then without waiting for an answer he gaily added, 'But, my dear Miss Percival, you are going out I am sure; and I am detaining you from your appointment. How can I ever expect to be forgiven for such injustice! Yet how can I, so circumstanced, forbear to offend! You seem dressed for a ball? But this is the land of gaiety, I know; I have for many years been desirous of visiting it. You have dances, I suppose, at least every week. But where are the rest of your party gone, and what kind angel in compassion to me has excluded *you* from it?'

'Perhaps, sir,' said Kitty, extremely confused by his manner of speaking to her, and highly displeased with the freedom of his conversation towards one who had never seen him before and did not *now* know his name, 'perhaps, sir, you are acquainted with Mr and Mrs Stanley; and your business may be with *them*?'

'You do me too much honour, ma'am,' replied he laughing, 'in supposing me to be acquainted with Mr and Mrs Stanley; I merely know them by sight; very distant relations; only my father and mother. Nothing more I assure you.'

'Gracious heaven!' said Kitty, 'are *you* Mr Stanley then? I beg a thousand pardons – though really upon recollection I do not know for what – for you never told me your name – '

'I beg your pardon – I made a very fine speech when you entered the room, all about introducing myself; I assure you it was very great for *me*.'

'The speech had certainly great merit,' said Kitty smiling; 'I thought so at the time; but since you never mentioned your name in it, as an *introductory* one, it might have been better.'

There was such an air of good humour and gaiety in Stanley, that Kitty, though perhaps not authorised to address him with so much familiarity on so short an acquaintance, could not forbear indulging the natural unreserve and vivacity of her own disposition in speaking to him as he spoke to her. She was intimately acquainted too with his family, who were her relations, and she chose to consider herself entitled by the connection to forget how little a while they had known each other. 'Mr and Mrs Stanley and your sister are extremely well,' said she, 'and will, I dare say, be very much surprised to see you – But I am sorry to hear that your return to England has been occasioned by an unpleasant circumstance.'

'Oh, don't talk of it,' said he, 'it is a most confounded shocking affair, and makes me miserable to think of it. But where are my father and mother, and your aunt gone? Oh! Do you know that I met the prettiest little waiting-maid in the world, when I came here; she let me into the house; I took her for you at first.'

'You did me a great deal of honour, and give me more credit for good nature than I deserve, for I *never* go to the door[299] when anyone comes.'

'Nay, do not be angry; I mean no offence. But tell me, where are you going to so smart[300] Your carriage is just coming round.'

'I am going to a dance at a neighbour's, where your family and my aunt are already gone.'

'Gone, without you! what's the meaning of *that*? But I suppose you are like myself, rather long in dressing.'

'I must have been so indeed, if that were the case, for they have been gone nearly these two hours. The reason, however, was not what you suppose – I was prevented going by a pain – '

'By a pain!' interrupted Stanley. 'Oh! heavens, that is dreadful indeed! No matter where the pain was. But, my dear Miss Percival, what do you say to my accompanying you? And suppose you were to dance with me too? *I* think it would be very pleasant.'

'I can have no objection to either, I am sure,' said Kitty, laughing to find how near the truth her maid's conjecture had been; 'on the contrary I shall be highly honoured by both, and I can answer for your being extremely welcome to the family who give the ball.'

'Oh! hang them; who cares for that; they cannot turn me out of the house. But I am afraid I shall cut a sad figure among all your Devonshire beaux in this dusty, travelling apparel,[301] and I have not wherewithal to change it. You can procure me some powder, perhaps, and I must get a pair of shoes from one of the men, for I was in such a devil of a hurry to leave Lyons that I had not time to have anything packed up but some linen.'

Kitty very readily undertook to procure for him everything he wanted, and telling the footman to show him into Mr Stanley's dressing-room, gave Nanny orders to send in some powder and pomatum,[302] which orders Nanny chose to execute in person. As Stanley's preparations in dressing were confined to such very trifling articles, Kitty of course expected him in about ten minutes; but she found that it had not been merely a boast of vanity in saying that he was dilatory in that respect, as he kept her waiting for him above half an hour, so that the clock had struck ten before he entered the room, and the rest of the party had gone by eight.

'Well,' said he as he came in, 'have not I been very quick? I never hurried so much in my life before.'

'In that case you certainly have,' replied Kitty, 'for all merit, you know, is comparative.'

'Oh! I knew you would be delighted with me for making so much haste. But come, the carriage is ready; so, do not keep me waiting.' And so saying he took her by the hand, and led her out of the room. 'Why, my dear cousin,' said he when they were seated, 'this will be a most agreeable surprise to everybody to see you enter the room with such a smart young fellow as I am – I hope your aunt won't be alarmed.'

'To tell you the truth,' replied Kitty, 'I think the best way to prevent it will be to send for her, or your mother, before we go into the room,

especially as you are a perfect stranger, and must of course be introduced to Mr and Mrs Dudley – '

'Oh! nonsense,' said he; 'I did not expect *you* to stand upon such
ceremony; our acquaintance with each other renders all such prudery
ridiculous; besides, if we go in together, we shall be the whole talk of
the country – '

'To *me*,' replied Kitty, 'that would certainly be a most powerful
inducement; but I scarcely know whether my aunt would consider it as
such. Women at her time of life have odd ideas of propriety, you know.'

'Which is the very thing that you ought to break them of; and why
should you object to entering a room with me where all our relations
are, when you have done me the honour to admit me without any
chaperone[303] into your carriage? Do not you think your aunt will be as
much offended with you for one as for the other of these mighty crimes.'

'Why really,' said Catharine, 'I do not know but that she may; however, it is no reason that I should offend against decorum a second time,
because I have already done it once.'

'On the contrary, that is the very reason which makes it impossible
for you to prevent it, since you cannot offend for the *first time* again.'

'You are very ridiculous,' said she laughing, 'but I am afraid your
arguments divert me too much to convince me.'

'At least they will convince you that I am very agreeable, which, after
all, is the happiest conviction for me, and as to the affair of propriety we
will let that rest till we arrive at our journey's end. This is a monthly
ball,[304] I suppose. Nothing but dancing here.'

'I thought I had told you that it was given by a Mr Dudley – '

'Oh! aye, so you did; but why should not Mr Dudley give one every
month? By the by, who is that man? Everybody gives balls now I think;
I believe I must give one myself soon. Well, but how do you like my
father and mother? And poor little Camilla, too, has not she plagued
you to death with the Halifaxes?'

Here the carriage fortunately stopped at Mr Dudley's, and Stanley
was too much engaged in handing her out of it to wait for an answer, or
to remember that what he had said required one. They entered the
small vestibule, which Mr Dudley had raised to the dignity of a hall,[305]
and Kitty immediately desired the footman who was leading the way
upstairs to inform either Mrs Percival or Mrs Stanley of her arrival, and
beg them to come to her; but Stanley, unused to any contradiction and
impatient to be among them, would neither allow her to wait, or listen
to what she said, and forcibly seizing her arm within his, overpowered
her voice with the rapidity of his own, and Kitty, half angry and half

laughing, was obliged to go with him upstairs, and could even with difficulty prevail on him to relinquish her hand before they entered the room.

Mrs Percival was at that very moment engaged in conversation with a lady at the upper end of the room, to whom she had been giving a long account of her niece's unlucky disappointment, and the dreadful pain that she had with so much fortitude endured the whole day. 'I left her, however,' said she, 'thank heaven! a little better, and I hope she has been able to amuse herself with a book, poor thing! for she must otherwise be very dull. She is probably in bed by this time, which while she is so poorly is the best place for her, you know, ma'am.'

The lady was going to give her assent to this opinion, when the noise of voices on the stairs, and the footman's opening the door as if for the entrance of company, attracted the attention of everybody in the room; and as it was in one of those intervals between the dances when everyone seemed glad to sit down, Mrs Percival had a most unfortunate opportunity of seeing her niece, whom she had supposed in bed or amusing herself as the height of gaiety with a book, enter the room most elegantly dressed, with a smile on her countenance, and a glow of mingled cheerfulness and confusion on her cheeks, attended by a young man uncommonly handsome, and who, without any of her confusion, appeared to have all her vivacity. Mrs Percival colouring with anger and astonishment, rose from her seat, and Kitty walked eagerly towards her, impatient to account for what she saw appeared wonderful to everybody but extremely offensive to *her*, while Camilla, on seeing her brother, ran instantly towards him, and very soon explained who he was by her words and her actions.

Mr Stanley, who so fondly doted on his son that the pleasure of seeing him again after an absence of three months prevented his feeling for the time any anger against him for returning to England without his knowledge, received him with equal surprise and delight; and soon comprehending the cause of his journey, forbore any further conversation with him, as he was eager to see his mother, and it was necessary that he should be introduced to Mr Dudley's family. This introduction to anyone but Stanley would have been highly unpleasant, for they considered their dignity injured by his coming uninvited to their house and received him with more than their usual haughtiness: but Stanley, who with a vivacity of temper seldom subdued and a contempt of censure not to be overcome, possessed an opinion of his own consequence and a perseverance in his own schemes which were not to be damped by the conduct of others, appeared not to perceive it.

The civilities therefore which they coldly offered, he received with a gaiety and ease peculiar to himself, and then attended by his father and sister walked into another room where his mother was playing at cards, to experience another meeting, and undergo a repetition of pleasure, surprise and explanations.

While these were passing, Camilla, eager to communicate all she felt to someone who would attend to her, returned to Catharine, and seating herself by her, immediately began – 'Well, did you ever know anything so delightful as this? But it always is so; I never go to a ball in my life but what something or other happens unexpectedly that is quite charming!'

'A ball,' replied Kitty, 'seems to be a most eventful thing to you – '

'Oh! Lord, it is indeed. But only think of my brother's returning so suddenly – and how shocking a thing it is that has brought him over! I never heard anything so dreadful!'

'What is it pray that has occasioned his leaving France? I am sorry to find that it is a melancholy event.'

'Oh! it is beyond anything you can conceive! His favourite hunter,[306] who was turned out in the park on his going abroad, somehow or other fell ill – No, I believe it was an accident, but however it was something or other, or else it was something else, and so they sent an express[307] immediately to Lyons where my brother was, for they knew that he valued this mare more than anything else in the world besides; and so my brother set off directly for England, and without packing up another coat! I am quite angry with him about it; it was so shocking, you know, to come away without a change of clothes – '

'Why indeed,' said Kitty, 'it seems to have been a very shocking affair from beginning to end.'

'Oh! it is beyond anything you can conceive! I would rather have had *anything* happen than that he should have lost that mare.'

'Except his coming away without another coat.'

'Oh! yes, that has vexed me more than you can imagine. Well, and so Edward got to Brampton[308] just as the poor thing was dead; but as he could not bear to remain there *then*, he came off directly to Chetwynde on purpose to see us. I hope he may not go abroad again.'

'Do you think he will not?'

'Oh! dear, to be sure he must, but I wish he may not with all my heart. You cannot think how fond I am of him! By the by, are not you in love with him yourself?'

'To be sure I am,' replied Kitty laughing, 'I am in love with every handsome man I see.'

'That is just like me – *I* am always in love with every handsome man in the world.'

'There you outdo me,' replied Catharine, 'for I am only in love with those I *do* see.'

Mrs Percival, who was sitting on the other side of her, and who began now to distinguish the words *love* and *handsome man*, turned hastily towards them, and said, 'What are you talking of Catharine?'

To which Catharine immediately answered with the simple artifice of a child, 'Nothing, ma'am.'

She had already received a very severe lecture from her aunt on the imprudence of her behaviour during the whole evening; she blamed her for coming to the ball, for coming in the same carriage with Edward Stanley, and still more for entering the room with him. For the last-mentioned offence Catharine knew not what apology to give, and though she longed in answer to the second to say that she had not thought it would be civil to make Mr Stanley *walk*, she dared not so to trifle with her aunt, who would have been but the more offended by it. The first accusation, however, she considered as very unreasonable, as she thought herself perfectly justified in coming.

This conversation continued till Edward Stanley, entering the room, came instantly towards her, and telling her that everyone waited for *her* to begin the next dance, led her to the top of the room[309] – for Kitty, impatient to escape from so unpleasant a companion, without the least hesitation or one civil scruple at being so distinguished, immediately gave him her hand, and joyfully left her seat.

This conduct, however, was highly resented by several young ladies present, among them Miss Stanley, whose regard for her brother, though *excessive*, and whose affection for Kitty, though *prodigious*, were not proof against such an injury to her importance and her peace. Edward had, however, only consulted his own inclinations in desiring Miss Percival to begin the dance, nor had he any reason to know that it was either wished or expected by anyone else in the party. As an heiress, she was certainly of consequence, but her birth gave her no other claim to it, for her father had been a merchant. It was this very circumstance which rendered this unfortunate affair so offensive to Camilla, for though she would sometimes boast, in the pride of her heart and her eagerness to be admired, that she did not know who her grandfather had been, and was as ignorant of everything relative to genealogy as to astronomy (and she might have added, geography), yet she was really proud of her family and connections, and easily offended if they were treated with neglect.

'I should not have minded it,' said she to her mother, if she had been *anybody* else's daughter; but to see her pretend to be above *me*, when her father was only a tradesman, is too bad! It is such an affront to our whole family! I declare I think papa ought to interfere in it, but he never cares about anything but politics. If I were Mr Pitt or the Lord Chancellor,[310] he would take care I should not be insulted, but he never thinks about *me*. And it is so provoking that *Edward* should let her stand there. I wish with all my heart that he had never come to England! I hope she may fall down and break her neck, or sprain her ankle.'

Mrs Stanley perfectly agreed with her daughter concerning the affair, and, though with less violence, expressed almost equal resentment at the indignity. Kitty in the meantime remained insensible of having given anyone offence, and therefore was unable either to offer an apology or make a reparation; her whole attention was occupied by the happiness she enjoyed in dancing with the most elegant young man in the room, and everyone else was equally unregarded. The evening indeed, to *her*, passed off delightfully; he was her partner during the greatest part of it, and the united attractions that he possessed of person, address and vivacity had easily gained that preference from Kitty which they seldom failed of obtaining from everyone. She was too happy to care either for her aunt's ill humour, which she could not help remarking, or for the alteration in Camilla's behaviour, which forced itself at last on her observation. Her spirits were elevated above the influence of displeasure in anyone, and she was equally indifferent as to the cause of Camilla's or the continuance of her aunt's.

Though Mr Stanley could never be really offended by any imprudence or folly in his son that had given him the pleasure of seeing him, he was yet perfectly convinced that Edward ought not to remain in England, and was resolved to hasten his leaving it as soon as possible; but when he talked to Edward about it, he found him much less disposed towards returning to France than to accompanying them in their projected tour, which he assured his father would be infinitely more pleasant to him; and that as to the affair of travelling, he considered it of no importance and capable of being pursued at any little odd time, when he had nothing better to do. He advanced these objections in a manner which plainly showed that he had scarcely a doubt of their being complied with, and appeared to consider his father's arguments in opposition to them as merely given with a view to keeping up his authority, and as being such as he should find little difficulty in combating. He concluded at last by saying, as the chaise in which they returned together from Mr Dudley's reached Mrs Percival's, 'Well, sir, we will settle this point some other time, and fortunately it is of so little consequence that an immediate discussion of it is unnecessary.' He then got out of the chaise and entered the house without waiting for his father's reply.

It was not till their return that Kitty could account for that coldness in Camilla's behaviour to her, which had been so pointed as to render it impossible to be entirely unnoticed. When, however, they were seated in the coach with the two other ladies, Miss Stanley's indignation was no longer to be suppressed from breaking out into words, and found the following vent: 'Well, I must say *this*, that I never was at a stupider[311] ball in my life! But it always is so; I am always disappointed in them for some reason or other. I wish there were no such things.'

'I am sorry, Miss Stanley,' said Mrs Percival, drawing herself up, 'that you have not been amused; everything was meant for the best, I am sure, and it is a poor encouragement for your mama to take you to another if you are so hard to be satisfied.'

'I do not know what you mean, ma'am, about mama's *taking* me to another. You know I am come out.'[312]

'Oh! dear Mrs Percival,' said Mrs Stanley, 'you must not believe everything that my lively Camilla says, for her spirits are prodigiously high sometimes, and she frequently speaks without thinking. I am sure it is impossible for *anyone* to have been at a more elegant or agreeable dance, and so she wishes to express herself, I am certain.'

'To be sure I do,' said Camilla very sulkily, 'only I must say that it is not very pleasant to have anybody behave so rude to me as to be quite shocking! I am sure I am not at all offended, and should not care if all the world were to stand above me, but still it is extremely abominable, and what I cannot put up with. It is not that I mind it in the least, for I had just as soon stand at the bottom as at the top all night long if it were not so very disagreeable. But to have a person come in the middle of the evening and take everybody's place is what I am not used to, and though I do not care a pin about it myself, I assure you I shall not easily forgive or forget it.'

This speech, which perfectly explained the whole affair to Kitty, was shortly followed on her side by a very submissive apology, for she had too much good sense to be proud of her family, and too much good nature to live at variance with anyone. The excuses she made were delivered with so much real concern for the offence, and such unaffected sweetness, that it was almost impossible for Camilla to retain that anger which had occasioned them; she felt indeed most highly gratified to find that no insult had been intended and that Catharine was very far from forgetting the difference in their birth for which she could *now* only pity her, and her good humour being restored with the same ease in which it had been affected, she spoke with the highest delight of the evening, and declared that she had never before been at so pleasant a ball. The same endeavours that had procured the forgiveness of Miss Stanley ensured to her the cordiality of her mother, and nothing was wanting but Mrs Percival's good humour to render the happiness of the others complete; but she, offended with Camilla for her affected superiority, still more so with her brother for coming to Chetwynde, and dissatisfied with the whole evening, continued silent and gloomy and was a restraint on the vivacity of her companions. She eagerly seized the very first opportunity which the next morning offered to her of speaking to Mr Stanley on the subject of his son's return, and after having expressed her opinion of its being a very silly affair that he came at all, concluded with desiring him to inform Mr Edward Stanley that it was a rule with her never to admit a young man into her house as a visitor for any length of time.

'I do not speak, sir,' she continued, 'out of any disrespect to you, but I could not answer it to myself to allow of his stay; there is no knowing what might be the consequence of it if he were to continue here, for girls nowadays will always give a handsome young man the preference before any other, though for why, I never could discover, for what after all is youth and beauty? It is but a poor substitute for real worth and merit; believe me, cousin, that, whatever people may say to the contrary, there is certainly nothing like virtue for making us what we ought to be, and as to a young man's being young and handsome and having an agreeable person, it is nothing at all to the purpose, for he had much better be respectable. I always *did* think so, and I always *shall*, and therefore you will oblige me very much by desiring your son to leave Chetwynde, or I cannot be answerable for what may happen between him and my niece. You will be surprised to hear *me* say it,' she continued, lowering her voice, 'but truth will out, and I must own that Kitty is one of the most impudent³¹³ girls that ever existed. I assure you, sir, that I have seen her sit and laugh and whisper with a young man whom she has not seen above half a dozen times. Her behaviour indeed is scandalous, and therefore I beg you will send your son away immediately, or everything will be at sixes and sevens.'

Mr Stanley, who from one part of her speech had scarcely known to what length her insinuations of Kitty's impudence were meant to extend, now endeavoured to quiet her fears on the occasion by assuring her that on every account he meant to allow only of his son's continuing that day with them, and that she might depend on his being more earnest in the affair from a wish of obliging her. He added also that he knew Edward to be very desirous himself of returning to France, as he wisely considered all time lost that did not forward the plans in which he was at present engaged, though he was but too well convinced of the contrary himself. His assurance in some degree quieted Mrs Percival, and left her tolerably relieved of her cares and alarms, and better disposed to behave with civility towards his son during the short remainder of his stay at Chetwynde.

Mr Stanley went immediately to Edward, to whom he repeated the conversation that had passed between Mrs Percival and himself, and strongly pointed out the necessity of his leaving Chetwynde the next day, since his word was already engaged for it. His son, however, appeared struck only by the ridiculous apprehensions of Mrs Percival; and highly delighted at having occasioned them himself, seemed engrossed alone in thinking how he might increase them, without attending to any other part of his father's conversation. Mr Stanley could get no determinate answer from him, and though he still hoped for the best, they parted almost in anger on his side.

His son, though by no means disposed to marry, or in any otherwise attached to Miss Percival than as a good-natured lively girl who seemed pleased with him, took infinite pleasure in alarming the jealous fears of her aunt by his attentions to her, without considering what effect they might have on the lady herself. He would always sit by her when she was in the room, appear dissatisfied if she left it, and was the first to enquire whether she meant soon to return. He was delighted with her drawings, and enchanted with her performance on the harpsichord; everything that she said appeared to interest him; his conversation was addressed to her alone, and she seemed to be the sole object of his attention. That such efforts should succeed with one so tremblingly alive to every alarm of the kind as Mrs Percival was by no means un-natural, and that they should have equal influence with her niece, whose imagination was lively and whose disposition romantic, who was already extremely pleased with him, and of course desirous that he might be so with her, was as little to be wondered at. Every moment as it added to the conviction of his liking her made him still more pleasing and strengthened in her mind a wish of knowing him better. As for Mrs Percival, she was in tortures the whole day; nothing that she had ever felt before on a similar occasion was to be compared to the sensations which now distracted her; her fears had never been so strongly, or indeed so reasonably, excited. Her dislike of Stanley, her anger at her niece, her impatience to have them separated conquered every idea of propriety and good-breeding, and though he had never mentioned any intention of leaving them the next day, she could not help asking him after dinner, in her eagerness to have him gone, at what time he meant to set out.

'Oh! ma'am,' replied he, 'if I am off by twelve at night, you may think yourself lucky; and if I am not, you can only blame yourself for having left so much as the hour of my departure to my own disposal.' Mrs Percival coloured very highly at this speech, and without addressing herself to anyone in particular, immediately began a long harangue on the shocking behaviour of modern young men, and the wonderful alteration that had taken place in them since her time, which she illustrated with many instructive anecdotes of the decorum and modesty which had marked the characters of those whom she had known when she had been young. This, however, did not prevent his walking in the garden with her niece, without any other companion, for nearly an hour in the course of the evening. They had left the room for that purpose with Camilla at a time when Mrs Percival had been out of it, nor was it for some time after her return to it that she could discover where they were. Camilla had taken two or three turns with them in the walk which led to the arbour, but soon growing tired of listening to a conversation in which she was seldom invited to join, and, from its turning occasionally on books, very little able to do it, she left them together in the arbour, to wander alone to some other part of the garden, to eat the fruit and examine Mrs Percival's greenhouse. Her absence was so far from being regretted that it was scarcely noticed by them, and they continued conversing together on almost every subject, for Stanley seldom dwelt long on any, and had something to say on all, till they were interrupted by her aunt.

Kitty was by this time perfectly convinced that both in natural abilities and acquired information Edward Stanley was infinitely superior to his sister. Her desire of knowing that he was so had induced her to take every opportunity of turning the conversation on history, and they were very soon engaged in an historical dispute, for which no one was more calculated[314] than Stanley, who was so far from being really of any party that he had scarcely a fixed opinion on the subject. He could therefore always take either side, and always argue with temper.[315] In his indifference on all such topics, he was very unlike his companion, whose judgement, being guided by her feelings which were eager and warm, was easily decided, and though it was not always infallible, she defended it with a spirit and enthusiasm which marked her own reliance on it. They had continued, therefore, for some time conversing in this manner on the character of Richard the Third,[316] which he was warmly defending, when he suddenly seized hold of her hand, and, exclaiming with great emotion, 'Upon my honour, you are entirely mistaken,' pressed it passionately to his lips, and ran out of the arbour.

Astonished at this behaviour, for which she was wholly unable to account, she continued for a few moments motionless on the seat where he had left her, and was then on the point of following him up the narrow walk through which he had passed, when on looking up the one that lay immediately before the arbour, she saw her aunt walking towards her with more than her usual quickness. This explained at once the reason of his leaving her, but his leaving her in such manner was rendered still more inexplicable by it. She felt a considerable degree of confusion at having been seen by her in such a place with Edward, and at having that part of his conduct, for which she could not herself account, witnessed by one to whom all gallantry was odious. She remained therefore confused and distressed and irresolute, and suffered her aunt to approach her without leaving the arbour. Mrs Percival's looks were by no means calculated to animate the spirits of her niece, who in silence waited her accusation, and in silence meditated her defence. After a few moments' suspense, for Mrs Percival was too much fatigued to speak immediately, she began, with great anger and asperity, the following harangue.

'Well; *this* is beyond anything I could have supposed. *Profligate*[317] as I *knew* you to be, I was not prepared for such a sight. This is beyond anything you ever did *before*; beyond anything I ever heard of in my life! Such impudence I never witnessed before in such a girl! And this is the reward for all the cares I have taken in your education; for all my troubles and anxieties; and heaven knows how many they have been! All I wished for was to breed you up virtuously; I never wanted you to play upon the harpsichord, or draw better than anyone else; but I had hoped to see you respectable, and good; to see you able and willing to give an example of modesty and virtue to the young people hereabouts. I bought you Blair's *Sermons*,[318] and *Coelebs in Search of a Wife*,[319] I gave you the key to my own library,[320] and borrowed a great many good books of my neighbours for you, all to this purpose. But I might have spared myself the trouble – Oh! Catharine, you are an abandoned creature, and I do not know what will become of you. I am glad, however,' she continued, softening into some degree of mildness, 'to see that you have some shame for what you have done, and if you are really sorry for it, and your future life is a life of penitence and reformation, perhaps you may be forgiven. But I plainly see that everything is going to sixes and sevens, and all order will soon be at an end throughout the kingdom.'

'Not, however, ma'am, the sooner, I hope, from any conduct of mine,' said Catharine in a tone of great humility, 'for upon my honour I have done nothing this evening that can contribute to overthrow the establishment of the kingdom.'

'You are mistaken, child,' replied she; 'the welfare of every nation depends upon the virtue of its individuals, and anyone who offends in so gross a manner against decorum and propriety is certainly hastening its ruin. You have been giving a bad example to the world, and the world is but too well disposed to receive such.'

'Pardon me, madam,' said her niece; 'but I *can* have given an example only to *you*, for you alone have seen the offence. Upon my word, however, there is no danger to fear from what I have done; Mr Stanley's behaviour has given me as much surprise as it has done to you, and I can only suppose that it was the effect of his high spirits, authorised in his opinion by our relationship. But do you consider, madam, that it is growing very late? Indeed you had better return to the house.'

This speech, as she well knew, would be unanswerable with her aunt, who instantly rose, and hurried away under so many apprehensions for her own health as banished for the time all anxiety about her niece, who walked quietly by her side, revolving within her own mind the occurrence that had given her aunt so much alarm.

'I am astonished at my own imprudence,' said Mrs Percival; 'how could I be so forgetful as to sit down out of doors at such a time of night. I shall certainly have a return of my rheumatism after it – I begin to feel very chill already. I must have caught a dreadful cold by this time; I am sure of being lain-up all the winter after it – ' Then, reckoning with her fingers, 'Let me see; this is July; the cold weather will soon be coming in – August – September – October – November – December – January – February – March – April – very likely I may not be tolerable again before May. I must and will have that arbour pulled down – it will be the death of me; who knows *now* but what I may never recover. Such things *have* happened. My particular friend Miss Sarah Hutchinson's death was occasioned by nothing more. She stayed out late one evening in April and got wet through, for it rained very hard, and never changed her clothes when she came home. It is unknown how many people have died in consequence of catching cold! I do not believe there is a disorder in the world, except the smallpox, which does not spring from it.'

It was in vain that Kitty endeavoured to convince her that her fears on the occasion were groundless; that it was not yet late enough to catch cold, and that even if it were, she might hope to escape any other complaint, and to recover in less than ten months. Mrs Percival only replied that she hoped she knew more of ill health than to be convinced in such a point by a girl who had always been perfectly well, and hurried upstairs, leaving Kitty to make her apologies to Mr and Mrs Stanley for going to bed. Though Mrs Percival seemed perfectly satisfied with the goodness of the apology herself, yet Kitty felt somewhat embarrassed to find that the only one she could offer to their visitors was that her aunt had *perhaps* caught cold, for Mrs Percival charged her to make light of it, for fear of alarming them. Mr and Mrs Stanley, however, who well knew that their cousin was easily terrified on that score, received the account of it with very little surprise, and all proper concern.

Edward and his sister soon came in, and Kitty had no difficulty in gaining an explanation of his conduct from him, for he was too warm on the subject himself, and too eager to learn its success, to refrain from making immediate enquiries about it; and she could not help feeling both surprised and offended at the ease and indifference with which he owned that all his intentions had been to frighten her aunt by pretending an affection for her, a design so very incompatible with that partiality which she had at one time been almost convinced of his feeling for her. It is true that she had not yet seen enough of him to be actually in love with him, yet she felt greatly disappointed that so handsome, so elegant, so lively a young man should be so perfectly free from any such sentiment as to make it his principal sport. There was a novelty in his character which to her was extremely pleasing; his person was uncommonly fine, his spirits and vivacity suited to her own, and his manners at once so animated and insinuating that she thought it must be impossible for him to be otherwise than amiable, and was ready to give him credit for being perfectly so. He knew the powers of them himself; to them he had often been indebted for his father's forgiveness of faults which had he been awkward and inelegant would have appeared very serious; to them, even more than to his person or his fortune, he owed the regard which almost everyone was disposed to feel for him, and which young women in particular were inclined to entertain.

Their influence was acknowledged on the present occasion by Kitty, whose anger they entirely dispelled, and whose cheerfulness they had power not only to restore, but to raise. The evening passed off as agreeably as the one that had preceded it; they continued talking to each other during the chief part of it, and such was the power of his address, and the brilliancy of his eyes, that when they parted for the night, though Catharine had but a few hours before totally given up the idea, yet she felt almost convinced again that he was really in love with her. She reflected on their past conversation, and though it had been on various and indifferent subjects, and she could not exactly recollect any speech on his side expressive of such a partiality, she was still however nearly certain of its being so; but fearful of being vain enough to suppose such a thing without sufficient reason, she resolved to suspend her final determination on it till the next day, and more especially till their parting, which she thought would infallibly explain his regard if any he had. The more she had seen of him, the more inclined was she to like him, and the more desirous that he should like *her*. She was convinced of his being naturally very clever and very well disposed, and that his thoughtlessness and negligence, which, though they appeared to *her* as very becoming in *him*, she was aware would by many people be considered as defects in his character, merely proceeded from a vivacity always pleasing in young men, and were far from testifying to a weak or vacant understanding.

Having settled this point within herself, and being perfectly convinced by her own arguments of its truth, she went to bed in high spirits, determined to study his character and watch his behaviour still more the next day. She got up with the same good resolutions and would probably have put them in execution had not Anne informed her as soon as she entered the room that Mr Edward Stanley was already gone. At first she refused to credit the information, but when her maid assured her that he had ordered a carriage the evening before to be there at seven o'clock in the morning and that she herself had actually seen him depart in it a little after eight, she could no longer deny her belief to it. 'And this,' thought she to herself, blushing with anger at her own folly, 'this is the affection for me of which I was so certain. Oh! what a silly thing is woman! How vain, how unreasonable! To suppose that a young man would be seriously attached, in the course of four-and-twenty hours, to a girl who has nothing to recommend her but a good pair of eyes! And he is really gone! Gone perhaps without bestowing a thought on me! Oh! why was not I up by eight o'clock? But it is a proper punishment for my laziness and folly, and I am heartily glad of it. I deserve it all, and ten times more for such insufferable vanity. It will at least be of service to me in that respect; it will teach me in future *not* to think everybody is in love with me. Yet I *should* like to have seen him before he went, for perhaps it may be many years before we meet again. By his manner of leaving us, however, he seems to have been perfectly indifferent about it. How very odd that he should go without giving us notice of it, or taking leave of anyone! But it is just like a young man, governed by the whim of the moment, or actuated merely by the love of doing anything oddly! Unaccountable beings indeed! And young women are equally ridiculous! I shall soon begin to think like my aunt that everything is going to sixes and sevens, and that the whole race of mankind is degenerating.'

She was just dressed, and on the point of leaving her room to make her personal enquiries after Mrs Percival, when Miss Stanley knocked at her door, and on her being admitted began in her usual strain a long harangue upon her father's being so shocking as to make Edward go at all, and upon Edward's being so horrid as to leave them at such an hour in the morning. 'You have no idea,' said she, 'how surprised I was, when he came into my room to bid me goodbye – '

'Have you seen him then, this morning?' said Kitty.

'Oh, yes! And I was so sleepy that I could not open my eyes. And so he said, "Camilla, goodbye to you, for I am going away. I have not time to take leave of anybody else, and I dare not trust myself to see Kitty, for then you know I should never get away" – '

'Nonsense,' said Kitty; 'he did not say that, or he was in joke if he did.'

'Oh! no, I assure you he was as much in earnest as he ever was in his life; he was too much out of spirits to joke *then*. And he desired me when we all met at breakfast to give his compliments to your aunt, and his love to you, for you were a nice girl, he said, and he only wished it were in his power to be more with you. You were just the girl to suit him, because you were so lively and good-natured, and he wished with all his heart that you might not be married before he came back, for there was nothing he liked better than being here. Oh! you have no idea what fine things he said about you, till at last I fell asleep and he went away. But he certainly is in love with you – I am sure he is – I have thought so a great while, I assure you.'

'How can you be so ridiculous?' said Kitty, smiling with pleasure; 'I do not believe him to be so easily affected. But he *did* desire his love to me[321] then? And wished I might not be married before his return? And said I was a nice girl, did he?'

'Oh! dear, yes, and I assure you it is the greatest praise, in his opinion, that he can bestow on anybody; I can hardly ever persuade him to call *me* one, though I beg him sometimes for an hour together.'

'And do you really think that he was sorry to go?'

'Oh! you can have no idea how wretched it made him. He would not have gone this month, if my father had not insisted on it; Edward told me so himself yesterday. He said that he wished with all his heart he had never promised to go abroad, for that he repented it more and more every day; that it interfered with all his other schemes, and that since papa had spoken to him about it, he was more unwilling to leave Chetwynde than ever.'

'Did he really say all this? And why would your father insist upon his going? "His leaving England interfered with all his other plans, and his conversation with Mr Stanley had made him still more averse to it." What can this mean?'

'Why, that he is excessively in love with you, to be sure; what other plans can he have? And I suppose my father said that if he had not been going abroad, he should have wished him to marry you immediately. But I must go and see your aunt's plants – there is one of them that I quite dote on – and two or three more besides – '

'Can Camilla's explanation be true?' said Catharine to herself, when her friend had left the room. 'And after all my doubts and uncertainties, can Stanley really be averse to leaving England for *my sake* only? "His plans interrupted." And what indeed can his plans be, but towards marriage? Yet *so soon* to be in love with me! – But it is the effect perhaps only of a warmth of heart, which to *me* is the highest recommendation in anyone. A heart disposed to love – and such under the appearance of so much gaiety and inattention – is Stanley's! Oh! how much does it endear him to me! But he is gone – gone perhaps for years. Obliged to tear himself from what he most loves, his happiness is sacrificed to the vanity of his father! In what anguish he must have left the house! Unable to see me, or to bid me adieu, while I, senseless wretch, was daring to sleep. This, then, explained his leaving us at such a time of day. He could not trust himself to see me. Charming young man! How much must you have suffered! I *knew* that it was impossible for one so elegant, and so well bred, to leave any family in such a manner but for a motive like this – unanswerable.' Satisfied, beyond the power of change, of this, she went in high spirits to her aunt's apartment, without giving a moment's recollection on the vanity of young women or the unaccountable conduct of young men.

Kitty continued in this state of satisfaction during the remainder of the Stanleys' visit – who took their leave with many pressing invitations to visit them in London, when, as Camilla said, she might have an opportunity of becoming acquainted with that sweet girl Augusta Halifax – 'or rather,' thought Kitty, 'of seeing my dear Mary Wynn again'. Mrs Percival, in answer to Mrs Stanley's invitation, replied that she looked upon London as the hothouse of vice, where virtue had long been banished from society and wickedness of every description was daily gaining ground; that Kitty was of herself sufficiently inclined to give way to, and indulge in, vicious inclinations, and therefore was the last girl in the world to be trusted in London, as she would be totally unable to withstand temptation –

After the departure of the Stanleys, Kitty returned to her usual occupations, but alas! they had lost their power of pleasing. Her bower alone retained its interest in her feelings, and perhaps that was owing to the particular remembrance it brought to her mind of Edward Stanley.

The summer passed away unmarked by any incident worth narrating, or any pleasure to Catharine save one which arose from the receipt of a letter from her friend Cecilia, now Mrs Lascelles, announcing the speedy return of herself and husband to England.

A correspondence, productive indeed of little pleasure to either party, had been established between Camilla and Catharine. The latter had now lost the only satisfaction she had ever received from the letters of Miss Stanley, as that young lady, having informed her friend of the departure of her brother to Lyons, now never mentioned his name. Her letters seldom contained any intelligence except a description of some new article of dress, an enumeration of various engagements, a panegyric on Augusta Halifax and perhaps a little abuse of the unfortunate Sir Peter –

The Grove, for so was the mansion of Mrs Percival at Chetwynde denominated, was situated within five miles from Exeter, but though that lady possessed a carriage and horses of her own, it was seldom that Catharine could prevail on her to visit that town for the purpose of shopping, on account of the many officers perpetually quartered[322] there and infesting the principal streets. A company of strolling players[323] in their way from some neighbouring races having opened a temporary theatre there, Mrs Percival was prevailed on by her niece to indulge her by attending the performance once during their stay. Mrs Percival insisted on paying Miss Dudley the compliment of inviting her to join the party, when a new difficulty arose, from the necessity of having some gentleman to attend them –

Lady Susan

Letter 1

Langford, December

MY DEAR BROTHER – I can no longer refuse myself the pleasure of profiting by your kind invitation when we last parted of spending some weeks with you at Churchhill, and, therefore, if quite convenient to you and Mrs Vernon to receive me at present, I shall hope within a few days to be introduced to a sister[324] whom I have so long desired to be acquainted with. My kind friends here are most affectionately urgent with me to prolong my stay, but their hospitable and cheerful dispositions lead them too much into society for my present situation and state of mind; and I impatiently look forward to the hour when I shall be admitted into your delightful retirement. I long to be made known to your dear little children, in whose hearts I shall be very eager to secure an interest. I shall soon have need for all my fortitude, as I am on the point of separation from my own daughter. The long illness of her dear father prevented my paying her that attention which duty and affection equally dictated, and I have too much reason to fear that the governess to whose care I consigned her was unequal to the charge. I have therefore resolved on placing her at one of the best private schools in town, where I shall have an opportunity of leaving her myself in my way to you. I am determined, you see, not to be denied admittance at Churchhill. It would indeed give me most painful sensations to know that it were not in your power to receive me.

Your most obliged and affectionate sister,

S. VERNON

Letter 2

Langford

You were mistaken, my dear Alicia, in supposing me fixed at this place for the rest of the winter: it grieves me to say how greatly you were mistaken, for I have seldom spent three months more agreeably than those which have just flown away. At present, nothing goes smoothly;

the females of the family are united against me. You foretold how it would be when I first came to Langford, and Mainwaring is so uncommonly pleasing that I was not without apprehensions for myself. I remember saying to myself, as I drove to the house, 'I like this man, pray heaven no harm come of it!' But I was determined to be discreet, to bear in mind my being only four months a widow, and to be as quiet as possible: and I have been so, my dear creature; I have admitted no one's attentions but Mainwaring's. I have avoided all general flirtation whatever; I have distinguished no creature besides, of all the numbers resorting hither, except Sir James Martin, on whom I bestowed a little notice, in order to detach him from Miss Mainwaring; but if the world could know my motive *there* they would honour me. I have been called an unkind mother, but it was the sacred impulse of maternal affection, it was the advantage of my daughter that led me on; and if that daughter were not the greatest simpleton on earth, I might have been rewarded for my exertions as I ought. Sir James did make proposals to me for Frederica; but Frederica, who was born to be the torment of my life, chose to set herself so violently against the match that I thought it better to lay aside the scheme for the present. I have more than once repented that I did not marry him myself; and were he but one degree less contemptibly weak I certainly should: but I must own myself rather romantic in that respect, and that riches only will not satisfy me. The event of all this is very provoking: Sir James is gone, Maria highly incensed, and Mrs Mainwaring insupportably jealous; so jealous, in short, and so enraged against me, that, in the fury of her temper, I should not be surprised at her appealing to her guardian, if she had the liberty of addressing him: but there your husband stands my friend; and the kindest, most amiable action of his life was his throwing her off for ever on her marriage. Keep up his resentment, therefore, I charge you. We are now in a sad state; no house was ever more altered; the whole party are at war, and Mainwaring scarcely dares speak to me. It is time for me to be gone; I have therefore determined on leaving them, and shall spend, I hope, a comfortable day with you in town within this week. If I am as little in favour with Mr Johnson as ever, you must come to me at 10 Wigmore Street;[325] but I hope this may not be the case, for as Mr Johnson, with all his faults, is a man to whom that great word 'respectable' is always given, and I am known to be so intimate with his wife, his slighting me has an awkward look. I take London in on my way to that insupportable spot, a country village; for I am really going to Churchhill. Forgive me, my dear friend, it is my last resource. Were there another place in England open to me I would prefer it. Charles

Vernon is my aversion; and I am afraid of his wife. At Churchhill, however, I must remain till I have something better in view. My young lady accompanies me to town, where I shall deposit her under the care of Miss Summers, in Wigmore Street, till she becomes a little more reasonable. She will make good connections there, as the girls are all of the best families. The price is immense, and much beyond what I can ever attempt to pay. Adieu, I will send you a line as soon as I arrive in town.

Yours ever,

S. Vernon

Letter 3

MRS VERNON TO LADY DE COURCY

Churchhill

My dear mother – I am very sorry to tell you that it will not be in our power to keep our promise of spending our Christmas with you; and we are prevented that happiness by a circumstance which is not likely to make us any amends. Lady Susan, in a letter to her brother-in-law, has declared her intention of visiting us almost immediately; and as such a visit is in all probability merely an affair of convenience, it is impossible to conjecture its length. I was by no means prepared for such an event, nor can I now account for her ladyship's conduct; Langford appeared so exactly the place for her in every respect, as well from the elegant and expensive style of living there as from her particular attachment to Mr Mainwaring, that I was very far from expecting so speedy a distinction, though I always imagined from her increasing friendship for us since her husband's death that we should, at some future period, be obliged to receive her. Mr Vernon, I think, was a great deal too kind to her when he was in Staffordshire; her behaviour to him, independent of her general character, has been so inexcusably artful and ungenerous since our marriage was first in agitation that no one less amiable and mild than himself could have overlooked it all; and though, as his brother's widow, and in narrow circumstances, it was proper to render her pecuniary assistance, I cannot help thinking his pressing invitation to her to visit us at Churchhill perfectly unnecessary. Disposed, however, as he always is to think the best of everyone, her display of grief, and professions of regret, and general resolutions of prudence, were sufficient to soften his heart and make him really confide in her sincerity; but, as for myself, I am still unconvinced, and plausibly as her ladyship has now written, I cannot make up my mind till I better understand her real meaning in coming to us. You may guess, therefore, my dear madam, with what feelings I look forward to her arrival. She will have occasion for all those attractive powers for which she is celebrated to gain any share of my regard; and I shall certainly endeavour to guard myself against their influence, if not accompanied by something more substantial. She expresses a most eager desire of being acquainted with me, and makes very gracious mention of my children but I am not quite weak enough to suppose a woman who has behaved with inattention, if not with unkindness, to her own child, should be attached to any of mine. Miss Vernon is to be placed at a school in London before her mother comes to us which I am glad of, for her sake and my own. It must be to her advantage to be separated from her mother, and a girl of sixteen who has received so wretched an education could not be a very desirable companion here. Reginald has long wished, I know, to see the captivating Lady Susan, and we shall depend on his joining our party soon.

I am glad to hear that my father continues so well; and am, with best love, &c.,

CATHERINE VERNON

Letter 4

MR DE COURCY TO MRS VERNON

Parklands

MY DEAR SISTER – I congratulate you and Mr Vernon on being about to receive into your family the most accomplished coquette in England. As a very distinguished flirt I have always been taught to consider her, but it has lately fallen in my way to hear some particulars of her conduct at Langford which prove that she does not confine herself to that sort of honest flirtation which satisfies most people, but aspires to the more delicious gratification of making a whole family miserable. By her behaviour to Mr Mainwaring she gave jealousy and wretchedness to his wife, and by her attentions to a young man previously attached to Mr Mainwaring's sister deprived an amiable girl of her lover. I learnt all this from Mr Smith, now in this neighbourhood (I have dined with him, at Hurst and Wilford), who is just come from Langford where he was a fortnight with her ladyship, and who is therefore well qualified to make the communication.

What a woman she must be! I long to see her, and shall certainly accept your kind invitation, that I may form some idea of those be-witching powers which can do so much – engaging at the same time, and in the same house, the affections of two men, who were neither of them at liberty to bestow them – and all this without the charm of youth! I am glad to find Miss Vernon does not accompany her mother to Churchhill, as she has not even manners to recommend her; and, according to Mr Smith's account, is equally dull and proud. Where pride and stupidity unite there can be no dissimulation worthy notice, and Miss Vernon shall be consigned to unrelenting contempt; but by all that I can gather, Lady Susan possesses a degree of captivating deceit which it must be pleasing to witness and detect. I shall be with you very soon, and am ever,

Your affectionate brother,

R. DE COURCY

Letter 5

LADY SUSAN VERNON TO MRS JOHNSON

Churchhill

I received your note, my dear Alicia, just before I left town, and rejoice to be assured that Mr Johnson suspected nothing of your engagement the evening before. It is undoubtedly better to deceive him entirely, and since he will be stubborn he must be tricked. I arrived here in safety, and have no reason to complain of my reception from Mr Vernon; but I confess myself not equally satisfied with the behaviour of his lady. She is perfectly well bred, indeed, and has the air of a woman of fashion, but her manners are not such as can persuade me of her being prepossessed in my favour. I wanted her to be delighted at seeing me. I was as amiable as possible on the occasion, but all in vain. She does not like me. To be sure when we consider that I *did* take some pains to prevent my brother-in-law's marrying her, this want of cordiality is not very surprising, and yet it shows an illiberal and vindictive spirit to resent a project which influenced me six years ago, and which never succeeded at last. I am sometimes disposed to repent that I did not let Charles buy Vernon Castle, when we were obliged to sell it; but it was a trying circumstance, especially as the sale took place exactly at the time of his marriage; and everybody ought to respect the delicacy of those feelings which could not endure that my husband's dignity should be lessened by his younger brother's having possession of the family estate.[326] Could matters have been so arranged as to prevent the necessity of our leaving the castle, could we have lived with Charles and kept him single, I should have been very far from persuading my husband to dispose of it elsewhere; but Charles was on the point of marrying Miss De Courcy, and the event has justified me. Here are children in abundance, and what benefit could have accrued to me from his purchasing Vernon? My having prevented it may perhaps have given his wife an unfavourable impression, but where there is a disposition to dislike, a motive will never be wanting; and as to money matters it has not withheld him from being very useful to me. I really have a regard for him, he is so easily imposed upon!

The house is a good one, the furniture fashionable, and everything announces plenty and elegance. Charles is very rich, I am sure; when a man has once got his name in a banking-house[327] he rolls in money; but they do not know what to do with it, keep very little company, and never go to London but on business. We shall be as stupid[328] as possible. I mean to win my sister-in-law's heart through the children; I know all their names already, and am going to attach myself with the greatest sensibility to one in particular, a young Frederic, whom I take on my lap and sigh over for his dear uncle's sake.

Poor Mainwaring! I need not tell you how much I miss him, how perpetually he is in my thoughts. I found a dismal letter from him on my arrival here, full of complaints of his wife and sister, and lamentations on the cruelty of his fate. I passed off the letter as his wife's, to the Vernons, and when I write to him it must be under cover to you.[329]

Ever yours,

S. VERNON

Letter 6

MRS VERNON TO MR DE COURCY

Churchhill

Well, my dear Reginald, I have seen this dangerous creature, and must give you some description of her, though I hope you will soon be able to form your own judgement. She is really excessively pretty; however you may choose to question the allurements of a lady no longer young, I must, for my own part, declare that I have seldom seen so lovely a woman as Lady Susan. She is delicately fair, with fine grey eyes and dark eyelashes; and from her appearance one would not suppose her more than five-and-twenty, though she must in fact be ten years older. I was certainly not disposed to admire her, though always hearing she was beautiful; but I cannot help feeling that she possesses an uncommon union of symmetry, brilliancy and grace. Her address to me was so gentle, frank, and even affectionate, that, if I had not known how much she has always disliked me for marrying Mr Vernon and that we had never met before, I should have imagined her an attached friend. One is apt, I believe, to connect assurance of manner with coquetry, and to expect that an impudent address will naturally attend an impudent mind; at least I was myself prepared for an improper degree of confidence in Lady Susan; but her countenance is absolutely sweet, and her voice and manner winningly mild. I am sorry it is so, for what is this but deceit? Unfortunately, one knows her too well. She is clever and agreeable, has all that knowledge of the world which makes conversation easy, and talks very well, with a happy command of language, which is too often used, I believe, to make black appear white. She has already almost persuaded me of her being warmly attached to her daughter, though I have been so long convinced to the contrary. She speaks of her with so much tenderness and anxiety, lamenting so bitterly the neglect of her education, which she represents however as wholly unavoidable, that I am forced to recollect how many successive springs her ladyship spent in town, while her daughter was left in Staffordshire to the care of servants, or a governess very little better, to prevent my believing what she says.

If her manners have so great an influence on my resentful heart, you may judge how much more strongly they operate on Mr Vernon's generous temper. I wish I could be as well satisfied as he is that it was really her choice to leave Langford for Churchhill; and if she had not stayed there for months before she discovered that her friends' manner of living did not suit her situation or feelings, I might have believed that concern for the loss of such a husband as Mr Vernon, to whom her own behaviour was far from unexceptionable, might for a time make her wish for retirement. But I cannot forget the length of her visit to the Mainwarings, and when I reflect on the different mode of life which she led with them from that to which she must now submit, I can only suppose that the wish of establishing her reputation by following, though late, the path of propriety, occasioned her removal from a family where she must in reality have been particularly happy. Your friend Mr Smith's story, however, cannot be quite correct, as she corresponds regularly with Mrs Mainwaring. At any rate it must be exaggerated. It is scarcely possible that two men should be so grossly deceived by her at once.

Yours, &c.,

S. VERNON

Letter 7

Churchhill

MY DEAR ALICIA – You are very good in taking notice of Frederica, and I am grateful for it as a mark of your friendship; but as I cannot have any doubt of the warmth of your affection, I am far from exacting so heavy a sacrifice. She is a stupid girl, and has nothing to recommend her. I would not, therefore, on my account, have you encumber one moment of your precious time by sending for her to Edward Street,[330] especially as every visit is so much deducted from the grand affair of education, which I really wish to have attended to while she remains at Miss Summers's. I want her to play and sing with some portion of taste and a good deal of assurance, as she has *my* hand and arm and a tolerable voice. *I* was so much indulged in my infant years that I was never obliged to attend to anything, and consequently am without the accomplishments which are now necessary to finish a pretty woman. Not that I am an advocate for the prevailing fashion of acquiring a perfect knowledge of all languages, arts, and sciences. It is throwing time away to be mistress of French, Italian, and German; music, singing, drawing, &c., will gain a woman some applause, but will not add one lover to her list. Grace and manner, after all, are of the greatest importance. I do not mean, therefore, that Frederica's acquirements should be more than superficial,[331] and I flatter myself that she will not remain long enough at school to understand anything thoroughly. I hope to see her the wife of Sir James within a twelvemonth. You know on what I ground my hope, and it is certainly a good foundation, for school must be very humiliating to a girl of Frederica's age.[332] And, by the by, you had better not invite her any more on that account, as I wish her to find her situation as unpleasant as possible. I am sure of Sir James at any time, and could make him renew his application by a line. I shall trouble you meanwhile to prevent his forming any other attachment when he comes to town. Ask him to your house occasionally, and talk to him of Frederica, that he may not forget her.

Upon the whole, I commend my own conduct in this affair extremely, and regard it as a very happy instance of circumspection and tenderness. Some mothers would have insisted on their daughter's accepting so good an offer on the first overture; but I could not reconcile it to myself to force Frederica into a marriage from which her heart revolted, and instead of adopting so harsh a measure merely propose to make it her own choice by rendering her thoroughly uncomfortable till she does accept him – but enough of this tiresome girl.

You may well wonder how I contrive to pass my time here, and for the first week it was insufferably dull. Now, however, we begin to mend; our party is enlarged by Mrs Vernon's brother, a handsome young man, who promises me some amusement. There is something about him which rather interests me, a sort of sauciness and familiarity which I shall teach him to correct. He is lively, and seems clever, and when I have inspired him with greater respect for me than his sister's kind offices have implanted, he may be an agreeable flirt. There is exquisite pleasure in subduing an insolent spirit, in making a person pre-determined to dislike acknowledge one's superiority. I have disconcerted him already by my calm reserve, and it shall be my endeavour to humble the pride of these self-important De Courcys still lower, to convince Mrs Vernon that her sisterly cautions have been bestowed in vain, and to persuade Reginald that she has scandalously belied me. This project will serve at least to amuse me, and prevent my feeling so acutely this dreadful separation from you and all whom I love.

Yours ever,

S. VERNON

Letter 8

MRS VERNON TO LADY DE COURCY

Churchhill

MY DEAR MOTHER – You must not expect Reginald back again for some time. He desires me to tell you that the present open[333] weather induces him to accept Mr Vernon's invitation to prolong his stay in Sussex that they may have some hunting together. He means to send for his horses immediately, and it is impossible to say when you may see him in Kent. I will not disguise my sentiments on this change from you, my dear mother, though I think you had better not communicate them to my father, whose excessive anxiety about Reginald would subject him to an alarm which might seriously affect his health and spirits. Lady Susan has certainly contrived, in the space of a fortnight, to make my brother like her. In short, I am persuaded that his continuing here beyond the time originally fixed for his return is occasioned as much by a degree of fascination towards her as by the wish of hunting with Mr

Vernon, and of course I cannot receive that pleasure from the length of his visit which my brother's company would otherwise give me. I am, indeed, provoked at the artifice of this unprincipled woman; what stronger proof of her dangerous abilities can be given than this perversion of Reginald's judgement, which when he entered the house was so decidedly against her! In his last letter he actually gave me some particulars of her behaviour at Langford, such as he received from a gentleman who knew her perfectly well, which, if true, must raise abhorrence against her, and which Reginald himself was entirely disposed to credit. His opinion of her, I am sure, was as low as of any woman in England; and when he first came it was evident that he considered her as one entitled neither to delicacy nor respect, and that he felt she would be delighted with the attentions of any man inclined to flirt with her.

Her behaviour, I confess, has been calculated to do away with such an idea; I have not detected the smallest impropriety in it – nothing of vanity, of pretension, of levity; and she is altogether so attractive that I should not wonder at his being delighted with her, had he known nothing of her previous to this personal acquaintance; but, against reason, against conviction, to be so well pleased with her as I am sure he is, does really astonish me. His admiration was at first very strong, but no more than was natural, and I did not wonder at his being much struck by the gentleness and delicacy of her manners; but when he has mentioned her of late it has been in terms of more extraordinary praise; and yesterday he actually said that he could not be surprised at any effect produced on the heart of man by such loveliness and such abilities; and when I lamented, in reply, the badness of her disposition, he observed that whatever might have been her errors they were to be imputed to her neglected education and early marriage, and that she was altogether a wonderful woman.

This tendency to excuse her conduct or to forget it, in the warmth of admiration, vexes me; and if I did not know that Reginald is too much at home at Churchhill to need an invitation for lengthening his visit, I should regret Mr Vernon's giving him any.

Lady Susan's intentions are of course those of absolute coquetry, or a desire of universal admiration; I cannot for a moment imagine that she has anything more serious in view; but it mortifies me to see a young man of Reginald's sense duped by her at all.

I am, &c.,

CATHERINE VERNON

Letter 9

Edward Street

MY DEAREST FRIEND – I congratulate you on Mr De Courcy's arrival, and I advise you by all means to marry him; his father's estate is, we know, considerable, and I believe certainly entailed.[334] Sir Reginald is very infirm, and not likely to stand in your way long. I hear the young man well spoken of, and though no one can really deserve you, my dearest Susan, Mr De Courcy may be worth having. Mainwaring will storm of course, but you may easily pacify him; besides, the most scrupulous point of honour could not require you to wait for *his* emancipation. I have seen Sir James; he came to town for a few days last week, and called several times in Edward Street. I talked to him about you and your daughter, and he is so far from having forgotten you, that I am sure he would marry either of you with pleasure. I gave him hopes of Frederica's relenting, and told him a great deal of her improvements. I scolded him for making love to Maria Mainwaring; he protested that he had been only in joke, and we both laughed heartily at her disappointment, and in short were very agreeable. He is as silly as ever.

Yours faithfully,

ALICIA

Letter 10

LADY SUSAN VERNON TO MRS JOHNSON

Churchhill

I am much obliged to you, my dear friend, for your advice respecting Mr De Courcy, which I know was given with the full conviction of its expediency, though I am not quite determined on following it. I cannot easily resolve on anything so serious as marriage; especially as I am not at present in want of money, and might perhaps, till the old gentleman's death, be very little benefited by the match. It is true that I am vain enough to believe it within my reach. I have made him sensible of my power, and can now enjoy the pleasure of triumphing over a mind prepared to dislike me, and prejudiced against all my past actions. His sister, too, is, I hope, convinced how little the ungenerous representations of any one to the disadvantage of another will avail when opposed by the immediate influence of intellect and manner. I see plainly that she is uneasy at my progress in the good opinion of her brother, and conclude that nothing will be wanting on her part to counteract me; but having once made him doubt the justice of her opinion of me, I think I may defy her. It has been delightful to me to watch his advances towards intimacy, especially to observe his altered manner in consequence of my repressing by the cool dignity of my deportment his insolent approach to direct familiarity. My conduct has been equally guarded from the first, and I never behaved less like a coquette in the whole course of my life, though perhaps my desire of dominion was never more decided. I have subdued him entirely by sentiment and serious conversation, and made him, I may venture to say, at least *half* in love with me, without the semblance of the most commonplace flirtation. Mrs Vernon's consciousness of deserving every sort of revenge that it can be in my power to inflict for her ill-offices could alone enable her to perceive that I am actuated by any design in behaviour so gentle and unpretending. Let her think and act as she chooses, however. I have never yet found that the advice of a sister could prevent a young man's being in love if he chose. We are advancing now to some kind of confidence, and in short are likely to be engaged in a sort of platonic friendship. On *my* side you may be sure of its never being more, for if I were not already attached to another person as much as I can be to anyone, I should make a point of not bestowing my affection on a man who had dared to think so meanly of me.

Reginald has a good figure and is not unworthy the praise you have heard given him, but is still greatly inferior to our friend at Langford. He is less polished, less insinuating than Mainwaring, and is comparatively deficient in the power of saying those delightful things which put one in good humour with oneself and all the world. He is quite agreeable enough, however, to afford me amusement, and to make many of those hours pass very pleasantly which would otherwise be spent in endeavouring to overcome my sister-in-law's reserve, and listening to the insipid talk of her husband.

Your account of Sir James is most satisfactory, and I mean to give Miss Frederica a hint of my intentions very soon.

Yours, &c.,

S. VERNON

Letter 11

Churchhill

I really grow quite uneasy, my dearest mother, about Reginald, from witnessing the very rapid increase of Lady Susan's influence. They are now on terms of the most particular friendship, frequently engaged in long conversations together; and she has contrived by the most artful coquetry to subdue his judgement to her own purposes. It is impossible to see the intimacy between them so very soon established without some alarm, though I can hardly suppose that Lady Susan's plans extend to marriage. I wish you could get Reginald home again on any plausible pretence; he is not at all disposed to leave us, and I have given him as many hints of my father's precarious state of health as common decency will allow me to do in my own house. Her power over him must now be boundless, as she has entirely effaced all his former ill-opinion, and persuaded him not merely to forget but to justify her conduct. Mr Smith's account of her proceedings at Langford, where he accused her of having made Mr Mainwaring and a young man engaged to Miss Mainwaring distractedly in love with her, which Reginald firmly believed when he came here, is now, he is persuaded, only a scandalous invention. He has told me so with a warmth of manner which spoke his regret at having believed the contrary himself.

How sincerely do I grieve that she ever entered this house! I always looked forward to her coming with uneasiness; but very far was it from originating in anxiety for Reginald. I expected a most disagreeable companion for myself, but could not imagine that my brother would be in the smallest danger of being captivated by a woman with whose principles he was so well acquainted, and whose character he so heartily despised. If you can get him away it will be a good thing.

Yours, &c.,

CATHERINE VERNON

Letter 12

Parklands

I know that young men in general do not admit of any enquiry even from their nearest relations into affairs of the heart, but I hope, my dear Reginald, that you will be superior to such as allow nothing for a father's anxiety, and think themselves privileged to refuse him their confidence and slight his advice. You must be sensible that as an only son, and the representative of an ancient family, your conduct in life is most interesting to your connections; and in the very important concern of marriage, especially, there is everything at stake – your own happiness, that of your parents, and the credit of your name. I do not suppose that you would deliberately form an absolute engagement of that nature without acquainting your mother and myself, or at least without being convinced that we should approve of your choice; but I cannot help fearing that you may be drawn in, by the lady who has lately attached you, to a marriage which the whole of your family, far and near, must highly reprobate.

Lady Susan's age is itself a material objection, but her want of character is one so much more serious that the difference of even twelve years becomes in comparison of small account. Were you not blinded by a sort of fascination, it would be ridiculous in me to repeat the instances of great misconduct on her side so very generally known. Her neglect of her husband, her encouragement of other men, her extravagance and dissipation, were so gross and notorious that no one could be ignorant of them at the time, nor can now have forgotten them. To our family she has always been represented in softened colours by the benevolence of Mr Charles Vernon, and yet, in spite of his generous endeavours to excuse her, we know that she did, from the most selfish motives, take all possible pains to prevent his marriage with Catherine.

My years and increasing infirmities make me very desirous of seeing you settled in the world. To the fortune of a wife, the goodness of my own will make me indifferent, but her family and character must be equally unexceptionable. When your choice is fixed so that no objection can be made to either, then I can promise you a ready and cheerful consent; but it is my duty to oppose a match which deep art only could render possible, and must in the end make wretched.

It is possible her behaviour may arise only from vanity, or the wish of gaining the admiration of a man whom she must imagine to be particularly prejudiced against her; but it is more likely that she should aim at something further. She is poor, and may naturally seek an alliance which must be advantageous to herself; you know your own rights, and that it is out of my power to prevent your inheriting the family estate. My ability of distressing you during my life would be a species of revenge to which I could hardly stoop under any circumstances. I honestly tell you my sentiments and intentions: I do not wish to work on your fears, but on your sense and affection. It would destroy every comfort of my life to know that you were married to Lady Susan Vernon; it would be the death of that honest pride with which I have hitherto considered my son; I should blush to see him, to hear of him, to think of him.

I may perhaps do no good but that of relieving my own mind by this letter, but I felt it my duty to tell you that your partiality for Lady Susan is no secret to your friends, and to warn you against her. I should be glad to hear your reasons for disbelieving Mr Smith's intelligence;[335] you had no doubt of its authenticity a month ago.

If you can give me your assurance of having no design beyond enjoying the conversation of a clever woman for a short period, and of yielding admiration only to her beauty and abilities, without being blinded by them to her faults, you will restore me to happiness; but if you cannot do this, explain to me, at least, what has occasioned so great an alteration in your opinion of her.

I am, &c., &c.,

REGINALD DE COURCY

Letter 13

Parklands

MY DEAR CATHERINE – Unluckily I was confined to my room when your last letter came, by a cold which affected my eyes so much as to prevent my reading it myself, so I could not refuse your father when he offered to read it to me, by which means he became acquainted, to my great vexation, with all your fears about your brother. I had intended to write to Reginald myself as soon as my eyes would let me, to point out, as well as I could, the danger of an intimate acquaintance with so artful a woman as Lady Susan to a young man of his age and high expectations. I meant, moreover, to have reminded him of our being quite alone now, and very much in need of him to keep up our spirits these long winter evenings. Whether it would have done any good can never be settled now, but I am excessively vexed that Sir Reginald should know anything of a matter which we foresaw would make him so uneasy. He caught all your fears the moment he had read your letter, and I am sure he has not had the business out of his head since. He wrote by the same post to Reginald a long letter full of it all, and particularly asking an explanation of what he may have heard from Lady Susan to contradict the late[336] shocking reports. His answer came this morning, which I shall enclose to you, as I think you will like to see it. I wish it was more satisfactory, but it seems written with such a determination to think well of Lady Susan that his assurances as to marriage, &c., do not set my heart at ease. I say all I can, however, to satisfy your father, and he is certainly less uneasy since Reginald's letter. How provoking it is, my dear Catherine, that this unwelcome guest of yours should not only prevent our meeting this Christmas, but be the occasion of so much vexation and trouble! Kiss the dear children for me.

Your affectionate mother,

C. DE COURCY

Churchhill

MY DEAR SIR – I have this moment received your letter, which has given me more astonishment than I ever felt before. I am to thank my sister, I suppose, for having represented me in such a light as to injure me in your opinion, and give you all this alarm. I know not why she should choose to make herself and her family uneasy by apprehending an event which no one but herself, I can affirm, would ever have thought possible. To impute such a design to Lady Susan would be taking from her every claim to that excellent understanding which her bitterest enemies have never denied her; and equally low must sink my pretensions to common sense if I am suspected of matrimonial views in my behaviour to her. Our difference of age must be an insuperable objection, and I entreat you, my dear father, to quiet your mind, and no longer harbour a suspicion which cannot be more injurious to your own peace than to our understandings.

I can have no other view in remaining with Lady Susan than to enjoy for a short time (as you have yourself expressed it) the conversation of a woman of high intellectual powers. If Mrs Vernon would allow something to my affection for herself and her husband in the length of my visit, she would do more justice to us all; but my sister is unhappily prejudiced beyond the hope of conviction against Lady Susan. From an attachment to her husband, which in itself does honour to both, she cannot forgive the endeavours at preventing their union, which have been attributed to selfishness in Lady Susan; but in this case, as well as in many others, the world has most grossly injured that lady by supposing the worst where the motives of her conduct have been doubtful.

Lady Susan had heard something so materially to the disadvantage of my sister as to persuade her that the happiness of Mr Vernon, to whom she was always much attached, would be wholly destroyed by the marriage. And this circumstance, while it explains the true motives of Lady Susan's conduct, and removes all the blame which has been so lavished on her, may also convince us how little the general report of anyone ought to be credited; since no character, however upright, can escape the malevolence of slander. If my sister, in the security of retirement, with as little opportunity as inclination to do evil, could not avoid censure, we must not rashly condemn those who, living in the world and surrounded with temptations, should be accused of errors which they are known to have the power of committing.

I blame myself severely for having so easily believed the slanderous tales invented by Charles Smith to the prejudice of Lady Susan, as I am now convinced how greatly they have traduced her. As to Mrs Mainwaring's jealousy, it was totally his own invention, and his account of her attaching Miss Mainwaring's lover was scarcely better founded. Sir James Martin had been drawn in by that young lady to pay her some attention; and as he is a man of fortune, it was easy to see *her* views extended to marriage. It is well known that Miss M. is absolutely on the catch for a husband, and no one therefore can pity her for losing, by the superior attractions of another woman, the chance of being able to make a worthy man completely wretched. Lady Susan was far from intending such a conquest, and on finding how warmly Miss Mainwaring resented her lover's defection, determined, in spite of Mr and Mrs Mainwaring's most urgent entreaties, to leave the family. I have reason to imagine she did receive serious proposals from Sir James, but her removing to Langford immediately on the discovery of his attachment must acquit her on that article with any mind of common candour. You will, I am sure, my dear sir, feel the truth of this, and will hereby learn to do justice to the character of a very injured woman.

I know that Lady Susan in coming to Churchhill was governed only by the most honourable and amiable intentions; her prudence and economy are exemplary, her regard for Mr Vernon equal even to *his* deserts, and her wish of obtaining my sister's good opinion merits a better return than it has received. As a mother she is unexceptionable; her solid affection for her child is shown by placing her in hands where her education will be properly attended to; but because she has not the blind and weak partiality of most mothers, she is accused of wanting maternal tenderness. Every person of sense, however, will know how to value and commend her well-directed affection, and will join me in wishing that Frederica Vernon may prove more worthy than she has yet done of her mother's tender care.

I have now, my dear father, written my real sentiments of Lady Susan; you will know from this letter how highly I admire her abilities, and esteem her character; but if you are not equally convinced by my full and solemn assurance that your fears have been most idly created, you will deeply mortify and distress me.

I am, &c., &c.,

R. De Courcy

Churchhill

MY DEAR MOTHER – I return you Reginald's letter, and rejoice with all my heart that my father is made easy by it: tell him so, with my congratulations; but, between ourselves, I must own it has only convinced *me* of my brother's having no *present* intention of marrying Lady Susan, not that he is in no danger of doing so three months hence. He gives a very plausible account of her behaviour at Langford; I wish it may be true, but his intelligence must come from herself, and I am less disposed to believe it than to lament the degree of intimacy subsisting between them implied by the discussion of such a subject.

I am sorry to have incurred his displeasure, but can expect nothing better while he is so very eager in Lady Susan's justification. He is very severe against me indeed, and yet I hope I have not been hasty in my judgement of her. Poor woman! though I have reasons enough for my dislike, I cannot help pitying her at present, as she is in real distress, and with too much cause. She had this morning a letter from the lady with whom she has placed her daughter, to request that Miss Vernon might be immediately removed, as she had been detected in an attempt to run away. Why, or whither she intended to go, does not appear; but as her situation seems to have been unexceptionable, it is a sad thing and of course highly distressing to Lady Susan.

Frederica must be as much as sixteen, and ought to know better; but from what her mother insinuates, I am afraid she is a perverse girl. She has been sadly neglected, however, and her mother ought to remember it.

Mr Vernon set off for London as soon as she had determined what should be done. He is, if possible, to prevail on Miss Summers to let Frederica continue with her; and if he cannot succeed, to bring her to Churchhill for the present, till some other situation can be found for her. Her ladyship is comforting herself meanwhile by strolling along the shrubbery[337] with Reginald, calling forth all his tender feelings, I suppose, on this distressing occasion. She has been talking a great deal about it to me. She talks vastly well; I am afraid of being ungenerous, or I should say, *too* well to feel so very deeply; but I will not look for her faults; she may be Reginald's wife! Heaven forbid it! – but why should I be quicker-sighted than anyone else? Mr Vernon declares that he never saw deeper distress than hers, on the receipt of the letter – and is his judgement inferior to mine?

She was very unwilling that Frederica should be allowed to come to Churchhill, and justly enough, as it seems a sort of reward to behaviour deserving very differently; but it was impossible to take her anywhere else, and she is not to remain here long.

'It will be absolutely necessary,' said she, 'as you, my dear sister, must be sensible, to treat my daughter with some severity while she is here; a most painful necessity, but I will *endeavour* to submit to it. I am afraid I have often been too indulgent, but my poor Frederica's temper could never bear opposition well: you must support and encourage me; you must urge the necessity of reproof if you see me too lenient.'

All this sounds very reasonable. Reginald is so incensed against the poor silly girl. Surely it is not to Lady Susan's credit that he should be so bitter against her daughter; his idea of her must be drawn from the mother's description.

Well, whatever may be his fate, we have the comfort of knowing that we have done our utmost to save him. We must commit the event to a higher power.

Yours ever, &c.,

CATHERINE VERNON

Letter 16

LADY SUSAN TO MRS JOHNSON

Churchhill

Never, my dearest Alicia, was I so provoked in my life as by a letter this morning from Miss Summers. That horrid girl of mine has been trying to run away. I had not a notion of her being such a little devil before, she seemed to have all the Vernon milkiness;[338] but on receiving the letter in which I declared my intention about Sir James, she actually attempted to elope; at least, I cannot otherwise account for her doing it. She meant, I suppose, to go to the Clarkes in Staffordshire, for she has no other acquaintances. But she *shall* be punished, she *shall* have him. I have sent Charles to town to make matters up if he can, for I do not by any means want her here. If Miss Summers will not keep her, you must find me out another school, unless we can get her married immediately. Miss S— writes word that she could not get the young lady to assign any cause for her extraordinary conduct, which confirms me in my own previous explanation of it.

Frederica is too shy, I think, and too much in awe of me to tell tales, but if the mildness of her uncle *should* get anything out of her, I am not afraid. I trust I shall be able to make my story as good as hers. If I am vain of anything, it is of my eloquence. Consideration and esteem as surely follow command of language as admiration waits on beauty, and here I have opportunity enough for the exercise of my talent, as the chief of my time is spent in conversation. Reginald is never easy unless we are by ourselves, and when the weather is tolerable, we pace the shrubbery for hours together. I like him on the whole very well; he is clever and has a good deal to say, but he is sometimes impertinent and troublesome. There is a sort of ridiculous delicacy about him which requires the fullest explanation of whatever he may have heard to my disadvantage, and he is never satisfied till he thinks he has ascertained the beginning and end of everything.

This is *one* sort of love, but I confess it does not particularly recommend itself to me. I infinitely prefer the tender and liberal spirit of Mainwaring, which, impressed with the deepest conviction of my merit, is satisfied that whatever I do must be right; and look with a degree of contempt on the inquisitive and doubtful fancies of that heart which seems always debating on the reasonableness of its emotions. Mainwaring is indeed, beyond all compare, superior to Reginald – superior in everything but the power of being with me! Poor fellow! he is quite distracted by jealousy, which I am not sorry for, as I know no better support of love. He has been teasing[339] me to allow of his coming into this country, and lodging somewhere near me *incog.*[340] – but I forbid anything of the kind. Those women are inexcusable who forget what is due to themselves, and the opinion of the world.

Yours ever,

S. Vernon

Letter 17

MRS VERNON TO LADY DE COURCY

Churchhill

My dear mother – Mr Vernon returned on Thursday night, bringing his niece with him. Lady Susan had received a line from him by that day's post, informing her that Miss Summers had absolutely refused to allow of Miss Vernon's continuance in her academy; we were therefore prepared for her arrival, and expected them impatiently the whole evening. They came while we were at tea, and I never saw any creature look so frightened as Frederica when she entered the room.

Lady Susan, who had been shedding tears before, and showing great agitation at the idea of the meeting, received her with perfect self-command, and without betraying the least tenderness of spirit. She hardly spoke to her, and on Frederica's bursting into tears as soon as we were seated, took her out of the room, and did not return for some time. When she did, her eyes looked very red and she was as much agitated as before. We saw no more of her daughter.

Poor Reginald was beyond measure concerned to see his fair friend in such distress, and watched her with so much tender solicitude, that I, who occasionally caught her observing his countenance with exultation, was quite out of patience. This pathetic[341] representation lasted the whole evening, and so ostentatious and artful a display has entirely convinced me that she did in fact feel nothing.

I am more angry with her than ever since I have seen her daughter; the poor girl looks so unhappy that my heart aches for her. Lady Susan is surely too severe, for Frederica does not seem to have the sort of temper to make severity necessary. She looks perfectly timid, dejected, and penitent.

She is very pretty, though not so handsome as her mother, nor at all like her. Her complexion is delicate, but neither so fair nor so blooming as Lady Susan's, and she has quite the Vernon cast of countenance, the oval face and mild dark eyes, and there is peculiar sweetness in her look when she speaks either to her uncle or me, for as we behave kindly to her we have of course engaged her gratitude. Her mother has insinuated that her temper is intractable, but I never saw a face less indicative of any evil disposition than hers; and from what I can see of the behaviour of each to the other, the invariable severity of Lady Susan and the silent dejection of Frederica, I am led to believe as heretofore that the former has no real love for her daughter, and has never done her justice or treated her affectionately.

I have not yet been able to have any conversation with my niece; she is shy, and I think I can see that some pains are taken to prevent her being much with me. Nothing satisfactory transpires as to her reason for running away. Her kind-hearted uncle, you may be sure, was too fearful of distressing her to ask many questions as they travelled. I wish it had been possible for me to fetch her instead of him. I think I should have discovered the truth in the course of a thirty-mile journey.

The small pianoforte has been removed within these few days, at Lady Susan's request, into her dressing-room, and Frederica spends the great part of the day there, *practising* as it is called; but I seldom hear any noise when I pass that way; what she does with herself there I do not know. There are plenty of books, but it is not every girl who has been running wild the first fifteen years of her life that can or will read. Poor creature! the prospect from her window is not very instructive, for that room overlooks the lawn, you know, with the shrubbery on one side, where she may see her mother walking for an hour together in earnest conversation with Reginald. A girl of Frederica's age must be childish indeed if such things do not strike her. Is it not inexcusable to give such an example to a daughter? Yet Reginald still thinks Lady Susan the best of mothers, and still condemns Frederica as a worthless girl! He is convinced that her attempt to run away proceeded from no justifiable cause, and had no provocation. I am sure I cannot say that it *had*, but while Miss Summers declares that Miss Vernon showed no signs of obstinacy or perverseness during her whole stay in Wigmore Street, till she was detected in this scheme, I cannot so readily credit what Lady Susan has made him and wants to make me believe, that it was merely an impatience of restraint and a desire of escaping from the tuition of masters which brought on the plan of an elopement. Oh, Reginald, how is your judgement enslaved! He scarcely dares even allow her to be handsome, and when I speak of her beauty, replies only that her eyes have no brilliancy!

Sometimes he is sure she is deficient in understanding, and at others that her temper only is in fault. In short, when a person is always to deceive, it is impossible to be consistent. Lady Susan finds it necessary that Frederica should be to blame, and probably has sometimes judged it expedient to excuse her of ill-nature and sometimes to lament her want of sense. Reginald is only repeating after her ladyship.

I remain, &c., &c.,

CATHERINE VERNON

Letter 18

From the same to the same

Churchhill

MY DEAR MOTHER – I am very glad to find that my description of Frederica Vernon has interested you, for I do believe her truly deserving of your regard; and when I have communicated a notion which has recently struck me, your kind impressions in her favour will, I am sure, be heightened. I cannot help fancying that she is growing partial to my brother. I so very often see her eyes fixed on his face with a remarkable expression of pensive admiration. He is certainly very handsome; and yet more, there is an openness in his manner that must be highly prepossessing, and I am sure she feels it so. Thoughtful and pensive in general, her countenance always brightens into a smile when Reginald says anything amusing; and, let the subject be ever so serious that he may be conversing on, I am much mistaken if a syllable of his uttering escapes her.

I want to make *him* sensible of all this, for we know the power of gratitude on such a heart as his; and could Frederica's artless affection detach him from her mother, we might bless the day which brought her to Churchhill. I think, my dear mother, you would not disapprove of her as a daughter. She is extremely young, to be sure, and has had a wretched education and a dreadful example of levity in her mother; but yet I can pronounce her disposition to be excellent, and her natural abilities very good.

Though totally without accomplishments, she is by no means so ignorant as one might expect to find her, being fond of books and spending the chief of her time in reading. Her mother leaves her more to herself than she did, and I have her with me as much as possible, and have taken great pains to overcome her timidity. We are very good friends, and though she never opens her lips before her mother, she talks enough when alone with me to make it clear that, if properly treated by Lady Susan, she would always appear to much greater advantage. There cannot be a more gentle, affectionate heart, or more obliging manners, when acting without restraint, and her little cousins are all very fond of her.

Your affectionate daughter,

CATHERINE VERNON

Letter 19

LADY SUSAN TO MRS JOHNSON

Churchhill

You will be eager, I know, to hear something further of Frederica, and perhaps may think me negligent for not writing before. She arrived with her uncle last Thursday fortnight, when, of course, I lost no time in demanding the cause of her behaviour; and soon found myself to have been perfectly right in attributing it to my own letter. The purport of it frightened her so thoroughly, that, with a mixture of true girlish perverseness and folly, without considering that she could not escape my authority by running away from Wigmore Street, she resolved on getting out of the house and proceeding directly by the stage[342] to her friends, the Clarkes; and had really got as far as the length of two streets in her journey when she was fortunately missed, pursued, and overtaken.

Such was the first distinguished exploit of Miss Frederica Susanna Vernon; and, if we consider that it was achieved at the tender age of sixteen, we shall have room for the most flattering prognostics of her future renown. I am excessively provoked, however, at the parade of propriety which prevented Miss Summers from keeping the girl; and it seems so extraordinary a piece of nicety, considering my daughter's family connections, that I can only suppose the lady to be governed by the fear of never getting her money. Be that as it may, however, Frederica is returned on my hands; and, having nothing else to employ her, is busy in pursuing the plan of romance begun at Langford. She is actually falling in love with Reginald De Courcy! To disobey her mother by refusing an unexceptionable offer is not enough; her affections must also be given without her mother's approbation. I never saw a girl of her age bid fairer to be the sport of mankind. Her feelings are tolerably acute, and she is so charmingly artless in their display as to afford the most reasonable hope of her being ridiculous, and despised by every man who sees her.

Artlessness will never do in love matters; and that girl is born a simpleton who has it either by nature or affectation. I am not yet certain that Reginald sees what she is about, nor is it of much consequence. She is now an object of indifference to him, and she would be one of contempt were he to understand her emotions. Her beauty is much admired by the Vernons, but it has no effect on him. She is in high favour with her aunt altogether, because she is so little like myself, of course. She is exactly the companion for Mrs Vernon, who dearly loves to be firm, and to have all the sense and all the wit of the conversation to herself: Frederica will never eclipse her. When she first came I was at some pains to prevent her seeing much of her aunt; but I have relaxed, as I believe I may depend on her observing the rules I have laid down for their discourse.

But do not imagine that with all this lenity I have for a moment given up my plan of her marriage. No; I am unalterably fixed on this point, though I have not yet quite decided on the manner of bringing it about. I should not choose to have the business brought on here, and canvassed by the wise heads of Mr and Mrs Vernon; and I cannot just now afford to go to town. Miss Frederica must therefore wait a little.

Yours ever,

S. VERNON

Letter 20

Churchhill

We have a very unexpected guest with us at present, my dear mother: he arrived yesterday. I heard a carriage at the door, as I was sitting with my children while they dined, and supposing I should be wanted, left the nursery soon afterwards, and was halfway downstairs, when Frederica, as pale as ashes, came running up, and rushed by me into her own room. I instantly followed, and asked her what was the matter. 'Oh!' said she, 'he is come – Sir James is come, and what shall I do?' This was no explanation; I begged her to tell me what she meant. At that moment we were interrupted by a knock at the door: it was Reginald, who came, by Lady Susan's direction, to call Frederica down. 'It is Mr De Courcy!' said she, colouring violently. 'Mamma has sent for me; I must go.'

We all three went down together; and I saw my brother examining the terrified face of Frederica with surprise. In the breakfast-room we found Lady Susan, and a young man of gentlemanlike appearance, whom she introduced by the name of Sir James Martin – the very person, as you may remember, whom it was said she had been at pains to detach from Miss Mainwaring; but the conquest, it seems, was not designed for herself, or she has since transferred it to her daughter, for Sir James is now desperately in love with Frederica, and with full encouragement from mamma. The poor girl, however, I am sure, dislikes him; and though his person and address are very well, he appears, both to Mr Vernon and me, a very weak young man.

Frederica looked so shy, so confused, when we entered the room, that I felt for her exceedingly. Lady Susan behaved with great attention to her visitor; and yet I thought I could perceive that she had no particular pleasure in seeing him. Sir James talked a great deal, and made many civil excuses to me for the liberty he had taken in coming to Churchhill – mixing more frequent laughter with his discourse than the subject required – said many things over and over again, and told Lady Susan three times that he had seen Mrs Johnson a few evenings before. He now and then addressed Frederica, but more frequently her mother. The poor girl sat all this time without opening her lips – her eyes cast down, and her colour varying every instant – while Reginald observed all that passed in perfect silence.

At length Lady Susan, weary, I believe, of her situation, proposed walking; and we left the two gentlemen together to put on our pelisses.[343]

As we went upstairs Lady Susan begged permission to attend me for a few moments in my dressing-room, as she was anxious to speak with me in private. I led her thither accordingly, and as soon as the door was closed, she said: 'I was never more surprised in my life than by Sir James's arrival, and the suddenness of it requires some apology to *you*, my dear sister, though to *me*, as a mother, it is highly flattering. He is so extremely attached to my daughter that he could not exist longer without seeing her. Sir James is a young man of an amiable disposition and excellent character; a little too much of the *rattle*,[344] perhaps, but a year or two will rectify *that*; and he is in other respects so very eligible a match for Frederica that I have always observed his attachment with the greatest pleasure; and am persuaded that you and my brother will give the alliance your hearty approbation. I have never before mentioned the likelihood of its taking place to anyone, because I thought that while Frederica continued at school it had better not be known to exist; but now, as I am convinced that Frederica is too old ever to submit to school confinement, and have, therefore, begun to consider her union with Sir James as not very distant, I had intended within a few days to acquaint yourself and Mr Vernon with the whole business. I am sure, my dear sister, you will excuse my remaining silent so long, and agree with me that such circumstances, while they continue from any cause in suspense, cannot be too cautiously concealed. When you have the happiness of bestowing your sweet little Catherine, some years hence, on a man who in connection and character is alike unexceptionable, you will know what I feel now; though, thank heaven, you cannot have all my reasons for rejoicing in such an event. Catherine will be amply provided for, and not, like my Frederica, indebted to a fortunate establishment[345] for the comforts of life.'

She concluded by demanding my congratulations. I gave them somewhat awkwardly, I believe; for, in fact, the sudden disclosure of so important a matter took from me the power of speaking with any clearness. She thanked me, however, most affectionately, for my kind concern in the welfare of herself and daughter, and then said: 'I am not apt to deal in professions, my dear Mrs Vernon, and I never had the convenient talent of affecting sensations foreign to my heart; and therefore I trust you will believe me when I declare that much as I had heard in your praise before I knew you, I had no idea that I should ever love you as I now do; and I must further say that your friendship towards me is more particularly gratifying because I have reason to believe that some attempts were made to prejudice you against me. I only wish that they, whoever they are, to whom I am indebted for such kind intentions, could see the terms on which we now are together, and understand the real affection we feel for each other; but I will not detain you any longer. God bless you for your goodness to me and my girl, and continue to you all your present happiness.'

What can one say of such a woman, my dear mother? Such earnestness, such solemnity of expression! and yet I cannot help suspecting the truth of everything she says.

As for Reginald, I believe he does not know what to make of the matter. When Sir James came, he appeared all astonishment and perplexity; the folly of the young man and the confusion of Frederica entirely engrossed him; and though a little private discourse with Lady Susan has since had its effect, he is still hurt, I am sure, at her allowing of such a man's attentions to her daughter.

Sir James invited himself with great composure to remain here a few days – hoped we would not think it odd, was aware of its being very impertinent, but he took the liberty of a relation; and concluded by wishing, with a laugh, that he might be really one very soon. Even Lady Susan seemed a little disconcerted by this forwardness; in her heart I am persuaded she sincerely wishes him gone.

But something must be done for this poor girl, if her feelings are such as both I and her uncle believe them to be. She must not be sacrificed to policy or ambition, and she must not be left to suffer from the dread of it. The girl whose heart can distinguish Reginald De Courcy, deserves, however he may slight her, a better fate than to be Sir James Martin's wife. As soon as I can get her alone, I will discover the real truth; but she seems to wish to avoid me. I hope this does not proceed from anything wrong, and that I shall not find out I have thought too well of her. Her behaviour to Sir James certainly speaks the greatest consciousness and embarrassment, and I see nothing in it less like encouragement.

Adieu, my dear mother.

Yours, &c.,

C. VERNON

Letter 21

MISS VERNON TO MR DE COURCY

SIR – I hope you will excuse this liberty; I am forced upon it by the greatest distress, or I should be ashamed to trouble you. I am very miserable about Sir James Martin, and have no other way in the world of helping myself but by writing to you, for I am forbidden even speaking to my uncle and aunt on the subject; and this being the case, I am afraid my applying to you will appear no better than equivocation, and as if I attended to the letter and not the spirit of mamma's commands. But if *you* do not take my part and persuade her to break it off, I shall be half-distracted, for I cannot bear him. No human being but *you* could have any chance of prevailing with her. If you will, therefore, have the unspeakably great kindness of taking my part with her, and persuading her to send Sir James away, I shall be more obliged to you than it is possible for me to express. I always disliked him from the first: it is not a sudden fancy, I assure you, sir; I always thought him silly and impertinent and disagreeable, and now he is grown worse than ever. I would rather work for my bread than marry him. I do not know how to apologise enough for this letter; I know it is taking so great a liberty. I am aware how dreadfully angry it will make mamma, but I must run the risk.

I am, sir, your most humble servant,

F. S. V.

Letter 22

LADY SUSAN TO MRS JOHNSON

Churchhill

This is insufferable! My dearest friend, I was never so enraged before, and must relieve myself by writing to you, who I know will enter into all my feelings. Who should come on Tuesday but Sir James Martin! Guess my astonishment, and vexation – for, as you well know, I never wished him to be seen at Churchhill. What a pity that you should not have known his intentions! Not content with coming, he actually invited himself to remain here a few days. I could have poisoned him! I made the best of it, however, and told my story with great success to Mrs Vernon, who, whatever might be her real sentiments, said nothing in opposition to mine. I made a point also of Frederica's behaving civilly to Sir James, and gave her to understand that I was absolutely determined on her marrying him. She said something of her misery, but that was all. I have for some time been more particularly resolved on the match from seeing the rapid increase of her affection for Reginald, and from not feeling secure that a knowledge of such affection might not in the end awaken a return. Contemptible as a regard founded only on compassion must make them both in my eyes, I felt by no means assured that such might not be the consequence. It is true that Reginald has not in any degree grown cool towards me; but yet he has lately mentioned Frederica spontaneously and unnecessarily, and once said something in praise of her person.

He was all astonishment at the appearance of my visitor, and at first observed Sir James with an attention which I was pleased to see not unmixed with jealousy; but unluckily it was impossible for me really to torment him, as Sir James, though extremely gallant to me, very soon made the whole party understand that his heart was devoted to my daughter.

I had no great difficulty in convincing De Courcy, when we were alone, that I was perfectly justified, all things considered, in desiring the match; and the whole business seemed most comfortably arranged. They could none of them help perceiving that Sir James was no Solomon;[346] but I had positively forbidden Frederica complaining to Charles Vernon or his wife, and they had therefore no pretence for interference; though my impertinent sister, I believe, wanted only opportunity for doing so.

Everything, however, was going on calmly and quietly; and, though I counted the hours of Sir James's stay, my mind was entirely satisfied with the posture of affairs. Guess, then, what I must feel at the sudden disturbance of all my schemes; and that, too, from a quarter where I had least reason to expect it. Reginald came this morning into my dressing-room, with a very unusual solemnity of countenance, and after some preface informed me in so many words that he wished to reason with me on the impropriety and unkindness of allowing Sir James Martin to address my daughter, contrary to *her* inclinations. I was all amazement. When I found that he was not to be laughed out of his design, I calmly begged an explanation, and desired to know by what he was impelled, and by whom commissioned, to reprimand me. He then told me, mixing in his speech a few insolent compliments and ill-timed expressions of tenderness, to which I listened with perfect indifference, that my daughter had acquainted him with some circumstances, concerning herself, Sir James and me, which had given him great uneasiness.

In short, I found that she had in the first place actually written to him to request his interference, and that, on receiving her letter, he had conversed with her on the subject of it, in order to understand the particulars, and to assure himself of her real wishes.

I have not a doubt but that the girl took this opportunity of making downright love to him. I am convinced of it by the manner in which he spoke of her. Much good may such love do him! I shall ever despise the man who can be gratified by the passion which he never wished to inspire, nor solicited the avowal of. I shall always detest them both. He can have no true regard for me, or he would not have listened to her; and *she*, with her little rebellious heart and indelicate feelings, to throw herself into the protection of a young man with whom she has scarcely ever exchanged two words before! I am equally confounded at *her* impudence and *his* credulity. How dared he believe what she told him in my disfavour! Ought he not to have felt assured that I must have unanswerable motives for all that I had done? Where was his reliance on my sense and goodness then? Where the resentment which true love would have dictated against the person defaming me – that person, too, a chit,[347] a child, without talent or education, whom he had been always taught to despise?

I was calm for some time; but the greatest degree of forbearance may be overcome, and I hope I was afterwards sufficiently keen.[348] He endeavoured, long endeavoured, to soften my resentment; but that woman is a fool indeed who, while insulted by accusation, can be worked on by compliments. At length he left me, as deeply provoked as myself; and he showed his anger *more*. I was quite cool, but he gave way to the most violent indignation; I may therefore expect it will the sooner subside, and perhaps his may be vanished for ever, while mine will be found still fresh and implacable.

He is now shut up in his apartment, whither I heard him go on leaving mine. How unpleasant, one would think, must be his reflections! but some people's feelings are incomprehensible. I have not yet tranquillised myself enough to see Frederica. *She* shall not soon forget the occurrences of this day; she shall find that she has poured forth her tender tale of love in vain, and exposed herself for ever to the contempt of the whole world, and the severest resentment of her injured mother.

Your affectionate

S. VERNON

Letter 23

MRS VERNON TO LADY DE COURCY

Churchhill

Let me congratulate you, my dearest mother! The affair which has given us so much anxiety is drawing to a happy conclusion. Our prospect is most delightful, and since matters have now taken so favourable a turn, I am quite sorry that I ever imparted my apprehensions to you; for the pleasure of learning that the danger is over is perhaps dearly purchased by all that you have previously suffered.

I am so much agitated by delight that I can scarcely hold a pen, but am determined to send you a few short lines by James, that you may have some explanation of what must so greatly astonish you – that Reginald should be returning to Parklands.

I was sitting about half an hour ago with Sir James in the breakfast parlour, when my brother called me out of the room. I instantly saw that something was the matter; his complexion was raised, and he spoke with great emotion; you know his eager manner, my dear mother, when his mind is interested.[349]

'Catherine,' said he, 'I am going home today; I am sorry to leave you, but I must go: it is a great while since I have seen my father and mother. I am going to send James forward with my hunters[350] immediately; if you have any letter, therefore, he can take it. I shall not be at home myself till Wednesday or Thursday, as I shall go through London, where I have business; but before I leave you,' he continued, speaking in a lower tone, and with still greater energy, 'I must warn you of one thing – do not let Frederica Vernon be made unhappy by that Martin. He wants to marry her; her mother promotes the match, but *she* cannot endure the idea of it. Be assured that I speak from the fullest conviction of the truth of what I say; I *know* that Frederica is made wretched by Sir James's continuing here. She is a sweet girl, and deserves a better fate. Send him away immediately; *he* is only a fool, but what her mother can mean, heaven only knows! Goodbye,' he added, shaking my hand with earnestness; 'I do not know when you will see me again; but remember what I tell you of Frederica; you *must* make it your business to see justice done her. She is an amiable girl, and has a very superior mind to what we have ever given her credit for.'

He then left me, and ran upstairs. I would not try to stop him, for I know what his feelings must be. The nature of mine, as I listened to him, I need not attempt to describe; for a minute or two I remained in the same spot, overpowered by wonder of a most agreeable sort indeed; yet it required some consideration to be tranquilly happy.

In about ten minutes after my return to the parlour Lady Susan entered the room. I concluded, of course, that she and Reginald had been quarrelling, and looked with anxious curiosity for a confirmation of my belief in her face. Mistress of deceit, however, she appeared perfectly unconcerned, and after chatting on indifferent subjects for a

short time, said to me, 'I find from Wilson that we are going to lose Mr
De Courcy – is it true that he leaves Churchhill this morning?' I replied
that it was. 'He told us nothing of all this last night,' said she, laughing,
'or even this morning at breakfast; but perhaps he did not know it
himself. Young men are often hasty in their resolutions, and not more
sudden in forming than unsteady in keeping them. I should not be
surprised if he were to change his mind at last, and not go.'

She soon afterwards left the room. I trust, however, my dear mother,
that we have no reason to fear an alteration of his present plan; things
have gone too far. They must have quarrelled, and about Frederica,
too. Her calmness astonishes me. What delight will be yours in seeing
him again; in seeing him still worthy your esteem, still capable of
forming your happiness!

When next I write, I shall be able to tell you that Sir James is gone,
Lady Susan vanquished, and Frederica at peace. We have much to do,
but it shall be done. I am all impatience to hear how this astonishing
change was effected. I finish as I began, with the warmest congratulations.

Yours ever, &c.,

CATH. VERNON

Letter 24

From the same to the same

Churchhill

Little did I imagine, my dear mother, when I sent off my last letter, that
the delightful perturbation of spirits I was then in would undergo so
speedy, so melancholy a reverse. I never can sufficiently regret that I
wrote to you at all. Yet who could have foreseen what has happened?
My dear mother, every hope which made me so happy only two hours
ago has vanished. The quarrel between Lady Susan and Reginald is
made up, and we are all as we were before. One point only is gained. Sir
James Martin is dismissed. What are we now to look forward to? I am
indeed disappointed; Reginald was all but gone, his horse was ordered
and all but brought to the door; who would not have felt safe?

For half an hour I was in momentary expectation of his departure.
After I had sent off my letter to you, I went to Mr Vernon, and sat with
him in his room talking over the whole matter, and then determined to
look for Frederica, whom I had not seen since breakfast. I met her on
the stairs, and saw that she was crying.

'My dear aunt,' said she, 'he is going – Mr De Courcy is going, and it is all my fault. I am afraid you will be very angry with me, but indeed I had no idea it would end so.'

'My love,' I replied, 'do not think it necessary to apologise to me on that account. I shall feel myself under an obligation to anyone who is the means of sending my brother home, because,' recollecting myself, 'I know my father wants very much to see him. But what is it you have done to occasion all this?'

She blushed deeply as she answered: 'I was so unhappy about Sir James that I could not help – I have done something very wrong, I know; but you have not an idea of the misery I have been in, and mamma had ordered me never to speak to you or my uncle about it, and – ' 'You therefore spoke to my brother to engage his interference,' said I, to save her the explanation. 'No, but I wrote to him – I did indeed, I got up this morning before it was light, and was two hours about it; and when my letter was done, I thought I never should have courage to give it. After breakfast, however, as I was going to my room, I met him in the passage, and then, as I knew that everything must depend on that moment, I forced myself to give it. He was so good as to take it immediately. I dared not look at him, and ran away directly. I was in such a fright I could hardly breathe. My dear aunt, you do not know how miserable I have been.'

'Frederica,' said I, 'you ought to have told *me* all your distresses. You would have found in me a friend always ready to assist you. Do you think that your uncle or I should not have espoused your cause as warmly as my brother?'

'Indeed, I did not doubt your kindness,' said she, colouring again, 'but I thought Mr De Courcy could do anything with my mother; but I was mistaken: they have had a dreadful quarrel about it, and he is going away. Mamma will never forgive me, and I shall be worse off than ever.' 'No, you shall not,' I replied; 'in such a point as this your mother's prohibition ought not to have prevented your speaking to me on the subject. She has no right to make you unhappy, and she shall *not* do it. Your applying, however, to Reginald can be productive only of good to all parties. I believe it is best as it is. Depend upon it that you shall not be made unhappy any longer.'

At that moment, how great was my astonishment at seeing Reginald come out of Lady Susan's dressing-room. My heart misgave me instantly. His confusion at seeing me was very evident. Frederica immediately disappeared. 'Are you going?' I said. 'You will find Mr Vernon in his own room.' 'No, Catherine,' he replied, 'I am *not* going. Will you let me speak to you a moment?'

We went into my room. 'I find,' he continued, his confusion increasing as he spoke, 'that I have been acting with my usual foolish impetuosity. I have entirely misunderstood Lady Susan, and was on the point of leaving the house under a false impression of her conduct. There has been some very great mistake; we have been all mistaken, I fancy. Frederica does not know her mother. Lady Susan means nothing but her good, but Frederica will not make a friend of her. Lady Susan does not always know, therefore, what will make her daughter happy. Besides, *I* could have no right to interfere. Miss Vernon was mistaken in applying to me. In short, Catherine, everything has gone wrong, but it is now all happily settled. Lady Susan, I believe, wishes to speak to you about it, if you are at leisure.'

'Certainly,' I replied, deeply sighing at the recital of so lame a story. I made no comments, however, for words would have been vain. Reginald was glad to get away, and I went to Lady Susan, curious, indeed, to hear her account of it.

'Did I not tell you,' said she with a smile, 'that your brother would not leave us after all?' 'You did, indeed,' replied I very gravely; 'but I flattered myself you would be mistaken.' 'I should not have hazarded such an opinion,' returned she, 'if it had not at that moment occurred[351] to me that his resolution of going might be occasioned by a conversation in which we had been this morning engaged, and which had ended very much to his dissatisfaction, from our not rightly understanding each other's meaning. This idea struck me at the moment, and I instantly determined that an accidental dispute, in which I might probably be as much to blame as himself, should not deprive you of your brother. If you remember, I left the room almost immediately. I was resolved to lose no time in clearing up those mistakes as far as I could. The case was this – Frederica had set herself violently against marrying Sir James.' 'And can your ladyship wonder that she should?' cried I with some warmth; 'Frederica has an excellent understanding, and Sir James has none.' 'I am at least very far from regretting it, my dear sister,' said she; 'on the contrary, I am grateful for so favourable a sign of my daughter's sense. Sir James is certainly under par (his boyish manners make him appear worse); and had Frederica possessed the penetration and the abilities which I could have wished in my daughter, or had I even known her to possess as much as she does, I should not have been anxious for the match.' 'It is odd that you should alone be ignorant of your daughter's sense!' 'Frederica never does justice to herself; her manners are shy and childish, and besides she is afraid of me. During her poor father's life she was a spoilt child; the severity which it has since been necessary for me to show has alienated her affection; neither has she any of that brilliancy of intellect, that genius or vigour of mind which will force itself forward.' 'Say rather that she has been unfortunate in her education!' 'Heaven knows, my dearest Mrs Vernon, how fully I am aware of that; but I would wish to forget every circumstance that might throw blame on the memory of one whose name is sacred with me.'

Here she pretended to cry; I was out of patience with her. 'But what,' said I, 'was your ladyship going to tell me about your disagreement with my brother?' 'It originated in an action of my daughter's, which equally marks her want of judgement and the unfortunate dread of me I have been mentioning – she wrote to Mr De Courcy.' 'I know she did; you had forbidden her speaking to Mr Vernon or to me on the cause of her distress; what could she do, therefore, but apply to my brother?' 'Good God!' she exclaimed, 'what an opinion you must have of me! Can you possibly suppose that I was aware of her unhappiness! that it was my object to make my own child miserable, and that I had forbidden her speaking to you on the subject from a fear of your interrupting the diabolical scheme? Do you think me destitute of every honest, every natural feeling? Am I capable of consigning *her* to ever-lasting misery, whose welfare it is my first earthly duty to promote? The idea is horrible!' 'What, then, was your intention when you insisted on her silence?' 'Of what use, my dear sister, could be any application to you, however the affair might stand? Why should I subject you to entreaties which I refused to attend to myself? Neither for your sake, nor for hers, nor for my own, could such a thing be desirable. When my own resolution was taken, I could not wish for the interference, however friendly, of another person. I was mistaken, it is true, but I believed myself right.' 'But what was this mistake to which your ladyship so often alludes! from whence arose so astonishing a misconception of your daughter's feelings! Did you not know that she disliked Sir James?' 'I knew that he was not absolutely the man she would have chosen, but I was persuaded that her objections to him did not arise from any perception of his deficiency. You must not question me, however, my dear sister, too minutely on this point,' continued she, taking me affectionately by the hand; 'I honestly own that there is something to conceal. Frederica makes me very unhappy! Her applying to Mr De Courcy hurt me particularly.' 'What is it you mean to infer,' said I, 'by this appearance of mystery? If you think your daughter at all attached to Reginald, her objecting to Sir James could not less deserve to be attended to than if the cause of her objecting had been a con-sciousness of his folly; and why should your ladyship, at any rate, quarrel with my brother for an interference which, you must know, it is not in his nature to refuse when urged in such a manner?'

'His disposition, you know, is warm,[352] and he came to expostulate with me; his compassion all alive for this ill-used girl, this heroine in distress! We misunderstood each other: he believed me more to blame than I really was; I considered his interference less excusable than I now find it. I have a real regard for him, and was beyond expression mortified to find it, as I thought, so ill bestowed. We were both warm, and of course both to blame. His resolution of leaving Churchhill was consistent with his general eagerness. When I understood his intention, however, and at the same time began to think that we had been perhaps equally mistaken in each other's meaning, I resolved to have an explanation before it was too late. For any member of your family I must always feel a degree of affection, and I own it would have sensibly hurt me if my acquaintance with Mr De Courcy had ended so gloomily. I have now only to say further, that as I am convinced of Frederica's having a reasonable dislike to Sir James, I shall instantly inform him that he must give up all hope of her. I reproach myself for having even, though innocently, made her unhappy on that score. She shall have all the retribution in my power to make; if she value her own happiness as much as I do, if she judge wisely, and command herself as she ought, she may now be easy. Excuse me, my dearest sister, for thus trespassing on your time, but I owed it to my own character; and after this explanation I trust I am in no danger of sinking in your opinion.'

I could have said, 'Not much, indeed!' but I left her almost in silence. It was the greatest stretch of forbearance I could practise. I could not have stopped myself had I begun. Her assurance! her deceit! – but I will not allow myself to dwell on them; they will strike you sufficiently. My heart sickens within me.

As soon as I was tolerably composed I returned to the parlour. Sir James's carriage was at the door, and he, merry as usual, soon afterwards took his leave. How easily does her ladyship encourage or dismiss a lover!

In spite of this release, Frederica still looks unhappy: still fearful, perhaps, of her mother's anger; and though dreading my brother's departure, jealous,[353] it may be, of his staying. I see how closely she observes him and Lady Susan, poor girl! I have now no hope for her. There is not a chance of her affection being returned. He thinks very differently of her from what he used to do; he does her some justice, but his reconciliation with her mother precludes every dearer hope.

Prepare, my dear mother, for the worst! The probability of their marrying is surely heightened! He is more securely hers than ever. When that wretched event takes place, Frederica must belong wholly to us. I am thankful that my last letter will precede this by so little, as every moment that you can be saved from feeling a joy which leads only to disappointment is of consequence.

Yours ever, &c.,

CATHERINE VERNON

Letter 25

LADY SUSAN TO MRS JOHNSON

Churchhill

I call on you, dear Alicia, for congratulations: I am my own self, gay and triumphant! When I wrote to you the other day I was, in truth, in high irritation, and with ample cause. Nay, I know not whether I ought to be quite tranquil now, for I have had more trouble in restoring peace than I ever intended to submit to. This Reginald has a proud spirit of his own! – a spirit, too, resulting from a fancied sense of superior integrity, which is peculiarly insolent! I shall not easily forgive him, I assure you. He was actually on the point of leaving Churchhill! I had scarcely concluded my last, when Wilson brought me word of it. I found, therefore, that something must be done; for I did not choose to leave my character at the mercy of a man whose passions are so violent and so revengeful. It would have been trifling with my reputation to allow of his departing with such an impression in my disfavour; in this light, condescension was necessary.

I sent Wilson to say that I desired to speak with him before he went; he came immediately. The angry emotions which had marked every feature when we last parted were partially subdued. He seemed astonished at the summons, and looked as if half wishing and half fearing to be softened by what I might say.

If my countenance expressed what I aimed at, it was composed and dignified – and yet, with a degree of pensiveness which might convince him that I was not quite happy. 'I beg your pardon, sir, for the liberty I have taken in sending for you,' said I; 'but as I have just learnt your intention of leaving this place today, I feel it my duty to entreat that you will not on my account shorten your visit here even an hour. I am perfectly aware that after what has passed between us it would ill suit the feelings of either to remain longer in the same house: so very great, so total a change from the intimacy of friendship must render any future intercourse the severest punishment; and your resolution of quitting Churchhill is undoubtedly in unison with our situation, and with those lively feelings which I know you to possess. But, at the same time, it is not for me to suffer such a sacrifice as it must be to leave relations to whom you are so much attached, and are so dear. My remaining here cannot give that pleasure to Mr and Mrs Vernon which your society must; and my visit has already perhaps been too long. My removal, therefore, which must, at any rate, take place soon, may, with perfect convenience, be hastened; and I make it my particular request that I may not in any way be instrumental in separating a family so affectionately attached to each other. Where I go is of no consequence to anyone; of very little to myself; but you are of importance to all your connections.' Here I concluded, and I hope you will be satisfied with my speech. Its effect on Reginald justifies some portion of vanity, for it was no less favourable than instantaneous. Oh, how delightful it was to watch the variations of his countenance while I spoke! to see the struggle between returning tenderness and the remains of displeasure. There is something agreeable in feelings so easily worked on; not that I envy him their possession, nor would, for the world, have such myself; but they are very convenient when one wishes to influence the passions of another. And yet this Reginald, whom a very few words from me softened at once into the utmost submission, and rendered more tractable, more attached, more devoted than ever, would have left me in the first angry swelling of his proud heart without deigning to seek an explanation.

Humbled as he now is, I cannot forgive him such an instance of pride, and am doubtful whether I ought not to punish him by dismissing him at once after this reconciliation, or by marrying and teasing him for ever. But these measures are each too violent to be adopted without some deliberation; at present my thoughts are fluctuating between various schemes. I have many things to compass: I must punish Frederica, and pretty severely too, for her application to Reginald; I must punish him for receiving it so favourably, and for the rest of his conduct. I must torment my sister-in-law for the insolent triumph of her look and manner since Sir James has been dismissed: for, in reconciling Reginald to me, I was not able to save that ill-fated young man; and I must make myself amends for the humiliation to which I have stooped within these few days. To effect all this I have various plans. I have also an idea of being soon in town; and whatever may be my determination as to the rest, I shall probably put *that* project in execution; for London will be always the fairest field of action, however my views may be directed; and at any rate I shall there be rewarded by your society, and a little dissipation, for a ten weeks' penance at Churchhill.

I believe I owe it to my character to complete the match between my daughter and Sir James after having so long intended it. Let me know your opinion on this point. Flexibility of mind, a disposition easily biased by others, is an attribute which you know I am not very desirous of obtaining; nor has Frederica any claim to the indulgence of her notions at the expense of her mother's inclinations. Her idle love for Reginald, too! It is surely my duty to discourage such romantic nonsense. All things considered, therefore, it seems incumbent on me to take her to town and marry her immediately to Sir James.

When my own will is effected, contrary to his, I shall have some credit in being on good terms with Reginald, which at present, in fact, I have not; for though he is still in my power, I have given up the very article by which our quarrel was produced, and at best, the honour of victory is doubtful.

Send me your opinion on all these matters, my dear Alicia, and let me know whether you can get lodgings to suit me within a short distance of you.

Your most attached

S. VERNON

Letter 26

MRS JOHNSON TO LADY SUSAN

Edward Street

I am gratified by your reference, and this is my advice: that you come to town yourself, without loss of time, but that you leave Frederica behind. It would surely be much more to the purpose to get yourself well established by marrying Mr De Courcy, than to irritate him and the rest of his family by making her marry Sir James. You should think more of yourself and less of your daughter. She is not of a disposition to do you credit in the world, and seems precisely in her proper place at Churchhill, with the Vernons. But *you* are fitted for society, and it is shameful to have you exiled from it. Leave Frederica, therefore, to punish herself for the plague she has given you by indulging that romantic tender-heartedness which will always ensure her misery enough, and come to London as soon as you can.

I have another reason for urging this.

Mainwaring came to town last week, and has contrived, in spite of Mr Johnson, to make opportunities of seeing me. He is absolutely miserable about you, and jealous to such a degree of De Courcy that it would be highly unadvisable for them to meet at present. And yet, if you do not allow him to see you here, I cannot answer for his not committing some great imprudence – such as going to Churchhill, for instance, which would be dreadful! Besides, if you take my advice, and resolve to marry De Courcy, it will be indispensably necessary for you to get Mainwaring out of the way, and you only can have influence enough to send him back to his wife.

I have still another motive for your coming: Mr Johnson leaves London next Tuesday; he is going for his health to Bath, where, if the waters are favourable to his constitution and my wishes, he will be laid up with the gout[354] many weeks. During his absence we shall be able to choose our own society, and to have true enjoyment. I would ask you to Edward Street, but that once he forced from me a kind of promise never to invite you to my house; nothing but my being in the utmost distress for money should have extorted it from me. I can get you, however, a nice drawing-room apartment in Upper Seymour Street,[355] and we may be always together there or here; for I consider my promise to Mr Johnson as comprehending only (at least in his absence) your not sleeping in the house.

Poor Mainwaring gives me such histories of his wife's jealousy. Silly woman to expect constancy from so charming a man! but she always was silly – intolerably so in marrying him at all, she the heiress of a large fortune and he without a shilling! *One* title I know she might have had, besides Baronet's.[356] Her folly in forming the connection was so great that, though Mr Johnson was her guardian and I do not in general share his feelings, I never can forgive her.

Adieu. Yours ever,

ALICIA

Letter 27

MRS VERNON TO LADY DE COURCY

Churchhill

This letter, my dear mother, will be brought you by Reginald. His long visit is about to be concluded at last, but I fear the separation takes place too late to do us any good. She is going to London to see her particular friend, Mrs Johnson. It was at first her intention that Frederica should accompany her, for the benefit of masters, but we overruled her there. Frederica was wretched in the idea of going, and I could not bear to have her at the mercy of her mother; not all the masters in London could compensate for the ruin of her comfort. I should have feared, too, for her health, and for everything but her principles – *there* I believe she is not to be injured, even by her mother, or her mother's friends; but with those friends she must have mixed (a very bad set, I doubt not), or have been left in total solitude, and I can hardly tell which would have been worse for her. If she is with her mother, moreover, she must, alas! in all probability be with Reginald, and that would be the greatest evil of all.

Here we shall in time be in peace, and our regular employments, our books and conversations, with exercise, the children, and every domestic pleasure in my power to procure her, will, I trust, gradually overcome this youthful attachment. I should not have a doubt of it were she slighted for any other woman in the world than her own mother.

How long Lady Susan will be in town, or whether she returns here again, I know not. I could not be cordial in my invitation, but if she chooses to come no want of cordiality on my part will keep her away.

I could not help asking Reginald if he intended being in London this winter, as soon as I found her ladyship's steps would be bent thither; and though he professed himself quite undetermined, there was something in his look and voice as he spoke which contradicted his words. I have done with lamentation; I look upon the event as so far decided that I resign myself to it in despair. If he leaves you soon for London everything will be concluded.

Your affectionate, &c.,

C. VERNON

Letter 28

MRS JOHNSON TO LADY SUSAN

Edward Street

MY DEAREST FRIEND – I write in the greatest distress; the most unfortunate event has just taken place. Mr Johnson has hit on the most effectual manner of plaguing us all. He had heard, I imagine, by some means or other, that you were soon to be in London, and immediately contrived to have such an attack of the gout as must at least delay his journey to Bath, if not wholly prevent it. I am persuaded the gout is brought on or kept off at pleasure; it was the same when I wanted to join the Hamiltons to the Lakes;[357] and three years ago, when I had a fancy for Bath, nothing could induce him to have a gouty symptom.

I have received yours and have engaged the lodgings in consequence. I am pleased to find that my letter had so much effect on you, and that De Courcy is certainly your own. Let me hear from you as soon as you arrive, and in particular tell me what you mean to do with Mainwaring. It is impossible to say when I shall be able to come to you; my confinement must be great. It is such an abominable trick to be ill here instead of at Bath that I can scarcely command myself at all. At Bath his old aunts would have nursed him, but here it all falls upon me; and he bears pain with such patience that I have not the common excuse for losing my temper.

Yours ever,

ALICIA

Letter 29

LADY SUSAN VERNON TO MRS JOHNSON

Upper Seymour Street

MY DEAR ALICIA – There needed not this last fit of the gout to make me detest Mr Johnson, but now the extent of my aversion is not to be estimated. To have you confined as nurse in his apartment! My dear Alicia, of what a mistake were you guilty in marrying a man of his age! just old enough to be formal, ungovernable, and to have the gout; too old to be agreeable, too young to die.

I arrived last night about five, and had scarcely swallowed my dinner when Mainwaring made his appearance. I will not dissemble what real pleasure his sight afforded me, nor how strongly I felt the contrast between his person and manners and those of Reginald, to the infinite disadvantage of the latter. For an hour or two I was even staggered in my resolution of marrying him, and though this was too idle and nonsensical an idea to remain long on my mind, I do not feel very eager for the conclusion of my marriage, nor look forward with much impatience to the time when Reginald, according to our agreement, is to be in town. I shall probably put off his arrival under some pretence or other. He must not come till Mainwaring is gone.

I am still doubtful at times as to marrying; if the old man would die I might not hesitate, but a state of dependence on the caprice of Sir Reginald will not suit the freedom of my spirit; and if I resolve to wait for that event, I shall have excuse enough at present in having been scarcely ten months a widow.

I have not given Mainwaring any hint of my intention, or allowed him to consider my acquaintance with Reginald as more than the commonest flirtation, and he is tolerably appeased. Adieu, till we meet; I am enchanted with my lodgings.

Yours ever,

S. VERNON

Letter 30

LADY SUSAN VERNON TO MR DE COURCY

Upper Seymour Street

I have received your letter, and though I do not attempt to conceal that I am gratified by your impatience for the hour of meeting, I yet feel myself under the necessity of delaying that hour beyond the time originally fixed. Do not think me unkind for such an exercise of my power, nor accuse me of instability without first hearing my reasons. In the course of my journey from Churchhill, I had ample leisure for reflection on the present state of our affairs, and every review has served to convince me that they require a delicacy and cautiousness of conduct to which we have hitherto been too little attentive. We have been hurried on by our feelings to a degree of precipitation which ill accords with the claims of our friends or the opinion of the world. We have been unguarded in forming this hasty engagement, but we must not complete the imprudence by ratifying it while there is so much reason to fear the connection would be opposed by those friends on whom you depend.

It is not for us to blame any expectations on your father's side of your marrying to advantage; where possessions are so extensive as those of your family, the wish of increasing them, if not strictly reasonable, is too common to excite surprise or resentment. He has a right to require a woman of fortune in his daughter-in-law, and I am sometimes quarrelling with myself for suffering you to form a connection so imprudent; but the influence of reason is often acknowledged too late by those who feel like me.

I have now been but a few months a widow, and, however little indebted to my husband's memory for any happiness derived from him during a union of some years, I cannot forget that the indelicacy of so early a second marriage must subject me to the censure of the world, and incur, what would be still more insupportable, the displeasure of Mr Vernon. I might perhaps harden myself in time against the injustice of general reproach, but the loss of *his* valued esteem I am, as you well know, ill-fitted to endure; and when to this may be added the consciousness of having injured you with your family, how am I to support myself? With feelings so poignant as mine, the conviction of having divided the son from his parents would make me, even with you, the most miserable of beings.

It will surely, therefore, be advisable to delay our union – to delay it till appearances are more promising, till affairs have taken a more favourable turn. To assist us in such a resolution I feel that absence will be necessary. We must not meet. Cruel as this sentence may appear, the necessity of pronouncing it, which can alone reconcile it to myself, will be evident to you when you have considered our situation in the light in which I have found myself imperiously obliged to place it. You may be – you must be – well assured that nothing but the strongest conviction of duty could induce me to wound my own feelings by urging a lengthened separation, and of insensibility to yours you will hardly suspect me. Again, therefore, I say that we ought not, we must not, yet meet. By a removal for some months from each other we shall tranquillise the sisterly fears of Mrs Vernon, who, accustomed herself to the enjoyment of riches, considers fortune as necessary everywhere, and whose sensibilities are not of a nature to comprehend ours.

Let me hear from you soon – very soon. Tell me that you submit to my arguments, and do not reproach me for using such. I cannot bear reproaches: my spirits are not so high as to need being repressed. I must endeavour to seek amusement abroad,[358] and fortunately many of my friends are in town, among them the Mainwarings; you know how sincerely I regard both husband and wife.

I am, very faithfully, yours,

S. VERNON

Letter 31

LADY SUSAN TO MRS JOHNSON

Upper Seymour Street

MY DEAR FRIEND – That tormenting creature Reginald is here. My letter, which was intended to keep him longer in the country, has hastened him to town. Much as I wish him away, however, I cannot help being pleased with such a proof of attachment. He is devoted to me, heart and soul. He will carry this note himself, which is to serve as an introduction to you, with whom he longs to be acquainted. Allow him to spend the evening with you, that I may be in no danger of his returning here. I have told him that I am not quite well, and must be alone; and should he call again there might be confusion, for it is impossible to be sure of servants. Keep him, therefore, I entreat you, in Edward Street. You will not find him a heavy companion, and I allow you to flirt with him as much as you like. At the same time, do not forget my real interest; say all that you can to convince him that I shall be quite wretched if he remains here; you know my reasons – propriety, and so forth. I would urge them more myself, but that I am impatient to be rid of him, as Mainwaring comes within half an hour.

Adieu!

S. VERNON

Letter 32

MRS JOHNSON TO LADY SUSAN

Edward Street

MY DEAR CREATURE – I am in agonies, and know not what to do. Mr De Courcy arrived just when he should not. Mrs Mainwaring had that instant entered the house, and forced herself into her guardian's presence, though I did not know a syllable of it till afterwards, for I was out when both she and Reginald came, or I should have sent him away at all events; but *she* was shut up with Mr Johnson, while *he* waited in the drawing-room for me. She arrived yesterday in pursuit of her husband, but perhaps you know this already from himself. She came to this house to entreat my husband's interference, and before I could be aware of it, everything that you could wish to be concealed was known to him; and unluckily she had wormed out of Mainwaring's servant that he had visited you every day since your being in town, and had just watched him to your door herself! What could I do! Facts are such horrid things! All is by this time known to De Courcy, who is now alone with Mr Johnson. Do not accuse me; indeed, it was impossible to prevent it. Mr Johnson has for some time suspected De Courcy of intending to marry you, and would speak with him alone as soon as he knew him to be in the house.

That detestable Mrs Mainwaring, who, for your comfort, has fretted herself thinner and uglier than ever, is still here, and they have been all closeted together. What can be done? If Mainwaring is now with you, he had better be gone. At any rate, I hope he will plague his wife more than ever.

With anxious wishes,

Yours faithfully,

ALICIA

Letter 33

Upper Seymour Street

This *éclaircissement* [359] is rather provoking. How unlucky that you should have been from home! I thought myself sure of you at seven! I am undismayed however. Do not torment yourself with fears on my account; depend on it, I can make my own story good with Reginald. Mainwaring is just gone; he brought me the news of his wife's arrival. Silly woman, what does she expect by such manoeuvres? Yet I wish she had stayed quietly at Langford.

Reginald will be a little enraged at first, but by tomorrow's dinner, everything will be well again.

Adieu!

S. V.

Letter 34

MR DE COURCY TO LADY SUSAN

— Hotel

I write only to bid you farewell, the spell is removed: I see you as you are. Since we parted yesterday, I have received from indisputable authority such a history of you as must bring the most mortifying conviction of the imposition I have been under, and the absolute necessity of an immediate and eternal separation from you. You cannot doubt to what I allude. Langford! Langford! that word will be sufficient. I received my information in Mr Johnson's house, from Mrs Mainwaring herself.

You know how I have loved you; you can intimately judge of my present feelings; but I am not so weak as to find indulgence in describing them to a woman who will glory in having excited their anguish, but whose affection they have never been able to gain.

R. De Courcy

Letter 35

LADY SUSAN TO MR DE COURCY

Upper Seymour Street

I will not attempt to describe my astonishment in reading the note this moment received from you. I am bewildered in my endeavours to form some rational conjecture of what Mrs Mainwaring can have told you to occasion so extraordinary a change in your sentiments. Have I not explained everything to you with respect to myself which could bear a doubtful meaning, and which the ill-nature of the world had interpreted to my discredit? What can you now have heard to stagger your esteem for me? Have I ever had a concealment from you? Reginald, you agitate me beyond expression. I cannot suppose that the old story of Mrs Mainwaring's jealousy can be revived again, or at least be *listened* to again. Come to me immediately, and explain what is at present absolutely incomprehensible. Believe me, the single word *Langford* is not of such potent intelligence as to supersede the necessity of more. If we *are* to part, it will at least be handsome to take your personal leave – but I have little heart to jest; in truth, I am serious enough; for to be sunk, though but for an hour, in your esteem, is a humiliation to which I know not how to submit. I shall count every minute till your arrival.

S. V.

Letter 36

MR DE COURCY TO LADY SUSAN

— Hotel

Why would you write to me? Why do you require particulars? But, since it must be so, I am obliged to declare that all the accounts of your misconduct, during the life and since the death of Mr Vernon, which had reached me, in common with the world in general, and gained my entire belief before I saw you, but which you, by the exertion of your perverted abilities, had made me resolved to disallow, have been unanswerably proved to me; nay more, I am assured that a connection, of which I had never before entertained a thought, has for some time existed, and still continues to exist, between you and the man whose family you robbed of its peace in return for the hospitality with which you were received into it; that you have corresponded with him ever since your leaving Langford – not with his wife, but with him – and that he now visits you every day. Can you, dare you deny it? and all this at the time when I was an encouraged, an accepted lover! From what have I not escaped! I have only to be grateful. Far from me be all complaint, every sigh of regret. My own folly had endangered me, my preservation I owe to the kindness, the integrity of another; but the unfortunate Mrs Mainwaring, whose agonies while she related the past seemed to threaten her reason, how is *she* to be consoled?

After such a discovery as this, you will scarcely affect further wonder at my meaning in bidding you adieu. My understanding is at length restored, and teaches me no less to abhor the artifices which had subdued me than to despise myself for the weakness on which their strength was founded.

R. De Courcy

Letter 37

LADY SUSAN TO MR DE COURCY

Upper Seymour Street

I am satisfied, and will trouble you no more when these few lines are dismissed.[360] The engagement which you were eager to form a fortnight ago is no longer compatible with your views, and I rejoice to find that the prudent advice of your parents has not been given in vain. Your restoration to peace will, I doubt not, speedily follow this act of filial obedience, and I flatter myself with the hope of surviving my share in this disappointment.

S. V.

Letter 38

MRS JOHNSON TO LADY SUSAN VERNON

Edward Street

I am grieved, though I cannot be astonished at your rupture with Mr De Courcy; he has just informed Mr Johnson of it by letter. He leaves London, he says, today. Be assured that I partake in all your feelings, and do not be angry if I say that our intercourse, even by letter, must soon be given up. It makes me miserable, but Mr Johnson vows that if I persist in the connection, he will settle in the country for the rest of his life – and you know it is impossible to submit to such an extremity while any other alternative remains.

You have heard of course that the Mainwarings are to part, and I am afraid Mrs M. will come home to us again; but she is still so fond of her husband and frets so much about him that perhaps she may not live long.

Miss Mainwaring is just come to town to be with her aunt, and they say that she declares she will have Sir James Martin before she leaves London again. If I were you, I would certainly get him myself. I had almost forgot to give you my opinion of Mr De Courcy; I am really delighted with him; he is full as handsome, I think, as Mainwaring, and with such an open, good-humoured countenance that one cannot help loving him at first sight. Mr Johnson and he are the greatest friends in the world. Adieu, my dearest Susan, I wish matters did not go so perversely. That unlucky visit to Langford! but I dare say you did all for the best, and there is no defying destiny.

Your sincerely attached   ALICIA

Letter 39

LADY SUSAN TO MRS JOHNSON

Upper Seymour Street

MY DEAR ALICIA – I yield to the necessity which parts us. Under such circumstances you could not act otherwise. Our friendship cannot be impaired by it, and in happier times, when your situation is as independent as mine, it will unite us again in the same intimacy as ever. For this I shall impatiently wait, and meanwhile can safely assure you that I never was more at ease, or better satisfied with myself and everything about me, than at the present hour. Your husband I abhor, Reginald I despise, and I am secure of never seeing either again. Have I not reason to rejoice? Mainwaring is more devoted to me than ever; and were we at liberty, I doubt if I could resist even matrimony offered by *him*. This event, if his wife live with you, it may be in your power to hasten. The violence of her feelings, which must wear her out, may be easily kept in irritation. I rely on your friendship for this. I am now satisfied that I never could have brought myself to marry Reginald, and am equally determined that Frederica never shall. Tomorrow, I shall fetch her from Churchhill, and let Maria Mainwaring tremble for the consequence. Frederica shall be Sir James's wife before she quits my house, and she may whimper, and the Vernons may storm, I regard them not. I am tired of submitting my will to the caprices of others; of resigning my own judgement in deference to those to whom I owe no duty, and for whom I feel no respect. I have given up too much, have been too easily worked on, but Frederica shall now feel the difference.

Adieu, dearest of friends; may the next gouty attack be more favourable! and may you always regard me as unalterably yours,

S. VERNON

Letter 40

LADY DE COURCY TO MRS VERNON

Parklands

MY DEAR CATHERINE – I have charming news for you, and if I had not sent off my letter this morning you might have been spared the vexation of knowing of Reginald's being gone to London, for he is returned. Reginald is returned, not to ask our consent to his marrying Lady Susan, but to tell us they are parted for ever. He has been only an hour in the house, and I have not been able to learn particulars, for he is so very low that I have not the heart to ask questions, but I hope we shall soon know all. This is the most joyful hour he has ever given us since the day of his birth. Nothing is wanting but to have you here, and it is our particular wish and entreaty that you will come to us as soon as you can. You have owed us a visit many long weeks; I hope nothing will make it inconvenient to Mr Vernon; and pray bring all my grandchildren; and your dear niece is included, of course; I long to see her. It has been a sad, heavy winter hitherto, without Reginald, and seeing nobody from Churchhill. I never found the season so dreary before; but this happy meeting will make us young again. Frederica runs much in my thoughts, and when Reginald has recovered his usual good spirits (as I trust he soon will), we will try to rob him of his heart once more, and I am full of hopes of seeing their hands joined at no great distance.

Your affectionate mother,

C. DE COURCY

MRS VERNON TO LADY DE COURCY

Churchhill

MY DEAR MOTHER – Your letter has surprised me beyond measure! Can it be true that they are really separated – and for ever? I should be overjoyed if I dared depend on it, but after all that I have seen, how can one be secure? And Reginald really with you! My surprise is the greater because on Wednesday, the very day of his coming to Parklands, we had a most unexpected and unwelcome visit from Lady Susan, looking all cheerfulness and good-humour, and seeming more as if she were to marry him when she got back to town than as if parted from him for ever. She stayed nearly two hours, was as affectionate and agreeable as ever, and not a syllable, not a hint was dropped of any disagreement or coolness between them. I asked her whether she had seen my brother since his arrival in town; not, as you may suppose, with any doubt of the fact, but merely to see how she looked. She immediately answered, without any embarrassment, that he had been kind enough to call on her on Monday; but she believed he had already returned home, which I was very far from crediting.

Your kind invitation is accepted by us with pleasure, and on Thursday next, we and our little ones will be with you. Pray heaven, Reginald may not be in town again by that time!

I wish we could bring dear Frederica too, but I am sorry to say that her mother's errand hither was to fetch her away; and, miserable as it made the poor girl, it was impossible to detain her. I was thoroughly unwilling to let her go, and so was her uncle; and all that could be urged, we *did* urge; but Lady Susan declared that as she was now about to fix herself in London for several months, she could not be easy if her daughter were not with her, for masters, &c. Her manner, to be sure, was very kind and proper, and Mr Vernon believes that Frederica will now be treated with affection. I wish I could think so too.

The poor girl's heart was almost broke at taking leave of us. I charged her to write to me very often, and to remember that if she were in any distress we should be always her friends. I took care to see her alone, that I might say all this, and I hope made her a little more comfortable; but I shall not be easy till I can go to town and judge of her situation myself.

I wish there were a better prospect than now appears of the match which the conclusion of your letter declares your expectations of. At present, it is not very likely.

Yours ever, &c.,

C. VERNON

Conclusion

This correspondence, by a meeting between some of the parties, and a separation between the others, could not, to the great detriment of the Post Office revenue, be continued any longer. Very little assistance to the State[361] could be derived from the epistolary intercourse of Mrs Vernon and her niece, for the former soon perceived, by the style of Frederica's letters, that they were written under her mother's inspection, and therefore, deferring all particular enquiry till she could make it personally in London, ceased writing minutely or often.

Having learnt enough, in the meanwhile, from her open-hearted brother, of what had passed between him and Lady Susan to sink the latter lower than ever in her opinion, she was proportionably more anxious to get Frederica removed from such a mother, and placed under her own care; and, though with little hope of success, was resolved to leave nothing unattempted that might offer a chance of obtaining her sister-in-law's consent to it. Her anxiety on the subject made her press for an early visit to London; and Mr Vernon, who, as it must already have appeared, lived only to do whatever he was desired, soon found some accommodating business to call him thither. With a heart full of the matter, Mrs Vernon waited on Lady Susan shortly after her arrival in town, and was met with such an easy and cheerful affection as made her almost turn from her with horror. No remembrance of Reginald, no consciousness of guilt, gave one look of embarrassment; she was in excellent spirits, and seemed eager to show at once by every possible attention to her brother and sister her sense of their kindness, and her pleasure in their society.

Frederica was no more altered than Lady Susan; the same restrained manners, the same timid look in the presence of her mother as heretofore, assured her aunt of her situation being uncomfortable, and confirmed her in the plan of altering it. No unkindness, however, on the part of Lady Susan appeared. Persecution on the subject of Sir James was entirely at an end; his name merely mentioned to say that he was not in London; and indeed, in all her conversation, she was solicitous only for the welfare and improvement of her daughter, acknowledging, in terms of grateful delight, that Frederica was now growing every day more and more what a parent could desire.

Mrs Vernon, surprised and incredulous, knew not what to suspect, and, without any change in her own views, only feared greater difficulty in accomplishing them. The first hope of anything better was derived from Lady Susan's asking her whether she thought Frederica looked quite as well as she had done at Churchhill, as she must confess herself to have sometimes an anxious doubt of London's perfectly agreeing with her.

Mrs Vernon, encouraging the doubt, directly proposed her niece's returning with them into the country. Lady Susan was unable to express her sense of such kindness, yet knew not, from a variety of reasons, how to part with her daughter; and as, though her own plans were not yet wholly fixed, she trusted it would ere long be in her power to take Frederica into the country herself, concluded by declining entirely to profit by such unexampled attention. Mrs Vernon persevered, however, in the offer of it, and though Lady Susan continued to resist, her resistance in the course of a few days seemed somewhat less formidable.

The lucky alarm of an influenza decided what might not have been decided quite so soon. Lady Susan's maternal fears were then too much awakened for her to think of anything but Frederica's removal from the risk of infection; above all disorders in the world she most dreaded the influenza for her daughter's constitution! Frederica returned to Churchhill with her uncle and aunt; and three weeks afterwards, Lady Susan announced her marriage to Sir James Martin.

Mrs Vernon was then convinced of what she had only suspected before, that she might have spared herself all the trouble of urging a removal which Lady Susan had doubtless resolved on from the first. Frederica's visit was nominally for six weeks, but her mother, though inviting her to return in one or two affectionate letters, was very ready to oblige the whole party by consenting to a prolongation of her stay, and in the course of two months ceased to write of her absence, and in the course of two more, to write to her at all.

Frederica was therefore fixed in the family of her uncle and aunt, till such time as Reginald De Courcy could be talked, flattered and finessed[362] into an affection for her – which, allowing leisure for the conquest of his attachment to her mother, for his abjuring all future attachments and detesting the sex, might be reasonably looked for in the course of a twelvemonth. Three months might have done it in general, but Reginald's feelings were no less lasting than lively.

Whether Lady Susan was or was not happy in her second choice, I do not see how it can ever be ascertained; for who would take her assurance of it on either side of the question? The world must judge from probabilities; she had nothing against her but her husband and her conscience.

Sir James may seem to have drawn a harder lot than mere folly merited; I leave him, therefore, to all the pity that anybody can give him. For myself, I confess that *I* can pity only Miss Mainwaring, who, coming to town and putting herself to an expense in clothes, which impoverished her for two years, on purpose to secure him, was defrauded of her due by a woman ten years older than herself.

The Watsons

T HE FIRST WINTER ASSEMBLY[363] in the town of D— in Surrey[364] was to be held on Tuesday, October 13th, and it was generally expected to be a very good one. A long list of county families was confidently run over as sure of attending, and sanguine hopes were entertained that the Osbornes themselves would be there. The Edwardses' invitation to the Watsons followed, of course. The Edwardses were people of fortune, who lived in the town and kept their coach. The Watsons inhabited a village about three miles distant, were poor, and had no close carriage;[365] and ever since there had been balls in the place, the former were accustomed to invite the latter to dress, dine, and sleep at their house on every monthly return throughout the winter. On the present occasion, as only two of Mr Watson's children were at home, and one was always necessary as companion to himself, for he was sickly and had lost his wife, one only could profit by the kindness of their friends. Miss Emma Watson, who was very recently returned to her family from the care of an aunt who had brought her up, was to make her first public appearance in the neighbourhood, and her eldest sister, whose delight in a ball was not lessened by a ten years' enjoyment, had some merit in cheerfully undertaking to drive her and all her finery in the old chair to D— on the important morning.

As they splashed along the dirty lane, Miss Watson thus instructed and cautioned her inexperienced sister: 'I dare say it will be a very good ball, and among so many officers you will hardly want partners. You will find Mrs Edwards's maid very willing to help you, and I would advise you to ask Mary Edwards's opinion if you are at all at a loss, for she has very good taste. If Mr Edwards does not lose his money at cards, you will stay as late as you can wish for; if he does, he will hurry you home perhaps – but you are sure of some comfortable soup. I hope you will be in good looks. I should not be surprised if you were to be thought one of the prettiest girls in the room; there is a great deal in novelty. Perhaps Tom Musgrave may take notice of you; but I would advise you by all means not to give him any encouragement. He generally pays attention to every new girl; but he is a great flirt, and never means anything serious.'

'I think I have heard you speak of him before,' said Emma; 'who is he?' 'A young man of very good fortune, quite independent, and remarkably agreeable – a universal favourite wherever he goes. Most of the girls hereabouts are in love with him, or have been. I believe I am the only one among them that have escaped with a whole heart; and yet I was the first he paid attention to when he came into this country six years ago; and very great attention did he pay me. Some people say that he has never seemed to like any girl so well since, though he is always behaving in a particular way to one or another.'

'And how came *your* heart to be the only cold one?' said Emma, smiling.

'There was a reason for that,' replied Miss Watson, changing colour – 'I have not been very well used among them, Emma. I hope you will have better luck.'

'Dear sister, I beg your pardon if I have unthinkingly given you pain.'

'When first we knew Tom Musgrave,' continued Miss Watson, without seeming to hear her, 'I was very much attached to a young man of the name of Purvis, a particular friend of Robert's, who used to be with us a great deal. Everybody thought it would have been a match.'

A sigh accompanied these words, which Emma respected in silence; but her sister after a short pause went on.

'You will naturally ask why it did not take place, and why he is married to another woman, while I am still single. But you must ask her, not me – you must ask Penelope. Yes, Emma, Penelope was at the bottom of it all. She thinks everything fair for a husband. I trusted her; she set him against me, with a view of gaining him herself, and it ended in his discontinuing his visits, and soon after marrying somebody else. Penelope makes light of her conduct, but *I* think such treachery very bad. It has been the ruin of my happiness. I shall never love any man as I loved Purvis. I do not think Tom Musgrave should be named with him in the same day.'

'You quite shock me by what you say of Penelope,' said Emma. 'Could a sister do such a thing? Rivalry, treachery between sisters! I shall be afraid of being acquainted with her. But I hope it was not so; appearances were against her.'

'You do not know Penelope. There is nothing she would not do to get married. She would as good as tell you so herself. Do not trust her with any secrets of your own, take warning by me, do not trust her; she has her good qualities, but she has no faith, no honour, no scruples, if she can promote her own advantage. I wish with all my heart she was well married. I declare I had rather have her well married than myself.'

'Than yourself! yes, I can suppose so. A heart wounded like yours can have little inclination for matrimony.'

'Not much indeed – but you know we must marry. I could do very well single for my own part; a little company, and a pleasant ball now and then, would be enough for me, if one could be young for ever; but my father cannot provide for us, and it is very bad to grow old and be poor and laughed at.[366] I have lost Purvis, it is true; but very few people marry their first loves. I should not refuse a man because he was not Purvis. Not that I can ever quite forgive Penelope.'

Emma shook her head in acquiescence.

'Penelope, however, has had her troubles,' continued Miss Watson. 'She was sadly disappointed in Tom Musgrave, who afterwards transferred his attentions from me to her, and whom she was very fond of; but he never means anything serious, and when he had trifled with her long enough, he began to slight her for Margaret, and poor Penelope was very wretched. And since then she has been trying to make some match at Chichester – she won't tell us with whom; but I believe it is a rich old Dr Harding, uncle to the friend she goes to see; and she has taken a vast deal of trouble about him, and given up a great deal of time to no purpose as yet. When she went away the other day, she said it should be the last time. I suppose you did not know what her particular business was at Chichester, nor guess at the object which could take her away from Stanton[367] just as you were coming home after so many years' absence?'

'No indeed, I had not the smallest suspicion of it. I considered her engagement to Mrs Shaw just at that time as very unfortunate for me. I had hoped to find all my sisters at home, to be able to make an immediate friend of each.'

'I suspect the doctor to have had an attack of the asthma, and that she was hurried away on that account. The Shaws are quite on her side – at least, I believe so; but she tells me nothing. She professes to keep her own counsel; she says, and truly enough, that "too many cooks spoil the broth".'

'I am sorry for her anxieties,' said Emma; 'but I do not like her plans or her opinions. I shall be afraid of her. She must have too masculine and bold a temper. To be so bent on marriage, to pursue a man merely for the sake of situation, is a sort of thing that shocks me; I cannot understand it. Poverty is a great evil; but to a woman of education and feeling it ought not, it cannot be the greatest. I would rather be a teacher at a school[368] (and I can think of nothing worse) than marry a man I did not like.'

'I would rather do anything than be a teacher at a school,' said her sister. '*I* have been at school, Emma, and know what a life they lead; *you* never have. I should not like marrying a disagreeable man any more than yourself; but I do not think there *are* many very disagreeable men;

I think I could like any good-humoured man with a comfortable income. I suppose my aunt brought you up to be rather refined.'

'Indeed I do not know. My conduct must tell you how I have been brought up. I am no judge of it myself. I cannot compare my aunt's method with any other person's, because I know no other.'

'But I can see in a great many things that you are very refined. I have observed it ever since you came home, and I am afraid it will not be for your happiness. Penelope will laugh at you very much.'

'*That* will not be for my happiness, I am sure. If my opinions are wrong, I must correct them; if they are above my situation, I must endeavour to conceal them; but I doubt whether ridicule – Has Penelope much wit?'

'Yes; she has great spirits, and never cares what she says.'

'Margaret is more gentle, I imagine?'

'Yes; especially in company. She is all gentleness and mildness when anybody is by; but she is a little fretful and perverse among ourselves. Poor creature! She is possessed with the notion of Tom Musgrave's being more seriously in love with her than he ever was with anybody else, and is always expecting him to come to the point. This is the second time within this twelvemonth that she has gone to spend a month with Robert and Jane on purpose to egg him on by her absence; but I am sure she is mistaken, and that he will no more follow her to Croydon now than he did last March. He will never marry unless he can marry somebody very great – Miss Osborne, perhaps, or something in that style.'

'Your account of this Tom Musgrave, Elizabeth, gives me very little inclination for his acquaintance.'

'You are afraid of him; I do not wonder at you.'

'No, indeed; I dislike and despise him.'

'Dislike and despise Tom Musgrave! No, *that* you never can. I defy you not to be delighted with him if he takes notice of you. I hope he will dance with you; and I dare say he will, unless the Osbornes come with a large party, and then he will not speak to anybody else.'

'He seems to have most engaging manners!' said Emma. 'Well, we shall see how irresistible Mr Tom Musgrave and I find each other. I suppose I shall know him as soon as I enter the ballroom; he *must* carry some of his charm in his face.'

'You will not find him in the ballroom, I can tell you; you will go early, that Mrs Edwards may get a good place by the fire, and he never comes till late; if the Osbornes are coming, he will wait in the passage and come in with them. I should like to look in upon you, Emma. If it was but a good day with my father, I would wrap myself up, and James should drive me over as soon as I had made tea for him; and I should be with you by the time the dancing began.'

'What! Would you come late at night in this chair?'

'To be sure I would. There, I said you were very refined, and *that*'s an instance of it.'

Emma for a moment made no answer. At last she said – 'I wish, Elizabeth, you had not made a point of my going to this ball; I wish you were going instead of me. Your pleasure would be greater than mine. I am a stranger here, and know nobody but the Edwardses; my enjoyment, therefore, must be very doubtful. Yours, among all your acquaintance, would be certain. It is not too late to change. Very little apology could be requisite to the Edwardses, who must be more glad of your company than of mine, and I should most readily return to my father; and should not be at all afraid to drive this quiet old creature home. Your clothes I would undertake to find means of sending to you.'

'My dearest Emma,' cried Elizabeth, warmly, 'do you think I would do such a thing? Not for the universe! But I shall never forget your good nature in proposing it. You must have a sweet temper indeed! I never met with anything like it! And would you really give up the ball that I might be able to go to it? Believe me, Emma, I am not so selfish as that comes to. No; though I am nine years older than you are, I would not be the means of keeping you from being seen. You are very pretty, and it would be very hard that you should not have as fair a chance as we have all had to make your fortune. No, Emma, whoever stays at home this winter, it shan't be you. I am sure I should never have forgiven the person who kept me from a ball at nineteen.'

Emma expressed her gratitude, and for a few minutes they jogged on in silence. Elizabeth first spoke: 'You will take notice who Mary Edwards dances with?'

'I will remember her partners, if I can; but you know they will be all strangers to me.'

'Only observe whether she dances with Captain Hunter more than once – I have my fears in that quarter. Not that her father or mother like officers; but if she does, you know, it is all over with poor Sam. And I have promised to write him word whom she dances with.'

'Is Sam attached to Miss Edwards?'

'Did not you know *that*?'

'How should I know it? How should I know in Shropshire what is passing of that nature in Surrey? It is not likely that circumstances of such delicacy should have made any part of the scanty communication which passed between you and me for the last fourteen years.'

'I wonder I never mentioned it when I wrote. Since you have been at home, I have been so busy with my poor father and our great wash[369] that I have had no leisure to tell you anything; but, indeed, I concluded you knew it all. He has been very much in love with her these two years, and it is a great disappointment to him that he cannot always get away to our balls; but Mr Curtis won't often spare him, and just now it is a sickly time at Guildford.'

'Do you suppose Miss Edwards inclined to like him?'

'I am afraid not: you know she is an only child, and will have at least ten thousand pounds.'[370]

'But still she may like our brother.'

'Oh, no! The Edwardses look much higher. Her father and mother would never consent to it. Sam is only a surgeon,[371] you know. Sometimes I think she does like him. But Mary Edwards is rather prim and reserved; I do not always know what she would be at.'

'Unless Sam feels on sure grounds with the lady herself, it seems a pity to me that he should be encouraged to think of her at all.'

'A young man must think of somebody,' said Elizabeth, 'and why should not he be as lucky as Robert, who has got a good wife and six thousand pounds?'[372]

'We must not all expect to be individually lucky,' replied Emma. 'The luck of one member of a family is luck to all.'

'Mine is all to come, I am sure,' said Elizabeth, giving another sigh to the remembrance of Purvis. 'I have been unlucky enough; and I cannot say much for you, as my aunt married again so foolishly. Well, you will have a good ball, I dare say. The next turning will bring us to the turnpike: you may see the church tower over the hedge, and the White Hart is close by it. I shall long to know what you think of Tom Musgrave.'

Such were the last audible sounds of Miss Watson's voice, before they passed through the turnpike-gate,[373] and entered on the pitching[374] of the town, the jumbling and noise of which made further conversation most thoroughly undesirable. The old mare trotted heavily on, wanting no direction of the reins to take the right turning, and making only one blunder, in proposing to stop at the milliner's, before she drew up towards Mr Edwards's door. Mr Edwards lived in the best house in the street, and the best in the place, if Mr Tomlinson, the banker, might be indulged in calling his newly erected house at the end of the town, with a shrubbery and sweep, in the country.

Mr Edwards's house was higher than most of its neighbours, with four windows on each side the door, the windows guarded by posts and chain,[375] and the door approached by a flight of stone steps.

'Here we are,' said Elizabeth, as the carriage ceased moving, 'safely arrived, and by the market clock we have been only five-and-thirty minutes coming; which *I* think is doing pretty well, though it would be nothing for Penelope. Is not it a nice town? The Edwardses have a noble house, you see, and they live quite in style. The door will be opened by a man in livery, with a powdered head, I can tell you.'

Emma had seen the Edwardses only one morning at Stanton; they were therefore all but strangers to her; and though her spirits were by no means insensible to the expected joys of the evening, she felt a little uncomfortable in the thought of all that was to precede them. Her conversation with Elizabeth, too, giving her some very unpleasant feelings with respect to her own family, had made her more open to disagreeable impressions from any other cause, and increased her sense of the awkwardness of rushing into intimacy on so slight an acquaintance.

There was nothing in the manner of Mrs or Miss Edwards to give immediate change to these ideas. The mother, though a very friendly woman, had a reserved air, and a great deal of formal civility; and the daughter, a genteel-looking girl of twenty-two, with her hair in papers,[376] seemed very naturally to have caught something of the style of the mother who had brought her up. Emma was soon left to know what they could be by Elizabeth's being obliged to hurry away; and some very languid remarks on the probable brilliancy of the ball were all that broke, at intervals, a silence of half an hour, before they were joined by the master of the house. Mr Edwards had a much easier and more communicative air than the ladies of the family; he was fresh from the street, and he came ready to tell whatever might interest.

After a cordial reception of Emma, he turned to his daughter with – 'Well, Mary, I bring you good news: the Osbornes will certainly be at the ball tonight. Horses for two carriages are ordered from the White Hart to be at Osborne Castle by nine.'

'I am glad of it,' observed Mrs Edwards, 'because their coming gives a credit to our assembly. The Osbornes being known to have been at the first ball, will dispose a great many people to attend the second. It is more than they deserve; for in fact, they add nothing to the pleasure of the evening: they come so late and go so early; but great people have always their charm.'

Mr Edwards proceeded to relate every other little article of news which his morning's lounge[377] had supplied him with, and they chatted with greater briskness, till Mrs Edwards's moment for dressing arrived, and the young ladies were carefully recommended to lose no time. Emma was shown to a very comfortable apartment, and as soon as Mrs

Edwards's civilities could leave her to herself, the happy occupation, the first bliss of a ball, began. The girls, dressing in some measure together, grew unavoidably better acquainted. Emma found in Miss Edwards the show of good sense, a modest unpretending mind, and a great wish of obliging; and when they returned to the parlour where Mrs Edwards was sitting, respectably attired in one of the two satin gowns which went through the winter and a new cap from the milliner's, they entered it with much easier feelings and more natural smiles than they had taken away. Their dress was now to be examined: Mrs Edwards acknowledged herself too old-fashioned to approve of every modern extravagance, however sanctioned, and though complacently viewing her daughter's good looks, would give but a qualified admiration; and Mr Edwards, not less satisfied with Mary, paid some compliments of good-humoured gallantry to Emma at her expense. The discussion led to more intimate remarks, and Miss Edwards gently asked Emma if she were not often reckoned very like her youngest brother. Emma thought she could perceive a faint blush accompany the question, and there seemed something still more suspicious in the manner in which Mr Edwards took up the subject.

'You are paying Miss Emma no great compliment, I think, Mary,' said he, hastily. 'Mr Sam Watson is a very good sort of young man, and I dare say a very clever surgeon; but his complexion has been rather too much exposed to all weathers to make a likeness to him very flattering.'

Mary apologised, in some confusion – 'She had not thought a strong likeness at all incompatible with very different degrees of beauty. There might be resemblance in countenance, and the complexion and even the features be very unlike.'

'I know nothing of my brother's beauty,' said Emma, 'for I have not seen him since he was seven years old; but my father reckons us alike.'

'Mr Watson!' cried Mr Edwards; 'well, you astonish me. There is not the least likeness in the world; your brother's eyes are grey, yours are brown; he has a long face and a wide mouth. My dear, do *you* perceive the least resemblance?'

'Not the least. Miss Emma Watson puts me very much in mind of her eldest sister, and sometimes I see a look of Miss Penelope, and once or twice there has been a glance of Mr Robert, but I cannot perceive any likeness to Mr Samuel.'

'I see the likeness between her and Miss Watson,'[378] replied Mr Edwards, 'very strongly, but I am not sensible of the others. I do not much think she is like any of the family *but* Miss Watson; but I am very sure there is no resemblance between her and Sam.'

This matter was settled, and they went to dinner.

'Your father, Miss Emma, is one of my oldest friends,' said Mr Edwards, as he helped her to wine, when they were drawn round the fire to enjoy their dessert. 'We must drink to his better health. It is a great concern to me, I assure you, that he should be such an invalid. I know nobody who likes a game of cards, in a social way, better than he does, and very few people that play a fairer rubber.[379] It is a thousand pities that he should be so deprived of the pleasure. For now we have a quiet little Whist Club, that meets three times a week at the White Hart; and if he could but have his health, how much he would enjoy it!'

'I dare say he would, sir; and I wish, with all my heart, he were equal to it.'

'Your club would be better fitted for an invalid,' said Mrs Edwards, 'if you did not keep it up so late.'

This was an old grievance.

'So late, my dear! What are you talking of?' cried the husband, with sturdy pleasantry. 'We are always at home before midnight. They would laugh at Osborne Castle to hear you call *that* late; they are but just rising from dinner at midnight.'

'That is nothing to the purpose,' retorted the lady, calmly. 'The Osbornes are to be no rule for us. You had better meet every night, and break up two hours sooner.'

So far the subject was very often carried; but Mr and Mrs Edwards were so wise as never to pass that point; and Mr Edwards now turned to something else. He had lived long enough in the idleness of a town to become a little of a gossip, and having some anxiety to know more of the circumstances of his young guest than had yet reached him, he began with – 'I think, Miss Emma, I remember your aunt very well, about thirty years ago; I am pretty sure I danced with her in the old rooms at Bath,[380] the year before I married. She was a very fine woman then; but like other people, I suppose, she is grown somewhat older since that time. I hope she is likely to be happy in her second choice.'

'I hope so; I believe so, sir,' said Emma, in some agitation.

'Mr Turner had not been dead a great while, I think?'

'About two years, sir.'

'I forget what her name is now.'

'O'Brien.'

'Irish! ah, I remember; and she is gone to settle in Ireland. I do not wonder that you should not wish to go with her into *that* country, Miss Emma; but it must be a great deprivation to her, poor lady, after bringing you up like a child of her own.'

'I was not so ungrateful, sir,' said Emma, warmly, 'as to wish to be anywhere but with her. It did not suit them, it did not suit Captain O'Brien that I should be of the party.'

'Captain!' repeated Mrs Edwards. 'The gentleman is in the army then?'

'Yes, ma'am.'

'Aye, there is nothing like your officers for captivating the ladies, young or old. There is no resisting a cockade,[381] my dear.'

'I hope there is,' said Mrs Edwards, gravely, with a quick glance at her daughter; and Emma had just recovered from her own perturbation in time to see a blush on Miss Edwards's cheek, and in remembering what Elizabeth had said of Captain Hunter, to wonder and waver between his influence and her brother's.

'Elderly ladies should be careful how they make a second choice,' observed Mr Edwards.

'Carefulness – discretion – should not be confined to elderly ladies or to a second choice,' added his wife. 'They are quite as necessary to young ladies in their first.'

'Rather more so, my dear,' replied he; 'because young ladies are likely to feel the effects of it longer. When an old lady plays the fool, it is not in the course of nature that she should suffer from it many years.'

Emma drew her hand across her eyes; and Mrs Edwards, on perceiving it, changed the subject to one of less anxiety to all.

With nothing to do but to expect the hour of setting off, the afternoon was long to the two young ladies; and though Miss Edwards was rather discomposed at the very early hour which her mother always fixed for going, that early hour itself was watched for with some eagerness.

The entrance of the tea things at seven o'clock was some relief; and luckily Mr and Mrs Edwards always drank a dish extraordinary[382] and ate an additional muffin when they were going to sit up late, which lengthened the ceremony almost to the wished-for moment.

At a little before eight, the Tomlinsons' carriage was heard to go by – which was the constant signal for Mrs Edwards to order hers to the door; and in a very few minutes the party were transported from the quiet and warmth of a snug parlour to the bustle, noise and draughts of air of the broad entrance passage of an inn. Mrs Edwards, carefully guarding her own dress, while she attended with yet greater solicitude to the proper security of her young charges' shoulders and throats, led the way up the wide staircase, while no sound of a ball but the first scrape of one violin blessed the ears of her followers; and Miss Edwards, on hazarding the anxious enquiry of whether there were many people come yet, was told by the waiter, as she knew she should, that 'Mr Tomlinson's family were in the room'.

In passing along a short gallery to the assembly-room, brilliant in lights before them, they were accosted by a young man in morning dress and boots,[383] who was standing in the doorway of a bedchamber, apparently on purpose to see them go by.

'Ah! Mrs Edwards, how do you do? How do you do, Miss Edwards?' he cried, with an easy air. 'You are determined to be in good time, I see, as usual. The candles are but this moment lit.'

'I like to get a good seat by the fire, you know, Mr Musgrave,' replied Mrs Edwards.

'I am this moment going to dress,' said he. 'I am waiting for my stupid fellow. We shall have a famous ball.[384] The Osbornes are certainly coming; you may depend upon *that*, for I was with Lord Osborne this morning.'

The party passed on. Mrs Edwards's satin gown swept along the clean floor of the ballroom to the fireplace at the upper end, where one party only were formally seated, while three or four officers were lounging together, passing in and out from the adjoining card-room. A very stiff meeting between these near neighbours ensued; and as soon as they were all duly placed again, Emma, in the low whisper which became the solemn scene, said to Miss Edwards – 'The gentleman we passed in the passage was Mr Musgrave, then; he is reckoned remarkably agreeable, I understand?'

Miss Edwards answered hesitatingly, 'Yes; he is very much liked by many people; but *we* are not very intimate.'

'He is rich, is not he?'

'He has about eight or nine hundred pounds a year,[385] I believe. He came into possession of it when he was very young, and my father and mother think it has given him rather an unsettled turn. He is no favourite with them.'

The cold and empty appearance of the room and the demure air of the small cluster of females at one end of it began soon to give way. The inspiriting sound of other carriages was heard, and continual accessions of portly chaperons[386] and strings of smartly-dressed girls were received, with now and then a fresh gentleman straggler, who, if not enough in love to station himself near any fair creature, seemed glad to escape into the card-room.

Among the increasing number of military men, one now made his way to Miss Edwards with an air of *empressement*[387] which decidedly said to her companion, 'I am Captain Hunter'; and Emma, who could not but watch her at such a moment, saw her looking rather distressed, but by no means displeased, and heard an engagement formed for the two first dances, which made her think her brother Sam's a hopeless case.

Emma, in the meanwhile, was not unobserved or unadmired herself. A new face, and a very pretty one, could not be slighted. Her name was whispered from one party to another; and no sooner had the signal been given by the orchestra's striking up a favourite air, which seemed to call the young to their duty and people the centre of the room, than she found herself engaged to dance with a brother officer, introduced by Captain Hunter.

Emma Watson was not more than of the middle height, well made and plump, with an air of healthy vigour. Her skin was very brown, but clear, smooth, and glowing, which, with a lively eye, a sweet smile, and an open countenance, gave beauty to attract and expression to make that beauty improve on acquaintance. Having no reason to be dissatisfied with her partner, the evening began very pleasantly to her, and her feelings perfectly coincided with the reiterated observation of others, that it was an excellent ball. The two first dances were not quite over when the returning sound of carriages after a long interruption called general notice, and 'The Osbornes are coming! The Osbornes are coming!' was repeated round the room. After some minutes of extraordinary bustle without and watchful curiosity within, the important party, preceded by the attentive master of the inn to open a door which was never shut, made their appearance. They consisted of Lady Osborne; her son, Lord Osborne; her daughter, Miss Osborne; Miss Carr, her daughter's friend; Mr Howard, formerly tutor to Lord Osborne, now clergyman of the parish in which the castle stood; Mrs Blake, a widow sister who lived with him; her son, a fine boy of ten years old; and Mr Tom Musgrave, who probably, imprisoned within his own room, had been listening in bitter impatience to the sound of the music for the last half-hour. In their progress up the room, they paused almost immediately behind Emma to receive the compliments of some acquaintance; and she heard Lady Osborne observe that they had made a point of coming early for the gratification of Mrs Blake's little boy, who was uncommonly fond of dancing. Emma looked at them all as they passed, but chiefly and with most interest on Tom Musgrave, who was certainly a genteel, good-looking young man. Of the females, Lady Osborne had by much the finest person; though nearly fifty, she was very handsome, and had all the dignity of rank.

Lord Osborne was a very fine young man; but there was an air of coldness, of carelessness, even of awkwardness about him, which seemed to speak him out of his element in a ballroom. He came, in fact, only because it was judged expedient for him to please the borough;[388] he was not fond of women's company, and he never danced. Mr Howard was an agreeable-looking man, a little more than thirty.

At the conclusion of the two dances, Emma found herself, she knew not how, seated among the Osborne set; and she was immediately struck with the fine countenance and animated gestures of the little boy, as he was standing before his mother, wondering when they should begin.

'You will not be surprised at Charles's impatience,' said Mrs Blake, a lively, pleasant-looking little woman of five- or six-and-thirty, to a lady who was standing near her, 'when you know what a partner he is to have. Miss Osborne has been so very kind as to promise to dance the two first dances with him.'

'Oh, yes! we have been engaged this week,' cried the boy, 'and we are to dance down every couple.'[389]

On the other side of Emma, Miss Osborne, Miss Carr, and a party of young men were standing engaged in very lively consultation; and soon afterwards she saw the smartest officer of the set walking off to the orchestra to order the dance, while Miss Osborne, passing before her to her little expecting partner, hastily said: 'Charles, I beg your pardon for not keeping my engagement, but I am going to dance these two dances with Colonel Beresford. I know you will excuse me, and I will certainly dance with you after tea'; and without staying for an answer, she turned again to Miss Carr, and in another minute was led by Colonel Beresford to begin the set.[390] If the poor little boy's face had in its happiness been interesting[391] to Emma, it was infinitely more so under this sudden reverse; he stood the picture of disappointment, with crimsoned cheeks, quivering lips, and eyes bent on the floor. His mother, stifling her own mortification, tried to soothe his with the prospect of Miss Osborne's second promise; but though he contrived to utter, with an effort of boyish bravery, 'Oh, I do not mind it!' it was very evident, by the unceasing agitation of his features, that he minded it as much as ever.

Emma did not think or reflect; she felt and acted. 'I shall be very happy to dance with you, sir, if you like it,' said she, holding out her hand with the most unaffected good-humour. The boy, in one moment restored to all his first delight, looked joyfully at his mother; and stepping forwards with an honest and simple, 'Thank you, ma'am,' was instantly ready to attend his new acquaintance. The thankfulness of Mrs Blake was more diffuse; with a look most expressive of unexpected pleasure and lively gratitude, she turned to her neighbour with repeated and fervent acknowledgements of so great and condescending a kindness to her boy. Emma, with perfect truth, could assure her that she could not be giving greater pleasure than she felt herself; and Charles being provided with his gloves and charged to keep them on, they joined the set which was now rapidly forming, with nearly equal complacency. It was a partnership which could not be noticed without surprise. It gained her a broad stare from Miss Osborne and Miss Carr as they passed her in the dance. 'Upon my word, Charles, you are in luck,' said the former, as she turned him; 'you have got a better partner than me'; to which the happy Charles answered, 'Yes.'

Tom Musgrave, who was dancing with Miss Carr, gave her many inquisitive glances; and after a time Lord Osborne himself came, and under pretence of talking to Charles, stood to look at his partner. Though rather distressed by such observation, Emma could not repent what she had done, so happy had it made both the boy and his mother; the latter of whom was continually making opportunities of addressing her with the warmest civility. Her little partner, she found, though bent chiefly on dancing, was not unwilling to speak when her questions or remarks gave him anything to say; and she learnt, by a sort of inevitable enquiry, that he had two brothers and a sister, that they and their mama all lived with his uncle at Wickstead,[392] that his uncle taught him Latin, that he was very fond of riding, and had a horse of his own given him by Lord Osborne; and that he had been out once already with Lord Osborne's hounds.

At the end of these dances,[393] Emma found they were to drink tea; Miss Edwards gave her a caution to be at hand, in a manner which convinced her of Mrs Edwards's holding it very important to have them both close to her when she moved into the tea-room; and Emma was accordingly on the alert to gain her proper station. It was always the pleasure of the company to have a little bustle and crowd when they adjourned for refreshment. The tea-room was a small room within the card-room; and in passing through the latter, where the passage was straitened by tables, Mrs Edwards and her party were for a few moments hemmed in. It happened close by Lady Osborne's cassino[394] table; Mr Howard, who belonged to it, spoke to his nephew; and Emma, on perceiving herself the object of attention both to Lady Osborne and him, had just turned away her eyes in time to avoid seeming to hear her young companion delightedly whisper aloud, 'Oh, uncle! do look at my partner; she is so pretty!' As they were immediately in motion again, however, Charles was hurried off without being able to receive his uncle's suffrage.[395] On entering the tea-room, in which two long tables were prepared, Lord Osborne was to be seen quite alone at the end of one, as if retreating as far as he could from the ball to enjoy his own thoughts and gape[396] without restraint. Charles instantly pointed him out to Emma. 'There's Lord Osborne; let you and I go and sit by him.'

'No, no,' said Emma, laughing; 'you must sit with my friends.'[397]

Charles was now free enough to hazard a few questions in his turn. 'What o'clock is it?'

'Eleven.'

'Eleven! and I am not at all sleepy. Mama said I should be asleep before ten. Do you think Miss Osborne will keep her word with me, when tea is over?'

'Oh, yes! I suppose so'; though she felt that she had no better reason to give than that Miss Osborne had *not* kept it before.

'When shall you come to Osborne Castle?'

'Never, probably. I am not acquainted with the family.'

'But you may come to Wickstead and see mama, and she can take you to the castle. There is a monstrous curious stuffed fox there, and a badger; anybody would think they were alive. It is a pity you should not see them.'

On rising from tea, there was again a scramble for the pleasure of being first out of the room, which happened to be increased by one or two of the card-parties having just broken up, and the players being disposed to move exactly the different way. Among these was Mr Howard, his sister leaning on his arm; and no sooner were they within reach of Emma, than Mrs Blake, calling her notice by a friendly touch, said, 'Your goodness to Charles, my dear Miss Watson, brings all his family upon you. Give me leave to introduce my brother, Mr Howard.' Emma curtsied, the gentleman bowed, made a hasty request for the honour of her hand in the two next dances, to which as hasty an affirmative was given, and they were immediately impelled in opposite directions. Emma was very well pleased with the circumstance; there was a quietly cheerful, gentlemanlike air in Mr Howard which suited her; and in a few minutes afterwards the value of her engagement increased, when, as she was sitting in the card-room, somewhat screened by a door, she heard Lord Osborne, who was lounging on a vacant table near her, call Tom Musgrave towards him and say, 'Why do not you dance with that beautiful Emma Watson? I want you to dance with her, and I will come and stand by you.'

'I was determining on it this very moment, my lord; I'll be introduced and dance with her directly.'

'Aye, do; and if you find she does not want much talking to, you may introduce me by and by.'

'Very well, my lord; if she is like her sisters, she will only want to be listened to. I will go this moment. I shall find her in the tea-room. That stiff old Mrs Edwards has never done tea.'

Away he went, Lord Osborne after him; and Emma lost no time in hurrying from her corner exactly the other way, forgetting in her haste that she left Mrs Edwards behind.

'We had quite lost you,' said Mrs Edwards, who followed her with Mary in less than five minutes. 'If you prefer this room to the other, there is no reason why you should not be here; but we had better all be together.'

Emma was saved the trouble of apologising by their being joined at that moment by Tom Musgrave, who requesting Mrs Edwards aloud to do him the honour of presenting him[398] to Miss Emma Watson, left that good lady without any choice in the business but that of testifying by the coldness of her manner that she did it unwillingly. The honour of dancing with her was solicited without loss of time – and Emma, however she might like to be thought a beautiful girl by lord or commoner, was so little disposed to favour Tom Musgrave himself that she had considerable satisfaction in avowing her previous engagement. He was evidently surprised and discomposed. The style of her last partner had probably led him to believe her not over-powered with applications.

'My little friend Charles Blake,' he cried, 'must not expect to engross you the whole evening. We can never suffer this. It is against the rules of the assembly, and I am sure it will never be patronised[399] by our good friend here, Mrs Edwards; she is by much too nice a judge of decorum to give her licence to such a dangerous particularity – '[400]

'I am not going to dance with Master Blake, sir!'

The gentleman, a little disconcerted, could only hope he might be fortunate another time, and seeming unwilling to leave her, though his friend Lord Osborne was waiting in the doorway for the result, as Emma with some amusement perceived, he began to make civil enquiries after her family.

'How comes it that we have not the pleasure of seeing your sisters here this evening? Our assemblies have been used to be so well treated by them that we do not know how to take this neglect.'

'My eldest sister is the only one at home, and she could not leave my father.'

'Miss Watson the only one at home! You astonish me! It seems but the day before yesterday that I saw them all three in this town. But I am afraid I have been a very sad[401] neighbour of late. I hear dreadful complaints of my negligence wherever I go, and I confess it is a shameful length of time since I was at Stanton. But I shall *now* endeavour to make myself amends for the past.'

Emma's calm curtsey in reply must have struck him as very unlike the encouraging warmth he had been used to receive from her sisters, and gave him probably the novel sensation of doubting his own influence, and of wishing for more attention than she bestowed. The dancing now recommenced; Miss Carr being impatient to call,[402] everybody was required to stand up; and Tom Musgrave's curiosity was appeased on seeing Mr Howard come forward and claim Emma's hand.

'That will do as well for me,' was Lord Osborne's remark, when his friend carried him the news, and he was continually at Howard's elbow during the two dances.

The frequency of his appearance there was the only unpleasant part of the engagement, the only objection she could make to Mr Howard. In himself, she thought him as agreeable as he looked; though chatting on the commonest topics, he had a sensible, unaffected way of expressing himself, which made them all worth hearing, and she only regretted that he had not been able to make his pupil's manners as unexceptionable as his own. The two dances seemed very short, and she had her partner's authority for considering them so. At their conclusion the Osbornes and their train were all on the move.

'We are off at last,' said his lordship to Tom. 'How much longer do *you* stay in this heavenly place – till sunrise?'

'No, faith! my lord; I have had quite enough of it. I assure you, I shall not show myself here again when I have had the honour of attending Lady Osborne to her carriage. I shall retreat in as much secrecy as possible to the most remote corner of the house, where I shall order a barrel of oysters, and be famously snug.'

'Let me see you soon at the castle, and bring me word how she looks by daylight.'

Emma and Mrs Blake parted as old acquaintances, and Charles shook her by the hand, and wished her goodbye at least a dozen times. From Miss Osborne and Miss Carr she received something like a jerking curtsey as they passed her; even Lady Osborne gave her a look of complacency, and his lordship actually came back, after the others were out of the room, to 'beg her pardon', and look in the window-seat behind her for the gloves which were visibly compressed in his hand. As Tom Musgrave was seen no more, we may suppose his plan to have succeeded, and imagine him mortifying with his barrel of oysters in dreary solitude, or gladly assisting the landlady in her bar to make fresh negus[403] for the happy dancers above. Emma could not help missing the party by whom she had been, though in some respects unpleasantly, distinguished; and the two dances which followed and concluded the ball were rather flat in comparison with the others. Mr Edwards having played with good luck, they were some of the last in the room.

'Here we are back again, I declare,' said Emma, sorrowfully, as she walked into the dining-room, where the table was prepared, and the neat upper maid was lighting the candles. 'My dear Miss Edwards, how soon it is at an end! I wish it could all come over again.'

A great deal of kind pleasure was expressed in her having enjoyed the evening so much; and Mr Edwards was as warm as herself in the praise of the fullness, brilliancy and spirit of the meeting, though as he had been fixed the whole time at the same table in the same room, with only one change of chairs, it might have seemed a matter scarcely perceived; but he had won four rubbers out of five, and everything went well. His daughter felt the advantage of this gratified state of mind in the course of the remarks and retrospections which now ensued over the welcome soup.

'How came you not to dance with either of the Mr Tomlinsons, Mary?' said her mother.

'I was always engaged when they asked me.'

'I thought you were to have stood up with Mr James the two last dances; Mrs Tomlinson told me he was gone to ask you, and I had heard you say two minutes before that you were *not* engaged.'

'Yes, but there was a mistake; I had misunderstood. I did not know I was engaged. I thought it had been for the two dances after, if we stayed so long; but Captain Hunter assured me it was for those very two.'

'So you ended with Captain Hunter, Mary, did you?' said her father. 'And whom did you begin with?'

'Captain Hunter,' was repeated in a very humble tone.

'Hum! That is being constant, however. But who else did you dance with?'

'Mr Norton and Mr Styles.'

'And who are they?'

'Mr Norton is a cousin of Captain Hunter's.'

'And who is Mr Styles?'

'One of his particular friends.'

'All in the same regiment,' added Mrs Edwards. 'Mary was surrounded by red coats[404] all the evening. I should have been better pleased to see her dancing with some of our old neighbours, I confess.'

'Yes, yes; we must not neglect our old neighbours. But if these soldiers are quicker than other people in a ballroom, what are young ladies to do?'

'I think there is no occasion for their engaging themselves so many dances beforehand, Mr Edwards.'

'No, perhaps not; but I remember, my dear, when you and I did the same.'

Mrs Edwards said no more, and Mary breathed again. A good deal of good-humoured pleasantry followed; and Emma went to bed in charming spirits, her head full of Osbornes, Blakes and Howards.

* * *

The next morning brought a great many visitors. It was the way of the place always to call on Mrs Edwards the morning after a ball, and this neighbourly inclination was increased in the present instance by a general spirit of curiosity on Emma's account, as everybody wanted to look again at the girl who had been admired the night before by Lord Osborne. Many were the eyes, and various the degrees of approbation with which she was examined. Some saw no fault, and some no beauty. With some her brown skin was the annihilation of every grace, and others could never be persuaded that she was half so handsome as Elizabeth Watson had been ten years ago. The morning passed quickly away in discussing the merits of the ball with all this succession of company; and Emma was at once astonished by finding it two o'clock and considering that she had heard nothing of her father's chair. After this discovery, she had walked twice to the window to examine the street, and was on the point of asking leave to ring the bell and make enquiries, when the light sound of a carriage driving up to the door set her heart at ease. She stepped again to the window, but instead of the convenient though very un-smart family equipage, perceived a neat curricle.[405] Mr Musgrave was shortly afterwards announced, and Mrs Edwards put on her very stiffest look at the sound. Not at all dismayed, however, by her chilling air, he paid his compliments to each of the ladies with no unbecoming ease, and continuing to address Emma, presented her a note, which 'he had the honour of bringing from her sister, but to which he must observe a verbal postscript from himself would be requisite'.

The note, which Emma was beginning to read rather *before* Mrs Edwards had entreated her to use no ceremony, contained a few lines from Elizabeth importing that their father, in consequence of being unusually well, had taken the sudden resolution of attending the visitation[406] that day, and that as his road lay quite wide from D—,[407] it was impossible for her to come home till the following morning, unless the Edwardses would send her, which was hardly to be expected, or she could meet with any chance conveyance, or did not mind walking so far. She had scarcely run her eye through the whole, before she found herself obliged to listen to Tom Musgrave's further account.

'I received that note from the fair hands of Miss Watson only ten minutes ago,' said he; 'I met her in the village of Stanton, whither my good stars prompted me to turn my horses' heads. She was at that moment in quest of a person to employ on the errand, and I was fortunate enough to convince her that she could not find a more willing or speedy messenger than myself. Remember, I say nothing of my disinterestedness. My reward is to be the indulgence of conveying you to Stanton in my curricle. Though they are not written down, I bring your sister's orders for the same.'

Emma felt distressed; she did not like the proposal – she did not wish to be on terms of intimacy with the proposer; and yet, fearful of encroaching on the Edwardses, as well as wishing to go home herself, she was at a loss how entirely to decline what he offered. Mrs Edwards continued silent, either not understanding the case, or waiting to see how the young lady's inclination lay. Emma thanked him, but professed herself very unwilling to give him so much trouble. 'The trouble was, of course, honour, pleasure, delight – what had he or his horses to do?' Still she hesitated – 'She believed she must beg leave to decline his assistance; she was rather afraid of the sort of carriage. The distance was not beyond a walk.' Mrs Edwards was silent no longer. She enquired into the particulars, and then said, 'We shall be extremely happy, Miss Emma, if you can give us the pleasure of your company till tomorrow; but if you cannot conveniently do so, our carriage is quite at your service, and Mary will be pleased with the opportunity of seeing your sister.'

This was precisely what Emma had longed for, and she accepted the offer most thankfully, acknowledging that as Elizabeth was entirely alone, it was her wish to return home to dinner. The plan was warmly opposed by their visitor – 'I cannot suffer it, indeed. I must not be deprived of the happiness of escorting you. I assure you there is not a possibility of fear with my horses. You might guide them yourself. *Your sisters* all know how quiet they are; they have none of them the smallest scruple in trusting themselves with me, even on a racecourse. Believe me,' added he, lowering his voice, '*you* are quite safe – the danger is only *mine*.'

Emma was not more disposed to oblige him for all this.

'And as to Mrs Edwards's carriage being used the day after a ball, it is a thing quite out of rule, I assure you – never heard of before. The old coachman will look as black as his horses – won't he Miss Edwards?'

No notice was taken. The ladies were silently firm, and the gentleman found himself obliged to submit.

'What a famous ball we had last night!' he cried, after a short pause. 'How long did you keep it up after the Osbornes and I went away?'

'We had two dances more.'

'It is making it too much of a fatigue, I think, to stay so late. I suppose your set was not a very full one.'

'Yes; quite as full as ever, except the Osbornes. There seemed no vacancy anywhere; and everybody danced with uncommon spirit to the very last.'

Emma said this, though against her conscience.

'Indeed! perhaps I might have looked in upon you again if I had been aware of as much, for I am rather fond of dancing than not. Miss Osborne is a charming girl, is not she?'

'I do not think her handsome,' replied Emma, to whom all this was chiefly addressed.

'Perhaps she is not critically[408] handsome, but her manners are delightful. And Fanny Carr is a most interesting little creature. You can imagine nothing more *naïve* or *piquante*;[409] and what do you think of *Lord Osborne*, Miss Watson?'

'He would be handsome even though he were *not* a lord, and perhaps, better bred; more desirous of pleasing and showing himself pleased in a right place.'

'Upon my word, you are severe upon my friend! I assure you Lord Osborne is a very good fellow.'

'I do not dispute his virtues, but I do not like his careless air.'

'If it were not a breach of confidence,' replied Tom, with an important look, 'perhaps I might be able to win a more favourable opinion of poor Osborne.'

Emma gave him no encouragement, and he was obliged to keep his friend's secret. He was also obliged to put an end to his visit, for, Mrs Edwards having ordered her carriage, there was no time to be lost on Emma's side in preparing for it. Miss Edwards accompanied her home; but as it was dinner-hour at Stanton, stayed with them only a few minutes.

'Now, my dear Emma,' said Miss Watson, as soon as they were alone, 'you must talk to me all the rest of the day without stopping, or I shall not be satisfied; but, first of all, Nanny shall bring in the dinner. Poor thing! You will not dine as you did yesterday, for we have nothing but some fried beef. How nice Mary Edwards looks in her new pelisse![410] And now tell me how you like them all, and what I am to say to Sam. I have begun my letter; Jack Stokes is to call for it tomorrow, for his uncle is going within a mile of Guildford the next day.'

Nanny brought in the dinner.

'We will wait upon ourselves,' continued Elizabeth, 'and then we shall lose no time. And so, you would not come home with Tom Musgrave?'

'No, you had said so much against him that I could not wish either for the obligation or the intimacy which the use of his carriage must have created. I should not even have liked the appearance of it.'

'You did very right; though I wonder at your forbearance, and I do not think I could have done it myself. He seemed so eager to fetch you that I could not say no, though it rather went against me to be throwing you together, so well as I knew his tricks; but I did long to see you, and it was a clever way of getting you home. Besides, it won't do to be too nice. Nobody could have thought of the Edwardses' letting you have their coach, after the horses being out so late. But what am I to say to Sam?'

'If you are guided by me, you will not encourage him to think of Miss Edwards. The father is decidedly against him, the mother shows him no favour, and I doubt his having any interest with Mary. She danced twice with Captain Hunter, and I think shows him in general as much encouragement as is consistent with her disposition and the circumstances she is placed in. She once mentioned Sam, and certainly with a little confusion; but that was perhaps merely owing to the consciousness of his liking her, which may very probably have come to her knowledge.'

'Oh, dear! yes. She has heard enough of that from us all. Poor Sam! he is out of luck as well as other people. For the life of me, Emma, I cannot help feeling for those that are crossed in love. Well, now begin, and give me an account of everything as it happened.'

Emma obeyed her, and Elizabeth listened with very little interruption till she heard of Mr Howard as a partner.

'Dance with Mr Howard! Good heavens! you don't say so! Why, he is quite one of the great and grand ones. Did you not find him very high?'[411]

'His manners are of a kind to give *me* much more ease and confidence than Tom Musgrave's.'

'Well, go on. I should have been frightened out of my wits to have had anything to do with the Osbornes' set.'

Emma concluded her narration.

'And so you really did not dance with Tom Musgrave at all; but you must have liked him – you must have been struck with him altogether.'

'I do *not* like him, Elizabeth. I allow his person and air to be good, and that his manner to a certain point – his address[412] rather – is pleasing, but I see nothing else to admire in him. On the contrary, he seems very vain, very conceited, absurdly anxious for distinction, and absolutely contemptible in some of the measures he takes for becoming so. There is a ridiculousness about him that entertains me, but his company gives me no other agreeable emotion.'

'My dearest Emma! You are like nobody else in the world. It is well Margaret is not by. You do not offend *me*, though I hardly know how to believe you; but Margaret would never forgive such words.'

'I wish Margaret could have heard him profess his ignorance of her being out of the country; he declared it seemed only two days since he had seen her.'

'Aye, that is just like him; and yet this is the man she *will* fancy so desperately in love with her. He is no favourite of mine, as you well know, Emma; but you must think him agreeable. Can you lay your hand on your heart, and say you do not?'

'Indeed, I can, both hands, and spread to their widest extent.'

'I should like to know the man you *do* think agreeable.'

'His name is Howard.'

'Howard! Dear me; I cannot think of *him* but as playing cards with Lady Osborne, and looking proud. I must own, however, that it *is* a relief to me to find you can speak as you do of Tom Musgrave. My heart did misgive me that you would like him too well. You talked so stoutly beforehand that I was sadly afraid your brag would be punished. I only hope it will last, and that he will not come on to pay you much attention. It is a hard thing for a woman to stand against the flattering ways of a man, when he is bent upon pleasing her.'

As their quietly sociable little meal concluded, Miss Watson could not help observing how comfortably it had passed.

'It is so delightful to me,' said she, 'to have things going on in peace and good-humour. Nobody can tell how much I hate quarrelling. Now, though we have had nothing but fried beef, how good it has all seemed! I wish everybody were as easily satisfied as you; but poor Margaret is very snappish, and Penelope owns she had rather have quarrelling going on than nothing at all.'

Mr Watson returned in the evening not the worse for the exertion of the day, and consequently pleased with what he had done, and glad to talk of it over his own fireside. Emma had not foreseen any interest to herself in the occurrences of a visitation; but when she heard Mr Howard spoken of as the preacher, and as having given them an excellent sermon, she could not help listening with a quicker ear.

'I do not know when I have heard a discourse more to my mind,' continued Mr Watson, 'or one better delivered. He reads extremely well, with great propriety, and in a very impressive manner, and at the same time without any theatrical grimace or violence. I own I do not like much action in the pulpit; I do not like the studied air and artificial inflexions of voice which your very popular and most admired preachers generally have. A simple delivery is much better calculated to inspire devotion, and shows a much better taste. Mr Howard read like a scholar and a gentleman.'

'And what had you for dinner, sir?' said his eldest daughter.

He related the dishes, and told what he had ate himself.

'Upon the whole,' he added, 'I have had a very comfortable day. My old friends were quite surprised to see me among them, and I must say that everybody paid me great attention, and seemed to feel for me as an invalid. They would make me sit near the fire; and as the partridges were pretty high,[413] Dr Richards would have them sent away to the other end of the table, "that they might not offend Mr Watson", which I thought very kind of him. But what pleased me as much as anything was Mr Howard's attention. There is a pretty steep flight of steps up to the room we dine in, which do not quite agree with my gouty[414] foot; and Mr Howard walked by me from the bottom to the top, and would make me take his arm. It struck me as very becoming in so young a man; but I am sure I had no claim to expect it, for I never saw him before in my life. By the by, he enquired after one of my daughters; but I do not know which. I suppose you know among yourselves.'

*   *   *

On the third day after the ball, as Nanny, at five minutes before three, was beginning to bustle into the parlour with the tray and the knife-case, she was suddenly called to the front door by the sound of as smart a rap as the end of a riding-whip could give; and though charged by Miss Watson to let nobody in, returned in half a minute with a look of awkward dismay to hold the parlour door open for Lord Osborne and Tom Musgrave. The surprise of the young ladies may be imagined. No visitors would have been welcome at such a moment, but such visitors as these – such a one as Lord Osborne, at least, a nobleman and a stranger – was really distressing.

He looked a little embarrassed himself, as, on being introduced by his easy, voluble friend, he muttered something of doing himself the honour of waiting upon Mr Watson. Though Emma could not but take the compliment of the visit to herself, she was very far from enjoying it. She felt all the inconsistency of such an acquaintance with the very humble style in which they were obliged to live; and having in her aunt's family been used to many of the elegancies of life, was fully sensible of all that must be open to the ridicule of richer people in her present home. Of the pain of such feelings, Elizabeth knew very little. Her simple mind, or juster reason, saved her from such mortification; and though shrinking under a general sense of inferiority, she felt no particular shame. Mr Watson, as the gentlemen had already heard from Nanny, was not well enough to be downstairs. With much concern they took their seats; Lord Osborne near Emma, and the convenient Mr Musgrave, in high spirits at his own importance, on the other side of the fireplace, with Elizabeth. *He* was at no loss for words; but when Lord Osborne had hoped that Emma had not caught cold at the ball, he had nothing more to say for some time, and could only gratify his eye by occasional glances at his fair neighbour. Emma was not inclined to give herself much trouble for his entertainment; and after hard labour of mind, he produced the remark of its being a very fine day, and followed it up with the question of, 'Have you been walking this morning?'

'No, my lord; we thought it too dirty.'

'You should wear half-boots.'[415] After another pause: 'Nothing sets off a neat ankle more than a half-boot; nankin galoshed with black[416] looks very well. Do not you like half-boots?'

'Yes; but unless they are so stout as to injure their beauty, they are not fit for country walking.'

'Ladies should ride in dirty weather. Do you ride?'

'No, my lord.'

'I wonder every lady does not; a woman never looks better than on horseback.'

'But every woman may not have the inclination, or the means.'

'If they knew how much it became them, they would all have the inclination; and I fancy, Miss Watson, when once they had the inclination, the means would soon follow.'

'Your lordship thinks we always have our own way. *That* is a point on which ladies and gentlemen have long disagreed; but without pretending to decide it, I may say that there are some circumstances which even *women* cannot control. Female economy will do a great deal, my lord: but it cannot turn a small income into a large one.'

Lord Osborne was silenced. Her manner had been neither sententious nor sarcastic, but there was a something in its mild seriousness, as well as in the words themselves, which made his lordship think; and when he addressed her again, it was with a degree of considerate propriety totally unlike the half-awkward, half-fearless style of his former remarks. It was a new thing with him to wish to please a woman; it was the first time that he had ever felt what was due to a woman in Emma's situation;

but as he wanted neither in sense nor a good disposition, he did not feel it without effect.

'You have not been long in this country, I understand,' said he, in the tone of a gentleman. 'I hope you are pleased with it.'

He was rewarded by a gracious answer, and a more liberal full view of her face than she had yet bestowed. Unused to exert himself, and happy in contemplating her, he then sat in silence for some minutes longer, while Tom Musgrave was chattering to Elizabeth, till they were interrupted by Nanny's approach, who, half-opening the door and putting in her head, said – 'Please, ma'am, master wants to know why he ben't to have his dinner?'

The gentlemen, who had hitherto disregarded every symptom, however positive, of the nearness of that meal, now jumped up with apologies, while Elizabeth called briskly after Nanny to 'tell Betty to take up the fowls'.

'I am sorry it happens so,' she added, turning good-humouredly towards Musgrave, 'but you know what early hours we keep.'

Tom had nothing to say for himself; he knew it very well, and such honest simplicity, such shameless truth, rather bewildered him. Lord Osborne's parting compliments took some time, his inclination for speech seeming to increase with the shortness of the term for indulgence. He recommended exercise in defiance of dirt; spoke again in praise of half-boots; begged that his sister might be allowed to send Emma the name of her shoemaker; and concluded with saying, 'My hounds will be hunting this country next week. I believe they will throw off [417] at Stanton Wood on Wednesday at nine o'clock. I mention this in hopes of your being drawn out to see what's going on. If the morning's tolerable, pray do us the honour of giving us your good wishes in person.'

The sisters looked on each other with astonishment when their visitors had withdrawn.

'Here's an unaccountable honour!' cried Elizabeth, at last. 'Who would have thought of Lord Osborne's coming to Stanton? He is very handsome; but Tom Musgrave looks all to nothing the smartest and most fashionable man of the two. I am glad he did not say anything to me; I would not have had to talk to such a great man for the world. Tom was very agreeable, was not he? But did you hear him ask where Miss Penelope and Miss Margaret were, when he first came in? It put me out of patience. I am glad Nanny had not laid the cloth, however – it would have looked so awkward; just the tray did not signify.' To say that Emma was not flattered by Lord Osborne's visit would be to assert a very unlikely thing, and describe a very odd young lady; but the gratification was by no means unalloyed: his coming was a sort of notice which might please her vanity, but did not suit her pride; and she would rather have known that he wished the visit without presuming to make it, than have seen him at Stanton.

Among other unsatisfactory feelings, it once occurred to her to wonder why Mr Howard had not taken the same privilege of coming, and accompanied his lordship; but she was willing to suppose that he had either known nothing about it, or had declined any share in a measure which carried quite as much impertinence in its form as good-breeding.

Mr Watson was very far from being delighted when he heard what had passed; a little peevish under immediate pain, and ill-disposed to be pleased, he only replied – 'Phoo! phoo! what occasion could there be for Lord Osborne's coming? I have lived here fourteen years without being noticed by any of the family. It is some foolery of that idle fellow, Tom Musgrave. I cannot return the visit. I would not if I could.' And when Tom Musgrave was met with again, he was commissioned with a message of excuse to Osborne Castle, on the too-sufficient plea of Mr Watson's infirm state of health.

A week or ten days rolled quietly away after this visit before any new bustle arose to interrupt even for half a day the tranquil and affectionate intercourse of the two sisters, whose mutual regard was increasing with the intimate knowledge of each other which such intercourse produced. The first circumstance to break in on this security was the receipt of a letter from Croydon to announce the speedy return of Margaret, and a visit of two or three days from Mr and Mrs Robert Watson, who undertook to bring her home and wished to see their sister Emma.

It was an expectation to fill the thoughts of the sisters at Stanton, and to busy the hours of one of them at least; for as Jane had been a woman of fortune, the preparations for her entertainment were considerable, and as Elizabeth had at all times more goodwill than method in her guidance of the house, she could make no change without a bustle. An absence of fourteen years had made all her brothers and sisters strangers to Emma, but in her expectation of Margaret there was more than the awkwardness of such an alienation; she had heard things which made her dread her return; and the day which brought the party to Stanton seemed to her the probable conclusion of almost all that had been comfortable in the house.

Robert Watson was an attorney at Croydon, in a good way of business; very well satisfied with himself for the same, and for having married the only daughter of the attorney to whom he had been clerk, with a fortune of six thousand pounds.[418] Mrs Robert was not less pleased with herself for having had that six thousand pounds, and for being now in possession of a very smart house in Croydon, where she gave genteel parties and wore fine clothes. In her person there was nothing remarkable; her manners were pert and conceited. Margaret was not without beauty; she had a slight pretty figure, and rather wanted countenance[419] than good features; but the sharp and anxious expression of her face made her beauty in general little felt. On meeting her long-absent sister, as on every occasion of show, her manner was all affection and her voice all gentleness; continual smiles and a very slow articulation being her constant resource when determined on pleasing.

She was now so 'delighted to see dear, dear Emma', that she could hardly speak a word in a minute. 'I am sure we shall be great friends,' she observed with much sentiment, as they were sitting together. Emma scarcely knew how to answer such a proposition, and the manner in which it was spoken she could not attempt to equal. Mrs Robert Watson eyed her with much familiar curiosity and triumphant compassion: the loss of the aunt's fortune was uppermost in her mind at the moment of meeting; and she could not but feel how much better it was to be the daughter of a gentleman of property in Croydon than the niece of an old woman who threw herself away on an Irish captain. Robert was carelessly kind, as became a prosperous man and a brother; more intent on settling with the post-boy, inveighing against the exorbitant advance in posting,[420] and pondering over a doubtful half-crown, than on welcoming a sister who was no longer likely to have any property for him to get the direction of.

'Your road through the village is infamous, Elizabeth,' said he; 'worse than ever it was. By heaven! I would indict it if I lived near you. Who is surveyor now?'

There was a little niece at Croydon to be fondly enquired after by the kind-hearted Elizabeth, who regretted very much her not being of the party.

'You are very good,' replied her mother, 'and I assure you it went very hard with Augusta to have us come away without her. I was forced to say we were only going to church and promise to come back for her directly. But you know it would not do to bring her without her maid, and I am as particular as ever in having her properly attended to.'

'Sweet little darling!' cried Margaret. 'It quite broke my heart to leave her.'

'Then why were you in such a hurry to run away from her?' cried Mrs Robert. 'You are a sad, shabby[421] girl. I have been quarrelling with you all the way we came, have not I? Such a visit as this, I never heard of!

You know how glad we are to have any of you with us, if it be for months together; and I am sorry' (with a witty smile) 'we have not been able to make Croydon agreeable this autumn.'

'My dearest Jane, do not overpower me with your raillery. You know what inducements I had to bring me home. Spare me, I entreat you. I am no match for your arch sallies.'

'Well, I only beg you will not set your neighbours against the place. Perhaps Emma may be tempted to go back with us and stay till Christmas, if you don't put in your word.'

Emma was greatly obliged.

'I assure you we have very good society at Croydon. I do not much attend the balls, they are rather too mixed; but our parties are very select and good. I had seven tables last week in my drawing-room. Are you fond of the country? How do you like Stanton?'

'Very much,' replied Emma, who thought a comprehensive answer most to the purpose. She saw that her sister-in-law despised her immediately. Mrs Robert Watson was indeed wondering what sort of a home Emma could possibly have been used to in Shropshire, and setting it down as certain that the aunt could never have had six thousand pounds.[422]

'How charming Emma is,' whispered Margaret to Mrs Robert, in her most languishing tone. Emma was quite distressed by such behaviour; and she did not like it better when she heard Margaret five minutes afterwards say to Elizabeth in a sharp, quick accent, totally unlike the first, 'Have you heard from Pen since she went to Chichester? I had a letter the other day. I don't find she is likely to make anything of it. I fancy she'll come back "Miss Penelope", as she went.'

Such, she feared, would be Margaret's common voice when the novelty of her own appearance were over; the tone of artificial sensibility[423] was not recommended by the idea. The ladies were invited upstairs to prepare for dinner.

'I hope you will find things tolerably comfortable, Jane,' said Elizabeth, as she opened the door of the spare bedchamber.

'My good creature,' replied Jane, 'use no ceremony with me, I entreat you. I am one of those who always take things as they find them. I hope I can put up with a small apartment for two or three nights without making a piece of work. I always wish to be treated quite *en famille* when I come to see you. And now I do hope you have not been getting a great dinner for us. Remember, we never eat suppers.'

'I suppose,' said Margaret, rather quickly to Emma, 'you and I are to be together; Elizabeth always takes care to have a room to herself.'

'No. Elizabeth gives me half hers.'

'Oh!' in a softened voice, and rather mortified to find that she was not ill-used, 'I am sorry I am not to have the pleasure of your company, especially as it makes me nervous to be much alone.'

Emma was the first of the females in the parlour again; on entering it she found her brother alone.

'So, Emma,' said he, 'you are quite a stranger at home. It must seem odd enough for you to be here. A pretty piece of work your Aunt Turner has made of it! By heaven! a woman should never be trusted with money. I always said she ought to have settled something on you as soon as her husband died.'

'But that would have been trusting *me* with money,' replied Emma; 'and *I* am a woman too.'

'It might have been secured to your future use, without your having any power over it now. What a blow it must have been upon you! To find yourself, instead of heiress of eight or nine thousand pounds,[424] sent back a weight upon your family, without a sixpence. I hope the old woman will smart for it.'

'Do not speak disrespectfully of her; she was very good to me, and if she has made an imprudent choice, she will suffer more from it herself than *I* can possibly do.'

'I do not mean to distress you, but you know everybody must think her an old fool. I thought Turner had been reckoned an extraordinarily sensible, clever man. How the devil came he to make such a will?'

'My uncle's sense is not at all impeached in my opinion by his attachment to my aunt. She had been an excellent wife to him. The most liberal and enlightened minds are always the most confiding. The event has been unfortunate; but my uncle's memory is, if possible, endeared to me by such a proof of tender respect for my aunt.'

'That's odd sort of talking. He might have provided decently for his widow without leaving everything that he had to dispose of, or any part of it, at her mercy.'

'My aunt may have erred,' said Emma, warmly; 'she *has* erred, but my uncle's conduct was faultless. I was her own niece, and he left to herself the power and the pleasure of providing for me.'

'But unluckily she has left the pleasure of providing for you to your father, and without the power. That's the long and short of the business. After keeping you at a distance from your family for such a length of time as must do away all natural affection among us, and breeding you up (I suppose) in a superior style, you are returned upon their hands without a sixpence.'

'You know,' replied Emma, struggling with her tears, 'my uncle's melancholy state of health. He was a greater invalid than my father. He could not leave home.'

'I do not mean to make you cry,' said Robert, rather softened – and after a short silence, by way of changing the subject he added: 'I am just come from my father's room; he seems very indifferent.[425] It will be a sad break up[426] when he dies. Pity you can none of you get married! You must come to Croydon, as well as the rest, and see what you can do there. I believe if Margaret had had a thousand or fifteen hundred pounds[427] there was a young man who would have thought of her.'

Emma was glad when they were joined by the others; it was better to look at her sister-in-law's finery than listen to Robert, who had equally irritated and grieved her. Mrs Robert, exactly as smart as she had been at her own party, came in with apologies for her dress.

'I would not make you wait,' said she; 'so I put on the first thing I met with. I am afraid I am a sad figure. My dear Mr W.,' to her husband, 'you have not put any fresh powder in your hair.'

'No, I do not intend it. I think there is powder enough in my hair for my wife and sisters.'

'Indeed, you ought to make some alteration in your dress before dinner when you are out visiting, though you do not at home.'

'Nonsense.'

'It is very odd you should not like to do what other gentlemen do. Mr Marshall and Mr Hemmings change their dress every day of their lives before dinner. And what was the use of my putting up[428] your last new coat, if you are never to wear it?'

'Do be satisfied with being fine yourself, and leave your husband alone.'

To put an end to this altercation and soften the evident vexation of her sister-in-law, Emma (though in no spirits to make such nonsense easy) began to admire her gown. It produced immediate complacency. 'Do you like it?' said she. 'I am very happy. It has been excessively admired; but sometimes I think the pattern too large. I shall wear one tomorrow that I think you will prefer to this. Have you seen the one I gave Margaret?'

Dinner came, and except when Mrs Robert looked at her husband's head, she continued gay and flippant, chiding Elizabeth for the profusion on the table, and absolutely protesting against the entrance of the roast turkey, which formed the only exception to, 'You see your dinner.' 'I do beg and entreat that no turkey may be seen today. I am really frightened out of my wits with the number of dishes we have already. Let us have no turkey, I beseech you.'

'My dear,' replied Elizabeth, 'the turkey is roasted, and it may just as well come in as stay in the kitchen. Besides, if it is cut, I am in hopes my father may be tempted to eat a bit, for it is rather a favourite dish.'

'You may have it in, my dear; but I assure you I shan't touch it.'

Mr Watson had not been well enough to join the party at dinner, but was prevailed on to come down and drink tea with them.

'I wish we may be able to have a game of cards tonight,' said Elizabeth to Mrs Robert, after seeing her father comfortably seated in his armchair.

'Not on my account, my dear, I beg. You know I am no card-player. I think a snug chat infinitely better. I always say cards are very well sometimes to break a formal circle, but one never wants them among friends.'

'I was thinking of its being something to amuse my father,' said Elizabeth, 'if it was not disagreeable to you. He says his head won't bear whist, but perhaps if we make a round game he may be tempted to sit down with us.'

'By all means, my dear creature. I am quite at your service; only do not oblige me to choose the game, that's all. Speculation[429] is the only round game at Croydon now, but I can play anything. When there is only one or two of you at home, you must be quite at a loss to amuse him. Why do you not get him to play at cribbage?[430] Margaret and I have played at cribbage most nights that we have not been engaged.'

A sound like a distant carriage was at this moment caught; everybody listened; it became more decided; it certainly drew nearer. It was an unusual sound for Stanton at any time of the day, for the village was on no very public road, and contained no gentleman's family but the rector's. The wheels rapidly approached; in two minutes the general expectation was answered; they stopped beyond a doubt at the garden-gate of the parsonage. 'Who could it be? It was certainly a post-chaise.[431] Penelope was the only creature to be thought of; she might perhaps have met with some unexpected opportunity of returning.' A pause of suspense ensued. Steps were distinguished along the paved footway, which led under the windows of the house to the front door, and then within the passage. They were the steps of a man. It could not be Penelope. It must be Samuel. The door opened, and displayed Tom Musgrave in the wrap[432] of a traveller. He had been in London, and was now on his way home, and he had come half a mile out of his road merely to call for ten minutes at Stanton. He loved to take people by surprise with sudden visits at extraordinary seasons, and, in the present instance, had had the additional motive of being able to tell the Miss Watsons, whom he depended on finding sitting quietly employed after tea, that he was going home to an eight-o'clock dinner.

As it happened, however, he did not give more surprise than he received, when, instead of being shown into the usual little sitting-room, the door of the best parlour (a foot larger each way than the other) was thrown open, and he beheld a circle of smart people whom he could not immediately recognise arranged, with all the honours of visiting, round the fire, and Miss Watson seated at the best Pembroke table,[433] with the best tea things before her. He stood a few seconds in silent amazement.

'Musgrave!' ejaculated Margaret, in a tender voice.

He recollected himself, and came forward, delighted to find such a circle of friends, and blessing his good fortune for the unlooked-for indulgence. He shook hands with Robert, bowed and smiled to the ladies, and did everything very prettily; but as to any particularity of address or emotion towards Margaret, Emma, who closely observed him, perceived nothing that did not justify Elizabeth's opinion, though Margaret's modest smiles imported that she meant to take the visit to herself. He was persuaded without much difficulty to throw off his greatcoat and drink tea with them. For 'whether he dined at eight or nine,' as he observed, 'was a matter of very little consequence;' and without seeming to seek, he did not turn away from the chair close by Margaret, which she was assiduous in providing him. She had thus secured him from her sisters, but it was not immediately in her power to preserve him from her brother's claims; for as he came avowedly from London, and had left it only four hours ago, the last current report as to public news, and the general opinion of the day, must be understood before Robert could let his attention be yielded to the less national and important demands of the women.

At last, however, he was at liberty to hear Margaret's soft address, as she spoke her fears of his having had a most terrible cold, dark, dreadful journey. 'Indeed, you should not have set out so late.'

'I could not be earlier,' he replied. 'I was detained chatting at the Bedford[434] by a friend. All hours are alike to me. How long have you been in the country, Miss Margaret?'

'We only came this morning; my kind brother and sister brought me home this very morning. 'Tis singular, is not it?'

'You were gone a great while, were not you? A fortnight, I suppose?'

'*You* may call a fortnight a great while, Mr Musgrave,' said Mrs Robert, sharply, 'but *we* think a month very little. I assure you we bring her home at the end of a month much against our will.'

'A month! Have you really been gone a month? 'Tis amazing how time flies.'

'You may imagine,' said Margaret, in a sort of whisper, 'what are my

sensations in finding myself once more at Stanton; you know what a sad
visitor I make. And I was so excessively impatient to see Emma; I
dreaded the meeting, and at the same time longed for it. Do you not
comprehend the sort of feeling?'

'Not at all,' cried he, aloud. 'I could never dread a meeting with Miss
Emma Watson – or any of her sisters.'

It was lucky that he added that finish.

'Were you speaking to me?' said Emma, who had caught her own
name.

'Not absolutely,' he answered; 'but I was thinking of you, as many at
a greater distance are probably doing at this moment. Fine open[435]
weather, Miss Emma, charming season for hunting.'

'Emma is delightful, is not she?' whispered Margaret; 'I have found
her more than answer my warmest hopes. Did you ever see anything
more perfectly beautiful? I think even *you* must be a convert to a brown
complexion.'

He hesitated. Margaret was fair herself, and he did not particularly
want to compliment her; but Miss Osborne and Miss Carr were likewise
fair, and his devotion to them carried the day.

'Your sister's complexion,' said he, at last, 'is as fine as a dark complexion can be; but I still profess my preference of a white skin. You have
seen Miss Osborne? She is my model for a truly feminine complexion,
and she is very fair.'

'Is she fairer than me?'

Tom made no reply. 'Upon my honour, ladies,' said he, giving a
glance over his own person, 'I am highly indebted to your condescension
for admitting me in such dishabille[436] into your drawing-room. I really
did not consider how unfit I was to be here, or I hope I should have kept
my distance. Lady Osborne would tell me that I was growing as careless
as her son, if she saw me in this condition.'

The ladies were not wanting in civil returns, and Robert Watson,
stealing a view of his own head in an opposite glass, said with equal
civility – 'You cannot be more in dishabille than myself. We got here so
late that I had not time even to put a little fresh powder in my hair.'
Emma could not help entering into what she supposed her sister-in-
law's feelings at that moment.

When the tea things were removed, Tom began to talk of his carriage;
but the old card-table being set out, and the fish and counters,[437] with
a tolerably clean pack, brought forward from the buffet[438] by Miss
Watson, the general voice was so urgent with him to join their party that
he agreed to allow himself another quarter of an hour. Even Emma was

pleased that he would stay, for she was beginning to feel that a family party might be the worst of all parties; and the others were delighted.

'What's your game?' cried he, as they stood round the table.

'Speculation, I believe,' said Elizabeth. 'My sister recommends it, and I fancy we all like it. I know *you* do, Tom.'

'It is the only round game played at Croydon now,' said Mrs Robert; 'we never think of any other. I am glad it is a favourite with you.'

'Oh, me!' said Tom. 'Whatever you decide on will be a favourite with *me*. I have had some pleasant hours at speculation in my time, but I have not been in the way of it now for a long while. Vingt-un[439] is the game at Osborne Castle. I have played nothing but vingt-un of late. You would be astonished to hear the noise we make there – the fine old lofty drawing-room rings again. Lady Osborne sometimes declares she cannot hear herself speak. Lord Osborne enjoys it famously, and he makes the best dealer without exception that I ever beheld – such quickness and spirit, he lets nobody dream over their cards. I wish you could see him overdraw himself on both his own cards.[440] It is worth anything in the world!'

'Dear me!' cried Margaret, 'why should not we play at vingt-un? I think it is a much better game than speculation. I cannot say I am very fond of speculation.'

Mrs Robert offered not another word in support of the game. She was quite vanquished, and the fashions of Osborne Castle carried it over the fashions of Croydon.

'Do you see much of the parsonage family at the castle, Mr Musgrave?' said Emma, as they were taking their seats.

'Oh, yes; they are almost always there. Mrs Blake is a nice little good-humoured woman; she and I are sworn friends; and Howard's a very gentlemanlike, good sort of fellow! You are not forgotten, I assure you, by any of the party. I fancy you must have a little cheek-glowing now and then, Miss Emma. Were not you rather warm last Saturday about nine or ten o'clock in the evening? I will tell you how it was – I see you are dying to know. Says Howard to Lord Osborne – '

At this interesting moment he was called on by the others to regulate the game and determine some disputable point; and his attention was so totally engaged in the business, and afterwards by the course of the game, as never to revert to what he had been saying before; and Emma, though suffering a good deal from curiosity, dared not remind him.

He proved a very useful addition to their table. Without him, it would have been a party of such very near relations as could have felt little interest, and perhaps maintained little complaisance; but his presence gave variety and secured good manners. He was, in fact, excellently qualified to shine at a round game, and few situations made him appear to greater advantage. He played with spirit, and had a great deal to say; and, though no wit himself, could sometimes make use of the wit of an absent friend, and had a lively way of retailing a commonplace or saying a mere nothing, that had great effect at a card-table. The ways and good jokes of Osborne Castle were now added to his ordinary means of entertainment. He repeated the smart sayings of one lady, detailed the oversights of another, and indulged them even with a copy of Lord Osborne's style of overdrawing himself on both cards.

The clock struck nine while he was thus agreeably occupied; and when Nanny came in with her master's basin of gruel, he had the pleasure of observing to Mr Watson that he should leave him at supper while he went home to dinner himself. The carriage was ordered to the door, and no entreaties for his staying longer could now avail; for he well knew that if he stayed he must sit down to supper in less than ten minutes, which, to a man whose heart had been long fixed on calling his next meal a dinner, was quite insupportable. On finding him determined to go, Margaret began to wink and nod at Elizabeth to ask him to dinner for the following day, and Elizabeth at last not able to resist hints which her own hospitable, social temper more than half seconded, gave the invitation: 'Would he give Robert the meeting,[441] they should be very happy?'

'With the greatest pleasure,' was his first reply. In a moment afterwards, 'That is, if I can possibly get here in time; but I shoot with Lord Osborne, and therefore must not engage. You will not think of me unless you see me.' And so he departed, delighted with the uncertainty in which he had left it.

*　　　*　　　*

Margaret, in the joy of her heart under circumstances which she chose to consider as peculiarly propitious, would willingly have made a confidante of Emma when they were alone for a short time the next morning, and had proceeded so far as to say, 'The young man who was here last night, my dear Emma, and returns today, is more interesting to me than perhaps you may be aware – '; but Emma, pretending to understand nothing extraordinary in the words, made some very inapplicable reply, and jumping up, ran away from a subject which was odious to her feelings. As Margaret would not allow a doubt to be repeated of Musgrave's coming to dinner, preparations were made for his entertainment much exceeding what had been deemed necessary the day before; and taking the office of superintendence entirely from her sister, she was half the morning in the kitchen herself, directing and scolding.

After a great deal of indifferent cooking and anxious suspense, however, they were obliged to sit down without their guest. Tom Musgrave never came; and Margaret was at no pains to conceal her vexation under the disappointment, or repress the peevishness of her temper. The peace of the party for the remainder of that day and the whole of the next, which comprised the length of Robert's and Jane's visit, was continually invaded by her fretful displeasure and querulous attacks. Elizabeth was the usual object of both. Margaret had just respect enough for her brother's and sister's opinion to behave properly by *them*, but Elizabeth and the maids could never do anything right; and Emma, whom she seemed no longer to think about, found the continuance of the gentle voice beyond her calculation short. Eager to be as little among them as possible, Emma was delighted with the alternative of sitting above with her father, and warmly entreated to be his constant companion each evening; and as Elizabeth loved company of any kind too well not to prefer being below at all risks; as she had rather talk of Croydon with Jane, with every interruption of Margaret's perverseness, than sit with only her father, who frequently could not endure talking at all – the affair was so settled, as soon as she could be persuaded to believe it no sacrifice on her sister's part. To Emma, the change was most acceptable and delightful. Her father, if ill, required little more than gentleness and silence, and being a man of sense and education, was, if able to converse, a welcome companion. In *his* chamber Emma was at peace from the dreadful mortifications of unequal society and family discord; from the immediate endurance of hard-hearted prosperity, low-minded conceit and wrong-headed folly, engrafted on an untoward disposition. She still suffered from them in the contemplation of their existence, in memory and in prospect, but for the moment she ceased to be tortured by their effects. She was at leisure; she could read and think, though her situation was hardly such as to make reflection very soothing. The evils arising from the loss of her uncle were neither trifling nor likely to lessen; and when thought had been freely indulged, in contrasting the past and the present, the employment of mind and dissipation of unpleasant ideas which only reading could produce made her thankfully turn to a book.

The change in her home, society and style of life, in consequence of the death of one friend and the imprudence of another, had indeed been striking. From being the first object of hope and solicitude to an uncle who had formed her mind with the care of a parent, and of tenderness to an aunt whose amiable temper had delighted to give her every indulgence, from being the life and spirit of a house where all had been comfort and elegance, and the expected heiress of an easy independence, she was become of importance to no one – a burden on those whose affections she could not expect, an addition in a house already overstocked, surrounded by inferior minds, with little chance of domestic comfort, and as little hope of future support. It was well for her that she was naturally cheerful, for the change had been such as might have plunged weak spirits in despondence.

She was very much pressed by Robert and Jane to return with them to Croydon, and had some difficulty in getting a refusal accepted, as they thought too highly of their own kindness and situation to suppose the offer could appear in a less advantageous light to anybody else. Elizabeth gave them her interest, though evidently against her own, in privately urging Emma to go. 'You do not know what you refuse, Emma,' said she, 'nor what you have to bear at home. I would advise you by all means to accept the invitation; there is always something lively going on at Croydon. You will be in company almost every day, and Robert and Jane will be very kind to you. As for me, I shall be no worse off without you than I have been used to be; but poor Margaret's disagreeable ways are new to *you*, and they would vex you more than you think for if you stay at home.'

Emma was of course uninfluenced, except to greater esteem for Elizabeth, by such representations, and the visitors departed without her.

Editorial Note

When the author's sister, Cassandra, showed the manuscript of this work to some of her nieces, she also told them something of the intended story; for with this dear sister – though, I believe, with no one else – Jane seems to have talked freely of any work she might have in hand. Mr Watson was soon to die; and Emma to become dependent for a home on her narrow-minded sister-in-law and brother. She was to decline an offer of marriage from Lord Osborne, and much of the interest of the tale was to arise from Lady Osborne's love for Mr Howard, and his counter affection for Emma, whom he was finally to marry.

from the second edition of *A Memoir of Jane Austen*
by James Austen-Leigh, 1871

Sanditon

Chapter 1

A gentleman and a lady travelling from Tunbridge towards that part of the Sussex coast which lies between Hastings and Eastbourne,[442] being induced by business to quit the high road and attempt a very rough lane, were overturned in toiling up its long ascent, half rock, half sand. The accident happened just beyond the only gentleman's house near the lane – a house which their driver, on being first required to take that direction, had conceived to be necessarily their object and had with most unwilling looks been constrained to pass by. He had grumbled and shaken his shoulders and pitied and cut[443] his horses so sharply that he might have been open to the suspicion of overturning them on purpose (especially as the carriage was not his master's[444] own) if the road had not indisputably become worse than before, as soon as the premises of the said house were left behind – expressing with a most portentous countenance that, beyond it, no wheels but cart wheels could safely proceed. The severity of the fall was broken by their slow pace and the narrowness of the lane; and the gentleman having scrambled out and helped out his companion, they neither of them at first felt more than shaken and bruised. But the gentleman had, in the course of the extrication, sprained his foot; and soon becoming sensible of it, was obliged in a few moments to cut short both his remonstrances to the driver and his congratulations to his wife and himself and sit down on the bank, unable to stand.

'There is something wrong here,' said he, putting his hand to his ankle. 'But never mind, my dear,' looking up at her with a smile, 'it could not have happened, you know, in a better place. Good out of evil. The very thing perhaps to be wished for. We shall soon get relief. *There*, I fancy, lies my cure,' pointing to the neat-looking end of a cottage, which was seen romantically[445] situated among woods on a high eminence at some little distance. 'Does not *that* promise to be the very place?'

His wife fervently hoped it was, but stood, terrified and anxious, neither able to do or suggest anything, and receiving her first real comfort from the sight of several persons now coming to their assistance. The accident had been discerned from a hayfield adjoining the house they had passed. And the persons who approached were a well-looking, hale, gentlemanlike man of middle age, the proprietor of the place, who happened to be among his haymakers at the time, and three or four of the ablest of them summoned to attend their master – to say nothing of all the rest of the field, men, women and children, not very far off.

Mr Heywood, such was the name of the said proprietor, advanced with a very civil salutation, much concern for the accident, some surprise at anybody's attempting that road in a carriage, and ready offers of assistance. His courtesies were received with good breeding and gratitude, and while one or two of the men lent their help to the driver in getting the carriage upright again, the traveller said, 'You are extremely obliging, sir, and I take you at your word. The injury to my leg is, I dare say, very trifling. But it is always best in these cases, you know, to have a surgeon's opinion without loss of time; and as the road does not seem in a favourable state for my getting up to his house myself, I will thank you to send off one of these good people for the surgeon.

'The surgeon!' exclaimed Mr Heywood. 'I am afraid you will find no surgeon at hand here, but I dare say we shall do very well without him.'

'Nay, sir, if he is not in the way, his partner will do just as well – or rather better. I would rather see his partner. Indeed I would prefer the attendance of his partner. One of these good people can be with him in three minutes, I am sure. I need not ask whether I see the house,' looking towards the cottage, 'for excepting your own, we have passed none in this place which can be the abode of a gentleman.'

Mr Heywood looked very much astonished. 'What, sir! Are you expecting to find a surgeon in that cottage? We have neither surgeon nor partner in the parish, I assure you.'

'Excuse me, sir,' replied the other. 'I am sorry to have the appearance of contradicting you, but from the extent of the parish or some other cause you may not be aware of the fact. Stay – can I be mistaken in the place? Am I not in Willingden?[446] Is not this Willingden?'

'Yes, sir, this is certainly Willingden.'

'Then, sir, I can bring proof of your having a surgeon in the parish, whether you may know it or not. Here, sir,' taking out his pocket book, 'if you will do me the favour of casting your eye over these advertisements, which I cut out myself from the *Morning Post* and the *Kentish Gazette*[447] only yesterday morning in London, I think you will be convinced that I am not speaking at random. You will find in it an advertisement of the dissolution of a partnership in the medical line – in your own parish – extensive business – undeniable character – respectable references – wishing to form a separate establishment. You will find it at full length, sir,' offering him the two little oblong extracts.

'Sir, if you were to show me all the newspapers that are printed in one week throughout the kingdom, you would not persuade me of there being a surgeon in Willingden,' said Mr Heywood, with a good-humoured smile. 'Having lived here ever since I was born, man and boy fifty-seven years, I think I must have known of such a person. At least I may venture to say that he has not much business. To be sure, if gentlemen were to be often attempting this lane in post-chaises,[448] it might not be a bad speculation for a surgeon to get a house at the top of the hill. But as to that cottage, I can assure you, sir, that it is in fact, in spite of its spruce air at this distance, as indifferent a double tenement[449] as any in the parish, and that my shepherd lives at one end and three old women at the other.'

He took the pieces of paper as he spoke, and, having looked them over, added, 'I believe I can explain it, sir. Your mistake is in the place. There are two Willingdens in this country. And your advertisements must refer to the other, which is Great Willingden or Willingden Abbots, and lies seven miles off on the other side of Battle.[450] Quite down in the Weald.[451] And *we*, sir,' he added, speaking rather proudly, 'are not in the Weald.'

'Not *down* in the Weald, I am sure,' replied the traveller pleasantly. 'It took us half an hour to climb your hill. Well, I dare say it is as you say and I have made an abominably stupid blunder. All done in a moment. The advertisements did not catch my eye till the last half-hour of our being in town – when everything was in the hurry and confusion which always attend a short stay there. One is never able to complete anything in the way of business, you know, till the carriage is at the door. So, satisfying myself with a brief enquiry, and finding we were actually to pass within a mile or two of *a* Willingden, I sought no further . . . My dear,' to his wife, 'I am very sorry to have brought you into this scrape. But do not be alarmed about my leg. It gives me no pain while I am quiet. And as soon as these good people have succeeded in setting the carriage to rights and turning the horses round, the best thing we can do will be to measure back our steps into the turnpike road[452] and proceed to Hailsham, and so home without attempting anything further. Two hours take us home from Hailsham.[453] And once at home, we have our remedy at hand, you know. A little of our own bracing sea air will soon set me on my feet again. Depend upon it, my dear, it is exactly a case for the sea. Saline air and immersion will be the very thing. My sensations tell me so already.'

In a most friendly manner, Mr Heywood here interposed, entreating them not to think of proceeding till the ankle had been examined and some refreshment taken, and very cordially pressing them to make use of his house for both purposes.

'We are always well stocked,' said he, 'with all the common remedies for sprains and bruises. And I will answer for the pleasure it will give my wife and daughters to be of service to you in every way in their power.'

A twinge or two, in trying to move his foot, disposed the traveller to think rather more than he had done at first of the benefit of immediate assistance; and consulting his wife in the few words of, 'Well, my dear, I believe it will be better for us,' he turned again to Mr Heywood. 'Before we accept your hospitality, sir, and in order to do away with any unfavourable impression which the sort of wild-goose chase you find me in may have given rise to – allow me to tell you who we are. My name is Parker, Mr Parker of Sanditon; this lady, my wife, Mrs Parker. We are on our road home from London. *My* name perhaps – though I am by no means the first of my family holding landed property in the parish of Sanditon – may be unknown at this distance from the coast. But Sanditon itself – everybody has heard of Sanditon. The favourite – for a young and rising bathing-place – certainly the favourite spot of all that are to be found along the coast of Sussex; the most favoured by nature, and promising to be the most chosen by man.'

'Yes, I have heard of Sanditon,' replied Mr Heywood. 'Every five years, one hears of some new place or other starting up by the sea and growing the fashion. How they can half of them be filled is the wonder! *Where* people can be found with money and time to go to them! Bad things for a country – sure to raise the price of provisions and make the poor good for nothing – as I dare say you find, sir.'

'Not at all, sir, not at all,' cried Mr Parker eagerly. 'Quite the contrary, I assure you. A common idea, but a mistaken one. It may apply to your large, overgrown places like Brighton or Worthing or Eastbourne – but *not* to a small village like Sanditon, precluded by its size from experiencing any of the evils of civilisation; while the growth of the place, the buildings, the nursery grounds,[454] the demand for everything and the sure resort of the very best company – those regular, steady, private families of thorough gentility and character who are a blessing every- where – excite the industry of the poor and diffuse comfort and improvement among them of every sort. No, sir, I assure you, Sanditon is not a place – '

'I do not mean to take exception to *any* place in particular,' answered Mr Heywood. 'I only think our coast is too full of them altogether. But had we not better try to get you – '

'Our coast too full!' repeated Mr Parker. 'On that point perhaps we may not totally disagree. At least there are *enough*. Our coast is abundant enough. It demands no more. Everybody's taste and everybody's finances may be suited. And those good people who are trying to add to the number are, in my opinion, excessively absurd and must soon find themselves the dupes of their own fallacious calculations. Such a place as Sanditon, sir, I may say was wanted, was called for. Nature had marked it out, had spoken in most intelligible characters. The finest, purest sea breeze on the coast – acknowledged to be so – excellent bathing – fine hard sand – deep water ten yards from the shore – no mud – no weeds – no slimy rocks. Never was there a place more palpably designed by nature for the resort of the invalid – the very spot which thousands seemed in need of! The most desirable distance from London! One complete, measured mile nearer than Eastbourne. Only conceive, sir, the advantage of saving a whole mile in a long journey. But Brinshore, sir, which I dare say you have in your eye – the attempts of two or three speculating people about Brinshore this last year to raise that paltry hamlet – lying as it does between a stagnant marsh, a bleak moor and the constant effluvia of a ridge of putrefying seaweed – can end in nothing but their own disappointment. What in the name of common sense is to *recommend* Brinshore? A most insalubrious air – roads proverbially detestable – water brackish beyond example, impossible to get a good dish of tea within three miles of the place. And as for the soil – it is so cold and ungrateful that it can hardly be made to yield a cabbage. Depend upon it, sir, that this is a most faithful description of Brinshore – not in the smallest degree exaggerated – and if you have heard it differently spoken of – '

'Sir, I never heard it spoken of in my life before,' said Mr Heywood. 'I did not know there was such a place in the world.'

'You did not! There, my dear,' turning with exultation to his wife, 'you see how it is. So much for the celebrity of Brinshore! This gentleman did not know there was such a place in the world. Why, in truth, sir, I fancy we may apply to Brinshore that line of the poet Cowper in his description of the religious cottager, as opposed to Voltaire – "*She*, never heard of half a mile from home.'[455]

'With all my heart, sir – apply any verses you like to it. But I want to see something applied to your leg. And I am sure by your lady's countenance that she is quite of my opinion and thinks it a pity to lose any more time. And here come my girls to speak for themselves and their mother.' Two or three genteel-looking young women, followed by as many maidservants, were now seen issuing from the house. 'I began to wonder the bustle should not have reached *them*. A thing of this kind soon makes a stir in a lonely place like ours, Now, sir, let us see how you can be best conveyed into the house.'

The young ladies approached and said everything that was proper to recommend their father's offers, and in an unaffected manner calculated to make the strangers easy. As Mrs Parker was exceedingly anxious for relief – and her husband by this time not much less disposed for it – a very few civil scruples were enough; especially as the carriage, being now set up, was discovered to have received such injury on the fallen side as to be unfit for present use. Mr Parker was therefore carried into the house and his carriage wheeled off to a vacant barn.

Chapter 2

The acquaintance, thus oddly begun, was neither short nor unimportant. For a whole fortnight the travellers were fixed at Willingden, Mr Parker's sprain proving too serious for him to move sooner. He had fallen into very good hands. The Heywoods were a thoroughly respectable family and every possible attention was paid, in the kindest and most unpretending manner, to both husband and wife. *He* was waited on and nursed, and *she* cheered and comforted with unremitting kindness; and as every office of hospitality and friendliness was received as it ought, as there was not more goodwill on one side than gratitude on the other, nor any deficiency of generally pleasant manners on either, they grew to like each other in the course of that fortnight exceedingly well.

Mr Parker's character and history were soon unfolded. All that he understood of himself, he readily told, for he was very open-hearted; and where he might be himself in the dark, his conversation was still giving information to such of the Heywoods as could observe. By such he was perceived to be an enthusiast – on the subject of Sanditon, a complete enthusiast. Sanditon, the success of Sanditon as a small, fashionable bathing place, was the object for which he seemed to live. A very few years ago, it had been a quiet village of no pretensions; but some natural advantages in its position and some accidental circumstances having suggested to himself and the other principal land holder the probability of its becoming a profitable speculation, they had engaged in it, and planned and built, and praised and puffed,[456] and raised it to something of a young renown; and Mr Parker could now think of very little besides.

The facts which, in more direct communication, he laid before them were that he was about five-and-thirty, had been married – very happily married – seven years, and had four sweet children at home; that he was of a respectable family and easy, though not large, fortune; no profession – succeeding as eldest son to the property which two or three generations had been holding and accumulating before him; that he had two brothers and two sisters, all single and all independent – the eldest of the two former indeed, by collateral inheritance,[457] quite as well provided for as himself.

His object in quitting the high road to hunt for an advertising surgeon was also plainly stated. It had not proceeded from any intention of spraining his ankle or doing himself any other injury for the good of such surgeon, nor (as Mr Heywood had been apt to suppose) from any design of entering into partnership with him; it was merely in consequence of a wish to establish some medical man at Sanditon, which the nature of the advertisement induced him to expect to accomplish in Willingden. He was convinced that the advantage of a medical man at hand would very materially promote the rise and prosperity of the place, would in fact tend to bring a prodigious influx; nothing else was wanting. He had *strong* reason to believe that *one* family had been deterred last year from trying Sanditon on that account – and probably very many more – and his own sisters, who were sad invalids and whom he was very anxious to get to Sanditon this summer, could hardly be expected to hazard themselves in a place where they could not have immediate medical advice.

Upon the whole, Mr Parker was evidently an amiable family man, fond of wife, children, brothers and sisters, and generally kind-hearted; liberal, gentlemanlike, easy to please; of a sanguine turn of mind, with more imagination than judgement. And Mrs Parker was as evidently a gentle, amiable, sweet-tempered woman, the properest wife in the world for a man of strong understanding but not of a capacity to supply the cooler reflection which her own husband sometimes needed; and so entirely waiting to be guided on every occasion that whether he was risking his fortune or spraining his ankle she remained equally useless.

Sanditon was a second wife and four children to him, hardly less dear, and certainly more engrossing. He could talk of it for ever. It had indeed the highest claims, not only those of birthplace, property and home: it was his mine, his lottery, his speculation and his hobby horse;[458] his occupation, his hope and his futurity. He was extremely desirous of drawing his good friends at Willingden thither; and his endeavours in the cause were as grateful and disinterested as they were warm.

He wanted to secure the promise of a visit, to get as many of the family as his own house would contain to follow him to Sanditon as soon as possible; and, healthy as they all undeniably were, foresaw that every one of them would be benefited by the sea. He held it indeed as certain that no person could be really well, no person (however upheld for the present by fortuitous aids of exercise and spirits in a semblance of health) could be really in a state of secure and permanent health without spending at least six weeks by the sea every year. The sea air and sea bathing together were nearly infallible, one or the other of them being a match for every disorder of the stomach, the lungs or the blood. They were anti-spasmodic, anti-pulmonary, anti-septic, anti-billious and anti-rheumatic.[459] Nobody could catch cold by the sea; nobody wanted appetite by the sea; nobody wanted spirits; nobody wanted strength. Sea air was healing, softening,[460] relaxing – fortifying and bracing – seemingly just as was wanted – sometimes one, sometimes the other. If the sea breeze failed, the sea bath was the certain corrective; and where bathing disagreed, the sea air alone was evidently designed by nature for the cure.

His eloquence, however, could not prevail. Mr and Mrs Heywood never left home. Marrying early and having a very numerous family, their movements had long been limited to one small circle; and they were older in habits than in age. Excepting two journeys to London in the year to receive his dividends, Mr Heywood went no farther than his feet or his well-tried old horse could carry him; and Mrs Heywood's adventurings were only now and then to visit her neighbours in the old coach which had been new when they married and fresh-lined on their eldest son's coming of age ten years ago. They had a very pretty property – enough, had their family been of reasonable limits, to have allowed them a very gentlemanlike share of luxuries and change; enough for them to have indulged in a new carriage and better roads, an occasional month at Tunbridge Wells, and symptoms of the gout[461] and a winter at Bath. But the maintenance, education and fitting out of fourteen children demanded a very quiet, settled, careful course of life, and obliged them to be stationary and healthy at Willingden.

What prudence had at first enjoined was now rendered pleasant by habit. They never left home and they had gratification in saying so. But very far from wishing their children to do the same, they were glad to promote *their* getting out into the world as much as possible. *They* stayed at home that their children *might* get out; and, while making that home extremely comfortable, welcomed every change from it which could give useful connections or respectable acquaintance to sons or daughters. When Mr and Mrs Parker, therefore, ceased from soliciting a family visit and bounded their views to carrying back one daughter with them, no difficulties were started. It was general pleasure and consent.

Their invitation was to Miss Charlotte Heywood, a very pleasing young woman of two-and-twenty, the eldest of the daughters at home and the one who, under her mother's directions, had been particularly useful and obliging to them; who had attended them most and knew them best. Charlotte was to go: with excellent health, to bathe and be better if she could; to receive every possible pleasure which Sanditon could be made to supply by the gratitude of those she went with; and to buy new parasols, new gloves and new brooches for her sisters and herself at the library,[462] which Mr Parker was anxiously wishing to support.

All that Mr Heywood himself could be persuaded to promise was that he would send everyone to Sanditon who asked his advice, and that nothing should ever induce him (as far as the future could be answered for) to spend even five shilling at Brinshore.

Chapter 3

Every neighbourhood should have a great lady. The great lady of Sanditon was Lady Denham; and in their journey from Willingden to the coast, Mr Parker gave Charlotte a more detailed account of her than had been called for before. She had been necessarily often mentioned at Willingden – for being his colleague in speculation, Sanditon itself could not be talked of long without the introduction of Lady Denham. That she was a very rich old lady who had buried two husbands, who knew the value of money, was very much looked up to and had a poor cousin living with her were facts already known; but some further particulars of her history and her character served to lighten the tediousness of a long hill, or a heavy bit of road, and to give the visiting young lady a suitable knowledge of the person with whom she might now expect to be daily associating.

Lady Denham had been a rich Miss Brereton, born to wealth but not to education. Her first husband had been a Mr Hollis, a man of considerable property in the country, of which a large share of the parish of Sanditon, with manor and mansion house, made a part. He had been an elderly man when she married him, her own age about thirty. Her motives for such a match could be little understood at the distance of forty years, but she had so well nursed and pleased Mr Hollis that at his death he left her everything – all his estates, and all at her disposal. After a widowhood of some years, she had been induced to marry again. The late Sir Harry Denham, of Denham Park in the neighbourhood of Sanditon, had succeeded in removing her and her large income to his own domains, but he could not succeed in the views of permanently enriching his family which were attributed to him. She had been too wary to put anything out of her own power and when, on Sir Harry's decease, she returned again to her own house at Sanditon, she was said to have made this boast to a friend: 'that though she had *got* nothing but her title from the family, still she had *given* nothing for it'.

For the title, it was to be supposed, she had married; and Mr Parker acknowledged there being just such a degree of value for it apparent now as to give her conduct that natural explanation. 'There is at times,' said he, 'a little self-importance – but it is not offensive – and there are moments, there are points, when her love of money is carried greatly too far. But she is a good-natured woman, a very good-natured woman – a very obliging, friendly neighbour; a cheerful, independent, valuable character – and her faults may be entirely imputed to her want of education. She has good natural sense, but quite uncultivated. She has a fine active mind as well as a fine healthy frame for a woman of seventy, and enters into the improvement of Sanditon with a spirit truly admirable – though now and then, a littleness *will* appear. She cannot look forward quite as I would have her – and takes alarm at a trifling present expense without considering what returns it will make her in a year or two. That is, we think *differently*. We now and then see things *differently*, Miss Heywood. Those who tell their own story, you know, must be listened to with caution. When you see us in contact, you will judge for yourself.'

Lady Denham was indeed a great lady beyond the common wants of society, for she had many thousands a year to bequeath, and three distinct sets of people to be courted by: her own relations, who might very reasonably wish for her original thirty thousand pounds[463] among them; the legal heirs of Mr Hollis, who must hope to be more indebted to her sense of justice than he had allowed them to be to his; and those members of the Denham family whom her second husband had hoped to make a good bargain for. By all of these, or by branches of them, she had no doubt been long, and still continued to be, well attacked; and of these three divisions, Mr Parker did not hesitate to say that Mr Hollis's kindred were the *least* in favour and Sir Harry Denham's the *most*. The former, he believed, had done themselves irremediable harm by expressions of very unwise and unjustifiable resentment at the time of

Mr Hollis's death; the latter had the advantage of being the remnant of a connection which she certainly valued, of having been known to her from their childhood and of being always at hand to preserve their interest by reasonable attention. Sir Edward, the present baronet, nephew to Sir Harry, resided constantly at Denham Park; and Mr Parker had little doubt that he and his sister, Miss Denham, who lived with him, would be principally remembered in her will. He sincerely hoped it. Miss Denham had a very small provision; and her brother was a poor man for his rank in society. 'He is a warm friend to Sanditon,' said Mr Parker, 'and his hand would be as liberal as his heart, had he the power. He would be a noble coadjutor! As it is, he does what he can and is running up a tasteful little cottage *ornée* [464] on a strip of waste ground[465] Lady Denham has granted him, which I have no doubt we shall have many a candidate for before the end even of *this* season.'

Till within the last twelvemonth, Mr Parker had considered Sir Edward as standing without a rival, as having the fairest chance of succeeding to the greater part of all that she had to give; but there were now another person's claims to be taken into account – those of the young female relation whom Lady Denham had been induced to receive into her family. After having always protested against any such addition, and long and often enjoyed the repeated defeats she had given to every attempt of her relations to introduce this young lady or that young lady as a companion[466] at Sanditon House, she had brought back with her from London last Michaelmas a Miss Brereton, who bid fair by her merits to vie in favour with Sir Edward and to secure for herself and her family that share of the accumulated property which they had certainly the best right to inherit.

Mr Parker spoke warmly of Clara Brereton, and the interest of his story increased very much with the introduction of such a character. Charlotte listened with more than amusement now; it was with solicitude and enjoyment, as she heard her described to be lovely, amiable, gentle, unassuming, conducting herself uniformly with great good sense, and evidently gaining by her innate worth on the affections of her patroness. Beauty, sweetness, poverty and dependence do not want the imagination of a man to operate upon; with due exceptions, woman feels for woman very promptly and compassionately. He gave the particulars which had led to Clara's admission at Sanditon as no bad exemplification of that mixture of character – that union of littleness with kindness and good sense, even liberality – which he saw in Lady Denham.

After having avoided London for many years, principally on account of these very cousins who were continually writing, inviting and tormenting her, and whom she was determined to keep at a distance, she had been obliged to go there last Michaelmas with the certainty of being detained at least a fortnight. She had gone to a hotel, living by her own account as prudently as possible to defy the reputed expensiveness of such a home, and at the end of three days calling for her bill that she might judge of her state. Its amount was such as determined her on staying not another hour in the house, and she was preparing – in all the anger and perturbation of her belief in very gross imposition and her ignorance of where to go for better usage – to leave the hotel at all hazards, when the cousins, the politic and lucky cousins, who seemed always to have a spy on her, introduced themselves at this important moment; and learning her situation, persuaded her to accept such a home for the rest of her stay as their humbler house in a very inferior part of London could offer.

She went, was delighted with her welcome and the hospitality and attention she received from everybody; found her good cousins, the Breretons, beyond her expectation worthy people; and finally was impelled by a personal knowledge of their narrow income and pecuniary difficulties to invite one of the girls of the family to pass the winter with her. The invitation was to *one*, for six months, with the probability of another being then to take her place; but in *selecting* the one, Lady Denham had shown the good part of her character – for, passing by the actual *daughters* of the house, she had chosen Clara, a niece, more helpless and more pitiable, of course, than any – a dependent on poverty – an additional burden on an encumbered circle; and one who had been so low in every worldly view as, with all her natural endowments and powers, to have been preparing for a situation little better than a nursery maid.

Clara had returned with her and by her good sense and merit had now, to all appearance, secured a very strong hold in Lady Denham's regard. The six months had long been over and not a syllable was breathed of any change or exchange. She was a general favourite. The influence of her steady conduct and mild, gentle temper was felt by everybody. The prejudices which had met her at first, in some quarters, were all dissipated. She was felt to be worthy of trust, to be the very companion who would guide and soften Lady Denham, who would enlarge her mind and open her hand. She was as thoroughly amiable as she was lovely; and since having had the advantage of their Sanditon breezes, that loveliness was complete.

Chapter 4

'And whose very snug-looking place is this?' said Charlotte as, in a sheltered dip within two miles of the sea, they passed close by a moderate-sized house, well fenced and planted, and rich in the garden, orchard and meadows which are the best embellishments of such a dwelling. 'It seems to have as many comforts about it as Willingden.'

'Ah,' said Mr Parker. 'This is my old house, the house of my fore-fathers, the house where I and all my brothers and sisters were born and bred, and where my own three eldest children were born; where Mrs Parker and I lived till within the last two years, till our new house was finished. I am glad you are pleased with it. It is an honest old place; and Hillier keeps it in very good order. I have given it up, you know, to the man who occupies the chief of my land. He gets a better house by it, and I, a rather better situation! One other hill brings us to Sanditon – modern Sanditon – a beautiful spot. Our ancestors, you know, always built in a hole. Here were we, pent down in this little contracted nook, without air or view, only one mile and three quarters from the noblest expanse of ocean between the South Foreland and Land's End,[467] and without the smallest advantage from it. You will not think I have made a bad exchange when we reach Trafalgar House – which, by the by, I almost wish I had not named Trafalgar – for Waterloo[468] is more the thing now. However, Waterloo is in reserve; and if we have encouragement enough this year for a little crescent to be ventured on (as I trust we shall), then we shall be able to call it Waterloo Crescent – and the name joined to the form of the building, which always takes, will give us the command of lodgers. In a good season we should have more applications than we could attend to.'

'It was always a very comfortable house,' said Mrs Parker, looking at it through the back window with something like the fondness of regret. 'And such a nice garden – such an excellent garden.'

'Yes, my love, but *that* we may be said to carry with us. It supplies us, as before, with all the fruit and vegetables we want. And we have, in fact, all the comfort of an excellent kitchen garden without the constant eyesore of its formalities or the yearly nuisance of its decaying vegetation. Who can endure a cabbage bed in October?'

'Oh dear, yes. We are quite as well off for garden stuff as ever we were; for if it is forgot to be brought at any time, we can always buy what we want at Sanditon House. The gardener there is glad enough to supply us. But it was a nice place for the children to run about in. So shady in summer!'

'My dear, we shall have shade enough on the hill, and more than enough in the course of a very few years. The growth of my plantations[469] is a general astonishment. In the meanwhile we have the canvas awning which gives us the most complete comfort within doors. And you can get a parasol at Whitby's for little Mary at any time, or a large bonnet at Jebb's. And as for the boys, I must say I would rather *they* ran about in the sunshine than not. I am sure we agree, my dear, in wishing our boys to be as hardy as possible.'

'Yes, indeed, I am sure we do. And I will get Mary a little parasol, which will make her as proud as can be. How grave she will walk about with it and fancy herself quite a little woman. Oh, I have not the smallest doubt of our being a great deal better off where we are now. If we any of us want to bathe, we have not a quarter of a mile to go. But you know,' still looking back, 'one loves to look at an old friend at a place where one has been happy. The Hilliers did not seem to feel the storms last winter at all. I remember seeing Mrs Hillier after one of those dreadful nights, when *we* had been literally rocked in our bed, and she did not seem at all aware of the wind being anything more than common.'

'Yes, yes, that's likely enough. *We* have all the grandeur of the storm with less real danger because the wind, meeting with nothing to oppose or confine it around our house, simply rages and passes on; while down in this gutter, nothing is known of the state of the air below the tops of the trees; and the inhabitants may be taken totally unawares by one of those dreadful currents, which do more mischief in a valley when they *do* arise than an open country ever experiences in the heaviest gale. But, my dear love, as to garden stuff, you were saying that any accidental omission is supplied in a moment by Lady Denham's gardener. But it occurs to me that we ought to go elsewhere upon such occasions, and that old Stringer and his son have a higher claim. I encouraged him to set up, you know, and am afraid he does not do very well. That is, there has not been time enough yet. He *will* do very well beyond a doubt. But at first it is uphill work, and therefore we must give him what help we can. When any vegetables or fruit happen to be wanted – and it will not be amiss to have them often wanted, to have something or other forgotten most days; just to have a nominal supply, you know, that poor old Andrew may not lose his daily job – but in fact to buy the chief of our consumption from the Stringers.'

'Very well, my love, that can be easily done. And cook will be satisfied, which will be a great comfort, for she is always complaining of old

Andrew now and says he never brings her what she wants. There – now the old house is quite left behind. What is it your brother Sidney says about its being a hospital?'[470]

'Oh, my dear Mary, merely a joke of his. He pretends to advise me to make a hospital of it. He pretends to laugh at my improvements. Sidney says anything, you know. He has always said what he chose, of and to us all. Most families have such a member among them, I believe, Miss Heywood. There is someone in most families privileged by superior abilities or spirits to say anything. In ours, it is Sidney, who is a very clever young man and with great powers of pleasing. He lives too much in the world to be settled; that is his only fault. He is here and there and everywhere. I wish we may get him to Sanditon. I should like to have you acquainted with him. And it would be a fine thing for the place! Such a young man as Sidney, with his neat equipage[471] and fashionable air. You and I, Mary, know what effect it might have. Many a respectable family, many a careful mother, many a pretty daughter might it secure us to the prejudice of Eastbourne and Hastings.'

They were now approaching the church and neat village of old Sanditon, which stood at the foot of the hill they were afterwards to ascend – a hill whose side was covered with the woods and enclosures of Sanditon House and whose height ended in an open down where the new buildings might soon be looked for. A branch only of the valley, winding more obliquely towards the sea, gave a passage to an inconsiderable stream, and formed at its mouth a third habitable division in a small cluster of fishermen's houses.

The original village contained little more than cottages; but the spirit of the day had been caught, as Mr Parker observed with delight to Charlotte, and two or three of the best of them were smartened up with a white curtain and 'Lodgings to let'; and farther on, in the little green court of an old farmhouse, two females in elegant white were actually to be seen with their books and camp stools; and in turning the corner of the baker's shop, the sound of a harp might be heard through the upper casement.

Such sights and sounds were highly blissful to Mr Parker. Not that he had any personal concern in the success of the village itself; for considering it as too remote from the beach, he had done nothing there; but it was a most valuable proof of the increasing fashion of the place altogether. If the *village* could attract, the hill might be nearly full. He anticipated an amazing season. At the same time last year (late in July) there had not been a single lodger in the village! Nor did he remember any during the whole summer, excepting one family of children who came from London for sea air after the whooping cough,[472] and whose mother would not let them be nearer the shore for fear of their tumbling in.

'Civilisation, civilisation indeed!' cried Mr Parker, delighted. 'Look, my dear Mary, look at William Heeley's windows. Blue shoes, and nankin boots![473] Who would have expected such a sight at a shoemaker's in old Sanditon! This is new within the month. There was no blue shoe when we passed this way a month ago. Glorious indeed! Well, I think I *have* done something in my day. Now, for our hill, our health-breathing hill.'

In ascending, they passed the lodge gates of Sanditon House and saw the top of the house itself among its groves. It was the last building of former days in that line of the parish. A little higher up, the modern began; and in crossing the down, a Prospect House, a Bellevue Cottage and a Denham Place were to be looked at by Charlotte with the calmness of amused curiosity, and by Mr Parker with the eager eye which hoped to see scarcely any empty houses. More bills at the windows[474] than he had calculated on, and a smaller show of company on the hill – fewer carriages, fewer walkers. He had fancied it just the time of day for them to be all returning from their airings to dinner; but the sands and The Terrace always attracted some, and the tide must be flowing – about half-tide now.

He longed to be on the sands, the cliffs, at his own house, and everywhere out of his house at once. His spirits rose with the very sight of the sea and he could almost feel his ankle getting stronger already. Trafalgar House, on the most elevated spot on the down, was a light, elegant building, standing in a small lawn with a very young plantation round it, about a hundred yards from the brow of a steep but not very lofty cliff, and the nearest to it of every building, excepting one short row of smart-looking houses called The Terrace, with a broad walk in front, aspiring to be the Mall of the place. In this row were the best milliner's shop and the library and, a little detached from it, the hotel and billiard-room. Here began the descent to the beach and to the bathing machines.[475] And this was therefore the favourite spot for beauty and fashion.

At Trafalgar House, rising at a little distance behind The Terrace, the travellers were safely set down; and all was happiness and joy between papa and mama and their children; while Charlotte, having received possession of her apartment, found amusement enough in standing at her ample Venetian window[476] and looking over the miscellaneous foreground of unfinished buildings, waving linen and tops of houses to the sea, dancing and sparkling in sunshine and freshness.

Chapter 5

When they met before dinner, Mr Parker was looking over letters.

'Not a line from Sidney!' said he. 'He is an idle fellow. I sent him an account of my accident from Willingden and thought he would have vouchsafed me an answer. But perhaps it implies that he is coming himself. I trust it may. But here is a letter from one of my sisters. *They* never fail me. Women are the only correspondents to be depended on. Now, Mary,' smiling at his wife, 'before I open it, what shall we guess as to the state of health of those it comes from – or rather what would Sidney say if he were here? Sidney is a saucy fellow, Miss Heywood. And you must know, he will have it there is a good deal of imagination in my two sisters' complaints. But it really is not so – or very little. They have wretched health, as you have heard us say frequently, and are subject to a variety of very serious disorders. Indeed, I do not believe they know what a day's health is. And at the same time, they are such excellent useful women and have so much energy of character that where any good is to be done, they force themselves on exertions which, to those who do not thoroughly know them, have an extraordinary appearance. But there is really no affectation about them, you know. They have only weaker constitutions and stronger minds than are often met with, either separate or together. And our youngest brother, who lives with them and who is not much above twenty, I am sorry to say is almost as great an invalid as themselves. He is so delicate that he can engage in no profession. Sidney laughs at him. But it really is no joke, though Sidney often makes me laugh at them all in spite of myself. Now, if he were here, I know he would be offering odds that either Susan, Diana or Arthur would appear by this letter to have been at the point of death within the last month.'

Having run his eye over the letter, he shook his head and began, 'No chance of seeing them at Sanditon, I am sorry to say. A very indifferent account of them indeed. Seriously, a very indifferent account. Mary, you will be quite sorry to hear how ill they have been and are. Miss Heywood, if you will give me leave, I will read Diana's letter aloud. I like to have my friends acquainted with each other and I am afraid this is the only sort of acquaintance I shall have the means of accomplishing between you. And I can have no scruple on Diana's account; for her letters show her exactly as she is, the most active, friendly, warm-hearted being in existence, and therefore must give a good impression.' He read:

'My DEAR TOM – we were all much grieved at your accident, and if you had not described yourself as fallen into such very good hands, I should have been with you at all hazards the day after the receipt of your letter, though it found me suffering under a more severe attack than usual of my old grievance, spasmodic bile,[477] and hardly able to crawl from my bed to the sofa. But how were you treated? Send me more particulars in your next. If indeed a simple sprain, as you denominate it, nothing would have been so judicious as friction, friction by the hand alone, supposing it could be applied *instantly*. Two years ago I happened to be calling on Mrs Sheldon when her coachman sprained his foot as he was cleaning the carriage and could hardly limp into the house, but by the immediate use of friction alone steadily persevered in (and I rubbed his ankle with my own hand for six hours without intermission) he was well in three days. Many thanks, my dear Tom, for the kindness with respect to us, which had so large a share in bringing on your accident. But pray never run into peril again in looking for an apothecary on our account, for had you the most experienced man in his line settled at Sanditon, it would be no recommendation to us. We have entirely done with the whole medical tribe. We have consulted physician after physician in vain, till we are quite convinced that they can do nothing for us and that we must trust to our own knowledge of our own wretched constitutions for any relief. But if you think it advisable for the interest of the *place* to get a medical man there, I will undertake the commission with pleasure, and have no doubt of succeeding. I could soon put the necessary irons in the fire. As for getting to Sanditon myself, it is quite an impossibility. I grieve to say that I dare not attempt it, for my feelings tell me too plainly that, in my present state, the sea air would probably be the death of me. And neither of my dear companions will leave me or I would promote their going down to you for a fortnight. But in truth, I doubt whether Susan's nerves would be equal to the effort. She has been suffering much from the headache, and six leeches[478] a day for ten days together relieved her so little that we thought it right to change our measures, and being convinced on examination that much of the evil lay in her gum, I persuaded her to attack the disorder there. She has accordingly had three teeth drawn, and is decidedly better, but her nerves are a good deal deranged. She can only speak in a whisper and fainted away twice this morning on poor Arthur's trying to suppress a cough. He, I am happy to say, is tolerably well though more languid than I like and I fear for his liver. I have heard nothing of Sidney since your being together in town, but conclude his scheme to the Isle of Wight has not taken place or we should have seen him in his way. Most sincerely do we wish you a good season at Sanditon, and though we cannot contribute to your *beau monde*[479] in person, we are doing our utmost to send you company worth having and think we may safely reckon on securing you two large families. One a rich West Indian[480] from Surrey, the other a most respectable girls' boarding school, or academy, from Camberwell.[481] I will not tell you how many people I have employed in the business – wheel within wheel. But success more than repays.

Yours most affectionately, &c.

'Well,' said Mr Parker, as he finished. 'Though I dare say Sidney might find something extremely entertaining in this letter and make us laugh for half an hour together, I declare, by myself can see nothing in it but what is either very pitiable or very creditable. With all their sufferings, you perceive how much they are occupied in promoting the good of others! So anxious for Sanditon! Two large families – one for Prospect House probably, the other for Number 2, Denham Place, or the end house of The Terrace, with extra beds at the hotel. I told you my sisters were excellent women, Miss Heywood.'

'And I am sure they must be very extraordinary ones,' said Charlotte. 'I am astonished at the cheerful style of the letter, considering the state in which both sisters appear to be. Three teeth drawn at once – frightful! Your sister Diana seems almost as ill as possible, but those three teeth of your sister Susan's are more distressing than all the rest.'

'Oh, they are so used to the operation – to every operation – and have such fortitude!'

'Your sisters know what they are about, I dare say, but their measures seem to touch on extremes. I feel that in any illness I should be so anxious for professional advice, so very little venturesome for myself or anybody I loved! But then, *we* have been so healthy a family that I can be no judge of what the habit of self-doctoring may do.'

'Why to own the truth,' said Mrs Parker, 'I *do* think the Miss Parkers carry it too far sometimes. And so do you, my love, you know. You often think they would be better if they would leave themselves more alone – and especially Arthur. I know you think it a great pity they should give *him* such a turn for being ill.'

'Well, well, my dear Mary, I grant you, it *is* unfortunate for poor Arthur that at his time of life he should be encouraged to give way to indisposition. It *is* bad that he should be fancying himself too sickly for any profession and sit down at one-and-twenty, on the interest of his own little fortune, without any idea of attempting to improve it or of engaging in any occupation that may be of use to himself or others. But let us talk of pleasanter things. These two large families are just what we wanted. But here is something at hand pleasanter still – Morgan with his, "Dinner on table." '

Chapter 6

The party were very soon moving after dinner. Mr Parker could not be satisfied without an early visit to the library, and the library subscription book;[482] and Charlotte was glad to see as much as possible, and as quickly as possible, where all was new. They were out in the very quietest part of a watering-place day, when the important business of dinner or of sitting after dinner was going on in almost every inhabited lodging. Here and there might be seen a solitary elderly man, who was forced to move early and walk for health; but in general, it was a thorough pause of company. It was emptiness and tranquillity on The Terrace, the cliffs and the sands.

The shops were deserted. The straw hats and pendant lace seemed left to their fate both within the house and without, and Mrs Whitby at the library was sitting in her inner room, reading one of her own novels for want of employment. The list of subscribers was but commonplace. The Lady Denham, Miss Brereton, Mr and Mrs Parker, Sir Edward Denham and Miss Denham, whose names might be said to lead off the season, were followed by nothing better than: Mrs Mathews, Miss Mathews, Miss E. Mathews, Miss H. Mathews; Dr and Mrs Brown; Mr Richard Pratt; Lieutenant Smith RN; Captain Little – Limehouse;[483] Mrs Jane Fisher, Miss Fisher; Miss Scroggs; Reverend Mr Hanking; Mr Beard – Solicitor, Grays Inn;[484] Mrs Davis and Miss Merryweather.

Mr Parker could not but feel that the list was not only without distinction but less numerous than he had hoped. It was but July, however, and August and September were the months. And besides, the promised large families from Surrey and Camberwell were an ever-ready consolation.

Mrs Whitby came forward without delay from her literary recess, delighted to see Mr Parker, whose manners recommended him to everybody, and they were fully occupied in their various civilities and communications; while Charlotte, having added her name to the list as the first offering to the success of the season, was busy in some immediate purchases for the further good of everybody – as soon as

Miss Whitby could be hurried down from her toilette,[485] with all her glossy curls and smart trinkets, to wait on her.

The library, of course, afforded everything: all the useless things in the world that could not be done without; and among so many pretty temptations, and with so much goodwill for Mr Parker to encourage expenditure, Charlotte began to feel that she must check herself – or rather, she reflected that at two-and-twenty there could be no excuse for her doing otherwise – and that it would not do for her to be spending all her money the very first evening. She took up a book; it happened to be a volume of *Camilla*.[486] She had not Camilla's youth, and had no intention of having her distress; so she turned from the drawers of rings and brooches, repressed further solicitation and paid for what she bought.

For her particular gratification, they were then to take a turn on the cliff; but as they quitted the library they were met by two ladies whose arrival made an alteration necessary: Lady Denham and Miss Brereton. They had been to Trafalgar House and been directed thence to the library; and though Lady Denham was a great deal too active to regard the walk of a mile as anything requiring rest, and talked of going home again directly, the Parkers knew that to be pressed into their house and obliged to take her tea with them would suit her best; and therefore the stroll on the cliff gave way to an immediate return home.

'No, no,' said her ladyship. 'I will not have you hurry your tea on my account. I know you like your tea late. My early hours are not to put my neighbours to inconvenience. No, no, Miss Clara and I will get back to our own tea. We came out with no other thought. We wanted just to see you and make sure of your being really come – but we get back to our own tea.'

She went on, however, towards Trafalgar House and took possession of the drawing-room very quietly, without seeming to hear a word of Mrs Parker's orders to the servant, as they entered, to bring tea directly. Charlotte was fully consoled for the loss of her walk by finding herself in company with those whom the conversation of the morning had given her a great curiosity to see. She observed them well. Lady Denham was of middle height, stout, upright and alert in her motions, with a shrewd eye and self-satisfied air but not an unagreeable countenance; and though her manner was rather downright and abrupt, as of a person who valued herself on being free-spoken, there was a good humour and cordiality about her – a civility and readiness to be acquainted with Charlotte herself and a heartiness of welcome towards her old friends – which was inspiring the goodwill she seemed to feel.

And as for Miss Brereton, her appearance so completely justified Mr Parker's praise that Charlotte thought she had never beheld a more lovely or more interesting young woman.

Elegantly tall, regularly handsome, with great delicacy of complexion and soft blue eyes, a sweetly modest and yet naturally graceful address, Charlotte could see in her only the most perfect representation of whatever heroine might be most beautiful and bewitching in all the numerous volumes they had left behind on Mrs Whitby's shelves; perhaps it might be partly owing to her having just issued from a circulating library, but she could not separate the idea of a complete heroine from Clara Brereton. Her situation with Lady Denham so very much in favour of it! She seemed placed with her on purpose to be ill-used. Such poverty and dependence joined to such beauty and merit seemed to leave no choice in the business.

These feelings were not the result of any spirit of romance in Charlotte herself. No, she was a very sober-minded young lady, sufficiently well read in novels to supply her imagination with amusement, but not at all unreasonably influenced by them; and while she pleased herself the first five minutes with fancying the persecution which *ought* to be the lot of the interesting Clara, especially in the form of the most barbarous conduct on Lady Denham's side, she found no reluctance to admit from subsequent observation that they appeared to be on very comfortable terms. She could see nothing worse in Lady Denham than the sort of old-fashioned formality of always calling her 'Miss Clara'; nor anything objectionable in the degree of observance and attention which Clara paid. On one side it seemed protecting kindness, on the other grateful and affectionate respect.

The conversation turned entirely upon Sanditon, its present number of visitants and the chances of a good season. It was evident that Lady Denham had more anxiety, more fears of loss, than her coadjutor. She wanted to have the place fill faster and seemed to have many harassing apprehensions of the lodgings being in some instances underlet. Miss Diana Parker's two large families were not forgotten.

'Very good, very good,' said her ladyship. 'A West Indy family and a school. That sounds well. That will bring money.'

'No people spend more freely, I believe, than West Indians,' observed Mr Parker.

'Aye, so I have heard; and because they have full purses, fancy themselves equal, maybe, to your old country families. But then, they who scatter their money so freely never think of whether they may not be doing mischief by raising the price of things. And I have heard that's

very much the case with your West Injines. And if they come among us
to raise the price of our necessaries of life, we shall not much thank
them, Mr Parker.'

'My dear madam, they can only raise the price of consumable articles
by such an extraordinary demand for them and such a diffusion of
money among us as must do us more good than harm. Our butchers
and bakers and traders in general cannot get rich without bringing
prosperity to us. If they do not gain, our rents must be insecure; and in
proportion to their profit must be ours eventually in the increased value
of our houses.'

'Oh! well. But I should not like to have butcher's meat raised, though.
And I shall keep it down as long as I can. Aye, that young lady smiles, I
see. I dare say she thinks me an odd sort of creature; but she will come
to care about such matters herself in time. Yes, yes, my dear, depend
upon it, you will be thinking of the price of butcher's meat in time,
though you may not happen to have quite such a servants' hall to feed as
I have. And I do believe those are best off that have fewest servants. I am
not a woman of parade as all the world knows, and if it was not for what
I owe to poor Mr Hollis's memory, I should never keep up Sanditon
House as I do. It is not for my own pleasure. Well, Mr Parker, and the
other is a boarding school, a French boarding school,[487] is it? No harm
in that. They'll stay their six weeks. And out of such a number, who
knows but some may be consumptive and want asses' milk;[488] and I have
two milch asses at this present time. But perhaps the little misses may
hurt the furniture. I hope they will have a good sharp governess to look
after them.'

Poor Mr Parker got no more credit from Lady Denham than he had
from his sisters for the object which had taken him to Willingden.

'Lord! my dear sir,' she cried. 'How could you think of such a thing?
I am very sorry you met with your accident, but upon my word, you
deserved it. Going after a *doctor*! Why, what should we do with a doctor
here? It would be only encouraging our servants and the poor to fancy
themselves ill if there was a doctor at hand. Oh! pray, let us have none
of the tribe at Sanditon. We go on very well as we are. There is the sea
and the downs and my milch asses. And I have told Mrs Whitby that if
anybody enquires for a chamber-horse,[489] they may be supplied at a fair
rate – poor Mr Hollis's chamber-horse, as good as new – and what can
people want for more? Here have I lived seventy good years in the
world and never took physic above twice – and never saw the face of a
doctor in all my life on my own account. And I verily believe if my poor
dear Sir Harry had never seen one neither, he would have been alive

now. Ten fees, one after another, did the man take who sent him out of the world. I beseech you, Mr Parker, no doctors here.'

The tea things were brought in.

'Oh, my dear Mrs Parker, you should not indeed – why would you do so? I was just upon the point of wishing you good-evening. But since you are so very neighbourly, I believe Miss Clara and I must stay.'

Chapter 7

The popularity of the Parkers brought them some visitors the very next morning; among them, Sir Edward Denham and his sister, who, having been at Sanditon House, drove on to pay their compliments; and the duty of letter-writing being accomplished, Charlotte was settled with Mrs Parker in the drawing-room in time to see them all.

The Denhams were the only ones to excite particular attention. Charlotte was glad to complete her knowledge of the family by an introduction to them, and found them, the better half at least (for while single, the *gentleman* may sometimes be thought the better half of the pair), not unworthy of notice. Miss Denham was a fine young woman, but cold and reserved, giving the idea of one who felt her consequence with pride and her poverty with discontent, and who was immediately gnawed by the want of a handsomer equipage than the simple gig in which they travelled, and which their groom[490] was leading about still in her sight. Sir Edward was much her superior in air and manner – certainly handsome, but yet more to be remarked for his very good address and wish of paying attention and giving pleasure. He came into the room remarkably well, talked much – and very much to Charlotte, by whom he chanced to be placed – and she soon perceived that he had a fine countenance, a most pleasing gentleness of voice and a great deal of conversation. She liked him. Sober-minded as she was, she thought him agreeable and did not quarrel with the suspicion of his finding her equally so, which would arise from his evidently disregarding his sister's motion to go, and persisting in his station and his discourse. I make no apologies for my heroine's vanity. If there are young ladies in the world at her time of life more dull of fancy and more careless of pleasing, I know them not and never wish to know them.

At last, from the low French windows[491] of the drawing-room which commanded the road and all the paths across the down, Charlotte and Sir Edward as they sat could not but observe Lady Denham and Miss Brereton walking by; and there was instantly a slight change in Sir

Edward's countenance – with an anxious glance after them as they proceeded – followed by an early proposal to his sister, not merely for moving, but for walking on together to The Terrace, which altogether gave a hasty turn to Charlotte's fancy, cured her of her half-hour's fever, and placed her in a more capable state of judging, when Sir Edward was gone, of how agreeable he had actually been. 'Perhaps there was a good deal in his air and address; and his title did him no harm.'

She was very soon in his company again. The first object of the Parkers, when their house was cleared of morning visitors, was to get out themselves. The Terrace was the attraction to all. Everybody who walked must begin with The Terrace; and there, seated on one of the two green benches by the gravel walk, they found the united Denham party; but though united in the gross,[492] very distinctly divided again: the two superior ladies being at one end of the bench, and Sir Edward and Miss Brereton at the other. Charlotte's first glance told her that Sir Edward's air was that of a lover. There could be no doubt of his devotion to Clara. How Clara received it was less obvious, but she was inclined to think not very favourably; for though sitting thus apart with him (which probably she might not have been able to prevent), her air was calm and grave.

That the young lady at the other end of the bench was doing penance was indubitable. The difference in Miss Denham's countenance, the change from Miss Denham sitting in cold grandeur in Mrs Parker's drawing-room, to be kept from silence by the efforts of others, to Miss Denham at Lady Denham's elbow, listening and talking with smiling attention or solicitous eagerness, was very striking – and very amusing or very melancholy, just as satire or morality might prevail. Miss Denham's character was pretty well decided with Charlotte. Sir Edward's required longer observation. He surprised her by quitting Clara immediately on their all joining and agreeing to walk, and by addressing his attentions entirely to herself.

Stationing himself close by her, he seemed to mean to detach her as much as possible from the rest of the party and to give her the whole of his conversation. He began, in a tone of great taste and feeling, to talk of the sea and the sea shore; and ran with energy through all the usual phrases employed in praise of their sublimity[493] and descriptive of the *undescribable* emotions they excite in the mind of sensibility.[494] The terrific grandeur of the ocean in a storm, its glass surface in a calm, its gulls and its samphire[495] and the deep fathoms of its abysses, its quick vicissitudes, its direful deceptions, its mariners tempting it in sunshine and overwhelmed by the sudden tempest – all were eagerly and fluently touched; rather commonplace perhaps, but doing very well from the lips of a handsome Sir Edward, and she could not but think him a man of feeling,[496] till he began to stagger her by the number of his quotations and the bewilderment of some of his sentences.

'Do you remember,' said he, 'Scott's beautiful lines on the sea? Oh! what a description they convey! They are never out of my thoughts when I walk here. That man who can read them unmoved must have the nerves of an assassin! Heaven defend me from meeting such a man unarmed.'

'What description do you mean?' said Charlotte. 'I remember none, at this moment, of the sea in either of Scott's poems.'

'Do you not indeed? Nor can I exactly recall the beginning at this moment. But you cannot have forgotten his description of woman –

> Oh! Woman in our hours of ease – [497]

Delicious! Delicious! Had he written nothing more, he would have been immortal. And then again, that unequalled, unrivalled address to parental affection –

> Some feelings are to mortals given
> With less of earth in them than heaven, &c.[498]

'But while we are on the subject of poetry, what think you, Miss Heywood, of Burns's lines to his Mary? Oh! there is pathos to madden one! If ever there was a man who *felt*, it was Burns. Montgomery has all the fire of poetry, Wordsworth has the true soul of it, Campbell[499] in his *Pleasures of Hope* has touched the extreme of our sensations –

> Like angels' visits, few and far between.

Can you conceive anything more subduing, more melting, more fraught with the deep sublime than that line? But Burns – I confess my sense of his pre-eminence, Miss Heywood. If Scott *has* a fault, it is the want of passion. Tender, elegant, descriptive – but *tame*. The man who cannot do justice to the attributes of woman is my contempt. Sometimes indeed a flash of feeling seems to irradiate him, as in the lines we were speaking of – "Oh! Woman in our hours of ease" – but Burns is always on fire. His soul was the altar in which lovely woman sat enshrined, his spirit truly breathed the immortal incense which is her due.'

'I have read several of Burns's poems with great delight,' said Charlotte as soon as she had time to speak. 'But I am not poetic enough to separate a man's poetry entirely from his character; and poor Burns's known irregularities[500] greatly interrupt my enjoyment of his lines. I have difficulty in depending on the *truth* of his feelings as a lover. I have not faith in the *sincerity* of the affections of a man of his description. He felt and he wrote and he forgot.'

'Oh! no, no,' exclaimed Sir Edward in an ecstasy. 'He was all ardour and truth! His genius and his susceptibilities might lead him into some aberrations – but who is perfect? It were hyper-criticism, it were pseudo-philosophy to expect from the soul of high-toned genius the grovellings of a common mind. The coruscations[501] of talent, elicited by impassioned feeling in the breast of man, are perhaps incompatible with some of the prosaic decencies of life; nor can you, loveliest Miss Heywood,' speaking with an air of deep sentiment, 'nor can any woman be a fair judge of what a man may be propelled to say, write or do by the sovereign impulses of illimitable ardour.'

This was very fine – but if Charlotte understood it at all, not very moral; and being, moreover, by no means pleased with his extraordinary style of compliment, she gravely answered, 'I really know nothing of the matter. This is a charming day. The wind, I fancy, must be southerly.'

'Happy, happy wind, to engage Miss Heywood's thoughts!'

She began to think him downright silly. His choosing to walk with her, she had learnt to understand. It was done to pique Miss Brereton. She had read it, in an anxious glance or two on his side; but why he should talk so much nonsense, unless he could do no better, was unintelligible. He seemed very sentimental, very full of some feeling or other, and very much addicted to all the newest-fashioned hard words, had not a very clear brain, she presumed, and talked a good deal by rote. The future might explain him further. But when there was a proposition for going into the library, she felt that she had had quite enough of Sir Edward for one morning and very gladly accepted Lady Denham's invitation of remaining on The Terrace with her.

The others all left them, Sir Edward with looks of very gallant despair in tearing himself away, and they united their agreeableness; that is, Lady Denham, like a true great lady, talked and talked only of her own concerns, and Charlotte listened, amused in considering the contrast between her two companions. Certainly there was no strain of doubtful sentiment nor any phrase of difficult interpretation in Lady Denham's discourse. Taking hold of Charlotte's arm with the ease of one who felt that any notice from her was an honour, and communicative from the influence of the same conscious importance or a natural love of talking, she immediately said in a tone of great satisfaction and with a look of arch sagacity, 'Miss Esther wants me to invite her and her brother to spend a week with me at Sanditon House, as I did last summer. But I shan't. She has been trying to get round me every way with her praise of this and her praise of that; but I saw what she was about. I saw through it all. I am not very easily taken in, my dear.'

Charlotte could think of nothing more harmless to be said than the simple enquiry of – 'Sir Edward and Miss Denham?'

'Yes, my dear. My young folks, as I call them sometimes, for I take them very much by the hand. I had them with me last summer, about this time, for a week; from Monday to Monday; and very delighted and thankful they were. For they are very good young people, my dear. I would not have you think that I only notice them for poor dear Sir Harry's sake. No, no; they are very deserving themselves or, trust me, they would not be so much in my company. I am not the woman to help anybody blindfold. I always take care to know what I am about and whom I have to deal with before I stir a finger. I do not think I was ever over-reached in my life. And that is a good deal for a woman to say that has been married twice. Poor dear Sir Harry, between ourselves, thought at first to have got more. But,' with a bit of a sigh, 'he is gone, and we must not find fault with the dead. Nobody could live happier together than us – and he was a very honourable man, quite the gentleman of ancient family. And when he died, I gave Sir Edward his gold watch.'

She said this with a look at her companion which implied its right to produce a great impression; and seeing no rapturous astonishment in Charlotte's countenance, added quickly, 'He did not bequeath it to his nephew, my dear. It was no bequest. It was not in the will. He only told me, and that but once, that he should wish his nephew to have his watch; but it need not have been binding if I had not chose it.'

'Very kind indeed! Very handsome!' said Charlotte, absolutely forced to affect admiration.

'Yes, my dear, and it is not the only kind thing I have done by him. I have been a very liberal friend to Sir Edward. And poor young man, he needs it bad enough. For though I am only the dowager,[502] my dear, and he is the heir, things do not stand between us in the way they commonly do between those two parties. Not a shilling do I receive from the Denham estate. Sir Edward has no payments to make me. He don't stand uppermost, believe me. It is *I* that help *him*.

'Indeed! He is a very fine young man, particularly elegant in his address.'

This was said chiefly for the sake of saying something, but Charlotte directly saw that it was laying her open to suspicion by Lady Denham's giving a shrewd glance at her and replying, 'Yes, yes, he is very well to look at. And it is to be hoped that some lady of large fortune will think so, for Sir Edward *must* marry for money. He and I often talk that matter over. A handsome young fellow like him will go smirking and smiling about and paying girls compliments, but he knows he must marry for money. And Sir Edward is a very steady young man in the main and has got very good notions.

'Sir Edward Denham,' said Charlotte, 'with such personal advantages may be almost sure of getting a woman of fortune, if he chooses it.'

This glorious sentiment seemed quite to remove suspicion.

'Aye, my dear, that's very sensibly said,' cried Lady Denham. 'And if we could but get a young heiress to Sanditon! But heiresses are monstrous scarce! I do not think we have had an heiress here – or even a countess – since Sanditon has been a public place. Families come after families but, as far as I can learn, it is not one in a hundred of them that has any real property, landed or funded. An income, perhaps, but no property. Clergymen maybe, or lawyers from town, or half-pay officers,[503] or widows with only a jointure.[504] And what good can such people do anybody? Except just as they take our empty houses and, between ourselves, I think they are great fools for not staying at home. Now if we could get a young heiress to be sent here for her health – and if she was ordered to drink asses' milk, I could supply her – and, as soon as she got well, have her fall in love with Sir Edward!'

'That would be very fortunate indeed.'

'And Miss Esther must marry somebody of fortune too. She must get a rich husband. Ah, young ladies that have no money are very much to be pitied! But,' after a short pause, 'if Miss Esther thinks to talk me into inviting them to come and stay at Sanditon House, she will find herself mistaken. Matters are altered with me since last summer, you know. I have Miss Clara with me now which makes a great difference.'

She spoke this so seriously that Charlotte instantly saw in it the evidence of real penetration and prepared for some fuller remarks; but it was followed only by, 'I have no fancy for having my house as full as an hotel. I should not choose to have my two housemaids' time taken up all the morning in dusting out bedrooms. They have Miss Clara's room to put to rights as well as my own every day. If they had hard places,[505] they would want higher wages.'

For objections of this nature, Charlotte was not prepared. She found it so impossible even to affect sympathy that she could say nothing. Lady Denham soon added, with great glee, 'And besides all this, my dear, am I to be filling my house to the prejudice of Sanditon? If people want to be by the sea, why don't they take lodgings? Here are a great many empty houses – three on this very Terrace. No fewer than three lodging papers staring me in the face at this very moment, Numbers 3, 4 and 8. Eight, the corner house, may be too large for them, but either of the two others are nice little snug houses, very fit for a young gentleman and his sister. And so, my dear, the next time Miss Esther begins talking about the dampness of Denham Park and the good bathing always does her, I shall advise them to come and take one of these lodgings for a fortnight. Don't you think that will be very fair? Charity begins at home, you know.'

Charlotte's feelings were divided between amusement and indignation, but indignation had the larger and the increasing share. She kept her countenance and she kept a civil silence. She could not carry her forbearance further, but without attempting to listen longer, and only conscious that Lady Denham was still talking on in the same way, allowed her thoughts to form themselves into such a meditation as this: 'She is thoroughly mean. I had not expected anything so bad; Mr Parker spoke too mildly of her. His judgement is evidently not to be trusted. His own good nature misleads him. He is too kind-hearted to see clearly. I must judge for myself. And their very connection prejudices him. He has persuaded her to engage in the same speculation, and because their object in that line is the same, he fancies she feels like him in others. But she is very, very mean. I can see no good in her. Poor Miss Brereton! And she makes everybody mean about her. This poor Sir Edward and his sister – how far nature meant them to be respectable, I cannot tell – but they are obliged to be mean in their servility to her. And I am mean, too, in giving her my attention with the appearance of coinciding[506] with her. Thus it is, when rich people are sordid.'

Chapter 8

The two ladies continued walking together till rejoined by the others, who, as they issued from the library, were followed by a young Whitby, running off with five volumes under his arm to Sir Edward's gig; and Sir Edward, approaching Charlotte, said, 'You may perceive what has been our occupation. My sister wanted my counsel in the selection of some books. We have many leisure hours and read a great deal. I am no indiscriminate novel reader. The mere trash of the common circulating library I hold in the highest contempt. You will never hear me advocating those puerile emanations which detail nothing but discordant principles incapable of amalgamation, or those vapid tissues of ordinary occurrences from which no useful deductions can be drawn. In vain may we put them into a literary alembic;[507] we distil nothing which can add to science. You understand me, I am sure?'

'I am not quite certain that I do. But if you will describe the sort of novels which you do approve, I dare say it will give me a clearer idea.'

'Most willingly, fair questioner. The novels which I approve are such as display human nature with grandeur; such as show her in the sublimities of intense feeling; such as exhibit the progress of strong passion from the first germ of incipient susceptibility to the utmost energies of reason half-dethroned; where we see the strong spark of woman's captivations elicit such fire in the soul of man as leads him – though at the risk of some aberration from the strict line of primitive obligations – to hazard all, dare all, achieve all to obtain her. Such are the works which I peruse with delight and, I hope I may say, with amelioration. They hold forth the most splendid portraitures of high conceptions, unbounded views, illimitable ardour, indomitable decision. And even when the event is mainly anti-prosperous to the high-toned machinations of the prime character – the potent, pervading hero of the story – it leaves us full of generous emotions for him; our hearts are paralysed. It would be pseudo-philosophy to assert that we do not feel more enwrapped by the brilliancy of his career than by the tranquil and morbid virtues of any opposing character. Our approbation of the latter is but eleemosynary. These are the novels which enlarge the primitive capabilities of the heart, and which it cannot impugn the sense or be any dereliction of the character of the most anti-puerile man to be conversant with.'

'If I understand you aright,' said Charlotte, 'our taste in novels is not at all the same.'

And here they were obliged to part, Miss Denham being much too tired of them all to stay any longer.

The truth was that Sir Edward, whom circumstances had confined very much to one spot, had read more sentimental novels than agreed with him. His fancy had been early caught by all the impassioned and most exceptionable parts of Richardson's.[508] And such authors as had since appeared to tread in Richardson's steps (so far as man's determined pursuit of woman in defiance of every opposition of feeling and convenience was concerned) had since occupied the greater part of his literary hours, and formed his character. With a perversity of judgement which must be attributed to his not having by nature a very strong head, the graces, the spirit, the sagacity and the perseverance of the villain of the story outweighed all his absurdities and all his atrocities with Sir Edward. With him such conduct was genius, fire and feeling. It interested and inflamed him. And he was always more anxious for its success, and mourned over its discomfitures with more tenderness, than could ever have been contemplated by the authors.

Though he owed many of his ideas to this sort of reading, it would be unjust to say that he read nothing else or that his language was not formed on a more general knowledge of modern literature. He read all the essays, letters, tours and criticisms of the day; and with the same ill-luck which made him derive only false principles from lessons of morality, and incentives to vice from the history of its overthrow, he gathered only hard words and involved sentences from the style of our most approved writers.

Sir Edward's great object in life was to be seductive. With such personal advantages as he knew himself to possess, and such talents as he did also give himself credit for, he regarded it as his duty. He felt that he was formed to be a dangerous man, quite in the line of the Lovelaces. The very name of Sir Edward, he thought, carried some degree of fascination with it. To be generally gallant and assiduous about the fair, to make fine speeches to every pretty girl, was but the inferior part of the character he had to play. Miss Heywood, or any other young woman with any pretensions to beauty, he was entitled (according to his own views of society) to approach with high compliment and rhapsody on the slightest acquaintance. But it was Clara alone on whom he had serious designs; it was Clara whom he meant to seduce – her seduction was quite determined on. Her situation in every way called for it. She was his rival in Lady Denham's favour; she was young, lovely and dependent. He had very early seen the necessity of the case, and had now been long trying with cautious assiduity to make an impression on her heart and to undermine her principles. Clara saw through him and had not the least intention of being seduced; but she bore with him patiently enough to confirm the sort of attachment which her personal charms had raised. A greater degree of discouragement indeed would not have affected Sir Edward. He was armed against the highest pitch of disdain or aversion. If she could not be won by affection, he must carry her off. He knew his business.

Already had he had many musings on the subject. If he *were* constrained so to act, he must naturally wish to strike out something new, to exceed those who had gone before him; and he felt a strong curiosity to ascertain whether the neighbourhood of Timbuktu[509] might not afford some solitary house adapted for Clara's reception. But the expense, alas! of measures in that masterly style was ill-suited to his purse, and prudence obliged him to prefer the quietest sort of ruin and disgrace for the object of his affections to the more renowned.

Chapter 9

One day, soon after Charlotte's arrival at Sanditon, she had the pleasure of seeing, just as she ascended from the sands to The Terrace, a gentleman's carriage with post horses[510] standing at the door of the hotel, as very lately arrived, and by the quantity of luggage being taken off, bringing, it might be hoped, some respectable family determined on a long residence.

Delighted to have such good news for Mr and Mrs Parker, who had both gone home some time before, she proceeded to Trafalgar House with as much alacrity as could remain after having contended for the last two hours with a very fine wind blowing directly on shore. But she had not reached the little lawn when she saw a lady walking nimbly behind her at no great distance; and convinced that it could be no acquaintance of her own, she resolved to hurry on and get into the house if possible before her. But the stranger's pace did not allow this to be accomplished. Charlotte was on the steps and had rung but the door was not open when the other crossed the lawn; and when the servant appeared, they were just equally ready for entering the house.

The ease of the lady, her 'How do you do, Morgan?' and Morgan's looks on seeing her were a moment's astonishment; but another moment brought Mr Parker into the hall to welcome the sister he had seen from the drawing-room; and Charlotte was soon introduced to Miss Diana Parker. There was a great deal of surprise but still more pleasure in seeing her. Nothing could be kinder than her reception from both husband and wife. How did she come? And with whom? And they were so glad to find her equal to the journey! And that she was to belong to them was taken as a matter of course. Miss Diana Parker was about four-and-thirty, of middling height and slender; delicate-looking rather than sickly; with an agreeable face and a very animated eye; her manners resembling her brother's in their ease and frankness, though with more decision and less mildness in her tone. She began an account of herself without delay, thanking them for their invitation but declaring 'that to accept was quite out of the question for they were all three come and meant to get into lodgings and make some stay'.

'All three come! What! Susan and Arthur! Susan able to come too! This is better and better.'

'Yes, we are actually all come. Quite unavoidable. Nothing else to be done. You shall hear all about it. But, my dear Mary, send for the children – I long to see them.'

'And how has Susan borne the journey? And how is Arthur? And why do we not see him here with you?'

'Susan has borne it wonderfully. She had not a wink of sleep either the night before we set out or last night at Chichester, and as this is not so common with her as with me, I have had a thousand fears for her. But she has kept up wonderfully – no hysterics of consequence till we came within sight of poor old Sanditon – and the attack was not very violent – nearly over by the time we reached your hotel – so that we got her out of the carriage extremely well with only Mr Woodcock's assistance. And when I left her she was directing the disposal of the luggage and helping old Sam uncord the trunks. She desired her best love with a thousand regrets at being so poor a creature that she could not come with me. And as for poor Arthur, he would not have been unwilling himself, but there is so much wind that I did not think he could safely venture – for I am *sure* there is lumbago hanging about him; and so I helped him on with his greatcoat and sent him off to The Terrace to take us lodgings. Miss Heywood must have seen our carriage standing at the hotel. I knew Miss Heywood the moment I saw her before me on the down. My dear Tom, I am so glad to see you walk so well. Let me feel your ankle. That's right; all right and clean. The play of your sinews a *very* little affected, barely perceptible. Well, now for the explanation of my being here. I told you in my letter of the two considerable families I was hoping to secure for you, the West Indians and the seminary.'

Here Mr Parker drew his chair still nearer to his sister and took her hand again most affectionately as he answered, 'Yes, yes, how active and how kind you have been!'

'The West Indians,' she continued, 'whom I look upon as the most desirable of the two, as the best of the good, prove to be a Mrs Griffiths and her family. I know them only through others. You must have heard me mention Miss Capper, the particular friend of my very particular friend Fanny Noyce. Now, Miss Capper is extremely intimate with a Mrs Darling, who is on terms of constant correspondence with Mrs Griffiths herself. Only a *short* chain, you see, between us, and not a link wanting. Mrs Griffiths meant to go to the sea for her young people's benefit, had fixed on the coast of Sussex but was undecided as to the where, wanted something private, and wrote to ask the opinion of her friend Mrs Darling. Miss Capper happened to be staying with Mrs Darling when Mrs Griffiths' letter arrived and was consulted on the question. She wrote the same day to Fanny Noyce and mentioned it to her; and Fanny, all alive for *us*, instantly took up her pen and forwarded the circumstance to me – except as to *names*, which have but lately transpired. There was but *one* thing for *me* to do. I answered Fanny's letter by the same post and pressed for the recommendation of Sanditon. Fanny had feared your having no house large enough to receive such a family. But I seem to be spinning out my story to an endless length. You see how it was all managed. I had the pleasure of hearing soon afterwards by the same simple link of connection that Sanditon had been recommended by Mrs Darling, and that the West Indians were very much disposed to go thither. This was the state of the case when I wrote to you. But two days ago – yes, the day before yesterday – I heard again from Fanny Noyce, saying that she had heard from Miss Capper, who by a letter from Mrs Darling understood that Mrs Griffiths had expressed herself in a letter to Mrs Darling more doubtingly on the subject of Sanditon. Am I clear? I would be anything rather than not clear.'

'Oh, perfectly, perfectly. Well?'

'The reason of this hesitation was her having no connections in the place, and no means of ascertaining that she should have good accomodations on arriving there; and she was particularly careful and scrupulous on all those matters more on account of a certain Miss Lambe, a young lady (probably a niece) under her care, than on her own account or her daughters'. Miss Lambe has an immense fortune – richer than all the rest – and very delicate health. One sees clearly enough by all this, the *sort* of woman Mrs Griffiths must be – as helpless and indolent as wealth and a hot climate are apt to make us. But we are not all born to equal energy. What was to be done? I had a few moments' indecision – whether to offer to write to *you* or to Mrs Whitby to secure them a house; but neither pleased me. I hate to employ others, when I am equal to act myself; and my conscience told me that this was an occasion which called for me. Here was a family of helpless invalids whom I might essentially serve. I sounded Susan. The same thought had occurred to her. Arthur made no difficulties. Our plan was arranged immediately, we were off yesterday morning at six, left Chichester at the same hour today – and here we are.'

Excellent! Excellent!' cried Mr Parker. 'Diana, you are unequalled in serving your friends and doing good to all the world. I know nobody like you. Mary, my love, is not she a wonderful creature? Well, and now, what house do you design to engage for them? What is the size of their family?'

'I do not at all know,' replied his sister, 'have not the least idea, never heard any particulars; but I am very sure that the largest house at Sanditon cannot be too large. They are more likely to want a second. I shall take only one, however, and that but for a week certain. Miss Heywood, I astonish you. You hardly know what to make of me. I see by your looks that you are not used to such quick measures.'

The words 'unaccountable officiousness!' 'activity run mad!' had just passed through Charlotte's mind, but a civil answer was easy.

'I dare say I do look surprised,' said she, 'because these are very great exertions, and I know what invalids both you and your sister are.

'Invalids indeed. I trust there are not three people in England who have so sad a right to that appellation! But, my dear Miss Heywood, we are sent into this world to be as extensively useful as possible, and where some degree of strength of mind is given, it is not a feeble body which will excuse us – or incline us to excuse ourselves. The world is pretty much divided between the weak of mind and the strong; between those who can act and those who cannot; and it is the bounden duty of the capable to let no opportunity of being useful escape them. My sister's complaints and mine are happily not often of a nature to threaten existence *immediately*. And as long as we *can* exert ourselves to be of use to others, I am convinced that the body is the better for the refreshment the mind receives in doing its duty. While I have been travelling with this object in view, I have been perfectly well.' The entrance of the children ended this little panegyric on her own disposition; and after having noticed and caressed them all, she prepared to go.

'Cannot you dine with us? Is not it possible to prevail on you to dine with us?' was then the cry. And *that* being absolutely negatived, it was, 'And when shall we see you again? And how can we be of use to you?' And Mr Parker warmly offered his assistance in taking the house for Mrs Griffiths.

'I will come to you the moment I have dined,' said he, 'and we will go about together.'

But this was immediately declined.

'No, my dear Tom, upon no account in the world shall you stir a step on any business of mine. Your ankle wants rest. I see by the position of your foot that you have used it too much already. No, I shall go about my house-taking directly. Our dinner is not ordered till six; and by that time I hope to have completed it. It is now only half past four. As to seeing *me* again today, I cannot answer for it. The others will be at the hotel all the evening and delighted to see you at any time; but as soon as I get back I shall hear what Arthur has done about our own lodgings, and probably the moment dinner is over shall be out again on business relative to them, for we hope to get into some lodgings or other and be settled after breakfast tomorrow. I have not much confidence in poor Arthur's skill for lodging-taking, but he seemed to like the commission.'

'I think you are doing too much,' said Mr Parker. 'You will knock yourself up. You should not move again after dinner.'

'No, indeed you should not,' cried his wife, 'for dinner is such a mere *name* with you all that it can do you no good. I know what your appetites are.'

'My appetite is very much mended, I assure you, lately. I have been taking some bitters of my own decocting,[511] which have done wonders. Susan never eats, I grant you; and just at present *I* shall want nothing. I never eat for about a week after a journey. But as for Arthur, he is only too much disposed for food. We are often obliged to check him.'

'But you have not told me anything of the *other* family coming to Sanditon,' said Mr Parker, as he walked with her to the door of the house. 'The Camberwell seminary. Have we a good chance of *them*?'

'Oh, certain. Quite certain. I had forgotten them for the moment. But I had a letter three days ago from my friend Mrs Charles Dupuis, which assured me of Camberwell. Camberwell will be here to a certainty, and very soon. *That* good woman – I do not know her name – not being so wealthy and independent as Mrs Griffiths, can travel and choose for herself. I will tell you how I got at *her*. Mrs Charles Dupuis lives almost next door to a lady who has a relation lately settled at Clapham who actually attends the seminary and gives lessons on eloquence and *belles-lettres* to some of the girls. I got this man a hare from one of Sidney's friends; and he recommended Sanditon. Without *my* appearing, however – Mrs Charles Dupuis managed it all.'

Chapter 10

It was not a week since Miss Diana Parker had been told by her feelings
that the sea air would probably, in her present state, be the death of her;
and now she was at Sanditon, intending to make some stay and without
appearing to have the slightest recollection of having written or felt any
such thing. It was impossible for Charlotte not to suspect a good deal of
fancy in such an extraordinary state of health. Disorders and recoveries
so very much out of the common way seemed more like the amusement
of eager minds in want of employment than of actual afflictions and
relief. The Parkers were no doubt a family of imagination and quick
feelings, and while the eldest brother found vent for his superfluity of
sensation as a projector, the sisters were perhaps driven to dissipate
theirs in the invention of odd complaints.

The *whole* of their mental vivacity was evidently not so employed;
part was laid out in a zeal for being useful. It would seem that they must
either be very busy for the good of others or else extremely ill themselves. Some natural delicacy of constitution, in fact, with an unfortunate
turn for medicine, especially quack medicine, had given them an early
tendency at various times to various disorders; the rest of their sufferings
was from fancy, the love of distinction and the love of the wonderful.
They had charitable hearts and many amiable feelings; but a spirit of
restless activity, and the glory of doing more than anybody else, had
their share in every exertion of benevolence; and there was vanity in all
they did, as well as in all they endured.

Mr and Mrs Parker spent a great part of the evening at the hotel; but
Charlotte had only two or three views of Miss Diana posting[512] over the
down after a house for this lady whom she had never seen and who had
never employed her. She was not made acquainted with the others till
the following day when, being removed into lodgings and all the party
continuing quite well, their brother and sister and herself were entreated
to drink tea with them.

They were in one of The Terrace houses; and she found them
arranged for the evening in a small neat drawing-room, with a beautiful
view of the sea if they had chosen it; but though it had been a very fair
English summer day, not only was there no open window, but the sofa
and the table and the establishment in general was all at the other end
of the room by a brisk fire. Miss Parker, whom, remembering the three
teeth drawn in one day, Charlotte approached with a peculiar degree
of respectful compassion, was not very unlike her sister in person or

manner, though more thin and worn by illness and medicine, more relaxed in air and more subdued in voice. She talked, however, the whole evening as incessantly as Diana; and excepting that she sat with salts in her hand, took drops[513] two or three times from one out of several phials already at home on the mantelpiece and made a great many odd faces and contortions, Charlotte could perceive no symptoms of illness which she, in the boldness of her own good health, would not have undertaken to cure by putting out the fire, opening the window, and disposing of the drops and the salts by means of one or the other. She had had considerable curiosity to see Mr Arthur Parker; and having fancied him a very puny, delicate-looking young man, materially the smallest of a not very robust family, was astonished to find him quite as tall as his brother and a great deal stouter, broad-made and lusty, and with no other look of an invalid than a sodden[514] complexion.

Diana was evidently the chief of the family – principal mover and actor. She had been on her feet the whole morning, on Mrs Griffiths' business or their own, and was still the most alert of the three. Susan had only superintended their final removal from the hotel, bringing two heavy boxes herself, and Arthur had found the air so cold that he had merely walked from one house to the other as nimbly as he could, and boasted much of sitting by the fire till he had cooked up a very good one. Diana, whose exercise had been too domestic to admit of calculation, but who, by her own account, had not once sat down during the space of seven hours, confessed herself a little tired. She had been too successful, however, for much fatigue; for not only had she – by walking and talking down a thousand difficulties – at last secured a proper house at eight guineas[515] per week for Mrs Griffiths; she had also opened so many treaties with cooks, housemaids, washerwomen and bathing women[516] that Mrs Griffiths would have little more to do on her arrival than to wave her hand and collect them around her for choice. Her concluding effort in the cause had been a few polite lines of information to Mrs Griffiths herself, time not allowing for the circuitous train of intelligence which had been hitherto kept up; and she was now regaling in the delight of opening the first trenches[517] of an acquaintance with such a powerful discharge of unexpected obligation.

Mr and Mrs Parker and Charlotte had seen two post-chaises crossing the down to the hotel as they were setting off, a joyful sight and full of speculation. The Miss Parkers and Arthur had also seen something; they could distinguish from their window that there *was* an arrival at the hotel, but not its amount. Their visitors answered for two hack chaises.[518] Could it be the Camberwell seminary? No, no. Had there been a third carriage, perhaps it might; but it was very generally agreed that two hack chaises could never contain a seminary. Mr Parker was confident of another new family.

When they were all finally seated, after some removals to look at the sea and the hotel, Charlotte's place was by Arthur, who was sitting next to the fire with a degree of enjoyment which gave a good deal of merit to his civility in wishing her to take his chair. There was nothing dubious in her manner of declining it and he sat down again with much satisfaction. She drew back her chair to have all the advantage of his person as a screen and was very thankful for every inch of back and shoulders beyond her preconceived idea. Arthur was heavy in eye as well as figure, but by no means indisposed to talk; and while the other four were chiefly engaged together, he evidently felt it no penance to have a fine young woman next to him, requiring in common politeness some attention – as his brother, who felt the decided want of some motive for action, some powerful object of animation for him, observed with considerable pleasure.

Such was the influence of youth and bloom that he began even to make a sort of apology for having a fire. 'We should not have had one at home,' said he, 'but the sea air is always damp. I am not afraid of anything so much as damp.'

'I am so fortunate,' said Charlotte, 'as never to know whether the air is damp or dry. It has always some property that is wholesome and invigorating to me.'

'I like the air too, as well as anybody can,' replied Arthur. 'I am very fond of standing at an open window when there is no wind. But, unluckily, a damp air does not like me. It gives me the rheumatism. You are not rheumatic, I suppose?'

'Not at all.'

'That's a great blessing. But perhaps you are nervous?'[519]

'No, I believe not. I have no idea that I am.'

'I am very nervous. To say the truth, nerves are the worst part of my complaints in *my* opinion. My sisters think me bilious,[520] but I doubt it.'

'You are quite in the right to doubt it as long as you possibly can, I am sure.'

'If I were bilious,' he continued, 'you know, wine would disagree with me, but it always does me good. The more wine I drink – in moderation – the better I am. I am always best of an evening. If you had seen me today before dinner, you would have thought me a very poor creature.'

Charlotte could believe it. She kept her countenance, however, and said, 'As far as I can understand what nervous complaints are, I have a great idea of the efficacy of air and exercise for them – daily, regular exercise – and I should recommend rather more of it to *you* than I suspect you are in the habit of taking.'

'Oh, I am very fond of exercise myself,' he replied, 'and I mean to walk a great deal while I am here, if the weather is temperate. I shall be out every morning before breakfast and take several turns upon The Terrace, and you will often see me at Trafalgar House.'

'But you do not call a walk to Trafalgar House much exercise?'

'Not as to mere distance, but the hill is so steep! Walking up that hill, in the middle of the day, would throw me into such a perspiration! You would see me all in a bath by the time I got there! I am very subject to perspiration, and there cannot be a surer sign of nervousness.'

They were now advancing so deep in physics[521] that Charlotte viewed the entrance of the servant with the tea things as a very fortunate interruption. It produced a great and immediate change. The young man's attentions were instantly lost. He took his own cocoa from the tray, which seemed provided with almost as many teapots, &c., as there were persons in the company – Miss Parker drinking one sort of herb tea and Miss Diana another – and turning completely to the fire, sat coddling and cooking it to his own satisfaction and toasting some slices of bread, brought up ready-prepared in the toast rack; and till it was all done, she heard nothing of his voice but the murmuring of a few broken sentences of self-approbation and success.

When his toils were over, however, he moved back his chair into as gallant a line as ever, and proved that he had not been working only for himself by his earnest invitation to her to take both cocoa and toast. She was already helped to tea – which surprised him, so totally self-engrossed had he been.

'I thought I should have been in time,' said he, 'but cocoa takes a great deal of boiling.'

'I am much obliged to you,' replied Charlotte. 'But I *prefer* tea.'

'Then I will help myself,' said he. 'A large dish of rather weak cocoa every evening agrees with me better than anything.'

It struck her, however, as he poured out this rather weak cocoa, that it came forth in a very fine, dark-coloured stream; and at the same moment, his sisters' both crying out, 'Oh, Arthur, you get your cocoa stronger and stronger every evening,' with Arthur's somewhat conscious reply of, ''Tis rather stronger than it should be tonight,' convinced her that Arthur was by no means so fond of being starved as they could desire or as he felt proper himself. He was certainly very happy to turn the conversation on dry toast and hear no more of his sisters.

'I hope you will eat some of this toast,' said he. 'I reckon myself a very good toaster. I never burn my toasts, I never put them too near the fire at first. And yet, you see, there is not a corner but what is well browned. I hope you like dry toast.

'With a reasonable quantity of butter spread over it, very much,' said Charlotte, 'but not otherwise.'

'No more do I,' said he, exceedingly pleased. 'We think quite alike there. So far from dry toast being wholesome, I think it a very bad thing for the stomach. Without a little butter to soften it, it hurts the coats of the stomach. I am sure it does. I will have the pleasure of spreading some for you directly, and afterwards I will spread some for myself. Very bad indeed for the coats of the stomach – but there is no convincing *some* people. It irritates and acts like a nutmeg grater.'

He could not get command of the butter, however, without a struggle, his sisters accusing him of eating a great deal too much and declaring he was not to be trusted, and he maintaining that he only ate enough to secure the coats of his stomach, and besides, he only wanted it now for Miss Heywood.

Such a plea must prevail. He got the butter and spread away for her with an accuracy of judgement which at least delighted himself. But when her toast was done and he took his own in hand, Charlotte could hardly contain herself as she saw him watching his sisters while he scrupulously scraped off almost as much butter as he put on and then seized an odd moment for adding a great dab just before it went into his mouth. Certainly, Mr Arthur Parker's enjoyments in invalidism were very different from his sisters' – by no means so spiritualised. A good deal of earthy dross hung about him. Charlotte could not but suspect him of adopting that line of life principally for the indulgence of an indolent temper, and to be determined on having no disorders but such as called for warm rooms and good nourishment.

In one particular, however, she soon found that he had caught something from *them*. 'What!' said he. 'Do you venture upon two dishes of strong green tea[522] in one evening? What nerves you must have! How I envy you. Now, if *I* were to swallow only one such dish, what do you think its effect would be upon me?'

'Keep you awake perhaps all night,' replied Charlotte, meaning to overthrow his attempts at surprise by the grandeur of her own conceptions.

'Oh, if that were all!' he exclaimed. 'No. It acts on me like poison and would entirely take away the use of my right side before I had swallowed it five minutes. It sounds almost incredible, but it has happened to me so often that I cannot doubt it. The use of my right side is entirely taken away for several hours!'

'It sounds rather odd to be sure,' answered Charlotte coolly, 'but I dare say it would be proved to be the simplest thing in the world by those who have studied right sides and green tea scientifically and thoroughly understand all the possibilities of their action on each other.'

Soon after tea, a letter was brought to Miss Diana Parker from the hotel.

'From Mrs Charles Dupuis,' said she, 'some private hand;'[523] and having read a few lines, exclaimed aloud, 'Well, this is very extraordinary! Very extraordinary indeed! That both should have the same name. Two Mrs Griffithses! This is a letter of recommendation and introduction to me of the lady from Camberwell – and *her* name happens to be Griffiths too.'

A few more lines, however, and the colour rushed into her cheeks and with much perturbation, she added, 'The oddest thing that ever was! A Miss Lambe too! A young West Indian of large fortune. But it cannot be the same. Impossible that it should be the same.'

She read the letter aloud for comfort. It was merely to introduce the bearer, Mrs Griffiths from Camberwell, and the three young ladies under her care to Miss Diana Parker's notice. Mrs Griffiths, being a stranger at Sanditon, was anxious for a respectable introduction; and Mrs Charles Dupuis, therefore, at the instance of the intermediate friend, provided her with this letter, knowing that she could not do her dear Diana a greater kindness than by giving her the means of being useful. 'Mrs Griffiths' chief solicitude would be for the accommodation and comfort of one of the young ladies under her care, a Miss Lambe, a young West Indian of large fortune, in delicate health.'

It was very strange! Very remarkable! Very extraordinary! But they were all agreed in determining it to be *impossible* that there should not be two families; such a totally distinct set of people as were concerned in the reports of each made that matter quite certain. There *must* be two families. Impossible to be otherwise. 'Impossible' and 'Impossible' were repeated over and over again with great fervour. An accidental resemblance of names and circumstances, however striking at first, involved nothing really incredible; and so it was settled.

Miss Diana herself derived an immediate advantage to counterbalance her perplexity. She must put her shawl over her shoulders and be running about again. Tired as she was, she must instantly repair to the hotel to investigate the truth and offer her services.

Chapter 11

It would not do. Not all that the whole Parker race could say among themselves could produce a happier catastrophe[524] than that the family from Surrey and the family from Camberwell were one and the same. The rich West Indians and the young ladies' seminary had all entered Sanditon in those two hack chaises. The Mrs Griffiths who, in her friend Mrs Darling's hands, had wavered as to coming and been unequal to the journey, was the very same Mrs Griffiths whose plans were at the same period (under another representation) perfectly decided, and who was without fears or difficulties.

All that had the appearance of incongruity in the reports of the two might very fairly be placed to the account of the vanity, the ignorance or the blunders of the many engaged in the cause by the vigilance and caution of Miss Diana Parker. Her intimate friends must be officious like herself; and the subject had supplied letters and extracts and messages enough to make everything appear what it was not. Miss Diana probably felt a little awkward on being first obliged to admit her mistake. A long journey from Hampshire taken for nothing, a brother disappointed, an expensive house on her hands for a week must have been some of her immediate reflections; and much worse than all the rest must have been the sensation of being less clear-sighted and infallible than she had believed herself.

No part of it, however, seemed to trouble her for long. There were so many to share in the shame and the blame that probably, when she had divided out their proper portions to Mrs Darling, Miss Capper, Fanny Noyce, Mrs Charles Dupuis and Mrs Charles Dupuis's neighbour, there might be a mere trifle of reproach remaining for herself. At any rate, she was seen all the following morning walking about after lodgings with Mrs Griffiths as alert as ever.

Mrs Griffiths was a very well-behaved, genteel kind of woman, who supported herself by receiving such great girls and young ladies as wanted either masters for finishing their education or a home for beginning their displays.[525] She had several more under her care than the three who were now come to Sanditon, but the others all happened to be absent. Of these three, and indeed of all, Miss Lambe was beyond comparison the most important and precious, as she paid in proportion to her fortune. She was about seventeen, half mulatto,[526] chilly and tender, had a maid of her own, was to have the best room in the lodgings, and was always of the first consequence in every plan of Mrs Griffiths.

The other girls, two Miss Beauforts, were just such young ladies as may be met with in at least one family out of three throughout the kingdom. They had tolerable complexions, showy figures, an upright decided carriage and an assured look; they were very accomplished and very ignorant, their time being divided between such pursuits as might attract admiration, and those labours and expedients of dexterous ingenuity by which they could dress in a style much beyond what they *ought* to have afforded; they were some of the first in every change of fashion. And the object of all was to captivate some man of much better fortune than their own.

Mrs Griffiths had preferred a small, retired place like Sanditon on Miss Lambe's account; and the Miss Beauforts, though naturally preferring anything to smallness and retirement, having in the course of the spring been involved in the inevitable expense of six new dresses each for a three days' visit, were constrained to be satisfied with Sanditon also till their circumstances were retrieved. There, with the hire of a harp for one and the purchase of some drawing paper for the other, and all the finery they could already command, they meant to be very economical, very elegant and very secluded; with the hope, on Miss Beaufort's side, of praise and celebrity from all who walked within the sound of her instrument, and on Miss Letitia's, of curiosity and rapture in all who came near her while she sketched; and to both, the consolation of meaning to be the most stylish girls in the place. The particular introduction of Mrs Griffiths to Miss Diana Parker secured them immediately an acquaintance with the Trafalgar House family and with the Denhams; and the Miss Beauforts were soon satisfied with 'the circle in which they moved in Sanditon', to use a proper phrase, for everybody must now 'move in a circle' – to the prevalence of which rotatory motion is perhaps to be attributed the giddiness and false steps of many.

Lady Denham had other motives for calling on Mrs Griffiths besides attention to the Parkers. In Miss Lambe, here was the very young lady, sickly and rich, whom she had been asking for; and she made the acquaintance for Sir Edward's sake and the sake of her milch asses. How it might answer with regard to the baronet remained to be proved, but as to the animals, she soon found that all her calculations of profit would be vain. Mrs Griffiths would not allow Miss Lambe to have the smallest symptom of a decline[527] or any complaint which asses' milk could possibly relieve. Miss Lambe was 'under the constant care of an experienced physician', and his prescriptions must be their rule. And, except in favour of some tonic pills, which a cousin of her own had a property in,[528] Mrs Griffiths never deviated from the strict medicinal page.

The corner house of The Terrace was the one in which Miss Diana Parker had the pleasure of settling her new friends; and considering that it commanded in front the favourite lounge[529] of all the visitors at Sanditon, and on one side whatever might be going on at the hotel, there could not have been a more favourable spot for the seclusion of the Miss Beauforts. And accordingly, long before they had suited themselves with an instrument or with drawing paper, they had, by the frequency of their appearance at the low windows upstairs, in order to close the blinds or open the blinds, to arrange a flower pot on the balcony or look at nothing through a telescope, attracted many an eye upwards and made many a gazer gaze again.

A little novelty has a great effect in so small a place. The Miss Beauforts, who would have been nothing at Brighton, could not move here without notice. And even Mr Arthur Parker, though little disposed for supernumerary exertion, always quitted The Terrace in his way to his brother's by this corner house for the sake of a glimpse of the Miss Beauforts – though it was half a quarter of a mile round about and added two steps to the ascent of the hill.

Chapter 12

Charlotte had been ten days at Sanditon without seeing Sanditon House, every attempt at calling on Lady Denham having been defeated by meeting with her beforehand. But now it was to be more resolutely undertaken, at a more early hour, that nothing might be neglected of attention to Lady Denham or amusement to Charlotte.

'And if you should find a favourable opening, my love,' said Mr Parker, who did not mean to go with them, 'I think you had better mention the poor Mullinses' situation and sound her ladyship as to a subscription[530] for them. I am not fond of charitable subscriptions in a place of this kind – it is a sort of tax upon all that come. Yet as their distress is very great and I almost promised the poor woman yesterday to get something done for her, I believe we must set a subscription on foot, and, therefore, the sooner the better; and Lady Denham's name at the head of the list will be a very necessary beginning. You will not dislike speaking to her about it, Mary?'

'I will do whatever you wish me,' replied his wife, 'but you would do it so much better yourself. I shall not know what to say.'

'My dear Mary,' he cried. 'It is impossible you can be really at a loss. Nothing can be more simple. You have only to state the present afflicted situation of the family, their earnest application to me, and my being willing to promote a little subscription for their relief, provided it meet with her approbation.'

'The easiest thing in the world,' cried Miss Diana Parker, who happened to be calling on them at the moment. 'All said and done in less time than you have been talking of it now. And while you are on the subject of subscriptions, Mary, I will thank you to mention a very melancholy case to Lady Denham which has been represented to me in the most affecting terms. There is a poor woman in Worcestershire, whom some friends of mine are exceedingly interested about, and I have undertaken to collect whatever I can for her. If you would mention the circumstance to Lady Denham! Lady Denham *can* give, if she is properly attacked. And I look upon her to be the sort of person who, when once she is prevailed on to undraw her purse, would as readily give ten guineas[531] as five. And therefore, if you find her in a giving mood, you might as well speak in favour of another charity which I and a few more have very much at heart – the establishment of a Charitable Repository[532] at Burton on Trent. And then there is the family of the poor man who was hung last assizes at York, though we really *have* raised the sum we wanted for putting them all out,[533] yet if you *can* get a guinea from her on their behalf, it may as well be done.'

'My dear Diana!' exclaimed Mrs Parker, 'I could no more mention these things to Lady Denham than I could fly.'

'Where's the difficulty? I wish I could go with you myself. But in five minutes I must be at Mrs Griffiths' to encourage Miss Lambe in taking her first dip. She is so frightened, poor thing, that I promised to come and keep up her spirits and go in the machine[534] with her if she wished it. And as soon as that is over, I must hurry home, for Susan is to have leeches at one o'clock – which will be a three hours' business.[535] Therefore I really have not a moment to spare. Besides that, between ourselves, I ought to be in bed myself at this present time for I am hardly able to stand; and when the leeches have done, I dare say we shall both go to our rooms for the rest of the day.'

'I am sorry to hear it, indeed. But if this is the case I hope Arthur will come to us.'

'If Arthur takes my advice, he will go to bed too, for if he stays up by himself he will certainly eat and drink more than he ought. But you see, Mary, how impossible it is for me to go with you to Lady Denham's.'

'Upon second thoughts, Mary,' said her husband. 'I will not trouble you to speak about the Mullinses. I will take an opportunity of seeing

Lady Denham myself. I know how little it suits you to be pressing matters upon a mind at all unwilling.'

His application thus withdrawn, his sister could say no more in support of hers, which was his object, as he felt all their impropriety and all the certainty of their ill effect upon his own better claim. Mrs Parker was delighted at this release and set off very happy, with her friend and her little girl, on this walk to Sanditon House.

It was a close, misty morning, and when they reached the brow of the hill, they could not for some time make out what sort of carriage it was which they saw coming up. It appeared at different moments to be everything from a gig to a phaeton, from one horse to four; and just as they were concluding in favour of a tandem,[536] little Mary's young eyes distinguished the coachman and she eagerly called out, 'It is Uncle Sidney, mama, it is indeed.' And so it proved.

Mr Sidney Parker, driving his servant in a very neat carriage, was soon opposite to them, and they all stopped for a few minutes. The manners of the Parkers were always pleasant among themselves; and it was a very friendly meeting between Sidney and his sister-in-law, who was most kindly taking it for granted that he was on his way to Trafalgar House. This he declined, however. He was 'just come from Eastbourne proposing to spend two or three days, as it might happen, at Sanditon'; but the hotel must be his quarters. He was expecting to be joined there by a friend or two.

The rest was common enquiries and remarks, with kind notice of little Mary, and a very well-bred bow and proper address to Miss Heywood on her being named to him. And they parted to meet again within a few hours. Sidney Parker was about seven- or eight-and-twenty, very good-looking, with a decided air of ease and fashion and a lively countenance. This adventure afforded agreeable discussion for some time. Mrs Parker entered into all her husband's joy on the occasion and exulted in the credit which Sidney's arrival would give to the place.

The road to Sanditon House was a broad, handsome, planted approach between fields, leading at the end of a quarter of a mile through second gates into grounds which, though not extensive, had all the beauty and respectability which an abundance of very fine timber could give. These entrance gates were so much in a corner of the grounds or paddock, so near to one of its boundaries, that an outside fence was at first almost pressing on the road, till an angle here and a curve there threw them to a better distance. The fence was a proper park paling[537] in excellent condition, with clusters of fine elms or rows of old thorns following its line almost everywhere.

Almost must be stipulated, for there were vacant spaces, and through one of these, Charlotte, as soon as they entered the enclosure, caught a glimpse over the pales of something white and womanish in the field on the other side. It was something which immediately brought Miss Brereton into her head; and stepping to the pales, she saw indeed – and very decidedly, in spite of the mist – Miss Brereton seated not far before her at the foot of the bank which sloped down from the outside of the paling and which a narrow path seemed to skirt along – Miss Brereton seated, apparently very composedly, and Sir Edward Denham by her side.

They were sitting so near each other and appeared so closely engaged in gentle conversation that Charlotte instantly felt she had nothing to do but to step back again and say not a word. Privacy was certainly their object. It could not but strike her rather unfavourably with regard to Clara; but hers was a situation which must not be judged with severity.

She was glad to perceive that nothing had been discerned by Mrs Parker. If Charlotte had not been considerably the taller of the two, Miss Brereton's white ribbons might not have fallen within the ken of her more observant eyes. Among other points of moralising reflection which the sight of this tête-à-tête produced, Charlotte could not but think of the extreme difficulty which secret lovers must have in finding a proper spot for their stolen interviews. Here, perhaps, they had thought themselves so perfectly secure from observation – the whole field open before them; a steep bank and pales never crossed by the foot of man at their back, and a great thickness of air to aid them as well! Yet here she had seen them. They were really ill-used.

The house was large and handsome. Two servants appeared to admit them and everything had a suitable air of property and order. Lady Denham valued herself upon her liberal establishment and had great enjoyment in the order and importance of her style of living. They were shown into the usual sitting-room, well proportioned and well furnished, though it was furniture rather originally good and extremely well kept than new or showy. And as Lady Denham was not there, Charlotte had leisure to look about her and to be told by Mrs Parker that the whole-length portrait of a stately gentleman which, placed over the mantelpiece, caught the eye immediately, was the picture of Sir Harry Denham; and that one among many miniatures in another part of the room, little conspicuous, represented Mr Hollis. Poor Mr Hollis! It was impossible not to feel him hardly used: to be obliged to stand back in his own house and see the best place by the fire constantly occupied by Sir Harry Denham.

NOTES

Abbreviations

Bree and Todd (2008)

Jane Austen, *Later Manuscripts*, edited by Janet Todd and Linda Bree, *The Cambridge Edition of the Works of Jane Austen* (general editor Janet Todd), Cambridge University Press, Cambridge, 2008

JA   Jane Austen

Le Faye (2004)   Deirdre Le Faye, *Jane Austen: A Family Record*, 2nd edition, Cambridge University Press, Cambridge 2004

Letters   *Jane Austen's Letters*, edited by Deirdre Le Faye, Oxford University Press, Oxford, 1995

OED   *Oxford English Dictionary*

Sabor (2006)   Jane Austen, *Juvenilia*, edited by Peter Sabor, *The Cambridge Edition of the Works of Jane Austen* (general editor Janet Todd), Cambridge University Press, Cambridge, 2008

Southam (1964)   B. C. Southam, *Jane Austen's Literary Manuscripts: A Study of the Novelist's Development Through the Surviving Papers*, Oxford University Press, Oxford, 1964

Note on Money

Money in JA's period was not decimalised. The following list of denominations uses three abbreviations or symbols (*d.* = pence; *s.* = shillings; £ = pounds):

4 farthings = 1*d.*	12*d.* = 1*s.*
5*s.* = 1 crown	4 crowns = £1
21*s.* = 1 guinea	

One sees, for example, that there were 240 pence in the pound. In the notes, I follow Robert D. Hume, 'Money in Jane Austen', *Review of English Studies*, forthcoming (2013), in using a multiplier of between 100 and 150 to get from the value of money in JA's period to an approximate range for an early-twenty-first-century purchasing-power equivalent. As Hume indicates, however, this gives only a very rough equivalent, and its validity wanes at the extremes. For example, Mr. Rushworth's annual income of £12,000 in *Mansfield Park* would put him among the two or three hundred wealthiest people in Britain: between £1.2m and £1.8m is of course a lot in 2012, but not quite comparable. Income was taxable at between five and ten per cent from 1798 to 1816.

Individuals are often described in JA's works as having a fortune, a lump sum, rather than an income; this applies particularly to women, for reasons detailed in the next note. From this amount, the individual derived an income by investing his or her money in order to earn interest, usually between four and five per cent, though the rate fluctuated and depended on the kind of investment. So, a woman with a fortune of £4,000 would have an annual income of between £160 and £200, somewhere between £16,000 and £30,000 in 2012. The width of this range indicates how difficult it is to compare the value of money then and now, and how income could fluctuate. The variance in costs then and now also complicates the attempt to establish equivalence; for instance, labour was cheap enough then for many modestly wealthy houses to be able to afford domestic servants

Note on Marriage and Property

The stories in this collection refer to aspects of marital and property law potentially unfamiliar to the modern reader. The key terms used by JA are placed in italics here. In the wake of Lord Hardwicke's Marriage Act (1753), the aim of which was to prevent *clandestine marriages* of those under twenty-one without parental consent, weddings required either a *special licence*, which could be issued only by the Archbishop of Canterbury; a *common licence*, which could be issued by a bishop for a wedding in his diocese; or the publication of *banns* announcing an impending marriage in the church on three successive Sundays prior to the ceremony. Because this Act did not apply to Scotland, which had its own legislature, Scotland (and Gretna Green in particular) became a common destination for elopers.

Married women, in general, did not legally own property; upon marriage, they entered a state of coverture, defined as 'the condition or position of a woman during her married life, when she is by law under the authority and protection of her husband' (*OED*). In some cases, a legal arrangement was made which allowed a married woman to retain her own property (Lady Denham's second marriage in *Sanditon* is an instance of this). At marriage, a woman often brought a *dowry*, sometimes called a *portion*, an amount of property or money, to her husband, which was generally negotiated between her father and her husband-to-be. *Pin money* was also settled at marriage: this was an allowance paid to the wife for everyday expenses. Widowed women often owned property outright: that which had been settled on them at marriage in the form of a *jointure* (or *settlement*) in the event of their husband's death. A widow in possession of a title or property that has come to her from her husband is a *dowager*.

The bulk of an estate would pass through the male line in the primogeniture system, whereby the eldest (male) inherits. A *provision* for younger sons and females could also be made in a will. However, an estate subject to an *entail* had a prescribed rule of descent unalterable by its present holder, which is the case with the De Courcy family in *Lady Susan*. Younger sons of the gentry generally entered a *profession*: the clergy, law, banking, army or navy, for example.

Note on Transportation

The stories refer to a number of modes of horse-drawn transport and related terms that are potentially unfamiliar to modern readers. The key terms used by JA are italicised here. The *stage wagon* was a slow and cheap form of transport: up to a dozen passengers were conveyed in a horse-drawn carriage at walking pace. The *stagecoach* was smaller, quicker and more genteel; it had a *coach box* – an elevated seat on which the driver sat – and a *basket*, a compartment on the back intended for luggage. A *chaise* was a small, expensive carriage with two or four wheels; hence, a *post-chaise* was a luxurious hired carriage, the horses of which were changed at *posts* to maximise speed: this is what characters mean when they say they will *travel post*. The *postilion*, or *post-boy*, was 'a person who rides the (leading) nearside (left-hand side) horse drawing a coach or carriage, especially when one pair only is used and there is no coach-man' (*OED*). The postilion also served as an attendant on the journey. A *groom* was a servant who attended to horses; a *coachman* was a driver.

Keeping one's own coach (as do the Edwardses in *The Watsons*, for instance) was a marker of substantial wealth. An *equipage* was the carriage, horses and attendant servants combined. A *phaeton* was a fashionable conveyance, defined as 'a type of light four-wheeled open carriage, usually drawn by a pair of horses, and having one or two seats facing forward' (*OED*). A bit smaller, a *curricle* was 'a light two-wheeled carriage, usually drawn by two horses abreast' (*OED*), and a *tandem* was a two-wheeled carriage drawn by two horses harnessed one behind the other. A *gig* was a light, two-wheeled open carriage drawn by a single horse. A *chair* was a simple open carriage, without springs or lining (so, less comfortable), drawn by a single horse. A *turnpike road* was a road on which turnpikes [toll-gates] were erected for the collection of tolls; hence, 'a main road or highway, [...] maintained by a toll levied on cattle and wheeled vehicles' (*OED*).

NOTES TO THE TEXT

Frederic and Elfrida

'Frederic and Elfrida' was probably written as early as 1787: see Southam (1964), p. 16.

1 (p. 3 dedication) *Martha Lloyd* (1765–1843) She was a friend and neighbour of JA at Steventon. In 1828 she married JA's brother, Francis. The dedication is in a later hand than the story, so may have been added after the transcription of *Volume the First*.

2 (p. 4) *rules of propriety* Marriage between first cousins was not uncommon in JA's day; the reference is probably to displays of affection, which were frowned upon.

3 (p. 4) *Crankhumdunberry ... Valley of Tempe* The valley is between the mountains of Olympus and Ossa in Greece, making it a comically impossible source for a stream in a village with a mock-Irish name.

4 (p. 5) *Damon* conventional name for a rustic lover in pastoral poetry

5 (p. 5) *muslins* garments made of this fashionable, finely woven cotton

6 (p. 5) *patches, powder, pomatum and paint* Black patches were applied to the face to resemble beauty spots; white powder coloured the hair; pomatum kept hair plastered in place; paint coloured the face (white for the neck and red for the cheeks).

7 (p. 5) *a post-chaise* In the manuscript, JA makes this specification in a footnote; see Note on Transportation.

8 (p. 6) *postilion* See Note on Transportation.

9 (p. 6) *Portland Place* fashionable street in Marylebone, London

10 (p. 6) *brace ... leash* group of two and of three, respectively

11 (p. 6) *pleasure grounds* land on an estate set aside for recreation, such as walking. The relatively narrow houses of central London did not feature pleasure grounds.

12 (p. 7) *smelling bottle* containing smelling salts, used in case of fainting

13 (p. 7) *Corydon* conventional name for a rustic lover in pastoral poetry

14 (p. 7) *fess*   smart

15 (p. 8) *stage-waggon*   See Note on Transportation.

Jack and Alice

'Jack and Alice' likely dates from early 1790: see Le Faye (2004), pp. 69–70.

16 (p. 10 dedication) *Francis William Austen*   JA's brother (1774–1865), who served in the navy from December 1789 to November 1791.

17 (p. 11) *masquerade … tickets*   a masked ball, for which tickets, serving as invitations, were issued

18 (p. 11) *Pammydiddle*   a mock-Welsh place name. Sabor (2006), p. 384, suggests it is 'a portmanteau word, formed from "pam", a card game, and "diddle", to cheat or waste time'.

19 (p. 11) *jointure*   See Note on Marriage and Property.

20 (p. 11) *sultana*   concubine of a sultan

21 (p. 12) *dominoes*   those dressed in a domino, a long, black Venetian gown for both sexes, worn by masquerade attendees not impersonating a character

22 (p. 12) *Flora*   Roman goddess of flowers

23 (p. 12) *Virtue … Envy*   Allegorical abstractions were represented at masquerades, though a positive one like Virtue was more common than a negative one such as Envy.

24 (p. 12) *tout ensemble*   all taken together; full picture; overall effect

25 (p. 13) *Sir Charles Grandison … bigamy*   Samuel Richardson's exemplary character, from the 1753–4 novel of that name, decries lying, exemplified in the custom of denying one is at home to unwelcome visitors. The comparison to bigamy alludes to Sir Charles's need to negotiate the predicament of having attracted the affections of two women at once.

26 (p. 14) *winter … in town*   It was fashionable to spend winter in London and summer in the country.

27 (p. 15) *'from words she almost came to blows'*   These lines are adapted from James Merrick's poem 'The Camelion: A Fable after Monsieur De La Motte', published in Volume 5 of Robert Dodsley's verse miscellany *A Collection of Poems* (1758). The original reads: 'From words they almost came to blows.'

28 (p. 17) *rents of the estate*   Gentlemen derived part of their income from the rents of tenant farmers on their land; they usually employed a steward to collect the rents.

29 (p. 17) *place*   employment as a servant

30 (p. 17) *offering him … my hand and heart*   It is unconventional for a woman to propose marriage, but there are other examples in 1790s' fiction, so the issue was up for debate.

31 (p. 18) *steel traps*   placed to catch trespassers and poachers

32 (p. 21) *ill health … Bath*   As well as those who went to Bath for the social scene, the bathing was considered beneficial for a number of health issues.

33 (p. 22) *raised to the gallows*   euphemism for hanged: the punishment for murder

34 (p. 23) *engaged*   It was an open secret that the Prince Regent, later King George IV (1762–1830; reigned 1820–30), had in 1785 married the widowed Catholic, Maria Fitzherbert (1756–1837). JA here alludes to his and his brothers' attachments.

35 (p. 23) *Great Mogul*   the Emperor of Delhi, who ruled most of the Indian subcontinent

Edgar and Emma

'Edgar and Emma' was probably written in 1787: see Le Faye (2004), p. 66. There is no dedication in the manuscript.

36 (p. 27) *three pair of stairs high*   The upper storeys of town houses were usually the servants' quarters or, if above a shop, where the shop-owners lived.

37 (p. 27) *consumption*   tuberculosis: a wasting disease of the lungs

38 (p. 27) *ninepence*   with an equivalent value of around £5 in 2012: not much to share between maybe nine bellringers. (See Note on Money.)

39 (p. 28) *villa*   country mansion

40 (p. 28) *ticket in the lottery*   The state lottery funded public projects; tickets were expensive (and hence often jointly-owned) but could produce large dividends.

41 (p. 28) *confidante*   Emma's selection of Henry for her 'confidante' breaches linguistic rules (JA uses the feminine form of the word), social decorum (Henry is the footman) and fictional convention (heroines in novels usually have young female confidantes).

42 (p. 29) *Eton … Winchester*   the colleges of those names

43 (p. 29) *Queen's Square*   Queen Square in Bloomsbury, where there was a girls' boarding school

44 (p. 29) *convent at Brussels*   Roman Catholic families commonly sent
    their children to foreign convent schools, of which there were none
    in England.

45 (p. 29) *college*   either one of the colleges of the Universities of
    Oxford and Cambridge, or a public school like Eton or Winchester

46 (p. 29) *at nurse*   Wealthy families often had their babies suckled by
    a wet-nurse, as was the case with the Austen children.

Henry and Eliza

'Henry and Eliza' was probably written in December 1788 or
January 1789: see Le Faye (2004), p. 67. The title refers to JA's
brother Henry (1771–1850) and her cousin Eliza de Feuillide, née
Hancock (1761–1813); the real Henry and Eliza eventually married
in 1797, after Eliza's first husband, a French nobleman, had been
guillotined in 1794.

47 (p. 32) *Miss Cooper*   Jane Cooper (1771–98) was JA's cousin.

48 (p. 33) *haycock*   conical heap of hay

49 (p. 33) *£50*   with an equivalent value of between £5,000 and £7,500
    in 2012. (See Note on Money.)

50 (p. 33) *humble companion*   a position for an impoverished gentle-
    woman, who would accompany and entertain a wealthier woman
    upon whom she was dependent; sometimes disparagingly called a
    'toad-eater' or 'toady'

51 (p. 34) *private union*   marriage with a licence, rather than the
    publication of banns. (See Note on Marriage and Property.)

52 (p. 35) *£12,000 a year*   with an equivalent value of between £1.2m
    and £1.8m in 2012. (See Note on Money.)

53 (p. 35) *derangement*   disarrangement

54 (p. 35) *Newgate*   a figurative usage here for a private dungeon, after
    the famous prison in London, demolished in 1904, now the site of
    the Old Bailey

55 (p. 36) *cold collation*   a meal of assorted cold meats and salad

56 (p. 36) *junketings*   feasts; banquets; merrymaking

57 (p. 36) *postilion*   See Note on Transportation.

Love and Friendship

'Love and Friendship' is dated in the manuscript 'June 13th 1790'. See Sabor (2006), pp. 427–8, on the possible sources of the title. The source of the motto 'Deceived in Friendship and Betrayed in Love' is unidentified, though Sabor (2006), p. 428, gives a 1799 usage of the same phrase. JA spells 'friendship' as 'freindship' throughout.

58 (p. 40 dedication) *la Comtesse de Feuillide* JA's cousin, Eliza de Feuillide: see headnote, above, to *Henry and Eliza*. She was probably staying with the Austens at Steventon in June 1790, having returned from France after the start of the Revolution the previous year.

59 (p. 41) *natural* illegitimate

60 (p. 41) *opera girl* dancer between the acts of an opera: a disreputable position

61 (p. 42) *romantic … Vale of Uske* now Usk; in Monmouthshire, south Wales. It is 'romantic' in the eighteenth-century sense that it features wild scenery.

62 (p. 42) *accustomary* archaic form, even then, of 'customary'

63 (p. 42) *rendezvous* JA crossed out 'the place of appointment' in the manuscript, deeming the explanation superfluous.

64 (p. 42) *sensibility* The eighteenth-century culture of sensibility – or cult of sentiment – privileged sympathy for other people's suffering, but was double-edged as it also suggested an excessive or affected sensitivity that was disabling or ridiculous.

65 (p. 42) *Minuet Dela Cour* a formal dance of the court

66 (p. 42) *neighbourhood was small* in the sense of having few people, rather than a small area

67 (p. 43) *cot* cottage

68 (p. 44) *baronet* lowest hereditary rank, ranking just above a knight

69 (p. 44) *Polydore … Claudia* names that recall outmoded romances

70 (p. 44) *studying novels* Novels were still considered pernicious; JA denounces this attitude in *Northanger Abbey* (1817), where she defends the novel as a form 'in which the greatest powers of the mind are displayed, in which the most thorough knowledge of human nature, the happiest delineation of its varieties, the liveliest effusions of wit and humour, are conveyed to the world in the best-chosen language'.

71 (p. 44) *a tolerable proficient in geography* Edward's journeying from Bedfordshire to Middlesex via south Wales indicates that his confidence in his geographical proficiency is misplaced.

72 (p. 45) *taken orders*   ordained as a minister of the Church

73 (p. 47) *postilions*   See Note on Transportation.

74 (p. 48) *pathetic*   moving

75 (p. 49) *clandestine marriage*   See Note on Marriage and Property.

76 (p. 49) *escritoire*   writing desk

77 (p. 50) *execution in the house*   seizure of goods on creditors' orders. The goods would be sold to satisfy debts.

78 (p. 50) *Officers of Justice*   sheriff's officers, enforcing the execution

79 (p. 50) *Newgate*   See Note 54.

80 (p. 51) *annuity*   annual payment to a person during his or her lifetime

81 (p. 51) *to travel post*   See Note on Transportation.

82 (p. 52) *a coroneted coach and four*   The coronet, an emblem of a crown on the coach, indicates the owner is a peer; the four horses (instead of two) indicate his wealth.

83 (p. 54) *The Sorrows of Werther*   An epistolary novel of 1774 by Johann Wolfgang von Goethe, the hero of which exemplifies the delicate feelings associated with the culture of sensibility that prevailed in the late eighteenth century. (See Note 64.)

84 (p. 55) *Gretna Green*   southern Scottish town (see Note on Marriage and Property). Janetta and McKenzie do not need to elope there, as they are already in Scotland.

85 (p. 57) *turnpike road*   See Note on Transportation.

86 (p. 57) *eastern zephyr*   Zephyr is the west wind in classical mythology, making this nonsense.

87 (p. 58) *phaeton*   See Note on Transportation.

88 (p. 58) *Cardinal Wolsey*   Thomas Wolsey (1473–1530), Archbishop of York from 1514 and a cardinal of the Roman Catholic Church from 1515, was assigned the role of petitioning Pope Clement VII for the annulment of King Henry VIII's marriage to Catherine of Aragon; his failure to procure Henry's divorce led to his political downfall shortly before his death. He is a byword here for the vagaries of fortune.

89 (p. 59) *Cupid's thunderbolts … piercing shafts of Jupiter*   In Roman mythology, Cupid is the god of love, armed with a bow and arrows that induce desire, whereas Jupiter is the king of the gods and god of thunder, who hurls thunderbolts. In her madness, Laura mixes them up.

90 (p. 60) *consumption*   See Note 37.

91 (p. 61) *coach box … basket*   See Note on Transportation.

92 (p. 62) *Gilpin's Tour to the Highlands*   William Gilpin's *Observations, Relative Chiefly to Picturesque Beauty … On Several Parts of Great Britain; Particularly the High-Lands of Scotland* (1766)

93 (p. 62) *stagecoach*   See Note on Transportation.

94 (p. 63) *post-chaise*   See Note on Transportation.

95 (p. 63) *green tea*   'tea made from unfermented leaves, typically pale in colour and sometimes slightly astringent in flavour' (*OED*)

96 (p. 63) *stay-maker*   one who makes women's corsets

97 (p. 64) *nine thousand pounds … nine hundred … principal*   By a 2012 equivalent, Bertha and Agatha's fortune is reduced from between £900,000 and £1.35m to a tenth of that (see Note on Money). This diminution is because they spend the capital, rather than living on the interest, which at the rate of five per cent would have yielded £450 per annum (between £45,000 and £67,500 in 2012).

98 (p. 64) *strolling company of players*   travelling troupe of actors

99 (p. 65) *romantic*   See Note 61.

100 (p. 65) *Covent Garden … Lewis and Quick*   William Thomas Lewis (*c.*1746–1812) and John Quick (1748–1831) were comic actors at Covent Garden Theatre.

101 (p. 65) *paid the debt of nature*   died (euphemism)

The History of England

'The History of England' is dated in the manuscript to Saturday, November 26th, 1791. JA wrote extensive marginal comments on a copy of Oliver Goldsmith's four-volume *The History of England, from the Earliest Times to the Death of George II* (1771), the title of which she imitates here, and the details of which she takes up at various points. JA's annotations to Goldsmith are printed in Sabor (2006), pp. 316–51.

102 (p. 68 dedication) *Miss Austen … Revd George Austen*   JA's elder sister, Cassandra (1773–1845), who did the illustrations for *The History of England*, and their father (1731–1805)

103 (p. 69) Henry the 4th   (1367–1413; reigned 1399–1413)

104 (p. 69) *Pomfret Castle*   Pontefract Castle, in West Yorkshire

105 (p. 69) *wife*   Henry IV was married to Mary de Bohun (1368–94) before he became king, and they had six children, including Henry V. He married Joan of Navarre (1370–1437) in 1403.

106 (p. 69) *Shakespeare's plays* See Shakespeare's *Henry IV, Part 2* (*c.*1596–9), 4, 3, 221–305. Contrary to JA's assertion here, Henry IV's speech is actually slightly longer than Prince Hal's.

107 (p. 69) *Sir William Gascoigne* (1350–1419) Lord Chief Justice under Henry IV; for the incident to which JA alludes, see *Henry IV, Part 2*, 5, 2.

108 (p. 70) HENRY THE 5TH (1386–1422; reigned 1413–22)

109 (p. 70) *Lord Cobham* (d. 1417) formerly Sir John Oldcastle, the presumed model for Shakespeare's Falstaff, who was executed for heresy

110 (p. 70) *Battle of Agincourt* English victory in 1415 over France in the Hundred Years' War (1337–1453); a major part of Shakespeare's *Henry V* (*c.*1599)

111 (p. 70) *Catherine ... Shakespeare's account* Catherine of Valois (1401–37), daughter of King Charles VI of France, married Henry V in 1420; see *Henry V*, 5, 2 for Shakespeare's account of their meeting.

112 (p. 71) HENRY THE 6TH (1421–71; reigned 1422–61 and 1470–1)

113 (p. 71) *sense* Henry VI suffered bouts of insanity.

114 (p. 71) *wars ... Duke of York* The Wars of the Roses comprised dynastic fighting between the Lancastrian and Yorkist branches of the House of Plantagenet, which mainly occurred sporadically between 1455 and 1485. In the earlier phases of the Wars, the Lancastrian Henry VI's right to the throne was disputed by the Duke of York, who ousted Henry to become Edward IV in 1461; Henry VI re-attained the throne in 1470, but Edward resumed as king six months later following his victory at the Battle of Tewkesbury in 1471, after which Henry and his heir, Edward, Prince of Wales, were killed, allowing Edward IV to reign until his death in 1483.

115 (p. 71) *vent my spleen* freely express ill-humour (the spleen was considered the source of anger and melancholy)

116 (p. 71) *Margaret of Anjou* (1430–82) Henry VI's wife from 1445; imprisoned after the Lancastrian defeat and Henry's death in 1471, but ransomed by her native France in 1475, where she died seven years later

117 (p. 71) *Joan of Arc* (*c.*1412–31) the woman who inspired France to victories over the English in 1429. She was captured and burned at the stake by the English.

118 (p. 72) *EDWARD THE 4TH* (1442–83; reigned 1461–70 and 1471–83). See Note 114.

119 (p. 72) *engaged to another ... Elizabeth Woodville* Edward secretly married the widowed Elizabeth Woodville (*c.*1437–92) in 1464; he was presumed to be betrothed to Bona of Savoy.

120 (p. 72) *confined in a convent* Elizabeth resided at Bermondsey Abbey after Henry VII's accession in 1485; his marriage to her daughter, Elizabeth of York, made her his mother-in-law. Modern historians debate whether Henry forcibly removed her from court or whether she chose to retreat.

121 (p. 72) *Jane Shore* (*c.*1445–*c.*1527) The play is Nicholas Rowe's *The Tragedy of Jane Shore* (1714).

122 (p. 72) *EDWARD THE 5TH* (1470–83; reigned 1483) He succeeded his father at age twelve, but was deposed two months later and imprisoned in the Tower of London with his younger brother, Richard of Shrewsbury, Duke of York (1473–83). Edward and Richard are the fabled Princes in the Tower. They were presumably murdered, as JA suggests here, at Richard III's 'contrivance'; however, JA contradicts this on the following page. In the manuscript, JA left space and penned a caption for a portrait, and there is a portrait in Goldsmith's *History*, but Cassandra did not draw one.

123 (p. 73) *RICHARD THE 3RD* (1442–85; reigned 1483–5) the last Plantagenet king

124 (p. 73) *wife* Richard married Anne Neville (1456–85) in 1472.

125 (p. 73) *Perkin Warbeck* (*c.*1474–99) a pretender who, in 1499, during the reign of Henry VII, claimed to be Richard of Shrewsbury, son of Edward IV. He confessed the imposture and was executed.

126 (p. 73) *Lambert Simnel* (*c.*1477–*c.*1525) another imposter in Henry VII's reign, who, in 1487, was claimed by Yorkists first to be the son of Edward IV and then to be Edward, Earl of Warwick (1475–99), the son of Richard III's brother, George, Duke of Clarence (1449–78). The actual Warwick was still imprisoned in the Tower. Simnel was pardoned by Henry, as he was merely a child, and was subsequently employed in the royal kitchen, as JA states on the next page. In proposing him as Richard's widow, JA is joking about the convoluted conspiracies and dynastic dilemmas of this period.

127 (p. 73) *Battle of Bosworth*   In 1485, Richard III was defeated and killed by the supporters of Henry Tudor at the Battle of Bosworth Field in Leicestershire.

128 (p. 74) HENRY THE 7TH   (1457–1509; reigned 1485–1509) the first Tudor king

129 (p. 74) *Princess Elizabeth of York*   (1466–1503) daughter of the Yorkist Edward IV and Elizabeth Woodville (see Note 119). Her marriage to Henry VII in 1486 was an attempt to unify the warring houses of York and Lancaster.

130 (p. 74) *daughters ... King of Scotland ... first characters in the world*   Henry VII's elder daughter Margaret Tudor (1489–1541) married in 1503 James IV, King of Scotland (1473–1513; reigned 1488–1513); their granddaughter was Mary, Queen of Scots (1542–87; reigned 1542–67).

131 (p. 74) *Mary ... King of France ... Duke of Suffolk*   Mary Tudor (1496–1533) married Louis XII (1462–1515; reigned 1498–1515) in 1514, shortly before his death; her second marriage was to Charles Brandon, Duke of Suffolk (*c.*1484–1545) in 1515.

132 (p. 74) *mother ... Lady Jane Grey*   Lady Frances Brandon (1519–47) was the mother of Lady Jane Grey (1537/8–54). The latter was the Nine Days' Queen, so called because she was nominated by her cousin Edward VI as his successor over his half-sister, the Roman Catholic Mary, and became *de facto* monarch for nine days in July 1553, before Mary was proclaimed queen. Lady Jane was imprisoned and was executed in 1554.

133 (p. 74) *Beaulieu Abbey*   in the New Forest in Hampshire

134 (p. 74) *Earl of Warwick*   See Note 126.

135 (p. 75) HENRY THE 8TH   (1491–1547; reigned 1509–47)

136 (p. 75) *Cardinal Wolsey's ... bones among them*   See Note 88. Wolsey was buried in Leicester Abbey; Goldsmith is the likely source of the quotation.

137 (p. 75) *reformation in religion*   Henry VIII effected the Protestant Reformation in England between 1529 and 1537.

138 (p. 75) *Anna Bullen*   Anne Boleyn (1501–36) became Henry VIII's second wife in 1533 and was executed on the charge of adultery three years later.

139 (p. 76) *fifth wife was the Duke of Norfolk's niece*   Catherine Howard (*c.*1521–42) married Henry in 1540 and was executed on the charge of adultery two years later; she was the niece of Thomas Howard, Duke of Norfolk (1473–1554), as was Anne Boleyn.

140 (p. 76) *Duke of Norfolk*   Thomas Howard, Duke of Norfolk (1536–72), the 4th Duke, was grandson of his predecessor, the 3rd Duke (see previous Note); he was imprisoned in 1569 for scheming to marry Mary, Queen of Scots, and executed for treason in 1572 for plotting against Elizabeth I.

141 (p. 76) *king's last wife*   Catherine Parr (*c.*1512–48)

142 (p. 77) *EDWARD THE 6TH*   (1537–53; reigned 1547–53) The Boy King, he was the son of Henry VIII and his third wife, Jane Seymour (1509–37).

143 (p. 77) *Duke of Somerset*   Edward Seymour, Duke of Somerset (1500–52)

144 (p. 77) *Robert, Earl of Essex, Delamere, or Gilpin*   Robert Devereux, Earl of Essex (1565–1601), was a favourite of Elizabeth I. Frederic Delamere is the hero of Charlotte Smith's novel, *Emmeline, The Orphan of the Forest* (1788). For Gilpin, see Note 92: his travel book expresses sympathy for Mary, Queen of Scots.

145 (p. 77) *Duke of Northumberland*   John Dudley, Duke of Northumberland (1504–53). He prevailed in a power struggle with the Duke of Somerset and replaced his rival as Lord Protector during Edward VI's minority. He then married one of his sons to Lady Jane Grey and persuaded the dying king to settle the succession on Lady Jane (who was the great-granddaughter of Henry VII). He was executed for treason in 1553 after Queen Mary's succession.

146 (p. 78) *MARY*   (1516–58; reigned 1553–8) Henry VIII's daughter by his first wife, Catherine of Aragon (1485–1536)

147 (p. 78) *dozen*   Mary was a Roman Catholic, and accounts of the persecution of Protestants during her reign, most notably in John Foxe's *Book of Martyrs* (1563), earned her the nickname Bloody Mary.

148 (p. 79) *Philip King of Spain … Armadas*   Philip II of Spain (1527–98; reigned 1554–98) married Mary in 1554; after her death, in the reign of Elizabeth I, he led the Spanish Armada, a failed invasion of England in 1588.

149 (p. 79) *ELIZABETH*   (1533–1603; reigned 1558–1603) the daughter of Henry VIII and Anne Boleyn

150 (p. 79) *Lord Burleigh, Sir Francis Walsingham*   William Cecil, Baron Burghley (1521–98), and Walsingham (1532–90) were prominent politicians during Elizabeth's reign.

151 (p. 79) *scandalous death* Mary, Queen of Scots was imprisoned and eventually tried and executed in 1587 for allegedly plotting against her cousin, Elizabeth I. Burghley and Walsingham were her enemies.

152 (p. 79) *Duke of Norfolk* See Note 140.

153 (p. 79) *Mr Whitaker, Mrs Lefroy, Mrs Knight* John Whitaker was the author of *Mary Queen of Scots Vindicated* (1787). Anna Lefroy was JA's friend. For Catherine Knight, see Note 171.

154 (p. 80) *Fotheringay Castle … 1586* This castle, in Northamptonshire, was the prison of Mary, Queen of Scots and the place of her execution; the year should be 1587.

155 (p. 80) *Sir Francis Drake* (1540–96) circumnavigated the globe in 1577

156 (p. 80) *one who though now but young* JA alludes to another Francis, her brother, who was serving in the navy: see headnote to *Jack and Alice*.

157 (p. 80) *Robert Devereux, Lord Essex* See Note 144: he instigated a failed rebellion against Elizabeth and was executed in 1601.

158 (p. 81) *JAMES THE 1ST* (1566–1625; reigned 1603–25) the son of Mary, Queen of Scots, and Henry Stuart, Lord Darnley (1545–67). He was King James VI of Scotland from 1567, after his mother's enforced abdication, and he united the Scottish and English crowns when he succeeded Elizabeth I in 1603.

159 (p. 81) *Anne of Denmark* (1574–1619) married James in 1589.

160 (p. 81) *Prince Henry … unfortunate brother* Henry Frederick, Prince of Wales (1594–1612), predeceased his father, James I; his 'unfortunate brother' was Charles I, executed in 1649.

161 (p. 81) *Sir Henry Percy … Lord Mounteagle* Henry Percy, 9th Earl of Northumberland (1564–1632), was one of the Catholic conspirators behind the failed Gunpowder Plot (1605), an attempt to blow up the House of Lords with James I in it. The Plot came to light when an anonymous letter was received by William Parker, 4th Baron Monteagle (1575–1622), warning him to stay away that day; Goldsmith states that Percy wrote the letter, though modern historians incline towards Francis Tresham (*c.*1567–1605).

162 (p. 81) *Sir Walter Raleigh* (1554–1618) poet, courtier and explorer; a sometime favourite of Elizabeth I

163 (p. 81) *Mr Sheridan's play of The Critic* Richard Brinsley Sheridan's 1779 comedy features a play-within-the-play, entitled *The Spanish Armada*, which depicts Raleigh and Hatton.

164 (p. 81) *Sir Christopher Hatton* (1540–91) Lord Chancellor of England 1587–91

165 (p. 82) *charade … Car* Sir Robert Carr, 1st Earl of Somerset (1587–1645). A charade is a riddle playing with the syllables of a word, such as the one Mr Elton sets in JA's *Emma*. Here, the solution is 'carpet': 'Car' (Carr) was the 'pet' (favourite) of James I.

166 (p. 82) *George Villiers afterwards Duke of Buckingham* The 1st Duke of Buckingham (1592–1628) succeeded Carr as James's favourite. In her references to James's 'keener penetration' and to Carr as his 'pet', JA hints at James's rumoured sexual relations with these men.

167 (p. 83) *CHARLES THE 1ST* (1600–49; reigned 1625–49) He was beheaded by the Parliamentary forces with which he had been at civil war since 1642.

168 (p. 83) *grandmother* Mary, Queen of Scots

169 (p. 83) *Archbishop Laud, Earl of Strafford, Viscount Faulkland and Duke of Ormond* All adherents to Charles I. William Laud (1573–1645), Archbishop of Canterbury, was executed for treason by the Parliamentarians. Sir Thomas Wentworth, 1st Earl of Strafford (1593–1641), was impeached for high treason and Charles reluctantly signed his death warrant. Lucius Cary, 2nd Viscount Falkland (*c.*1610–1643), was killed in fighting after the outbreak of war; 'Faulkland' is JA's spelling. James Butler, 12th Duke of Ormonde (1610–88), commanded the Royalist forces in Ireland, and was a prominent political figure after the Restoration (1660), under Charles II.

170 (p. 83) *Cromwell, Fairfax, Hampden and Pym* All Parliamentarians: opponents of Charles I in the Civil War. Oliver Cromwell (1599–1658) was Lord Protector after 1653. Sir Thomas Fairfax (1612–71) was Parliamentary commander-in-chief. John Hampden (1595–1643) and John Pym (1584–1643) were both prominent members of the Long Parliament which, from 1640, opposed Charles, and then fought against him when war broke out.

The Three Sisters

'The Three Sisters' most likely dates from late 1791, based on the likelihood that it satirises the marital ambitions of the sisters of Elizabeth Bridges, the new wife of JA's brother Edward (the story's dedicatee – see following Note).

171 (p. 86 dedication) *Edward Austen Esquire* JA's brother (1767–1852) had been raised and, in 1783, formally adopted by the wealthy but childless Thomas and Catherine Knight (Thomas was the cousin of Revd George Austen, JA and Edward's father).

172 (p. 87) *settlements* See Note on Marriage and Property.

173 (p. 87) *low* High carriages were fashionable, because they provided a better view, but low ones were more stable and practical.

174 (p. 87) *chaperone* A married (or widowed) woman would accompany, for the sake of propriety, unmarried women on public occasions; Kitty Dutton later teases Mary by implying she will be like a governess chaperoning young women for pay, rather than as an elegant married woman.

175 (p. 88) *Lor* exclamation of surprise: 'Lord'. Written 'Law' in the manuscript. It would have been considered vulgar.

176 (p. 90) *heavy* grave, dull

177 (p. 90) *Three thousand a year* with an equivalent value of between £300,000 and £450,000 in 2012. (See Note on Money.)

178 (p. 91) *who keeps ... at behind?* This part is deleted in the manuscript. See the Note on Transportation. Mr Watts's possession of ('keeps') a 'post-chaise and pair' (i.e. of horses) would be odd, as the 'post' implies the horses are hired. The 'boot', as now, is a compartment for luggage.

179 (p. 91) *phaeton* See Note on Transportation.

180 (p. 91) *chaise* See Note on Transportation.

181 (p. 92) *jointure* See Note on Marriage and Property.

182 (p. 92) *pin money* See Note on Marriage and Property.

183 (p. 92) *two hundred a year* with an equivalent value of between £20,000 and £30,000 in 2012. (See Note on Money.)

184 (p. 93) *town* See Note 26.

185 (p. 93) *tour* either to the Continent or to a picturesque part of Britain, like the Lake District or Peak District

186 (p. 93) *watering place* a spa town, like Tunbridge Wells, or seaside town, like Brighton

187 (p. 93) *balls and masquerades* See Note 17.

188 (p. 93) *theatre* Private theatricals, sometimes with a purpose-built space or an improvised one, became fashionable in the later eighteenth century. The abortive play in JA's *Mansfield Park* is a famous fictional representation.

189 (p. 93) *Which is the Man ... Lady Bell Bloomer* a comedy from

1783 by Hannah Cowley, the heroine of which, Lady Bloomer, is a widow

190 (p. 93) *writings*   the aforementioned marriage settlement. (See Note on Marriage and Property.)

191 (p. 94) *special licence … banns … common licence*   See Note on Marriage and Property.

192 (p. 94) *saddle horse*   one used for riding

193 (p. 94) *Stoneham*   Sabor (2006), p. 421, suggests this is 'probably an imaginary village', but there is a parish of this name in south Hampshire.

194 (p. 94) *appearance*   first public engagement after marriage

195 (p. 95) *provision*   sum left to Mary by her late father. (See Note on Marriage and Property.)

196 (p. 95) *entrée*   public entrance

197 (p. 96) *blackguard*   'a person, *esp.* a man, who behaves in a dishonourable or contemptible way; someone worthless or despicable; a villain' (*OED*)

198 (p. 96) *dressed*   that is, for dinner in the evening

Lesley Castle

'Lesley Castle' apparently dates from early 1792, based on the dates of the letters in the story, which range from January to April 1792.

199 (p. 98 dedication) *Henry Thomas Austen Esq.*   See headnote to *Henry and Eliza*.

200 (p. 98) *the liberty you have frequently honoured me with*   As Southam observes, the phrasing here is ambiguous: it could be that Henry was generous enough to dedicate his own fictions to JA (if so, these are now lost); or that he had repeatedly requested she make him her dedicatee; or that JA had dedicated previous works to him (in which case these are now lost).

201 (p. 98) *H. T. Austen*   Henry apparently wrote and signed this mock note ordering his fictitious bank to pay JA. Henry in fact later became a banker.

202 (p. 99) *saluting*   bidding farewell to

203 (p. 99) *chaise*   See Note on Transportation.

204 (p. 99) *dishonour*   JA here added a footnote: 'Rakehelly Dishonor Esqre.' It makes the abstract noun, dishonour, into another man. 'Rakehell', from which 'rake' derives, means 'scoundrel'.

205 (p. 99) *work*   needlework, embroidery

206 (p. 100) *Tunbridge*   Tunbridge Wells, a fashionable spa town

207 (p. 101) *stewed soup*   broth made by boiling meat and bones in water

208 (p. 101) *whipped syllabub*   'a drink or dish made of milk [...] or cream, curdled by the admixture of wine, cider, or other acid, and often sweetened and flavoured'; also, 'something unsubstantial and frothy; *esp.* floridly vapid discourse or writing' (*OED*)

209 (p. 101) *Eloisa*   JA alludes to the legendary story of the anguished love between Héloïse d'Argenteuil and Pierre Abélard in twelfth-century France, reworked in Alexander Pope's *Eloisa to Abelard* (1717).

210 (p. 102) *decline*   a general failure of health, or a particular wasting disease, such as tuberculosis (consumption). See Note 37.

211 (p. 102) *Bristol*   Bristol Hotwells, a spa near Bristol

212 (p. 103) *mother-in-law*   stepmother

213 (p. 104) *Cumberland*   historic county; what is now the northern part of Cumbria

214 (p. 105) *Dunbeath*   either the fictional Lesley estate near Aberdeen or the actual coastal village in Caithness in the Scottish Highlands

215 (p. 105) *universities*   King's College and Marischal College; unified as the University of Aberdeen in 1860

216 (p. 105) *Bristol downs*   hilly areas in and around Bristol, thought like the spas to have restorative qualities

217 (p. 105) *charwomen*   'wom[e]n hired by the day to do odd jobs of household work' (*OED*)

218 (p. 105) *jellies*   aspic

219 (p. 106) *stupid*   bored and/or boring

220 (p. 106) *Brighthelmstone*   Brighton

221 (p. 106) *four thousand pounds ... every year*   with an equivalent value of between £400,000 and £600,000 in 2012, deriving an annual income – based on five-per-cent interest – of £200, which is between £20,000 and £30,000 in 2012. (See Note on Money.)

222 (p. 107) *set her cap at him*   aim to attract him as her suitor

223 (p. 108) *Portman Square*   fashionable square in Marylebone, London

224 (p. 109) *humoured*   spoilt

225 (p. 109) *toilette*   dressing table

226 (p. 112) *Vauxhall ... cold beef there is cut so thin*   Vauxhall pleasure gardens in Lambeth; the thinness of the slices of cold beef there was infamous in the period.

227 (p. 112) *receipts*   recipes

228 (p. 113) *Malbrouck*   the popular French nursery song 'Malbrouck s'en va-t-en guerre' (Marlborough is going to battle'), which celebrates the military success of John Churchill, 1st Duke of Marlborough (1650–1722), and shares the same tune as 'For he's a jolly good fellow'; spelled 'Malbrook' in JA's original

229 (p. 113) *Bravo ... Poco presto*   a mishmash of Italian musical terms, some of them inappropriate for an auditor to call out because they are instructions for performers

230 (p. 115) *Grosvenor Street*   one of the most prestigious streets in London, indicating the Marlowes' wealth

231 (p. 117) *toad-eater*   See Note 50.

232 (p. 117) *sensibility*   See Note 64.

233 (p. 117) *papers ... print shops*   Public figures and wealthy, beautiful, marriageable young women featured in newspaper gossip sections or one-off prints; Margaret Lesley is deluded.

234 (p. 118) *smallpox*   The disease can cause a rash that leaves scars; Margaret has had smallpox, but it has not affected her face, and having had it she is now immune to it.

235 (p. 118) *Last Monday se'night*   seven nights ago last Monday: the Monday before last

236 (p. 118) *rout*   evening party

237 (p. 118) *Lady Flambeau's*   A flambeau is 'a torch, *esp.* one made of several thick wicks dipped in wax' (*OED*), commonly used to light someone descending from a carriage at night.

238 (p. 119) *Pope's Bulls*   'a papal or episcopal edict or mandate' (*OED*). Because he has converted to Catholicism, Lesley can have his first marriage annulled on the grounds of his wife's adultery, and can remarry (as can Louisa). The papal edict would, however, not be recognised in Britain.

Evelyn

'Evelyn' was probably written in late 1791: see Le Faye (2004), p. 74.

239 (p. 122 dedication) *Miss Mary Lloyd*   (1771–1843) She was sister to Martha, the dedicatee of *Frederic and Elfrida*, and they were friends and neighbours of JA.

240 (p. 124) *paddock ... paling*   an enclosure of land demarcated by pales (wooden stakes in the ground)

241 (p. 124) *chocolate*   hot chocolate for drinking

242 (p. 124) *ices*   frozen confection

243 (p. 124) *a hundred pounds*   with an equivalent value of between £10,000 and £15,000 in 2012. (See Note on Money.)

244 (p. 125) *handsome portion*   large dowry. (See Note on Marriage and Property.)

245 (p. 125) *ten thousand pounds*   with an equivalent value of between £1m and £1.5m in 2012. (See Note on Money.)

246 (p. 128) *gout*   a kind of arthritis affecting the foot

247 (p. 128) *favourite character of Sir Charles Grandison's, a nurse* Richardson's hero in the novel of that name nurses several people from the brink of death, though he declares, 'Male nurses are unnatural creatures!', and advises his uncle to marry a younger woman who will serve him as a nurse.

248 (p. 129) *distracted*   insane

249 (p. 129) *August*   not especially late in the year, of course

250 (p. 130) *Hungary water*   rosemary flowers distilled in water

251 (p. 130) *nectar*   the drink of the gods in Roman mythology

252 (p. 130) *Anchor*   an inn of that name

253 (p. 131) *£30*   with an equivalent value of between £3,000 and £4,500 in 2012. (See Note on Money.)

Catharine, or the Bower

The dedication is dated from Steventon in August 1792. The contents page of *Volume the Third* lists the story as *Kitty, or the Bower*, but this title is corrected at the start of the story, along with some (but not all) instances of 'Kitty' in the story itself.

254 (p. 134 dedication) *Miss Austen ... threescore editions*   To her sister, Cassandra, JA jokes that the unpublished story has been published and has proved so popular that it has gone through sixty editions.

255 (p. 135) *bower*   'a place closed in or overarched with branches of trees, shrubs, or other plants; a shady recess, leafy covert, arbour' (*OED*)

256 (p. 135) *tenure*   tenor

257 (p. 136) *East Indies*   Women in search of a husband had a good chance of finding one in India, where the East India Company employed numerous young single men; the journey was generally

a last resort but was one undertaken in 1752 by JA's aunt, Philadelphia Austen.

258 (p. 136) *Bengal*   province of north-eastern India (and modern-day Bangladesh), where the East India Company was based

259 (p. 136) *Dowager*   See Note on Marriage and Property.

260 (p. 136) *companion*   See Note 50.

261 (p. 136) *living of Chetwynde*   Chetwynde is presumably fictitious, there being no such place in Devon; the living is the remunerated ecclesiastical office attached to the place.

262 (p. 137) *tithes*   tax of one-tenth of a farm's production, or the monetary value thereof, payable to the rector of the parish

263 (p. 137) *to take orders*   See Note 72.

264 (p. 137) *neighbourhood*   See Note 66.

265 (p. 137) *travels*   the Grand Tour of Europe, an essential part of a gentleman's education

266 (p. 138) *working*   See note 205.

267 (p. 138) *establishment*   domestic staff

268 (p. 138) *coach and four … sweep*   See Note on Transportation. A sweep is a semi-circular driveway in front of a house, which allows carriages to turn.

269 (p. 138) *half the year in town*   As a Member of Parliament, Mr Stanley resides in London from the New Year to early June, and resides for the remainder of the year at his home in the country.

270 (p. 139) *Mrs Smith's novels*   Charlotte Smith (1749–1806) was heretofore the author of *Emmeline, The Orphan of the Castle* (1788), *Ethelinde, or The Recluse of the Lake* (1789), *Celestina* (1791) and *Desmond* (1792), the first two of which are mentioned by Camilla here.

271 (p. 139) *Grasmere … Lakes*   Grasmere is a picturesque lake in the Lake District.

272 (p. 140) *travelling dress*   Doody and Murray (1993), p. 350, say this is probably a spencer, a short jacket; Sabor (2006), p. 493, suggests a riding habit of jacket, waistcoat and petticoat.

273 (p. 140) *go from Derbyshire to Matlock and Scarborough*   Camilla's geographical errors are multiplying. Matlock is *in* Derbyshire, and stopping there en route to the Lakes from Devon is viable; Scarborough, however, is not in the Lake District, as Camilla seems to think, nor a practicable via point.

274 (p. 140) *world*   The recent French Revolution, which began in 1789, is the source of Mrs Percival's political anxiety.

275 (p. 140) *Queen Elizabeth*   See Note 149. JA was extremely critical of Queen Elizabeth I in *The History of England*. The antagonistic characters in *Catharine* have names with Elizabethan associations: Dudley, Stanley and Devereux.

276 (p. 142) *Brook Street*   fashionable street in Mayfair, London

277 (p. 142) *find her in clothes*   provide her with clothes

278 (p. 142) *curacies*   Mr Wynne held additional livings to that of Chetwynde, in which he would have employed curates to carry out the clerical duties.

279 (p. 142) *Cheltenham*   a fashionable spa resort, particularly after George III's visit in 1788

280 (p. 143) *Ranelagh*   pleasure gardens in Chelsea, opened in 1742

281 (p. 143) *gout*   See Note 246.

282 (p. 144) *Barbados*   The Caribbean island was then a British colony.

283 (p. 144) *nice*   fastidious

284 (p. 144) *chaperoned*   See Note 174.

285 (p. 144) *draws in oils*   Painting with oil was considered more skilled than watercolour painting.

286 (p. 145) *gold net … pattern*   This is a cap with a hairnet made of golden thread, and a pattern is 'a model or design in dressmaking; a set of instructions to be followed in sewing or knitting an item' (*OED*).

287 (p. 146) *receipt book*   containing remedies for ailments

288 (p. 146) *mortality*   the human race

289 (p. 147) *sensibility*   See Note 64. Mrs Stanley uses the word in a positive way.

290 (p. 148) *Regency walking dress*   In the manuscript, 'pierrot' is excised and 'Regency walking dress' is inserted above the line. A pierrot was a type of jacket. The emendation was seemingly made after February 1811, the date of the Regency Act, which made the Prince of Wales regent when his father was incapacitated by mental illness. This was almost twenty years after the original composition of *Catharine*. A walking dress has a shorter skirt than an evening dress.

291 (p. 148) *pelisse*   'a woman's long cloak, with armhole slits and a shoulder cape or hood, often made of a rich fabric' (*OED*)

292 (p. 149) *Scotch steps*   Lively Scottish dancing was popular in the period.

293 (p. 150) *chaise and four* See Note on Transportation.

294 (p. 150) *done up* probably curled to resemble a wig

295 (p. 150) *livery* uniform for servants

296 (p. 150) *hack horses* hired from an inn

297 (p. 151) *reached* offered

298 (p. 151) *to be so* that is, surprised

299 (p. 152) *go to the door* gentlewomen did not answer the door

300 (p. 152) *smart* smartly dressed

301 (p. 153) *travelling apparel* overcoat and boots, not ball clothes

302 (p. 153) *powder and pomatum* See Note 6.

303 (p. 154) *chaperone* See Note 174.

304 (p. 154) *monthly ball* Provincial public assemblies, which took place in an inn, were held monthly and funded by subscriptions from attendees; a private ball, such as the one to which Catharine and Stanley are going, was given by an individual, like Mr Dudley, and required an invitation (which Stanley does not have).

305 (p. 154) *vestibule … hall* Stately homes featured large entrance halls for the reception of a large number of guests; Mr Dudley has decked out his smaller vestibule as though it were a larger hall.

306 (p. 156) *hunter* horse used for hunting

307 (p. 156) *express* messenger

308 (p. 156) *Brampton* the Stanleys' country seat

309 (p. 157) *the top of the room* the place of honour, leading the dance

310 (p. 158) *Mr Pitt or the Lord Chancellor* William Pitt the Younger (1759–1806) was Prime Minister from 1783–1801 and 1804–6. The Lord High Chancellor is the royally appointed head of the judiciary, who (before 2005) also presided over the House of Lords. Edward, 1st Lord Thurlow (1731–1806), held this office until 1792.

311 (p. 159) *stupider* See Note 219.

312 (p. 159) *come out* Camilla has made a formal entry into society, making her marriageability public knowledge.

313 (p. 160) *impudent* immodest

314 (p. 162) *calculated* suited

315 (p. 162) *temper* calmness; equanimity

316 (p. 163) *Richard the Third* See Note 123.

317 (p. 163) *Profligate* abandoned to vice

318 (p. 163) *Blair's Sermons* The published sermons of Hugh Blair (1718–1800) were widely read in the late eighteenth century.

319 (p. 163) *Coelebs in Search of a Wife*   JA originally wrote 'Seccar's explanation of the Catechism', which is Archbishop Thomas Secker's *Lectures on the Catechism of the Church of England* (1769), but replaced this with Hannah More's moralistic novel *Coelebs in Search of a Wife* (1809), which depicts a celibate bachelor in search of a perfect wife, rejecting young ladies for various moral flaws attributable to their inadequate education. JA criticised More's novel in her letters: see *Letters*, pp. 169–70, 172.

320 (p. 163) *key to my own library*   possibly a room, but more likely a locked bookcase

321 (p. 167) *he did desire his love to me*   he wished that his love would be relayed to Catharine

322 (p. 169) *quartered*   law required communities to lodge soldiers in private houses

323 (p. 169) *strolling players*   See Note 98.

Lady Susan

Lady Susan, which was almost certainly written in 1794, survived JA in a fair-copy manuscript she made in around 1805, which is now held in the Pierpont Morgan Library, New York. The title likely comes from JA's nephew and nieces, James Edward Austen-Leigh, Anna Lefroy and Caroline Austen, who used it in correspondence regarding the *Memoir*, in the second edition (1871) of which *Lady Susan* was first published.

324 (p. 173) *sister*   sister-in-law

325 (p. 174) *10 Wigmore Street*   in Marylebone, London, just north of Oxford Street

326 (p. 177) *husband's dignity … family estate*   The financial mismanagement of the elder Vernon, Lady Susan's deceased husband, necessitated the sale of the family estate; selling to his younger brother would have kept the estate in the family, but would have added to the embarrassment, which is evidently why Lady Susan blocked it.

327 (p. 178) *banking-house*   As a younger son, not standing to inherit the family estate, Charles Vernon has entered the banking profession.

328 (p. 178) *stupid*   See Note 219.

329 (p. 178) *under cover to you*   within a letter addressed to Mrs Johnson

330 (p. 180) *Edward Street* the former name of part of Wigmore Street, so effectively the same road

331 (p. 180) *superficial* Lady Susan advocates the form of education for girls – focusing on 'accomplishments' that would get them a husband and on domestic economy that would make them good wives – the limitations of which radicals like Catherine Macaulay and Mary Wollstonecraft were starting to critique.

332 (p. 180) *Frederica's age* Many girls would have finished their formal education at sixteen.

333 (p. 181) *open* mild; free from frost

334 (p. 182) *entailed* See Note on Marriage and Property: the property is legally bound to be inherited by the eldest son.

335 (p. 187) *intelligence* information

336 (p. 188) *late* recent

337 (p. 191) *shrubbery* small private garden by the house

338 (p. 192) *milkiness* meekness

339 (p. 193) *teasing* 'teizing' in JA's original, meaning pestering

340 (p. 193) *incog.* incognito

341 (p. 194) *pathetic* See Note 74 (used here ironically).

342 (p. 197) *stage* See Note on Transportation.

343 (p. 199) *pelisses* See Note 291.

344 (p. 199) *rattle* excessive talker; chatterer

345 (p. 199) *establishment* financial situation at marriage

346 (p. 202) *Solomon* Old Testament king, whose wisdom was proverbial

347 (p. 203) *chit* brat

348 (p. 203) *keen* sharp, piercing, causing pain

349 (p. 204) *interested* concerned, having an interest in something

350 (p. 204) *hunters* See Note 306.

351 (p. 207) *occurred to me* 'to' does not appear in the manuscript

352 (p. 209) *warm* ardent, impulsive

353 (p. 209) *jealous* zealous, eager for

354 (p. 213) *going for his health to Bath … gout* See Notes 32 (Bath) and 246 (gout).

355 (p. 213) *drawing-room apartment in Upper Seymour Street* the street is also in Marylebone; a drawing-room apartment is a suite of apartments in a town house

356 (p. 213) *Baronet's* See Note 68.

357 (p. 214) *Lakes*   See Note 185.

358 (p. 217) *abroad*   out of the house

359 (p. 219) *éclaircissement*   'a clearing up or revelation of what is obscure or unknown; an explanation' (*OED*)

360 (p. 221) *dismissed*   sent

361 (p. 225) *the Post Office revenue ... State*   Postal fees, paid by the recipient of a letter, went to the state.

362 (p. 226) *finessed*   'to conduct by artifice' (*OED*). JA's usage is the first cited by the *OED*.

The Watsons

The Watsons dates from 1803–4: see Todd and Bree (2008), pp. lxvii–lxix. The manuscript is untitled; the first known use of this title is in the second edition of James Edward Austen-Leigh's *Memoir of Jane Austen* (1871), which was the first time *The Watsons* was published. A transcription of the manuscript is given in Todd and Bree (2008), pp. 259–380. This is a working manuscript, with many revisions, like *Sanditon*, rather than a fair copy, like the juvenilia and *Lady Susan*.

363 (p. 231) *winter assembly*   Provincial towns had a formal social season in the winter, including monthly assemblies at inns, funded by subscriptions from attendees, at which there were refreshments, dancing and card-playing.

364 (p. 231) *D— in Surrey*   Dorking is most probably the place intended

365 (p. 231) *kept their coach ... close carriage*   Owning their own covered carriage is a sign of the Edwardses' considerable wealth, whereas the Watsons have a simple open-top vehicle, subsequently specified as an 'old chair' (see Note on Transportation).

366 (p. 233) *must marry ... father cannot provide for us ... laughed at*   Mr Watson's income will cease when he dies, so his daughters must marry, or face the humiliating situation of being poor, genteel spinsters.

367 (p. 233) *Stanton*   presumably fictitious, there being no Stanton in Surrey or West Sussex (in which county is Chichester)

368 (p. 233) *school*   Some genteel girls were educated entirely at home, but some attended a school for a period. Teaching was an occupation open to educated women, but it was low-income and hard work, and for gentlewomen it betokened a lower status than becoming a governess.

369 (p. 236) *great wash*   Elizabeth has supervised the thorough cleaning of the Watsons' house, which probably entailed several days' upheaval.

370 (p. 236) *ten thousand pounds*   with an equivalent value of between £1m and £1.5m in 2012. This could be Miss Edwards's dowry upon marriage or her inheritance upon her father's death. (See Note on Money.)

371 (p. 236) *surgeon*   a relatively low-status profession in the period

372 (p. 236) *six thousand pounds*   with an equivalent value of between £600,000 and £900,000 in 2012. (See Note on Money.)

373 (p. 236) *turnpike-gate*   See Note on Transportation.

374 (p. 236) *pitching*   stone road

375 (p. 236) *shrubbery and sweep … posts and chain*   See Notes 337 (shrubbery) and 268 (sweep); the chained posts would prevent carriages parking directly outside. These features signal a substantial town house.

376 (p. 237) *hair in papers*   Hair was twisted round paper (usually overnight) to produce curls.

377 (p. 237) *lounge*   stroll

378 (p. 238) *Miss Watson*   Elizabeth: only the eldest daughter would be called 'Miss Watson'; Emma would be addressed as Miss Emma or Miss Emma Watson.

379 (p. 239) *rubber*   a set of three or five games, in this case at whist. (Mr Edwards later specifies he won four of five.)

380 (p. 239) *old rooms at Bath*   The old or Lower Assembly Rooms were built in 1708; they had been joined by the larger new or Upper Assembly Rooms in 1777.

381 (p. 240) *cockade*   'a ribbon, knot of ribbons, rosette, or the like, worn in the hat as a badge of office or party, or as part of a livery dress' (*OED*). Here, this feature of the military uniform stands in for its wearer.

382 (p. 240) *extraordinary*   extra one

383 (p. 241) *morning dress and boots*   day wear, not yet having changed into his evening clothes

384 (p. 241) *famous*   splendid

385 (p. 241) *eight or nine hundred pounds*   with an equivalent value of between £80,000 and £135,000 in 2012. (See Note on Money.)

386 (p. 241) *chaperons*   See Note 174.

387 (p. 241) *empressement*   'animated display of cordiality' (*OED*); spelled 'empressément' by JA

388 (p. 243) *borough*   here, electorate. Lord Osborne is a peer, so automatically sits in the House of Lords, but he seeks to curry favour at the assembly with the senior male citizens who could vote because he may eventually wish to promote a favoured candidate for Parliament.

389 (p. 243) *dance down every couple*   Dancers stood in rows facing their partners, and as the dance progressed, the head couple would dance down to the end between the other pairs.

390 (p. 243) *begin the set*   The 'set' is the line of couples (see preceding Note). Miss Osborne leads the dance because she is the highest ranking lady present. Her breaking her engagement to dance first with Charles Blake is a major breach of etiquette, only unremarked upon because he is a child.

391 (p. 243) *interesting*   engaging the emotions

392 (p. 244) *Wickstead*   presumably fictitious

393 (p. 244) *dances*   To note a few aspects of the dance: Charles is told to keep his gloves on because white gloves are part of male ball attire; Miss Osborne 'turns' Charles because part of the dance involves temporarily stepping outside of one's own pairing but being restored to place; and dancing is evidently no bar to conversation, either between the dancers or even with one standing by, here Lord Osborne.

394 (p. 244) *cassino*   card game

395 (p. 244) *suffrage*   vote in support of a statement; assent

396 (p. 245) *gape*   It meant 'yawn' as well as 'stare', and both meanings may apply.

397 (p. 245) *you must sit with my friends*   Etiquette required the gentleman to join his partner's party in the interval.

398 (p. 246) *presenting him*   A formal introduction was required before a request to dance could be made.

399 (p. 246) *patronised*   approved

400 (p. 246) *nice ... particularity*   'nice' in the sense of 'particular'; 'particularity' in the sense of exceptionable behaviour

401 (p. 246) *sad*   bad

402 (p. 247) *call*   The leading lady of each dance – which role has passed from Miss Osborne to the second highest ranked female, Miss Carr – called which tunes would be played, which in turn determined the dance.

403 (p. 247) *negus* 'a drink made from wine (usually port or sherry) mixed with hot water, sweetened with sugar and sometimes flavoured' (*OED*)

404 (p. 249) *red coats* military men, designated metonymically by their uniform

405 (p. 249) *equipage … curricle* See Note on Transportation.

406 (p. 249) *visitation* ecclesiastical inspection of the parish's affairs by the bishop or archdeacon

407 (p. 249) *D—* written as 'R—' in the manuscript, which is apparently an error. JA may have been thinking of Reigate.

408 (p. 251) *critically* by accepted critical standards

409 (p. 251) *piquante* likely used here in the sense of 'stimulating or agreeable to the mind or senses; fascinating; charming' (*OED*)

410 (p. 251) *pelisse* See Note 291.

411 (p. 252) *high* haughty

412 (p. 252) *manner … address* This is quite a fine distinction, making Mary's self-correction significant in the analysis of Musgrave's character. 'Manner' signifies 'outward bearing, deportment; a person's characteristic style of attitude, gesture, or speech' (*OED*); but its other senses indicate a person's habitual behaviour, conduct and morals. 'Address' relates more concretely and specifically to outward behaviour and speech in formal situations.

413 (p. 254) *high* strong smelling

414 (p. 254) *gouty* See Note 246.

415 (p. 255) *half-boots* 'a boot reaching halfway to the knee, or con-siderably above the ankle' (*OED*)

416 (p. 255) *nankin galoshed with black* Nankin is 'a kind of pale yellowish cloth, originally made at Nanking [now Nanjing] in China from a yellow variety of cotton'; a galosh is 'a piece of leather or other material running round the lower part of a boot or shoe above the sole' (*OED*).

417 (p. 256) *throw off* release hounds from leashes to begin the hunt

418 (p. 257) *six thousand pounds* with an equivalent value of between £600,000 and £900,000 in 2012. (See Note on Money.)

419 (p. 258) *countenance* bearing; demeanour; comportment

420 (p. 258) *post-boy … posting* See Note on Transportation.

421 (p. 258) *sad, shabby* See Note 401 for 'sad'; 'shabby' is a gentle criticism for someone behaving in a mean or ungenerous way,

more common now in adverb form, as when someone behaves shabbily, for instance.

422 (p. 259) *six thousand pounds*   with an equivalent value of between £600,000 and £900,000 in 2012. (See Note on Money.)

423 (p. 259) *sensibility*   See Note 64.

424 (p. 260) *eight or nine thousand pounds*   with an equivalent value of between £800,000 and £1.35m in 2012. (See Note on Money.)

425 (p. 261) *indifferent*   in poor health

426 (p. 261) *break up*   division of the estate

427 (p. 261) *a thousand or fifteen hundred pounds*   with an equivalent value of between £100,000 and £225,000 in 2012. (See Note on Money.)

428 (p. 261) *putting up*   packing to bring

429 (p. 262) *round game ... Speculation*   A 'round game' at cards is one for individual players, not pairs; speculation is such a game,

430 (p. 262) *cribbage*   a game usually for two players

431 (p. 262) *post-chaise*   See Note on Transportation.

432 (p. 262) *wrap*   outer garment

433 (p. 263) *Pembroke table*   'a small table with a drop-leaf on each side, which may be raised and supported horizontally on a hinged bracket' (*OED*)

434 (p. 263) *Bedford*   Bedford Coffee House in Covent Garden

435 (p. 264) *open*   See Note 333.

436 (p. 264) *dishabille*   informal dress

437 (p. 264) *fish and counters*   Tokens with which to gamble or keep score in card games; the former were often shaped like fish and made of ivory or bone.

438 (p. 264) *buffet*   sideboard or side-table; spelled 'beaufit' in the manuscript

439 (p. 265) *Vingt-un*   card game, now commonly called pontoon, blackjack, twenty-one or vingt-et-un

440 (p. 265) *overdraw himself on both his own cards*   If in pontoon one is dealt two initial cards of the same value, one can split them and play two hands; Lord Osborne as dealer is described as overdrawing himself by taking more cards until he exceeds the target of twenty-one with both of his hands.

441 (p. 266) *give Robert the meeting*   Musgrave is invited, for form's sake, on Robert Watson's behalf.

Sanditon

What exists of *Sanditon* was written by JA into the surviving manuscript between January and March 1817, and was left unfinished at the time of JA's death that year. JA's sister Cassandra transcribed it after JA's death. Both manuscripts are untitled: on the title, which might have been intended to be *The Brothers*, see Todd and Bree (2008), pp. lxxx–lxxxi.

442 (p. 271) *Tunbridge … Hastings and Eastbourne*   Tunbridge Wells is about thirty miles inland from the coastal resorts of Hastings and Eastbourne.

443 (p. 271) *cut*   whipped

444 (p. 271) *not his master's*   In the manuscript, these words are written above the line, but of the words they are to replace – 'not the gentleman's' – only the first is deleted. It seems that the driver is Parker's employee, but that the carriage is hired.

445 (p. 271) *romantically*   See Note 61.

446 (p. 272) *Willingden*   There is a village called Willingdon in East Sussex, near Eastbourne, but not one of this name in the vicinity in which the Parkers are travelling.

447 (p. 272) *the Morning Post and the Kentish Gazette*   The former was a daily London newspaper, first published in 1772; the latter was a twice-weekly local paper, first published in 1768, which would have been read in the eastern part of Sussex as well as Kent.

448 (p. 273) *post-chaises*   See Note on Transportation.

449 (p. 273) *double tenement*   a single house divided for two separate tenants

450 (p. 273) *Great Willingden or Willingden Abbots … Battle*   This second Willingden is again fictitious (see Note 446 above), but Battle is a town near Hastings (its name commemorates the 1066 battle).

451 (p. 273) *the Weald*   an area of south-eastern England between the chalk escarpments of the North and South Downs

452 (p. 273) *turnpike road*   See Note on Transportation.

453 (p. 273) *Hailsham*   market town just north of Eastbourne in East Sussex

454 (p. 274) *nursery grounds*   'an area of land used for raising young plants' (*OED*)

455 (p. 275) *She, never heard of half a mile from home*   a line from 'Truth' (1782), by William Cowper, in which the sceptical, iconoclastic philosopher Voltaire is contrasted with a simple, pious peasant woman

456 (p. 276) *puffed*   advertised fulsomely

457 (p. 277) *collateral inheritance*   an inheritance from a relative with no direct heir; for example, a man with no children might choose to bequeath his wealth to the younger son of his brother

458 (p. 277) *his mine, his lottery, his speculation and his hobby horse* Investments in mining and the lottery connote get-rich-quick schemes or 'speculations': commercial ventures carrying the possibility of large profits, but involving considerable risk. A hobby horse was originally a model of a horse (or a wooden stick with a horse's head) used in entertainments or as a toy, but signifies figuratively a pursuit followed obsessively and delusionally, as most memorably in Uncle Toby's battle re-enactments in Laurence Sterne's *Tristram Shandy* (1759–67).

459 (p. 278) *anti-spasmodic … anti-rheumatic*   words that satirise the medical jargon of the time

460 (p. 278) *softening*   'softing' in the manuscript, though corrected to 'softening' in Cassandra's copy

461 (p. 278) *gout*   See Note 246.

462 (p. 279) *library*   The circulating library, which as well as lending books was an important social venue, and a place where items from perfume to pottery, and tickets for entertainments, could be purchased, and musical instruments hired, for example.

463 (p. 280) *thirty thousand pounds*   with an equivalent value of between £3m and £4.5m in 2012. (See Note on Money.)

464 (p. 281) *cottage ornée*   a picturesque detached country house

465 (p. 281) *waste ground*   land not in use for pasture or crops

466 (p. 281) *companion*   See Note 50.

467 (p. 283) *between the South Foreland and Land's End*   the full length of the south coast

468 (p. 283) *Trafalgar … Waterloo*   alluding to the Battles of Trafalgar (1805) and of Waterloo (1815), commemorated in the naming of houses in Sanditon

469 (p. 284) *plantations*   'an area planted with trees, *esp.* for commercial purposes' (*OED*)

470 (p. 285) *hospital*   housing invalids at watering places. Such hospitals were funded by charitable donations.

471 (p. 285) *equipage*   See Note on Transportation.

472 (p. 286) *whooping cough*   a contagious disease mainly affecting children

473 (p. 286) *nankin boots*   See Note 416.

474 (p. 286) *bills at the windows*   notices advertising available accommodation

475 (pp. 286) *bathing machines*   huts on wheels in which sea bathers changed into their bathing costumes and were drawn by horse to the water. This avoided the impropriety of being seen by members of the opposite sex so scantily clad.

476 (p. 286) *Venetian window*   'a window in three separate apertures, the two side ones being narrow, and separated from the centre by timber only' (an 1842 definition, cited by *OED*)

477 (p. 288) *spasmodic bile*   an excess or obstruction in the secretion of bile, causing spasms and pain

478 (p. 288) *leeches*   used in letting blood

479 (p. 289) *beau monde*   fashionable society

480 (p. 289) *West Indian*   a European settler in the West Indies (where large fortunes could be made)

481 (p. 289) *Camberwell*   then a village south of London (now a district of south London)

482 (p. 290) *library subscription book*   Being a register of subscribers, this would provide a list of genteel visitors to Sanditon.

483 (p. 290) *Limehouse*   dockland area of east London

484 (p. 290) *Grays Inn*   one of the four Inns of Court, professional associations of lawyers, in London

485 (p. 291) *toilette*   See Note 225.

486 (p. 291) *Camilla*   Frances Burney's 1796 novel *Camilla* depicts a young heroine who incurs debts through over-spending on a visit to Tunbridge Wells.

487 (p. 293) *French boarding school*   a boarding school run by a French-woman – or a pretended one. JA attended one run by 'Mrs La Tournelle', whose real name was Sarah Hackitt: see *Family Record*, p. 51.

488 (p. 293) *consumptive … asses' milk*   Ass's milk was recommended for those suffering with consumption (see Note 37).

489 (p. 293) *chamber-horse*   'a piece of exercise equipment which simulates the motion of horse riding, typically consisting of a sprung chair on which the user sits and bounces up and down' (*OED*)

490 (p. 294) *equipage … gig … groom*   See Note on Transportation.

491 (p. 294) *French windows* 'a pair of tall casement windows closing against each other with no frame between them, allowing access to the outside or to another room' (*OED*)

492 (p. 295) *in the gross*   in general

493 (p. 295) *sublimity* an aesthetic term, referring to the grand and awe-inspiring features of nature, which was popular during the Romantic period. Its reduction to convention is mocked here in Sir Edward's discussion of poetry.

494 (p. 295) *sensibility*   See Note 64.

495 (p. 295) *samphire*   a plant that grows on rocks by the sea

496 (p. 296) *man of feeling*   possibly an allusion to Henry Mackenzie's sentimental novel *The Man of Feeling* (1771), the excessively sensitive hero of which became a type character in later fiction

497 (p. 296) *Oh! ... ease*   from Sir Walter Scott's *Marmion* (1808), canto 6, verse 30

498 (p. 296) *Some ... &c.*   from Scott's *The Lady of the Lake: A Poem* (1810), canto 2, verse 22

499 (p. 296) *Burns ... Montgomery ... Wordsworth ... Campbell*   These are all popular poets of the time. Robert Burns addressed poetry to his fiancée, Mary Campbell, known as Highland Mary, before her premature death. James Montgomery, William Wordsworth and Thomas Campbell are the others mentioned, and a line from Campbell's *The Pleasures of Hope* (1799) is here quoted by Sir Edward Denham.

500 (p. 297) *poor Burns's known irregularities*   alluding to Burns's rumoured love affairs

501 (p. 297) *coruscations*   quivering flashes of light (used figuratively here)

502 (p. 298) *dowager*   See Note on Marriage and Property.

503 (p. 299) *half-pay officers*   Army and navy officers between assignments or debilitated were paid reduced wages.

504 (p. 299) *jointure*   See Note on Marriage and Property.

505 (p. 299) *places*   See Note 29.

506 (p. 300) *coinciding*   agreeing

507 (p. 301) *alembic*   a glass vessel for distilling chemicals, used here figuratively along with other haphazardly applied scientific terms in Sir Edward's criticism of bad fiction. The ridiculously inflated language continues in his next speech, and is explained by his having read too many sentimental novels.

508 (p. 301) *impassioned and most exceptionable parts of Richardson's* The rakes, Mr B. and Lovelace, relentlessly pursue the eponymous heroines of Samuel Richardson's *Pamela* (1740) and *Clarissa* (1747–8), respectively.

509 (p. 302) *Timbuktu* city in present-day Mali, on the edge of the Sahara Desert, used figuratively for the most distant place imaginable

510 (p. 303) *post horses* See Note on Transportation.

511 (p. 307) *bitters of my own decocting* medicinal substance made by boiling down (decocting) herbs, such as camomile

512 (p. 308) *posting* hurrying (alluding to the swiftness of the post-chaise)

513 (p. 309) *salts … drops* respectively, smelling salts, used in case of fainting (see Note 12), and medicinal preparations taken in the form of drops of liquid

514 (p. 309) *sodden* 'characterised by heaviness, dullness, or want of vivacity' (*OED*)

515 (p. 309) *eight guineas* Todd and Bree (2008), p. 671, suggest this is the equivalent of £500 in 2012; using the multiplier of 100 to 150 proposed by Hume (2012), it is between £840 and £1,260 (see Note on Money).

516 (p. 309) *bathing women* employed to assist bathers to get in and out of the water

517 (p. 309) *trenches* figurative use, perhaps denoting 'a path or track cut through a wood or forest' (*OED*), or perhaps the more common military sense, which would be reinforced by the 'powerful *discharge* of unexpected obligations' later in the sentence

518 (p. 309) *hack chaises* hired ones

519 (p. 310) *nervous* suffering from a disorder attributable to the nerves, affecting the mind too. Many considered such disorders as either what we could call psychosomatic, a result of hypochondria, or a self-induced consequence of indolence or over-indulgence. JA's Mrs Bennet in the opening chapter of *Pride and Prejudice* pleads for compassion for her nerves, which is not forthcoming from her husband.

520 (p. 310) *bilious* See Note 477.

521 (p. 311) *physics* natural sciences in general

522 (p. 312) *green tea* See Note 95.

523 (p. 313) *private hand*   delivered by a private carrier, signifying a personal letter

524 (p. 314) *catastrophe*   in drama, the denouement; the solution of the complication in the plot

525 (p. 314) *displays*   learning the accomplishments (dancing, drawing, playing music) that would help them to get husbands. (See Note 331.)

526 (p. 314) *half mulatto*   A mulatto is 'a person having one white and one black parent. Freq. more generally: a person of mixed race resembling a mulatto' (*OED*). Being 'half mulatto' makes Miss Lambe a 'quadroon', having one black and three white grandparents, though the designation was not always used with precision, so it might be one black great-grandparent, for example. These terms are now offensive.

527 (p. 315) *decline*   See Note 210.

528 (p. 315) *property in*   a financial investment in

529 (p. 316) *lounge*   place for strolling

530 (p. 316) *subscription*   a charitable subscription: an arrangement whereby money is pledged to a fund. The signature of a prominent person like Lady Denham would encourage others to contribute.

531 (p. 317) *ten guineas*   with an equivalent value of between £1,050 and £1,575 in 2012. (See Note on Money.)

532 (p. 317) *Charitable Repository*   where donated goods were sold for the benefit of the poor

533 (p. 317) *putting them all out*   that is, to apprenticeships or paid work, which would have required an initial payment

534 (p. 317) *machine*   See Note 475.

535 (p. 317) *leeches ... three hours' business*   The application of leeches (see Note 478) was a delicate operation.

536 (p. 318) *gig ... phaeton ... tandem*   See Note on Transportation.

537 (p. 318) *paling*   See Note 240.